Praise for
The Wolfe Pack I: Strong Arm Tactics

"Nye, already well-known for her humor, offers an amusing but effective military sf novel in the story of Lieutenant David Wolfe...The book has something in common with the Phule's Company series by Nye's occasional collaborator Robert Asprin but is in many ways more straightforward, better developed, and not less amusing. The conclusion gives Wolfe a couple of nasty surprises, darkening the overall tone but also strongly suggesting that Wolfe and the Cockroaches will be back."
—Roland Green, *Booklist*, September 2005

"Even if you are inordinately fond of chow mien, you'll find this book engrossing, funny, ingeniously clever and a very good read. Indeed, this will be the book I tout at all conventions I'll be attending this Summer. I'd love to buttonhole a lot of weary readers and say, "Try *Wolfe Pack 1* by Jody Lynn Nye—you'll be glad you did." But that sort of strong-arm tactic has the reverse effect and I don't want people missing this yarn. I must say, after fifty year of reading how the good guys get saved, this has the most unusual army ever mobilized to save the day. Those scenes alone are worth the price of the book.

I'm hoping this is the first of several about this group of misfits, the Cockroach or X-ray Platoon in which all the screw-ups are lumped together. The hero, Daivid Wolfe, is as much as screw-up as everyone else but he has the good sense to take advantage of what other lieutenants were too green to appreciate. Read it! Before I buttonhole you to do so.

Ciao, Annie"—Anne McCaffrey

"Readers familiar with the military science fiction works of John Ringo and David Webber or the battle scenes form the Star Wars trilogy and the amusement in a Harry Harrison's

Stainless Steel Rat novel will thoroughly enjoy Jody Lynn Nye's latest work. Humor is used to relieve the tension during the battle scenes with the rebels who are not trying to overthrow an evil confederation but want to grab power for themselves which make them dangerous and uncaring about loss of civilian life. Ms. Nye's villains have no redeeming features which makes it easy for readers to want to see them fail. The audience will eagerly await the next book in this exciting series in which the characters especially the Wolf Pack are likeable, loyal and earthy."—*SFReview Online*

"Engaging characters, a clever plot, and a fun—indeed, extremely funny—setting make Strong Arm Tactics a delight."
—Dave Drake

The Wolfe Pack Book I
STRONG ARM TACTICS

JODY LYNN NYE

Meisha Merlin Publishing, Inc.
Atlanta, GA

Strong Arm Tactics

Published by Meisha Merlin Publishing, Inc.
PO Box 7
Decatur, GA 30031

Editing by Stephen Pagel
Copyediting and Proofreading by Elizabeth Easter
Interior layout by Lynn Swetz
Cover art by Don Maitz
Cover design by Kevin Murphy

ISBN: Hard Cover   1-59222-045-2
ISBN: Soft Cover   1-59222-044-4

http://www.MeishaMerlin.com
First MM Publishing edition: November 2005

Printed in the United States of America
0 9 8 7 6 5 4 3 2 1

To Bill
All's fair in love and war
And this is both

TABLE OF CONTENTS

ONE GIANT PRACTICAL JOKE
The relationship between war and humor

SOLDIERS, COPS, PARAMEDICS, firemen, emergency services people everywhere. They all have things in common. They do an intensely stressful job while watching their pay and benefits being constantly eroded. And they do it with humor or they don't do it at all.

Why do humor and such intensely serious and stressful occupations go hand in glove? Looked at logically, policemen, firefighters and combat soldiers should be dour and humorless people. There is nothing more potentially sobering than watching the person next to you step on a mine. But the tales redound of soldiers that then pick up the leg of their buddy and waggle it back and forth. "Look! I'm Wally's Leg! Wheeee!" Firefighters are some of the most vicious practical jokers in the world. When policemen gather after going to the funeral for one of their brother officers, alcohol often flows free, but not as freely as the humorous stories and very sick jokes, often at the expense of the beloved deceased.

So the question remains, why?

Essentially, the answer is "self medication for stress." Humor has (finally) been recognized as one of the most psychologically successful forms of stress relief. It's the soldier, Marine, cop or firefighter that can laugh at the insanity around him or her that is the most likely to truly "come home." And often the most likely to survive the carnage around him or her, by being able to overcome and adapt to the horror. Laughter is not only the best medicine: laughter is a weapon in and of itself that acts as a combat enhancer.

Laughter is more than a visual and vocal behaviour. It is accompanied by a wide range of physiological changes. During vigorous laughter the body brings in extra oxygen, shudders the internal organs, causes muscles to contract, and activates the hypothalamus, pituitary, and adrenal glands. This results in an increase in the secretion of endorphines (internally produced morphine-like

molecules). This internal jogging produces an increase in oxygen absorption, increase in heart rate, relaxation of the muscles, and increases in the number of disease fighting immune cells (Cousins, 1989; Siegel, 1989).
Healingwithhumor.com
Cathy Fenwick, Ph. D.

In any study of methods of combating stress, especially post-traumatic stress, humor is repeatedly, pardon the pun, stressed. Humor is the quickest way of overcoming minor depression, anxiety and generalized stress. "It does you good to laugh" has been proven to be far more than just an old lady's saying, it is a provable treatment for even serious illness and has been used as therapy in cancer and autoimmune disease patients. But, most especially, it is useful in treating combat fatigue and similar traumatic stress syndromes.

Not to be neglected is the use of humor, which has its place in many forms of psychotherapy, but may be especially useful in working with law enforcement and emergency services personnel. In general, if the therapist and patient can share a laugh, this may lead to the sharing of more intimate feelings. Humor serves to bring a sense of balance, perspective, and clarity to a world that seems to have been warped and polluted by malevolence and horror. Humor, even sarcastic, gross, or callous humor, if handled appropriately and used constructively may allow the venting of anger, frustration, resentment, or sadness, and thereby lead to productive, reintegrative therapeutic work (Fullerton et al, 1992; Miller, 1994; Silva, 1991).
Law Enforcement Traumatic Stress: Clinical Syndromes and Intervention Strategies
Laurence Miller, Ph.D.

In terms of combat, there is a recognized psychological syndrome in which combat fatigue manifests in terms of black humor. It is a functional release, the chimpanzee within dealing with killing stress by using humor to deflect and treat itself. When there is nothing around but the insanity and irony of war, the ability to see the irony and find humor in it can keep a soldier alive and sane when others fall.

When combat veterans get together to tell stories, those that have handled the stresses of combat well almost always concentrate on the humorous (if bizarre) ones. Humor is found in the deaths of the enemies and even the deaths of buddies. This is neither "bad" nor "evil" but a functional human reaction. War, after all, is simply one giant practical joke, with the victims of the joke being both sides.

In terms of writing about combat, neglecting the bleak and black humor of combat veterans is a sure sign of either a combat veteran who never really "came home" or someone with little or no knowledge of how soldiers, sailors and Marines behave. I have occasionally been castigated by the unknowing for the humor my characters manifest. I know that they are "unknowing" when they react that way. Anyone who knows combat veterans that have truly "come home from the wars" knows that there's not a bigger group of jokers short of the stand-up comic circuit.

Jody has captured the insanity of a long-term combat unit well in this book. Such soldiers as survive, mentally and physically, survive to the most common extent by becoming the world's worst jokesters. It was a joy to see how well Jody captured that spirit. I hope you enjoy the tale as much as I.

John Ringo
1/508th Infantry (Airborne), 82nd Airborne Division
June 1983-February 1987
Author of the *Legacy of the Aldenata* series and *There Will Be Dragons* series

The Wolfe Pack Book I

STRONG ARM
TACTICS

JODY LYNN NYE

PROLOGUE

"YOU MADE IT," General Robin Petrovna Sams exclaimed, as a scruffy human male in a worn brown shipsuit staggered in to the desolate conference room. Colonel Inigo Ayala clasped hands with the red-haired human woman whose comfortable, plump figure and heart-shaped face were so at odds with the devious brain inside. She was the titular head of the Insurgency, and hoped one day to sit in the President's chair at the Senate Council of the newly reformed Thousand Worlds Confederation—reformed by her forces, of course. In the meantime, they were a rebellion on a budget. The space station in which they were meeting was nearly derelict. The Insurgency liked to say they captured it, but the fact was the Confederation had all but abandoned it during a fight with the nascent rebel forces.

"Missed a Con patrol by a scoche," Ayala said, flopping into a chair. The hydraulics had long ago gone flat, and the servos shrieked under his weight. His ivory skin, pleated from long years of staring at stars from behind inadequately shielded viewports, was paler than usual. "They're getting too close. We're going to have to abandon K-17 sector for a while."

"They're reading your power signatures," Itterim Van Yarrow grumbled. No ally to humankind could look less like it. Itter's homeworld had produced as many billions of intelligent, upright bipedal beings as Terra, who would have (and had) taken one look at the Itterim and thought, "praying mantis."

Ayala snorted at him. "Well, what do you expect? All we've got is crap ships, everybody's leftovers, anything we can capture or steal or adapt. Every time a closet rebel industrialist who claims he hates the Confederation promises us funding, they always find an excuse not to pay off. We might as well hover off the bows of Con dreadnoughts and throw stones."

Van Yarrow curled his green foreclaw and shook it. "By my exo, we will, if we must. The Confederation treats us like hive in-sects, all to be treated like one type of being. It is unnatural. How all our species and cultures have survived so long under its yoke I do not know."

"Never mind," Sams said. "We still have Benarli."

"Three rotten little planets circling three minor stars barely adequate for maintaining viable systems," Ayala said scornfully. "Look at us! We just don't have the headcount or the weaponry to attack. We need more soldiers, more ships, more money!"

Sams shrugged. "I've got everyone I can spare on procurement, Ayala."

Vareda Borenik growled. The old woman turned her one good eye toward him; the cloned replacement for her left had yet to grow to viable size and was still behind the sewn-closed lid. "The traders are getting smart. If they're carrying a valuable load, they travel with military transports. The little ones are hard to catch."

"The little ones often have the really worthwhile cargoes, like power supplies and nanocomputers! If we had better intelligence we could intercept those."

The itterim clicked his mandibles. "That is what I have come to tell the general," he said. "My spies have sent me the flight paths of five transports carrying goods that we will want." He pushed an infopad toward Sams and aimed a claw at the fourth entry. "This one is four thousand units of Tachytalk generators."

Sams nodded. Tachytalk was a brand name for a communications system that relied upon tachyons, particles that could not travel slower than light, to enable almost real-time information exchange within a few light years, and significantly cut down transfer time of more distant communiqués.

"That would go a long way in helping to coordinate our efforts. Go get them."

"As good as done, general," Van Yarrow clicked, crossing his paws to show how pleased he was with himself.

Sams pushed away from the table and half-floated toward the starchart that glowed softly on the only illuminated screen wall in the chamber. "The Benarli cluster will be ours soon. The populations of two of the remaining inhabited planets have submitted to our occupying forces. It will become an ideal base for us. No one in the Confederation will notice that they've stopped transmitting. Their communications were intermittent anyhow because of all the black holes surrounding the stars. The fact that they are small and unimportant helps us to make the rest of the Confederation forget them."

Her captains nodded. Travel through Benarli space was tricky. Craft traveling by means of interstellar strings avoided routing through the area; one missed calculation, and a ship could be sucked into eternity. The only reason the Benarlis had been interesting in the past was because such old systems yielded a ponderance of heavy minerals not as plentiful in younger stars. Over the thousands of years humanity and others had plied the spaceways, the easy sources in the cluster had been whittled down, and more mineral beds had opened up in other, safer parts of the galaxy. Benarli was like a ghost town, ideal for a gang that didn't want to attract notice.

"We still aren't addressing the problem," Ayala argued. "I need more trained pilots and better fighter ships. We have lots of volunteers. They're all newbies. I have plenty of cannon fodder, but no one I can really trust."

Borenik smiled, her sagging eye making the expression sinister. "I think I can fix the problem. If we had ships that could fight for us, then we wouldn't need to put more people at risk."

Ayala waved the suggestion away. "Fantasy. All the efforts to create AIs that are capable of sophisticated strategy without being plugged into the opposing system have had too many flaws."

"Ah," the old woman said. "What if I knew where a superprocessor was being developed that had the capacity not only to counter multiple-front input and deduce the strategy behind it, but read a situation and come up with its own ahead of time?"

"Now, I agree with the human," Van Yarrow chittered. "That's such a fantasy."

"But it's not. In fact, one of the greatest inventors in the galaxy is working on the problem."

"Who? Who's got the funding for that kind of R&D?" Ayala demanded.

Borenik leaned back in her chair and took a plastic sheet out of an upper pocket. "My intelligence sources inform me that he is almost finished. And when I tell you where he is you're going to kick yourself in the behind for not figuring it out for yourself."

"Where?" Sams asked greedily.

Borenik threw a brochure on the table. The plastic sheet immediately began to emit flickering lights that coalesced into happy costumed figures of humans, animals, cuddly monsters and animated objects smiling and dancing together.

"Oh, happy happy happy. All of us are happy. Come with us and sing a happy tune! Happy happy happy, all the world is happy. Dance with us, and you'll be happy soon!"

"You're joking," Sams said.

"No," Borenik smirked. "And if you hurry, you can get in before any of the other bidders."

Ayala grinned fiercely at his fellow officers. "It's decided, then. We're going to Wingle World."

CHAPTER 1

"LIEUTENANT WOLFE!"

"Ma'am!" The tawny-haired young man stood at attention before the uniformed, middle-aged woman behind the desk. His jaw was sharply delineated enough to suggest he might be related to the animal with whom he shared his name.

Certainly, Commander Voreca Mason thought with grim humor, his family's history displayed most of the traits associated with *canis lupus*. Or should she say, Family? Even his nose, straight yet blunted at the tip, suggested a muzzle. She imagined that the golden-hazel eyes, tilted up at the corners, long-lashed, almost yellow in his tawny-complected face, could burst into the savage fire of a wild creature. To be honest, Daivid Wolfe had never been reported baying at the moons or tearing his fellow troopers apart with his fangs, but he was every bit as dangerous to have around. She sincerely wished he was elsewhere.

None of her brother or sister officers wanted him, but *they* could say no. They had. Wolfe had been shifted from brigade to brigade as soon as his initial evolution had ended. *She* couldn't transfer him out. She was here on Treadmill for reasons she devoutly hoped no one outside Admin knew. She had no good choices: 1) Keep him, and risk her own career on handling a hot potato; 2) Boot him out, and risk annoying the Family. The army was taking that chance already.

By trying to show the Wolfe Family they weren't so tough, the upper brass had shifted the eldest child and scion of the Old Man to what amounted to punishment detail. If anything happened to him, she'd be the one to take the blame. She'd always thought that half the punishment going on around here was being visited on her. Resigned to the thankless situation she had been handed, she returned the salute, and ruffled her graying blond hair with her fingers before folding her hands together on the desk.

"At ease, Lieutenant," she said.

Eyes still straight ahead, Wolfe set his feet exactly shoulder-width apart and locked his hands behind his back. Ill at ease was more like it. Colonel Mason felt exactly the same as he did. "I should welcome you to Neutron Company and X-ray Platoon. Your first command. This is an irregular company. You won't be bored."

Wolfe's Adam's apple bobbed up and down. Mason nodded to herself. He knew what the shorthand meant—it meant his unit got all the jobs no one else would touch When a trooper was sent to X-ray Platoon, s/he knew what it was for. Every one of the men and women in it had been dumped into the detail by COs who didn't want them around any more, for whatever reason, but could not or did not want to discharge them. There should have been a place on the transfer form for "Whom did you piss off?" X-ray was the unit that was always sent in to attempt the unaccomplishable mission and take the blame, if need be, when it failed to be accomplished. Every soldier in it was considered expendable. About half the transferees were killed in the first twelve months of duty. Another fifty percent of the survivors died within three years. The ones who'd survived— she had no idea how they survived. The upper brass was obviously hoping Wolfe would quit the military and go home *before* he became one of those statistics. So was she.

"Your unit is waiting for your inspection on the parade ground. I'm going to give you a few days to break them in before I hand you an assignment. Do you have any questions?"

The Adam's apple bobbed again. "No, ma'am."

"Well, then, son, they're waiting for you. Dismissed!"

Wolfe spun on his heel and marched out of the room. Mason watched him go, feeling a little sorry for him. He was just a boy. It was only the accident of his birth that he'd ended up here in the Penalty Box.

"You want to join the *army*?" his father had asked him three years before, crinkling his thick black brows. "What are you? Crazy?"

"I'm not crazy," Daivid had protested, glaring at the old man. Both of them had the yellow-hazel eyes that went back thousands of years in family portraits, holovideos and threedeeo images. In Benjamin's narrow, bony face, they looked feral. Daivid's features were similar enough that people were always remarking on the resemblance to his father and their family's eponymous totem animal. Daivid hoped he looked more doglike. A dog was loyal, brave and, above all, honest. A friend to man, not a foe or a rival.

"Look," his father had pleaded, running both long-fingered hands through his thick hair and making it stand up. "You don't want to be associated with the family, but you can't run away from your destiny." "It's not my destiny!"

The old man patted the air with both palms. "All right, all right; your heritage, then. How about just going into one of the other businesses we own? Strictly legitimate."

Daivid remembered rounding on his father with all the fury of an idealistic youth. "The money still comes from one of the illicit operations, or rolls over into one of them. No. I don't want anything from this family! I want to make it on my own. *Completely* legal. No cheating, no pushing, no threats."

"You don't want to do that," his father assured him. The old man sat there like the mandarin he was, wise with the experience of his years. "Do you know what happens to people who never cheat on anything? They end up on public assistance. You don't want that, son. The government issue food's terrible."

Daivid's voice had risen to the ceiling in an outraged howl. "You're making fun of me!"

"Maybe," Benjamin Wolfe said indulgently. "But maybe your great dream isn't going to be all you think it is."

For once, Daivid Wolfe had to admit, his father might not have been all wrong. The scene before him now reminded him that the cosmos was not above making fun of its creations, either. He had once seen an ancient Earth flat-screen vid about a group of recruits so weird that none of them should ever have considered a career in the military. The assortment of odd body shapes, assorted costumes and odd weaponry worn by the group assembled under the hot noon sun on the parade ground reminded him strongly of it. Only one, a very tall, pale woman with scraped-back blond hair, wore the traditional parade dress, her white tunic collar turned up and stiffened at the edges, just like his. Not one of the others had on a whole uniform. Daivid had laughed at the vid. At the moment he felt like doing anything but.

Looming above the dusty square was the main reason Treadmill had its reputation as a dead end: the Space Service brig, a three-storey square structure of grim, gray-blue plascrete. Those spacers who had been sentenced to prison were sent here, a low-grade Terran-class world that would otherwise be an attractive planet for settlement since it was positioned along four active spaceways in between major systems of the Thousand Worlds Confederation. To avoid burnout caring for prisoners who might once have served beside them, units were usually stationed here in six-month rotations, except for X-ray Platoon. It had been here three years.

Wolfe had gotten an earful from the other officers on the transport that brought him here. The only reason that the spacers in the company he was inheriting weren't in the brig, or out of the service, was that, like him, no one could find an excuse for dismissing any of them that would stand up under scrutiny. A friendly commander had taken him aside in the hopper that had carried them both from the spaceport to the base, and warned him he was getting the worst unit in the vast Space Service. The man, in his fifties and secure in his ascent up the promotions ladder, wished him well, but suggested that Wolfe might want to start studying his options in the private sector.

Daivid knew the higher-ups wanted to scuttle his career. At the moment, he could have turned around and gone back in to request a discharge and passage home. No, he'd pay for his passage home. He'd work for his ticket, if he had to. He stepped backwards, preparing to turn around. But it was too late. They'd seen him. The tall woman barked out a command, and a few of the troops stood up straighter. He threw back his shoulders and marched forward.

"Company, tenn-nn hutt!" the woman barked out.

Daivid hesitated a moment before striding the rest of the way across the yard toward the people he was to command. He was met at the leading edge of the squared-off formation by the woman and a man, his officers by their insigne, who marched him down the rows. He'd been inspected a thousand times, so he knew how to do the inspection walk all the way across the face of the block. The men and women stared straight ahead, but their gazes followed him as soon as they thought he couldn't see them. He knew they did. He'd done the same thing. It was the longest walk he could ever imagine taking. Daivid knew what they saw: a very young man who was trying to act as though he was not scared bloodless. His uniform was spotless and perfectly ironed. That made two of them, him and the blonde. Everyone else was dressed in a jumble-sale collection of uniform pieces and items that had nothing to do with the military. He saw ski pants, pieces of cryo-suits, hospital greens, fatigues from half a dozen other services on twenty different worlds. One beefy, muscular man with a rounded belly like a hamburger bun appeared in just the general-issue skivvies, hacked off at the knees to show hairy shins and calloused feet clinging by the toes to worn flip-flop sandals. The skinny, tawny-skinned male beside him had on a dress tunic over soaked swim trunks.

The ensign saluted him snappily. Wolfe looked at him with resignation. The dark-skinned man's uniform pants were creased like knife blades down his long, skinny legs to spit-polished boots without a scuff or a scratch anywhere. Above the perfect trousers he had on a sleeveless knitted vest of brilliant pink. His insignia was clipped to one shoulder strap

"Ensign Thielind, sir. This is Lieutenant Borden. Ready for inspection, sir!"

"Carry on," Wolfe said, returning the salute.

"Yes, sir! Sound off!" Thielind barked.

The company reeled off its names. Wolfe listened to the rapid-fire roster, glad that all that data was in the chipboard that the adjutant carried and would be transferred to him at the end of roll call. Aaooorru, Adri'Leta, Ambering, Boland, Borden, Ewanowski, Gire, Haalten, Injaru, Jones, Lin, Meyers, Mose, Nuu Myi, Okumede, ParuizSoftware, Somulska, Streb, Theilind, D-45, Vacarole. Three nonhumans: an itterim in cutoff shorts and suspenders, a shrimplike corlist one meter high with ten jointed limbs wearing a toilet plunger on its stalk-eyed head, and a semicat, one of the race of tall, muscular inhabitants of a cluster of star systems that had been enveloped by the human-dominated empire five or six hundred years ago, in coveralls with a drop-seat to allow free movement of its long tail. Twenty-two in all. With him, twenty-three. Even for a platoon it was a small group: two squads of eleven, plus a communications officer who stayed aboard their transport vessel while the company was on a mission, or three platoons of six or seven spacers each. Barely large enough to function.

One very large man in the second row, a chief petty officer by the half of his insignia that still clung to his cap, was wearing the tunic of the elite fighter pilot company that flew the single-man warp fighters. The guy didn't look like a star ace. His thick, short fingers and heavy arms suggested he fought in deployed troops on shipboard or planetary surface. Curiosity got the better of Wolfe.

"Chief?"

The big man straightened up.

"Boland," the aide at his elbow advised.

"Where'd you get that uniform?"

"Traded for it, sir," Boland said. Instead of eyes-front, he turned to grin at Wolfe. His eyes were a startling shade of green, with stubby, pale lashes sticking out from thick, creased lids. The executive officer at Wolfe's elbow gave a deep-throated *hem!* of disapproval. Boland snapped back to eyes-front.

"What'd you trade?" Wolfe asked, even though he suspected he'd regret the answer.

"Admiral's runabout, sir," Boland said.

Wolfe almost asked 'surplus,' and realized that it could never be true, and the question would brand him as a hopeless neophyte. Better to assume the worst and let him plead innocent.

"You stole a flitter and traded it for a *tunic?*"

Boland looked at him, eyes wide with wounded pride. "Oh, no, sir, I got lots of other stuff! My mama didn't raise any fools."

"Uh-huh," Wolfe said helplessly, knowing that some kind of response was called for. He raised his voice. "Well, there will be no more stealing," he said, and instantly felt as though his words fell down the endless well of ignored orders that had come before. He continued on doggedly. "That book you threw away, find your copy, because we're going to be running by it from now on. No more disobeying rules. No more appearing on parade out of uniform. If you don't have one now, trade for it or put in for a replacement. I want to see you smartly turned out for the next inspection. Do I make myself clear?"

It didn't matter if he had, because they'd already tuned him out. He was too young, untried, possessed of no authority, and they knew it. He was off to a bad start trying to make a good impression on them. He glanced around, trying to find something that would reconnect him with them. He glanced over at the flagpoles. The first was the Galactic Union flag. The second was the army. The third was the brigade. The fourth was a gold field displaying a black, ovoid blob with legs. "And what the hell is that?"

"That's our company banner, sir," said the adjutant.

"What is it?" Wolfe demanded. "It looks like a cockroach."

"Got it in one guess," said Boland, grimly pleased. "That's what they call us. X-ray Platoon. Brand X. Penalty Box. Screwup Company. The Cockroaches. Welcome to hell. Sir."

"Your luggage is in your quarters," the ensign said. "Shall I arrange to have the cases unpacked, sir?"

"No, thanks," Wolfe said, grateful for the interruption. "I'll take care of it." He didn't want any hand-holding, and any babying he allowed himself to accept put him that many paces away from the spacers in his company. He needed to relate to them—not too closely, because he still had to be responsible for sending them into battle, and, when necessary, maybe to their deaths—but they were being thrown together under the worst possible circumstances. Their lives depended on one another. He needed to form a bond. Besides, he had a lot of questions about X-ray Company. He had a better chance of getting an honest response out of them than he was from the brass above him.

"Company quarters ready for inspection, sir," the adjutant said.

"Thank you, Ensign—?"

"Thielind, sir!"

"Good. Let's see them."

Thielind threw himself into one of his skull-shattering salutes. "Sir! Company, about face! March!"

Shrugging, X-ray more or less lined up and marched together toward the end of the parade ground where the barracks buildings stood. Wolfe trailed along behind them, his assistants on either side. The group veered away from the pristine buildings, heading instead toward a transportal.

"Uh, where are we going?" he asked the female lieutenant, as his soldiers popped open the last car on the three-pod train inside the transparent tube and found seats.

"Our quarters, sir," she replied crisply. "We're station-keeping on the launch facility. It's about half an hour from here. We commute in for occasions like this, and to visit the canteen and PX."

"Must suck," Wolfe observed, frankly.

"With considerable force, sir," she replied. The first hint of any kind of empathy appeared in her eyes for a second, but only a second. She climbed on board the transport and waited until he took his place on the blue-gray upholstered seat before she sat down herself.

He had wondered why the mapmakers had called this planet Treadmill. Once he got a look at the terrain, it wasn't much of a stretch to guess. Barren yellow and brown hills stretched out on either side of him, punctuated by the occasional green thornbush. It looked like a low-resolution animated treadmill workout with troughs and highs, seldom settling into flat plains. He'd gotten a look at the topography from above, eager to see the site of his first posting as a first lieutenant. Treadmill had looked kind of pretty from space, like a piece of ornate parquet-work in golds, greens and browns. Now that he could see all of it up close, the lines in between fields and hills and sorry excuses for forests were jagged fault zones.

A hiker trying to make his way in the dark was in danger of falling through the crust of the planet. Treadmill, according to Wolfe's friendly source, had fairly active tectonics, making it unsuitable for heavy industry or company farms or ranches, but it had a T-class atmosphere and gravity, and it was well placed to send troops out to the rest of the Confederation when needed. The base and launch station were separated because not enough flat land existed in either place to accommodate the entire facility.

In fact, it took them forty minutes to ride down the high-speed tube to the end of the line. If Wolfe needed any further reminders that his company was the brigade pariah, the fact that the supports and substations along the way got more and more seedy was one more checkmark off the list. Transport tubes were supposed to run smoothly. He noticed about three-fourths of the way through the ride that his troops gripped the arm-rests and lifted their butts subtly off the shock-padded seats.

When the train hit the first bump it felt like a shockwave striking his spine. Wolfe grabbed for a support, just in time to save himself from getting thrown out of his seat. Small wonder the officers had chosen to take a hopper from the spaceport directly to the base! No one would do this ride if s/he didn't have to. Every time he tried to sit down, the train bucked and juddered some more. He did the rest of the trip standing. Grins passed among the members of his company. He kept his face straight. They must do this to all the greenhorns, officers included. Well, he wasn't going to hand them an easy victory.

"Been on this station long?" he asked Borden. His voice wobbled with every fresh bounce.

The officer never changed expression. "Three years, sir."

The train swung wide to avoid a jagged fissure. Wolfe seesawed on one foot, swinging around helplessly. He grabbed for another ceiling loop with his free hand. The others bobbed gently on their seats like dressage riders. Daivid vowed to learn the topography of the route the very next time he rode this runaway whipsaw.

"When was X-ray's last mission?" he asked, bending his knees to keep his equilibrium as the train rode over hills he saw approaching.

The lieutenant wasn't impressed. "It's all in the briefing summary in your quarters, sir."

Wolfe suppressed a sigh and concentrated on not getting flung out the curved window.

In spite of the bright sunshine, X-ray's compound was dreary. Daivid hadn't been in a camp that grim since he'd visited his Great-Uncle Robbile's fishing hideaway in the wilds of the northern continent on Tokumine IV, but Robbile Wolfe liked his haven bleak, so as to put off casual tourists if any had ever dropped by. The Cockroaches were stuck with their décor: military beige, military gray and, for a final insult, military pink.

Beyond a compound fence from the top of which energy crackled, sentries in bubble flitters roved around and around the spaceport in which he had just arrived. The shuttle that had brought him down from the dreadnought still stood on the landing pad, its silver body sharply backlit by brilliant blue work-lights as coverall-clad engineers swarmed over it, performing maintenance and making sure the fuel rods were intact. Hangars as large as small moons lined the field, also under the watchful eye of human MPs, high-response alarm systems and guardbots.

Security measures around a spaceport were cursory in comparison with the watch kept on the surrounding spaceways: serious attacks upon a military base would almost certainly come from orbit, not ground level. Anyone who was already on planet could either fly the craft in the spaceport and were authorized to do so, or wouldn't know what to do to launch one if s/he managed to get into the cockpit in the first place. The most the ground-level military police usually did was prevent anyone from hurting him- or herself or damaging valuable systems. As a military base Treadmill's adminis-tration had the authority to oust any civilian who caused trouble, no matter how much investment that civilian had put into profit-making infrastructure. Just that knowledge kept down the active protests. Grubstakes on T-class planets were hard to come by.

"This way, sir," said the eager ensign in the knitted vest. Daivid followed him to a small building to the left of the barracks hall.

No trace remained of Daivid's predecessor's belongings in the officer's personal quarters. Wolfe looked around the drab beige chamber trying to get a sense of the former occupant. He couldn't find a clue. The rooms, a bedroom, a bath, a walk-in closet and a small office, had all been cleaned—hosed out, he guessed by the streaks on the blue-gray floor. Well, he couldn't smell anything unsavory. Chances were the former CO hadn't died there.

Wolfe unpacked his regulation trunk into the chest of drawers and closet provided. As usual, the closet contained five hangers, as per standard supply orders, sufficient for all his uniforms. Officers were expected to provide their own hangers for any civilian clothing they retained. Water glass, soap, towels, shaver and hair dryer in the lavatory, water saver-purifier, small storage cabinet behind the sink mirror. Impersonal. That was one of the things he liked about the military. He didn't have to make choices about what he wore or what his quarters looked like. It didn't offend anyone when he chose one kind of suit, or put a company out of business when he stopped buying their shoes. Those selections were made for him.

The briefing clipboard lay on the desk in the small office. He scrolled up the company rolls and had the information sent as an oral reading to his personal communications unit. The receiver screen every trooper in the TWC forces wore rode the back of the left sleeve ten centimeters above the wrist. When a company suited up in battle armor, the unit was inserted into a purpose-built protective slot to activate communications between troopers and command. They were all voice-activated, and had to be personally tuned so they couldn't be captured and used by the enemy to listen in on transmissions. For privacy, one could wear an ear-bud, though some officers had their audio receivers implanted in the mastoid bone behind the ear or in a piercing in the upper pinna. Daivid had decided to have a mastoid receiver. It didn't bang against the side of his head the way ear-implants did, he'd still be in touch with his command even if his ear got shot off, and the sound quality he got when he was listening to music through the unit was awesome.

"Aaooorru, Dompeter," the flat voice intoned directly into his aural nerves. "Corlist. Born Mishagui, Vom, Beta Antares system—"

He took off the uniform he had traveled in and put it in the cleaning trunk. Working just fine, he observed, listening to the hum that started up as soon as the lid dropped. His dress whites would come out spotless with perfect seams, perfect creases. Efficient. He brought out fatigues and laid them on the bed. Impersonal. Regulation. No hurt feelings involved.

He wrapped himself in his white, service-issued bath robe and turned on the shower. No sonic cleanser here, he was pleased to see. He hated having the outer layer of dead cells shivered off him by vibrations they told him he couldn't hear. They were wrong: he could hear the high-pitched whine just fine, and he hated it. Sonic cleansers were standard on all interplanetary transports except luxury liners. Space Service personnel didn't travel on those.

He almost missed the sonic cleanser when he observed the thin stream of water dribbling out of the showerhead, like the output of an incontinent dog. He felt the water; at least it wasn't cold. The heating elements still functioned correctly. He'd have to see about getting a plumber out here to check the pipes and the pressure feed. He stepped into the stall and pulled the curtain closed.

The only non-regulation thing he had in his possession was a card the size of a credit chit attached with a glue-square to the skin over his sternum. Before he turned into the weak spray of water, he examined the card. It was the only thing he owned that he didn't dare let out of his possession at any time.

Wolfe dried himself off and shouldered into the singlet that went under his uniform, making sure the card was still firmly attached to his skin. He started when the adjutant came into the room behind him and cleared his throat. Wolfe hastily lowered his undershirt and shrugged into his blue-gray fatigue jacket.

"They're ready for inspection, sir," the adjutant said, saluting smartly, and swung around again, heading out the door.

Wolfe brushed imaginary dust off his insignia. Just before he stepped outside he felt the middle of his chest to make sure the card was secure.

CHAPTER 2

RAUCOUS CONVERSATION DROPPED into silence as soon as they opened the door. X-ray Company leaped off unmade bunks, aged chairs and battered star chests to stand at attention as Wolfe came in behind Thielind.

He did the inspection walk again. This time it felt more real than it had on the parade ground. It was just dawning on him: he had a command—all right, the crappiest one in the space service, but it was all his. He had to swallow the grin he felt pinning back the corners of his mouth. Here was the beginning of his rise to the top. He'd show those doubters that he was more than just his father's son. Here was the beginning of the change for good that he could make in the universe. With a proprietary swagger, he sauntered down the center of the long room.

Like his quarters, the barracks was bog-standard. The biggest difference between this place and the barracks he'd last occupied, as a second lieutenant, had to be the wear and tear. Everything here must be hand-me-downs dating back decades, maybe even centuries. The lavatory facilities he could see through the open door bore the patina of ages, the porcelain riddled with small cracks and the chrome worn off the metal spigots.

Hovel, Sweet Hovel, he thought, *but it's mine, all mine.*

At least no one felt crowded. With a unit this small there was no need for tiered bunks. Everyone had a single bed, spaced from the ones on either side by upright lockers that also gave the sleeper a measure of privacy.

And now, to get to know the spacers who inhabited this dormitory. It wasn't going to be easy. The faces sized Wolfe up as he walked up and down the center aisle. Their expressions said they weren't impressed by what they saw.

"At ease," he ordered, looking around at them. He gave them a smile, hoping it didn't look nervous or insincere. "This is a casual visit. You all probably know this is my first command. The first-lieutenant bars are fresh off the card. I haven't got any bad habits to unlearn."

"Too bad," someone snickered under his breath. A low titter of laughter ran through the room. Wolfe decided to pretend he didn't hear it.

"I know a lot of you have been together for a long time. You'll have to adapt to my style, but I've got to learn about you if we're to work effectively together."

Dead silence. Wolfe shrugged. The words hadn't sounded sincere or convincing even to him. He wished he had gone ahead and written down the brilliant remarks he had conceived when he first learned he was getting a command. Those would've rocked 'em in the aisles. Instead, they looked at him as though he'd just piddled on the floor. Maybe he ought to—that would get their attention.

He continued walking up and down, the adjutant at his heels. The long barracks was divided into three sections, every fifteen meters, as per fire regulations, but during the day the partitions were pushed back to make one big room. The walls were the enameled panels standard in military facilities both shipside and dirtside for their durability and ease in cleaning. Most of it here was drab khaki-gray, except for one panel in drab coral. That one didn't quite fit into its modular frame. The edges were fire-scarred, and half the surface was etched with names. Some of them were scratched into the hard surface with some sharp object. Others had been laboriously cut, dot by dot, with a laser, all the way through the wall to the insulation. Wolfe ran his fingers along the names, feeling the minute impressions. He knew from experience that the enamel was practically indestructible. Each name had to have taken hours to incise.

"What's this?" he asked.

There was a defensive growl from the troops, but only Chief Boland stepped forward.

"Wall of honor, sir," he said. "Memory of the dead."

"Why not have their names decently engraved?"

"It's our custom," said another trooper, a tall woman with very long legs and sincere brown eyes. "We use the knife or the sidearm of the lost soldier to write his or her name. It's—more personal that way."

Wolfe nodded. "I see. The color—It didn't start here, did it?"

"No, sir," said the female lieutenant. "It came from Platoon X's first HQ on board the *Burnside*." Wolfe recognized the name of a dreadnought that had been destroyed in a territorial conflict on the

TWC borders several years before. "We've been moved a few times, whenever someone the brass likes better wants our location. We take it with us."

Wolfe raised an eyebrow. A piece of bulkhead that heavy wouldn't get shipped as part of a unit's regular kit. In fact, the loaders would raise hell if a company showed up with something like that in tow, and word got back up the line to the brass. In fact, there should have been at least one attempt to confiscate it. On the other hand, he wouldn't put it past the resourcefulness of X-ray to make a way to get their memorial on board their troop transport. The more experienced units would recognize and honor the effort for what it was and let it slip by, and the young ones couldn't outthink them long enough to stop them doing what they wanted.

"It's a Cockroach tradition," Boland said, staring Wolfe straight in the eye.

"You're not going to take it down, sir?" the diminutive woman chief asked. Though it was phrased like a question, it was a statement. Wolfe knew enough to take the warning.

"I wouldn't dream of taking it down," Wolfe said.

This time, the murmur that ran through the room was positive. Wolfe knew he'd scored a point, but he meant it sincerely. For all the crap they spouted about being in Platoon X, he knew they had their pride. Outsiders didn't realize that being the outcasts made this unit band together, form their own society, establish their own rules. The Cockroaches didn't like being questioned by anyone from a legitimate unit, one that had the backing of the regular Thousand Worlds' navy behind him or her. Because no one cared what happened to them. Because they really didn't seem to care themselves. Look at the way they lived! Not a single bunk had been made. The curtains at the windows were gray and cracking. The floor creaked when walked on, probably indicating cracked joists underneath. Look at their uniforms! If anyone had given a hoot about them they'd have had those worn fatigues replaced long ago. *Someone* had to care about these troopers, and resurrect any self-respect they had. That must be why he had been sent here.

A blooping sound interrupted his thoughts. The Cockroaches looked surprised then shamefaced. Then defensive. The bloop erupted again. Daivid followed the noise to a distant corner of the long room and grabbed for the handle of a well-traveled upright packing case two meters on a side that served the unit as a storage closet. The box wouldn't open. He shook the handle and looked for a locking mechanism.

"Thielind," he ordered, "open this box."

"Sir—"

BLOOP! A cloud spread out from the top of the box. Wolfe got a faceful of sharp fumes and started coughing.

"Open this damned box!" he gasped.

Two of the spacers jumped forward and thrust their fingers into apertures that he thought at first were projectile-weapon damage the old box had sustained in transit. The front divided into two halves and swung open.

Inside, though, the crate wasn't derelict, as it had appeared on the outside. It had been lined with the kind of sound-insulation foam that was found in TWC starship engine compartments. Ventilation holes had been drilled into the ceiling and rear walls of the closet to allow the flow of air and the occasional escape of warm liquor fumes, which were now rising from the contraption that was propped on a tripod at waist level. The device, for that was all he could find to call it, consisted of shiny copper tubing, gleaming metal vacuum flasks, twisted gray and white flexible piping and half a dozen pieces of laboratory glass. Underneath it all lay a survival stove, its orange heat circle glowing like a sunset, and a hundred liter tank, the recipient of the still's output.

"And the booze?" Wolfe asked as mildly as he could, considering the current ethanol content of his lungs. "I take it this is a tradition, too?"

"Uh-huh," Boland said, his face stony. "Long time, sir. Dating all the way back, sir."

"There's only one bar on the launch pad, lieutenant!" Thielind protested. "You oughta see what they charge for one watered-down beer. Four credits."

"Four credits!" Wolfe frowned at Thielind, who nodded vigorously. "Hell, I'd go into business for myself at prices like those." Eyebrows lifted all around the room

"So that's what we did, sir," Petty Officer Jones assured him in his musical voice. "I'm glad you feel the same way we do, sir. There's a longstanding trrr-adition of self-sufficiency in our unit. You wouldn't want us wasting our precious resources on overpriced booze, would you?"

Wolfe grinned. "That's a big tank for twenty-odd troopers. You're not supplying the bar, too, are you? That's not self-sufficiency, that'd be going into business for yourself on Space Service territory with Space Service property."

"Well—" Jones rolled the final 'l,' trying to find the words.

"It's not strictly against the rules," Borden said in her bloodless voice. By now, Wolfe had figured out that the XO was a bunkroom lawyer. She liked rules, good for a woman in her position. Normally, it wouldn't make her popular among the rank-and-file, but this company seemed to like her. She must have other redeeming traits. Wolfe had to get to know what those were. Clearly, one of them was being able to rationalize anything that the Cockroaches wanted to do that wasn't exactly in the books. "All of this material is salvage. Half of it we fished out of vacuum or grubbed up out of dumps, sir. As such, it is no longer Navy property, because the Navy has discarded it."

"Not like Boland's runabout, eh?"

"No, sir!" The XO's voice rose to an emphatic point, though she continued to stare at a spot on the wall.

"We're just being resourceful," Petty Officer Mose said. "Is there anything in the Space Service regs preventing resourcefulness?"

"Not exactly," Daivid began then realized 1) this was an argument that would go on for weeks and 2) he was being baited. "But there's resourcefulness, and there's going outside the lines."

Boland laid an innocent hand on his chest. "No one has ever caught us going outside the lines, sir."

Daivid laughed. "I bet they haven't."

"Want a snort, sir?" Chief Lin asked.

"No," Wolfe said. The others stared at him suspiciously until he smiled. "I have to finish the inspection first."

"At ease," Wolfe said, and winced as the scrawny adjutant relayed the order in a shout from under his right ear. He sat down on the nearest footlocker and took off his hat. At his signal, most of the troops resumed the seats they'd left when he entered, kicking back on their bunks with their boots up, sitting on reversed chairs, perching wherever a human buttocks or alien analog would fit. Thielind popped open the still closet and brought a beaker of liquor and a relatively clean glass to Wolfe. Gingerly, Daivid took a sip, and hastily sucked in a double lungful of air to cool his windpipe. The rotgut wasn't as bad as he'd feared, but it still burned its way down into his belly.

"So," he gasped, slinging a hip as casually as he could onto the nearest table while the others helped themselves to the booze. "Tell me about your last few missions. I hear this company gets the worst assignments, in the worst possible conditions. Where do we usually end up getting sent?"

The 'we' was accepted as a positive sign, too.

"You know how they say 'slag happens'?" the tall woman asked. She was called Adri'Leta Sixteen, which meant she was a clone, the sixteenth generation of her combination of genes. From her record Daivid had learned she was the first one to go into military service, and wondered why.

He nodded. "Uh-huh."

"Well, that's where we go. Where slag's happening."

"Right. Do we have to watch them make it, or do we just clean it up afterwards?" Wolfe asked reasonably. "We get to critique 'em on technique?"

Boland sputtered between his lips.

"No one cares about our opinion, sir," Borden informed him.

Wolfe shifted to face her, giving her his full attention. "I do. Yeah, I know I got sent here, same as you, but giving me these bars means that I have access to the chain of command. I don't want slag assignments, so I don't want you to get slag assignments, because we're all going there together." They all grumbled. They'd heard the speech before, probably one time per commanding officer. How was he going to get through to them? "So, where'd you get sent last? How come I'm here, and not your last CO?"

For a moment, no one said anything. Wolfe felt his heart sink, thinking he'd lost them again. He should have waited for the booze to kick in. It turned out they were all sucking in breath. They all started talking at once.

"We got pinned down on Sombel," Lin blurted out.

"The brass screwed us," Boland snarled, interrupting her. "No air cover—"

"We needed three platoons to cover, not two," Adri'Leta added.

"Heavy fire from guarded positions—" Borden explained.

Wolfe sat in the middle of it, letting them talk. Terran civilization had spent its first fifteen hundred years bringing itself into existence. Humanity had spread from the single world called Earth out to every T-class planet it could find, and adapted to hundreds of others with atmosphere domes, undersea habitats or orbiting space stations. During the Building Phase, as the historians liked to call it, spacefarers and settlers cooperated, seeing one another as fellow seekers in the drive to open up the galaxy to humanity. Explorers led the way, sending back reports to Earth Central, and later to Alpha Centauri and Delta Glius of viable systems. In their wake industry and colonists followed, as did traders, teachers and scientists, as well as those who saw their mission in life to take advantage of those who trusted in the basic goodness of human nature. Wolfe was ashamed to admit that many of his ancestors fell into the last category. He saw it as his goal to make amends by undoing some of the harm they had done.

Settlements grew into civilizations. The first Galactic Government arose. It lasted fifty years before it was obsolete, unable to keep up with the growth of its power base. It fell, to be replaced by the First Terran Empire. Which split up into the Power Enterprise, the Vargan Trade Union, and the Star Systems Alliance. Which reconformed into the Second Terran Empire. Which, after a few more reconfigurations, including the brief but colorful reign of Mad Emperor Haviland, elections, both crooked and otherwise, plenty of bullying, conquest, persuasion and preferential treatment in trade, became the Thousand Worlds Confederation.

Modeled upon the ancient Roman and American patterns of historic Terra, the TWC was a looser association than many of the past govermental structures, reestablishing a common defense, a common language, and a common currency. It allowed member systems to regulate themselves, with certain basic rights guaranteed to all citizens, such as the child protective system and the marriage rights act, which had held up for thousands of years though it was always attacked whenever there was a change of regime. (There weren't really a thousand worlds in the system yet, since the statute insisted only a viable planet with T-class characteristics and a breathable atmosphere qualified, but it sounded better to the founding members than the Six Hundred and Fifty-Three Worlds Confederation.)

But not everyone was happy with the status quo. Because the current government found itself loath to lean too heavily on individual worlds' administrations, sometimes excesses grew unchecked into abuses. TWC found itself having to send in troops to defend beings' rights or extract diplomats from a deteriorated situation. Word spread that TWC's over government was attempting to conquer member worlds and run them under a local governor from a central location, as had been done in the bad old days of the Empires.

Out of this misunderstanding, insurgency had flared a movement seeking to overturn the galactic government. TWC had been trying to quash the rebellion for years. Where diplomacy failed, armed intervention became necessary to prevent noncombatants from becoming prey to the rebel forces, and to prevent trade routes from being cut off. The main problem was that no matter how many ships or troopers that TWC had, the space service could be and was always being stretched too thin over too many fronts. Daivid had only been in the Space Service for three years, but even he saw that the galactic government was always fighting too many battles at once. X-ray had fallen victim to this latest round of bad planning.

With insufficient firepower to protect them while they tried to accomplish their task, they'd been sent into a location that had not been adequately scouted or even scoped.

"It ought to have been pretty straightforward," Lin said, her small face concentrated. "We were sent in to do a surgical shutdown of a major power plant. Not to destroy it, but to close it down. The Insurgency had taken over a factory in this city and was regearing it to use as a munitions plant."

D-45 made a disgusted gesture. "They weren't making weapons, they were making flitters. The trick is it was in a city sympathetic to the rebels, and they had plenty of notice that we were coming. They were ready for us. We started taking fire almost as soon as we were inserted."

"It turns out we were only a diversion," Thielind added bitterly. The normally cheerful adjutant wore a grim expression on his thin face. "Halfway around the globe, the big ships were pulling prisoners out of a bunker. They'd sent us in to draw the fire from the insurgents. It worked. We had half the local army on our asses. If they'd only told us we were the stalking horse, we could have dug in and given a good show, pot-shooting at the power plant without exposing ourselves. As it is, we lost Captain Scoley, who was a damned good officer."

"They wanted us all to die." Round-faced Jones clamped his lips shut after delivering his single opinion.

All of them crossed their arms and looked at Wolfe. He looked back, uncertain what to say.

They obviously didn't care if he reported the gossip up the line. Apart from being sent to the brig or a prison ship, what worse thing could happen to them? They were already being sent on death missions. Mustering out would be a favor, compared to what he was hearing.

"Tell me more," Wolfe said.

They hardly needed further encouragement. The cork was out of the bottle. They were dying to tell him more. The Cockroaches got all the bad duties: garbage detail, prisoner escort, munitions guard, hazardous waste cleanup—Name the task: if it was dangerous or disgusting, the Cockroaches had dealt with it. And, Wolfe thought as he listened, they dealt pretty admirably.

They didn't complain about the task itself, just about the lack of respect and support from the brass. And they were absolutely right. No one cared if they lived or died. By the reckoning of the powers that be, they had already been discarded. They caught hell if they failed or wasted Navy resources, and got precious little praise if they succeeded. They had to be their own cheering section. And now Wolfe was in the dumper with them. He was determined to raise their stock somehow. Let someone else be Brand X for a change. These were good people. He'd certainly met worse in his lifetime.

"…And that's how we got started with the bulkhead," Borden explained, at the end of a long narrative, interrupted along the way by half her fellows. "It's our way of coping."

"So's the still," Jones added in his lilting baritone.

Wolfe hated to admit it, but he was almost one hundred percent sure he could place the heavyset trooper's planet of origin. Cymrai had been settled thousands of years ago by people named Jones. Most of them were of Terran-Welsh descent, but the rest had assumed the name somewhere along the way or had it imposed on their ancestors by others. In the long run, Cymrai's culture had taken a Celtic turn, preserving ancient arts and music. The communications directory was strictly arranged by given names.

"And our interest in advanced education," put in D-45. He was a very tall man with sallow skin, shining black hair, and a prominent, pointed chin. Wolfe recognized the style of naming. It came from a world named Egalos on TWC's fringe where the liberal government abolished all family cognomens in an effort to put behind its people any of the disadvantages or bad memories of the past associated with their names. Instead, they gave each regional cluster a designation based upon the location of their city, town or neighborhood. One of Daivid's teachers had been Sarah N'Diya Q-333. He'd had a mad crush on her when he was eight years old.

"And our weekly smokers," said Thielind.

"And the ritual scarification—"

"And the limerick competitions—"

"All right," Wolfe laughed. "Now I know you're making these up to impress me. Come on! Limericks? Ritual scarification?"

"Yeah," Ambering said, rolling up her sleeve. She was a meaty woman with warm brown skin and gray eyes. She pointed to an irregular mass on the inside of her forearm, an oval with three or four little lines sticking out of one side. "There. You lift the skin with a knife. When it heals you lift it again. The color's office ink—very permanent. It's supposed to be a cockroach, but I was never very good at art."

"All right," Daivid said, shaken. "Now I am impressed."

"Ahem." Jones cleared his throat and raised a hand theatrically. "A surveyor in space, grade E-4, went out with an antigrav whore. Ten klicks over the ground, he spun her round and round, and centrifugally plumb-bobbed her core."

The others broke into applause and raucous cheers. Wolfe joined in.

Jones rose and bowed, a thick hand across his round belly. "That's one made up by Toco Bradon. She left us about four years ago. What a mind on that girl! She had a flair for the rhyming word. I can still recall a few more of her ditties—"

BLEE-ble. BLEE-ble. BLEE-ble.

Everyone immediately fell silent. Wolfe glanced around for the communications unit. Thielind clapped down his glass and looked at his wrist screen.

"Ancom!" he chirped, the signal to answer an incoming transmission on his personal communications unit. The noise ceased at once. Thielind listened for a moment then tapped at the bright yellow stud in his ear lobe. "Gotcha. I mean, aye aye, ma'am!" He looked up at Wolfe. "Inspection tomorrow morning at eleven hundred, sir. The commander wants to make sure you're checked in and ready, and everything's under control."

"Of course. Thanks, ensign," Wolfe said. He glanced at the rest of his command. "Okay, company, you heard it. I want this place ship-shape by eleven. That's an order."

Thielind's large eyes glanced around the room. He picked up the laboratory flask and filled Wolfe's glass with it. "Have another drink, Lieutenant."

"Here's to fallen comrades," Borden said as the chronometer clicked over to 00:00.

By now the booze had been joined on the battered table by mixers, cards and pows. Wolfe selected a caffeine pow two millimeters across and tucked it into the space between his cheek and gum. The heat and saliva melted the coating instantly, releasing a jolt of bitterness into his mouth. It'd be good to keep his wits alert. He held two pairs, jacks and sevens, in a game so ancient that he never even questioned why the guard card was called a jack, and fervently hoped no one else had anything useful in his or her hand. His luck was usually pretty good, but it was being sorely tested. He signalled for one card.

"Why do you have so many customs?" he asked, watching Jones deal. The Cymraeg's thick fingers were surprisingly deft. "I've been with a few units since I joined up. No one else seems to do it. Apart from the usual ones, breaking in new swabs by making them drink burning cocktails or ramming their new insigne into bare skin, that kind of thing."

They all looked at one another. "What, you writing a book?" Mose asked, a sour expression on his creased, pale face.

"No, officer-sir," Injaru called, his eyebrows high on his chocolate-dark forehead. "You don't want to do *that.*"

"Shut up," Mose growled. "Huh, lieutenant?"

A little puzzled, Wolfe watched the byplay. "No. Just curious. Where'd these all come from?"

"Boredom," Boland announced. "Boredom, maybe. Some of 'em we do for the hell of it, but a few do come from remembering old colleagues-in-arms. We've got nothing to do in between missions or on long space hauls except drink. In case you haven't noticed, they keep us pretty isolated out here. No one wants to associate with us. Afraid they'll get the stink, I don't doubt. We come up with things to keep our brains from dying in the isolation. We can't think ahead. We don't know where we're going, where they're sending us next. We *don't* want to think about the past. You wouldn't, if you had been through what we have. So we have our own ways. Keeps people guessing when they overhear us."

"Keeps us out of trouble," Meyers said. The curvaceous woman gathered up three cards with careful fingers. She looked up at him with a provocative eye. "In case you were wondering, we don't try to get into trouble."

"Maybe we have a little more imagination than most of those bobble-heads," Lin said fiercely.

"Hah!" Thielind barked. "That's how you ended up here! Well," he turned to Wolfe, "that's how I ended up here, anyway. Imagination." He poured another tot into Wolfe's glass. "Have a drink, lieutenant."

Wolfe eyed the glass, wishing there was a potted plant within reach. He didn't know how many more applications of that flensing acid his system could take before it shut down. "Maybe a little more," he agreed. "Thanks, ensign."

A few eyebrows were raised. "Don't you say 'enswine,' like the rest of them?" Thielind asked, curiously. "I'm used to it."

"Yeah. We even let him drink with us," Boland joked, bringing a huge hand around to impact jovially between the slight junior officer's shoulder blades. Thielind bounced into the table and fell back, but his eyes never left Wolfe's.

Daivid squirmed a little. "I know it's not corps practice, but I got so sick of it when I was an ensign that I promised myself I wouldn't use it. It's just respect. You're on the line, same as the rest of us."

"Respect, huh?" D-45 asked with a sound of the same in his voice.

To cover up what for the moment sounded like marshmallow-gooey sentimentality, Daivid took a huge swig of the company's rotgut, and let out an audible gasp as it hit the back of his throat.

"Too strong for you?" Jones asked. He emptied his own beaker, smacking his lips.

"It's fine," Wolfe assured him, trying not to gasp as the next sip found a portion of his esophagus that hadn't yet been cauterized. "Nice, but a little too rough to go to sleep on."

"Dilute it," Borden said, tossing him a beaker of mild mixer. To his own surprise Wolfe caught it one-handed. Coordination was not yet completely gone. "It's about 150 proof. What do you normally drink? Wine?"

"Yeah," the lieutenant admitted sheepishly, hoping he wouldn't sound like a wimp, but it was better to admit the truth than to pickle himself just to try and fit in.

"That's okay," she said with more friendliness than before. "We like wine, too."

"Yeah," Boland said, raising steadily reddening eyes from his current hand. "Do we ever! How come we can't get assignments escorting vintage booze, like the guy they caught with an unlicensed shipload of Earth wine the other day?

"Yeah, that guy! *His* name was Wolfe," Injaru said thoughtfully. "Nicol Sambor some-other-middle-names Wolfe. One of that big-time Family with all them connections. *You* know what kind I mean." The others nodded knowingly. "I bet that stuff they confiscated was pretty fine. Too bad we couldn't get a hold of some of that. He wouldn't be any relation to you, looey?" he joked.

Daivid cleared his throat and shifted uncomfortably. "As a matter of fact, he's my cousin."

"Yeah, right," Boland said, scornfully. He caught a yellow-eyed glance from his new commanding officer. "You're serious, aren't you?"

"Uh, yeah. I am. Nicol's a second cousin."

"*You're* one of *that* Wolfe Family?" the long-legged lieutenant asked, staring at him.

"Well, hell!" Lin said, as if everyone ought to know that. "They have connections all over!"

And indeed they did, as Daivid was all too aware, in shipping, gambling, smuggling, commodities trading, every money-making venture known to civilization. 'Whenever there's big money inside, there's a Wolfe at the door,' as the tired old joke went. Daivid tried to console himself with the thought that his family didn't commit murder for hire, or slaughter innocent people in pursuit of credits. They specialized in what were known as 'bloodless crimes': games of chance, control of shipping rights, exclusives on certain goods, influence with government officials, transport of desirable items or people who wished to go from point A to point B without drawing attention. Since the bad old days, when space had been totally lawless and a crackdown had ensued that left few members standing from any Family, the Wolfes had sworn off involvement with drugs, prostitution, animal smuggling, or anything that would trigger a quarantine or give the Thousand Worlds Confederation galactic government an excuse to toss one of their warehouses. Occasionally, some law-and-order candidate would shake things up upon coming into office, impounding ships whose ownership could be traced back to a family. But while the Wolfe family played rough to survive, its business practices were clean. They had a policy of charitable contributions, no strings attached, and ran a fine string of soup kitchens as well as their fabulous chain of restaurants. Wolfe took a perverse measure of pride in that; few of the other families could say the same. But rumor tarred all of them with the same brush.

It was the last thing he wanted to come out, but he might as well have handed a curriculum vitae out to everyone in camp. There was no way to get away from his Family.

"You knew, didn't you?" Thielind asked Lin accusingly.

Boland growled protectively—Wolfe suspected a personal interest—but the small woman tossed her head nonchalantly. "Sure I did, but why would I tell? There is no bad blood between our Families. We enjoy a centuries-old alliance. I am not in the inner circle anyhow." She gave her new CO a sloe-eyed glance. "I'm a bastard. My mother won't tell who my father is, so the Ancestors won't acknowledge me. I don't inherit anything from the Lin Family, and no one looks out for me. But if you didn't say who you were, I figured you didn't want to. It's your secret."

"Thanks," Wolfe mumbled, feeling more uncomfortable than ever in the frankly admiring glances some of his company was now giving him. "It'd have come out sooner or later."

"So, what the hell are you doing here," the broad-faced woman pressed, "if your family has all that money?"

"I don't really want to talk about it—Meyers, is it? How long have you been in the corps?"

Meyers gave him a funny look but let him distract her. "Five years. I was bonking my former CO. He happened to be in a strict marriage contract with an admiral he only saw about once every two months. When someone caught us and threatened to report him, he made up some offense to get me off the base. Wish I'd had some loathsome disease I could have left him with, as a parting gift. I like it here better, sir. No one cares who I sleep with, so long as I live through my assignments."

"Well, you can't sleep your way through missions with me. I expect everyone to be awake during missions."

The room fell silent. He looked around, feeling eyes peeling strips off him, though when he met anyone's gaze, it dropped. "What's the matter?"

Round-faced Jones cleared his throat. "With all due respect to your rank, sir, you don't have the right to make a crack like that. We've served together for years now. She has earned her right to be here. With respect," and the word was spat out, "you haven't. Yet."

It smarted, but Wolfe could take it. At least they hadn't fragged him and left him in the disintegration bin for a first offense. "Point taken, trooper," he said, pleasantly. "I apologize, Meyers. Perhaps I should take some lessons in humor. OTS was a little deficient in it."

"Accepted, sir." Meyers lifted her glass.

There seemed to be nothing left to say after that. He put down his cards, rose and made towards the door, hoping that it didn't look like a retreat. "Er. Well, then, good night."

"Night, sir," Boland called to him.

Just before the door shut behind him, he heard someone, probably Corporal Meyers, making a crack about his old man taking her out on a trip halfway to the moon and letting her walk the rest of the way back for making his little boy feel bad.

Meyers wasn't completely wrong, Daivid mused as he hiked hastily toward his quarters. Benjamin Wolfe was very protective of his only son. Except for one thing, the don of the Wolfe Family had paid Daivid the compliment of assuming that he could stand on his own feet. However, that one thing was as dangerous as carrying a planetkiller bomb around with him.

Daivid took a drink of water, hoping he could dilute the alcohol he had consumed somewhat before he went to sleep. After he undressed, he peeled the card off his chest and turned it over in his fingers. A tap on the touch-screen, which analyzed his DNA, scanned his retina and read his pulse, turned on the display. Here was what the others were joking about. This was the Wolfe Family power they meant.

Once old Wolfe had come to terms with Daivid's decision, he kept a calm expression on his face, but his eyes were worried. "I am not sending you out there unprotected."

"It's the space service, not a wildlife safari!" Daivid had flung himself up out of the armchair opposite his father's desk and stormed for the door.

"Don't do it." Benjamin held up a warning hand. "It may not be the wilderness, but you're still going to be out there with people. Strangers. You can't give me an absolute no. I still know people. You walk out of here without protection, and I will make some calls. They won't process you. You'll be back here in an hour." Daivid put out a hand to open the privacy lock. "And if you *don't* come back here, out of pique or I don't know what, pride, I will send Randy and Sven after you."

Daivid gave himself a moment to cool down. He knew that he'd been beaten. Randy and Sven were the most trusted of what in more respectable families would have been known as 'loyal retainers.' Where the Wolfes were concerned, they were more likely to be called henchmen. In fact, Randy, all 2.2 meters of him, had been Daivid's nurse and protector when he was little and had never let him forget it. It was hard to engender respect in someone who had taught him to wear 'big boy' underpants. Fealty and undying devotion, yes. Respect, no. If Randy decided to call him Bucktooth Boy or any of his many other embarrassing childhood nicknames in front of the recruiting officers, Daivid would shoot himself right there.

Sulkily, Daivid sank into the chair that his father indicated. "I don't know why I bothered to tell you I was going."

"I'd have found out anyhow," Benjamin assured him. "You wouldn't have gotten your clothes off for the physical before I'd be down there signing you out. So, are you going to take what I'm offering you, or not?"

"*What* protection do you want me to take? I can't bring bodyguards with me into the space service!"

Benjamin reached into an invisible pocket in the breast of his ten-thousand credit tunic and withdrew a small card, which he tucked into his son's hand. "This. It's a database of every single person in the galaxy who owes me a favor. There are more listings than any one man can use up in a hundred lifetimes. If you need it, use it. I don't want you out in the middle of the void with your bare *tuchas* hanging out when all you had to do was ask somebody for help. Someone who has to say yes. You take it, you promise me you'll use it if you need it, you can go. Otherwise, you might as well study viniculture, because I'm shipping you to your Aunt Hilda on Crekis. You can help her run the wine business out there."

It was the compulsory nature of that yes that grated on Daivid's psyche. But Benjamin Wolfe didn't hold onto control of the Wolfe Family purely through the charm of his personality. He knew how to get what he wanted, and how to get people to give him what he wanted. Daivid took the card, and promised to guard it with his life and check in periodically, but he had also promised himself that he would never use the database under any circumstances whatsoever.

So far, Daivid mused, lying in the dark of his quarters with only the tiny screen of the card for illumination, he'd been able to do without its help. For three years he had slogged his ass off. He had earned his promotions honestly—he hoped—and been able to call on others for assistance by doing favors for them. Simple ones. No blood oaths involved, no horrendous penalties if they failed to comply. He took pride in that. He was making his way in the universe.

There, Dad, he thought, *take that.*

Still, curiosity drove him to browse through the database from time to time, as now. The favors were graded from 1 to 6. In reverse order, class 6 favors were big favors the person owed the Don personally, the 'please will you blow up a planet for me' kind of favors. Next were big Family favors, generally incurred among members of the bloodline or owed to one of them. Then big friend-of-the-Family favors. Next came small personal favors, small Family favors and, lastly, small friend favors. (No one else got favors. If you asked for help, you became a friend. For life.)

Daivid could hear the voice of his father ringing in his ears, reminding him, "Ask! If you need something, it's stupid if you don't ask."

Ask! He didn't ask to be the Don's eldest and favorite child. For all his aspirations to make it honorably in life, there would always be the doubters, the ones whom he made nervous because he was who he was. X-ray must have heard all the rumors, and probably suspected that if he didn't like one of them he could arrange for a little 'accident,' as Meyers had implied when she thought he couldn't hear her.

He wished he could explain to them that he couldn't arrange anything. He had taken himself out of the line of succession. His middle sister Sherez, younger than he by two years, was now being groomed to take the top spot, but even she was certain that one day the old man would talk her brother into coming back. Daivid knew just as certainly that the old man couldn't. Sherez was one of the people he had been unable to convince.

In the card's memory there was also a complete address file of the Family and its connections across all inhabited worlds, including the people on the Family payroll who were deep in planetary governments. That he had also had reason to peruse, but largely for self-protection. The database also included those government workers who were on other Families' payrolls, who were not necessarily kindly inclined toward members of the Wolfe clan. A year ago he had almost gotten sent to an ice station outpost, until he realized that the clerk posting him there was an offshoot of the Franconi Family. Daivid had stretched out his neck and gone just a little over the clerk's head to have himself re-reassigned to the base he was supposed to have gone to in the first place. The one, he thought with a sigh, where he had been stationed before they had sent him to Treadmill.

The last section in the card's memory was a list. Daivid didn't like to read through it, didn't even like to think about it. It contained the names, images and last known addresses of people the Don would like to find, if his devoted son came across them, dead or alive. They were people who had skipped out on payments, committed some crime or outrage against the Family, or betrayed a trust that was not a prosecutable criminal offense. (Benjamin liked to let the courts do his work for him whenever possible.) His father had made it clear he didn't want Daivid to take any action on his own. He just wanted to know where those people were. Daivid read all his own sinister implications into the old man's breezy assurance. This section was really what made Daivid the most reluctant to use the cardbase. Nothing was free, he reflected. Even energy use led to entropy.

He flipped the card in the air, letting it land face down on his stomach. This list of favors cost a lot of lives, dating back from before human beings broke through the atmosphere on the mother planet. He had solemnly promised his father to stick the card in a communications box once a month ("Call collect," Benjamin had admonished him) to update the files, and to let the family know where and how he was.

He didn't mind checking in with his folks. In spite of their chosen 'professions,' he loved his family. He had always gotten along with his three sisters. His mother, who did not work in any of the Family businesses because she had her own career before she married Benjamin Wolfe, was Daivid's favorite person in the galaxy. She was proud of his attainments, praising him when he finished OTS at the top of his class (his father had been proud, too, but he had only confided this to Daivid's mother, never telling him so directly), sending a polished new infopad when he got his first promotion from ensign—enswine—to lieutenant (jg). He loved his family, but he was making his own way now. He had a purpose in life, probably one too big for a single lifetime, but it gave him *meaning*.

And he hadn't thought about Sesi in over a year.

He knew he was tough enough to make it in this assignment. He was young and inexperienced, but he had inherited enough of the family willpower to lead. The Cockroaches needed a good leader, but was he the one? What if behind the polished exterior he showed the world was a block of plaster instead of a chunk of ebony?

He tapped the card, wondering if there was any spot in his quarters where he could conceal it during those times it would be awkward to have it on him, such as if he had to shower with the troopers. Although the card's system was heavily encoded, with a heat-sensitive fingerprint switch and DNA scan as the primary triggers, he wasn't going to try and fool himself into believing the safeguards were foolproof. The databases' content was worth a large fortune on any black market inside the Thousand Worlds or outside. The Cockroaches had already proved they were willing to bend the rules and regard other people's property as their own.

He decided that, for the time being, he was going to have to wear the card on his chest and keep watch for where their eyes didn't go. Give them a few weeks to search his luggage for anything interesting or worth stealing—make that 'trading'—and perhaps he could figure out a safe hiding place.

CHAPTER 3

LOUD HONKING BROKE Wolfe out of a dream. Instantly, the visions of the victory in which he was leading a shining army into the midst of the rebel stronghold on Pteradon, where the insurgents greeted him with open arms, and the beautiful, scantily-clad women who had been held prisoner by the outlaws showered their rescuer with their gratitude, faded from colorful spectacle to the spider-web crackle of the ancient enameled ceiling in his new quarters.

With a gingerly forefinger, he poked the control that operated the window shading, trying to discover the source of the noise. The glass cleared. S-shaped white forms bustled around on the grassy slope just outside that led down to the river running around two sides of the spaceport. As his eyes grew used to the faint light of false dawn he realized they were geese. The birds, originally from Terra, were frequently employed as guard animals in low- to medium-security areas. They were cheap to feed and aggressively territorial. The only downsides were that they were noisy, and their droppings made traversing the green lawns an obstacle course.

He glanced at his chronometer. Oh four hundred hours! He groaned. That meant he'd only gotten three and a half hours of sleep. He jerked up into a sitting position, but the stabbing sensation in his head told him that fast movement was a very bad idea.

New rule, he told himself, moving more gingerly toward the dribbly shower. No more matching the troops drink for drink. They were used to the effects of their white lightning. He, most assuredly, was not.

He peered out the window for the source of the horn music. Was this a new form of reveille? No, it was Mother Nature. Just beyond the barrier fence was a broad wetland. He was being serenaded by a host of marsh hounds. They were local avians whose baying voices reminded the person who named them of howling dogs. By the look of the colony alighting on the water for a pre-dawn breakfast, their numbers were in no danger of decimation, except perhaps by annoyed service personnel whose precious sleep was interrupted by their noise.

He dragged himself to the bathroom to throw cold water on his face. PT started at 0500. Breakfast ran from 0700 to 0800. There ought to be plenty of time to get the barracks in order before Mason arrived for inspection at 1100. He pulled on a sleeveless tunic, light exercise pants and absorbent-insoled running shoes. No point in showering before he got sweaty.

Well before exercises were scheduled to begin, Wolfe ran out onto the yard, the paved area in between the barracks and the mess hall. Running a quick eye around the perimeter track in the twilight of false dawn, he judged that eight laps would be a kilometer. The morning was cold and damp, a bleak contrast to the hot sunny weather prediction that had showed up on his clipboard screen. He started jogging, gradually increasing his speed until his heartbeat pounded in his ears and he felt a healthy sweat break out on his skin. The headache faded, and he began to feel optimistic about the coming day.

The large chrono on the brow of the mess hall showed 0459 when Borden, also in a singlet, shorts and running shoes, emerged from the barracks. Behind her, in swim fins and a boiler suit, was Thielind. They jogged to the center of the exercise field and stood at attention. Their hands flew to their foreheads in salute. Wolfe joined them and threw them a jaunty salute in return.

"Are the others on their way out?" he asked.

"No, sir!" Thielind announced, snapping off the words like firecrackers.

"Why the hell not?"

"Not their day for it, sir!"

"Huh?"

"Rest day, sir!" the thin, darkskinned man explained, still eyes-front. "Firstday, Thirdday and Fifthday, half our force goes back to the main base to train at war games with the other units, and the rest of us help patrol the spaceport. Secondday, Fourthday and Sixthday, the halves alternate. This is our day off. Sir."

"They don't do PT on restdays?" Wolfe asked.

"Nossir! It's restday!" Thielind announced with conviction.

Wolfe shrugged. "Well, I guess that's reasonable. They come in for breakfast, then?"

"Nossir! They don't turn out until maybe ten or ten thirty on restday."

"That won't do!" Wolfe said with a frown. "The commander will be here in a few hours. I want everyone up and dressed in plenty of time." With purpose he strode toward the barracks. Borden caught up with him.

"I really wouldn't do that if I were you, sir," she said, trotting alongside him.

"Why the hell not?" He flung open the door. It crashed against the wall. Twenty bleary faces lifted from pillows or tank, and peered at him.

"Good morning!" he announced. "I know today's your day off, but we've got an inspection later on. Breakfast at 0700! See you there!"

He left Borden and Thielind behind and marched back to his quarters. The pathetic shower stream seemed even lighter than it had the night before. It took three times as long to soap up and scrub down. By the time he got dressed he was fully awake and feeling fit.

When he arrived in the mess, he was feeling rather jaunty. The grounds were tidy, his quarters were clean, and he had a hearty appetite for breakfast.

Borden and Thielind flanked an empty chair at the end of one of the two long tables next to the buffet servers. Borden gestured to him and pointed to the chair. He nodded, and turned his attention to the food bins.

One thing he had to hand the Space Service: they provided excellent coffee, and the servobots knew how to prepare it so it was hot and fragrant, never burned or bitter. He took a pot and mug, placing them on his tray with meat-filled rolls, wholegrain cereals, dairy blocks, pastries and a bunch of shiny red grapes. He took his time, enjoying each selection. Borden ate like an automaton. Thielind eyed each bite suspiciously before putting it into his mouth.

Nearly everyone in the room had availed themselves of the coffee, though he saw many a heavy head hung over the white china mugs. The three nonhumanoid troopers sat at the far end of the second table. The semicat gave Wolfe a look of slit-eyed annoyance and tore off the end of a meatroll with its pointed teeth as if dispatching prey. Boland, who had drunk plenty of home brew the night before, looked as though he could bleed to death through the eyeballs. Mose did not meet anyone's eyes directly. Lin held her spoon limply, dozing in between bites. Only Jones seemed to be in good spirits, buttering bread and chattering to his neighbors.

When he finished his meal, Daivid stood up and tapped on the side of his coffee mug for attention.

"Company, the commander arrives in three hours. I want everyone to give this inspection their full attention. Get everything sparkling, and I promise you won't regret it. Thank you. That is all. Fall out at will."

No one raised head, eyes or voice to reply. Things were looking up. No one was going to give him an argument. Then he noticed the glance between his two officers.

"What?" he asked.

"Nothing, sir," Borden replied, and took another precise spoonful of cereal.

Gradually, the troopers drifted out of the dining room, followed at last by Thielind and Borden. Alone in the hall, Daivid thought he would treat himself to just one more cup of the excellent coffee. He savored its aroma and complex, bitter taste, thinking command wasn't as hard as he had feared it would be.

He finished the last sip just as the wall chrono changed from 0759 to 0800. He set his tray in the hatch, where it was taken out of his hands by the robotic dishwasher. Leaving the machines to do their jobs, he strolled across the exercise yard to check on the progress of the cleanup.

Everyone must still be suffering from mighty hangovers. Daivid could hardly hear a sound as he stepped up into the barracks. It was too quiet. Looking in the door, he realized the big room was empty. Not a bunk had been made, nor had any other efforts to make the place neat been made. The square-bodied automatic sweeper was drifting around the floor, sucking up used pows and sorting fallen cards and gathering glasses. It hummed when it sensed him, and veered around his feet. He sidestepped it and headed for the bathrooms. Could they all be in the showers? He couldn't hear any water running.

The bathroom, too, was empty. And filthy.

He hurried out of the door and circled around to the junior officers' quarters. On the threshold he stood panting. Borden, her back to him, kicked the cleanerbot.

"Dammit, I said wipe the windows and sweep the floors, not the other way around!" The small robot paused in mid-movement waved its multiple arms at her. Fine sprays of cleaning fluid splashed her. "Gah! Stupid machine!" She lashed out with a foot again. Thielind looked up calmly from making his bed.

"Don't do that," he reproved her. "It will never learn from violence. You've got to treat them with love, Lizzie."

"Dammit, don't call me that! Sir!" She noticed Daivid and swung into a salute, regaining in an instant her stonefaced aplomb.

"Sir!" Thielind echoed, clapping his hand to his head. It was holding what looked like a solid-gold loving cup. Sheepishly, he lowered it and put it behind his back. "What can we do for you?"

"Where is everybody?" Wolfe demanded.

He didn't have to explain what he meant. The junior officers glanced at one another.

"It's restday, sir," Thielind offered. "Everyone's resting."

"Where are they 'resting'?" Daivid asked, apoplectic with fury. "We've got an inspection soon! I'll ream their asses. Where did they go?"

Thielind shook his head. "Maybe a dozen places. Maybe all over."

"Name them, ensign," Daivid insisted. "I'll get a flitter. No, I'll borrow a riot van from the brig. I'll handcuff and haul each and every one of them if I have to!"

"You can't take the time, sir." Borden shook her head. "One thing they are very good at is disappearing when they don't want to be found. They'll come back when they're good and ready. We'll help you clean. There's plenty of time."

"The bots will help us," Thielind promised. He hoisted the malfunctioning automaton and carried it with him.

"Damn them, what were they thinking?" Daivid stormed.

The junior officers followed him in silence, giving Daivid plenty of time to think about what he would do to the company when he found them. Keelhauling? If he could find a keel, he'd tie them all end to end and sling them underneath it until—

"Whoo!" Thielind whistled. "Someone musta had a party in here. It looks worse than when I left, around 0300." He put the cleanerbot on the floor and flipped open its maintenance lid. "There. It'll work like new."

"Good," said Wolfe. "Now I want you to go out and find them. Tell them that if they are not back here, clean, sober and in their dress whites by 1100 hours their asses will be grass. Is that clear?"

"Yessir!" Thielind said. "Aye aye." The skinny ensign scooted out of the door.

Borden put her hands on her hips. "It's not as bad as it looks, sir," she said. "Between us, we can get this done in an hour."

"Where do we start?" Wolfe asked, looking at the mess in dismay.

"Bathroom last," she suggested. "It's what we'll be clearing the rest of the mess into. Dusting first. The robots will take care of that. Then beds."

They turned the cleanerbots loose on the dusting and clearing up of the debris from the party, but the beds had to be done by hand. That was a longstanding service tradition. The custom of spacers, in fact members of all branches of the armed forces, straightening up their own sleeping pads was one that went back all the way to Old Earth. No matter what else, no matter what services or technology were available, each man or woman or whatever had to make the bed. Wolfe thought it was a stupid throwback, but rules were rules. Until he was in a position to change them, he had to follow them. He snapped out a sheet, the harsh sound reflecting his bad mood. *How dare the Cockroaches flout his order?* he thought, stuffing in loose ends with a knife-sharp hand. *What the hell was the matter with them?*

He was furious to realize that they held the cards on this one. He could report them. X-ray Company would all have to face dereliction of duty punishment, but they didn't care. They were already in the worst unit in the service. But he, *he* would be removed from command as being unable to hold his own with them. First impressions: if he was perceived as inept from the very beginning, he would have no chance of changing that perception once it got into the minds of the brass. As badly as the people upstairs wanted him out of the regular chain of command, they couldn't leave him in charge of a band of creative screwups. Listening to them last night had convinced him they were guilty of far more than the service had been able to prove. That uncertainty was why they continued to wear the uniform. They had outmaneuvered him first time out of the gate. He had to find a way to turn that around.

Still, there was a homey satisfaction to completing a simple task like making beds. By the third bunk, he found himself falling into a rhythm, bending, shaking out the sheets, tucking in the corners.

"This takes me all the way back to summer camp," he said to Borden, thumping a pillow between his hands. "My dad used to send us to Parker's Planet for eight weeks every year. It took a week's transit to get there, and another back again. Those were good times."

Ah, those were the days, he thought, slinging the pillow against the head rail. He had a vision of those carefree summers, full of swimming, hiking, sleeping out of doors, getting bitten by a range of insects and scraped by falling out of trees or off rocks, learning how to make annoying noises and how to tell even more annoying jokes, the bigger boys teaching but just as frequently picking on the younger boys. The counselors attempted to impose discipline from above, but things had a way of getting settled down in the lower echelons by means of minor torture and often cruel practical jokes. The perpetrators got away with it because to rat out a fellow camper was punishable by even more of the same. Camp and the Space Service had a lot in common. Simple times. Simple responsibilites. Simple relationships. Simple revenge.

He had held his own back on Parker's Planet, learning the bigger boys' techniques and turning it around on them. No one got the better of a Wolfe. No one *should*. Involuntarily, his upper lip drew back, showing his teeth. Suddenly, he caught Borden staring at him.

"What's the matter?" he asked.

"With respect, I don't like the look on your face, sir," the officer said. "You—looked for a moment like you might bite someone."

"Nothing like that. I just had an idea," he replied, unable to keep from grinning ferally. "I was just thinking that you learn a lot about coping with life from living with your peer group. Were you ever at sleepaway camp?" Borden nodded. "Ever heard of the Vortex?"

"No—I—"

"Well," Wolfe said, flicking out another bedsheet with practiced hands. "Watch and learn."

She did watch, respect dawning on her face for the first time. "Sir, we can't do that."

Daivid was in no mood to argue. "This is an order. If I have to earn the privilege from you, I'll do it later. For now, just do it."

Borden watched him again as he took all the bedclothes off Ewanowski's bunk and remade it deftly. "No, sir, you've earned this one just for teaching me something new. I never saw that before."

"Good."

Daivid made sure she knew all the steps then turned her loose to work on her own. The tall woman's hands were even more adept than his. Very shortly, the two of them had remade all the beds on one side of the room and were starting on the other.

"What's wrong with Lizzie?" Wolfe wondered aloud. "It's in your bio. At least, it's a derivative of one of your middle names—"

"With all due respect, sir," Borden's voice returned to its original ice-cold tone of the day before, "I don't care for the implication. Everyone in this unit has a combat name, a handle. If you perused the records, you have seen them all noted. Mine is not Lizzie."

In his mildest voice, Daivid said, "I just thought it was a nickname, lieutenant. No offense intended." He bent all of his natural charm on her, smiling warmly, willing her to thaw out. As one of the only people in the company to prove a trusted ally, he didn't want to lose her good will. He knew his yellow-hazel eyes could turn a mellow gold in some lights. He'd used the effect to beguile treats out of schoolmates, and less innocent favors out of dates. "Please. I've been here less than a day. You'll have to let me have more than one gotcha."

Borden hesitated. "Well—"

Daivid fluttered his eyelashes. "Pretty please?"

A brief smile lifted the corners of her mouth. "Aye, sir. Sorry to be so quick on the trigger. You've walked into an ancient minefield."

A bright *ping!* from the cleanerbots informed him that they had finished their assignments. Daivid went to inspect. All the windows glistened, the tabletops and even the locker tops had been cleared and wiped, and the lavatories looked pristine enough to do surgery on. The barracks was clean.

On the other hand, he wasn't. His neatly pressed dress uniform was now a mass of crumples and smudges from bumping into the edges of the bunks. It was a quarter to eleven. There wasn't time left to put the uniform through a full pressing cycle. He would be lucky if the box could sponge off the dirt spots. He felt his temper rising all over again. He glanced up at Borden.

"Lieutenant, why did they go off without cleaning up? Don't they *want* to look good for the brass? You'd think that they would want to gain some points, not lose them. Don't they give a damn?"

Borden hesitated, her cool eyes wary. "Permission to speak freely?"

Wolfe nodded.

"With respect, we," and Wolfe understood that he wasn't part of the 'we' yet, "really *don't* give a damn."

Wolfe eyed her. "Then why are *you* helping me?"

The harsh face softened just a little. "Permission to continue speaking freely? Because I feel sorry for you. You're so gung-ho. You're an idealist." Pain etched itself between the perfect eyebrows then smoothed out again. "I almost remember what that high feels like, before it got wrung out of me by—circumstances."

Ouch. That stung Daivid, remembering the bogus reasons that he had been sent here to X-ray. The others all had similar stories to tell, probably worse than his. He had been sheltered from a lot of bad treatment because of the command's fear of his family. He promised himself he would read the personnel records in more detail as soon as he could.

"The others sort of feel sorry for you, too."

"Then why aren't they here?" Daivid asked reasonably.

Her eyebrows went up. "Permission to express an opinion? Because you gave them an order."

Daivid felt outraged. "What? But that's my job! And it's theirs to obey!"

"Yeah, it is, in a way, but you haven't earned the right. The one thing that's missing in any military is a way to make sure that officers are worthy of leading the troops under them. You've read history—officers used to be nobles who bought their commissions. The peasants under them didn't have any choice but to follow. It didn't matter if the officers could lead their way out of a one-way door. Times have changed over the last few millenia. With few exceptions, the service has been all-volunteer. We're better educated, more experienced, and have more to offer than any army humankind has been able to muster since they started carrying sticks and stones. You've got guys in here who have been in the service since long before you were born. Look at Jones. How old do you think he is?"

Wolfe thought about the chunky man, mentally counted the few white hairs shot through the dark curls. "Fifty."

"Seventy-two. He's been *in* fifty years. He's going to go easier on you than a five-year spacer will, but why should he? He's buried about one officer every other year since he joined up."

Wolfe brushed at his tunic thoughtfully. "I had no idea troopers thought that way. Every other unit I've been in everyone is so young and inexperienced. All our officers were older than we were, and *their* CO's were older and had been in longer than they had."

The look Borden gave him had sympathy in it. "Well, the real thing is more messy than that. Once you really get out into the void you'll be serving with sixty-year-old recruits and twenty-year-old colonels. Nothing wrong with that. But if it was me walking in here I'd download the company records as a bedtime book. Sir."

"Don't mess with them, huh?"

"In my personal opinion. Sir."

"Well, that's good advice, but it goes both ways," Wolfe said, straightening his shoulders. "I'm here to do a job, and I'm serious about it, so they're going to have to respect that. If we have a little rough going on the maiden voyage, so be it."

"Fine, sir," Borden said tonelessly. "We'll see who breaks first."

"Yes, we will, lieutenant," Wolfe said with some satisfaction as Thielind led the sheepish-looking troopers back into the barracks. "Remember the Vortex." He smiled at the smug looks on the faces of his company as they looked around at the spotless room. Throwing salutes toward the officers, they shrugged out of their fatigues and headed for the showers to clean up. "Where'd you find 'em, ensign?"

"Oh, usual place," Thielind replied vaguely. "Permission to tidy up, sir?"

"Granted," Daivid said. "Let's make this an inspection to remember."

"Very nice, very nice," Mason said, ambling through the room. She wore white gloves that all but fluoresced in the acid lights. Occasionally, she ran a finger over the top of a doorjamb or underneath a bed frame. Not a mark. The cleanerbots had done a good job.

Daivid had done a hasty steam on his uniform tunic, hoping to hide most of the stains with a layer of soapcream. It would only convince if she didn't look too closely. A lot of things were going on underneath the surface in this unit. Mason might have locked them all up if she had had an inkling.

He marched stiffly behind her, pausing with hands folded behind his back every time she paused. The Cockroaches had turned out decently, though in everyday uniforms instead of dress. When he had started to fulminate over the omission, Thielind had caught his eye and dragged a forefinger across his throat. Wolfe had stopped his protest in mid-syllable. He would get an explanation from the ensign later. It was the only change upon which Mason commented.

"Though it is a restday," she amended. "And I didn't give you much time to polish up your best bibs and tuckers, did I?"

"Er, no, ma'am," Wolfe said without intonation.

He knew his troopers were watching him, trying to guess what he was thinking and wondering why he wasn't mad. The commander avoided the packing crate at the end of the room, which informed Wolfe that she knew its contents and had decided there were better battles to fight. At his insistence, the Cockroaches had turned off the heating element before she had arrived, so the still wasn't emitting either telltale steam or its burbling sound. No sense in throwing the commander's kind omission directly in her face. Mason went out the back door to the armory, where she praised the spotlessness of the company's weaponry and battle armor. One more pass through the barracks, and the commander swung around smartly to face him.

"Congratulations, Lieutenant Wolfe," she beamed. "Everything looks top drawer. A robot couldn't have done better. Anything I ought know about?"

"Most of the infrastructure is in pretty good repair, ma'am," Wolfe replied. "Most of the fixtures show a lot of wear, but they're working. With one exception, I'm afraid: the plumbing in my quarters seems to have no pressure."

One of the Cockroaches cleared his throat loudly. The trooper next to him hit him in the ribs with her elbow, never breaking her parade-ground stare.

Commander Mason glanced at her aide, who recorded a note. "I think you'll find that your water problems are largely due to the unstable ground conditions here, lieutenant," she said. "I have heard that complaint a lot. But maintenance will be out to take a look at it, and see if there's anything they can do. Anything else?"

"No, ma'am. Everything's shipshape." Mason was openly relieved. "Good! You have done well on your first day, Lieutenant. I'm very pleased to see that you have everything under control so soon." She raised her voice so everyone could hear. "That makes it much easier for me to inform you that I've got your orders for your first mission with X-ray Platoon."

The others looked wary, but Daivid felt pleased. A chance to prove himself, already!

"May I ask what it is, ma'am?" he asked, mentally kicking himself because he knew how eager he sounded.

Mason looked grave. "I'm afraid the orders are sealed until you are aboard the transport that's coming for you, lieutenant."

A groan erupted from the company. Daivid frowned, and Mason started nervously. Perhaps he was jumping the gun. Borden said he was too gung-ho. Slide it down a little, he warned himself.

"Aye, ma'am."

The commander glanced at the adjutant who waited by her elbow. "Five days, ma'am."

"The *Eastwood* will be here in five days," Mason repeated. "Get your unit ready. Again, well done, lieutenant."

The commander and her entourage marched out of the barracks. Wolfe almost enjoyed the aura of worried anticipation around him as he surveyed his company.

"We passed," he said, presenting a bland countenance. "I'll expect a little more cooperation from the rest of you next time. Borden, Thielind, Lin, will you come to my office with me?"

"Aye, sir!" the two junior officers chimed.

Back straight, he marched out of the door with the others behind him.

"You know what?" Injaru asked the others before he was quite out of hearing range, "I figured out why he's not in the Family business. He doesn't kick ass. He's too soft. We got away with it!"

"Yeah," Meyers smirked. "It sure was nice of him to make our beds for us."

Certain none of them could see his face by then, Wolfe allowed himself a grin.

CHAPTER 4

"SIT DOWN, PLEASE," Wolfe invited the three veterans. He set on the table a carafe of white lightning that he had abstracted from the still while he and Borden were cleaning up. "Drink?"

"No, thanks, sir," Borden said. Lin shook her head silently.

"Too early," Thielind agreed. "Lunch is in an hour. What's up, looey?"

Daivid settled himself down in the chair behind the desk. "You've already figured out I'm as green as they come, but I got one good piece of advice when I shipped out from my last posting. My commander told me to trust the experienced officers and the top noncom in my unit, so that's what I am doing. Let me put myself in your hands. I'm a newbie. Hell, I haven't been here a day yet. You've been around here for years. What can I do to help keep this unit running, or get it running better? I've noticed the morale around here sucks. How can I help raise it? What does X-ray really need? What do *you* need?"

"Need?" Thielind's open face showed astonishment then pleasure. "Really?"

Borden tented her hands together and leaned forward. "Sir, we need everything."

Wolfe blinked. "Everything?"

"Everything," Lin affirmed.

Borden nodded. "Yup. You wanted to know why we weren't wearing dress whites today. Ours are falling apart. I haven't had new ones in five years. Some of the others have gone longer. Supply always puts us off when we ask, saying that the request is going up the chain of command. Same goes for everything else. We need new field uniforms, updated weapons, updated software for the weapons, better communication gear—I guess we're okay on the condition of our body armor, but the CBS,Ps are bad, and Supply refuses to replace them. We've had the same units for almost eight months, now. They're supposed to be rotated every three months of use." Borden pushed her infopad towards the lieutenant, who frowned at the list.

Compression Body Stocking, Personal, was a neck-to-heels weblike garment that went on bare skin underneath the padded lining of combat armor. Its sensors read environmental data coming from outside and kept blood flowing out to the extremities, especially in deep-space conflicts, by means of gentle peristaltic pressure. His CBS,P had been worn on only three missions of a few days each. From the litany of missions the others had given him, theirs had seen service for more than ten times that long. By comparison, his was brand, spanking new.

"That's outrageous," Wolfe sputtered. "CBS,Ps are vital! They might be all that keeps you alive if your armor malfunctions."

Lin shook her head in pity. "Sir, they don't care if we come back alive, remember? We're an ancillary scout platoon, officially. Unofficially, well, this is where old troublemakers go to die."

Borden's bleak voice interrupted the master chief's. "We've made the request about once a week since we got back from our last mission, three months ago. If we only have five days until we ship out again, then those are our top priority. The others won't matter if we don't have fresh webs."

Resolutely, Wolfe shoved his infopad so the transfer eye faced Borden's. "Give me the whole list. I'll get new units for the company, and then we'll see about the rest."

"That," Thielind said, with his ready smile, "will do a lot to help morale."

"New CO of the Cockroaches?" the supply master chief asked, as he scrolled down the list on Daivid's infopad. He had thick, red-tinted hair that jarred violently with his ruddy-pink complexion and red irised eyes. His round belly strained against his gray-blue uniform tunic. "Welcome, I guess."

"Thanks," Daivid said, leaning over to read along with him. They were in the supply office, a square stub attached to the front of the vast warehouse that held everything from paperclips to armor-plated personnel carriers. "Will you be able to lend me a loader to get all these supplies to the transport, or do you deliver everything but the clothes directly to our transport?"

"Not so fast, not so fast!" Master Chief Sargus said, holding up a thick-fingered hand. "It's restday, admiral. You asking to see me, I thought this was urgent."

Daivid frowned. "Some of it is urgent. We're shipping in a few days."

"Uh-huh, so I hear." Sargus scrolled through the list again. "Well, I've got some of this, but some, maybe not. There's a hold against some of my stock for the other units here, see?"

Wolfe sighed. He had dealt with supply officers before. The game they always played bored him silly, but it seemed as though every one of them had gone through a training class in the same technique and insisted on using it. 'Obstruct, deny, refuse' was the unspoken motto of Supply Corps. "Right, and if you give it to me, then you'll be out of it, and you'll have to reorder. Is that it?"

"Right you are, admiral," Sargus agreed, with a grin that showed big square teeth. Daivid was surprised they weren't tinted red, too, but, no, they were gleaming yellow. The guy looked like a tropical island shirt. "No can do. And then what would I tell my other customers?"

"You'll tell them you gave them to me, because I asked," Daivid said, dropping his voice slightly.

"Yeah? And why would I do that?"

"Because I did ask. And while you're looking for the general list, why don't you see if you can find me some extra rounds for my Dockery 5002?" Suddenly moving closer to the counter, Daivid eased a sidearm out of his holster just so the big man could get a look at the maker's name, then briefly, just for shock value, the end of the barrel. He let his eyes flash dangerously, a glint of the gold showing. Sargus took an involuntary step backward as Daivid put the barrel practically up the other man's nose. "Isn't she a beauty? Eleven millimeter select-fire machine pistol with a twenty-round magazine. Caseless ammunition. With a suppressor like that no one would ever hear you die."

"Well!" Sargus exclaimed, with fresh heartiness, his color paled to light peach. "I heard you were one of those Wolfes. Wasn't sure. But you had to be a crazy bastard or canny as a fox to pull a gun on me in the middle of one of the most heavily secured buildings on the base, didn't you? Nice to be connected, huh, admiral? I'm an organized man, you know. I like to have my facts in order. Now, those rounds I'd have to send away for. No way I'll have them before you ship out, sir. No lie."

Daivid nodded slowly, backing away and putting the gun back into its holster. He deplored having to invoke the Family reputation, but it cut out at least forty minutes of the "I don't have it" dance and negotiations. Lin had told him everyone already knew who he was; he might as well use other people's imaginations to get what the company needed. It wasn't as if he was threatening to have his father's minions come down and wreck the chief's storehouse. Not that Benjamin wouldn't do it if Daivid had been stupid and rash enough to ask.

"But within, say, six weeks, sure," said Sargus. "I'm expecting at least three major shipments in that interval. By the time you get back, I'll have 'em."

"Good." Wolfe let his hand drop away from the holster. "I've still got two hundred rounds in magazines in my kit. What about the rest of it?"

"Your group isn't due for rotation into new dress gear for two more months," the master chief said, shaking his head. This time Daivid believed him. "Fatigues—I'm only authorized to replace worn items, not ones that were willfully damaged. Otherwise, it comes out of your people's pay. You know that. Ammo, yeah, Commander Mason sent me a message that you needed supplies. But fifty cases of P-130 shells, admiral! I can't give you fifty."

"We need fifty," Daivid insisted patiently, though he had inflated the numbers just because he expected to have to negotiate. "That's what my master chief said, and I want backups. I can't just walk into a trading post or a department store and ask for heavy artillery rounds."

"Thirty-five," Sargus countered. "And I'll make sure you get all ten rapid-charges for the dragons."

Daivid nodded slightly, satisfied. Dragons, the space service's light, one- or two-man hovertank, was the workhorse of small field units. X-ray had two. Lin had insisted that they couldn't do without at least five backup power sources per dragon, especially since they were working under blind orders. Like the ammunition, it would be too late to hunt for more once they were at their task site. He wondered what assignment was so important that it had to be kept secret even on the base but was being handed to a unit that everyone knew was considered expendable.

Sargus ran through the list. The two of them bantered back and forth over one item after another. Daivid noticed that the chief was purposely ignoring the item on the top.

"Well, that's it, admiral," Sargus said, slapping the infopad down on the counter. "Success to your mission. I'll have your special order ready when you get back. Forgot to ask—is it official, or will you be, er, making some other arrangement for reimbursement?" He leered, showing the big yellow teeth. "A—favor, maybe?"

"The Dockery ammunition is personal," Daivid said, cringing at the use of the word. The man really did understand who he was. "We can talk about what you'd like in exchange when you know what it's going to cost, but we're not done yet. You still have not signed off on one of my requests, and it's the most important of all."

"No can do, Lieutenant Wolfe," Sargus said, clapping his big hand down on the screen. His jovial manner evaporated and he was back to all business. "Sorry. No CBS,Ps."

"Sorry? What do you mean, sorry?" Wolfe asked, drawing his brows down over his eyes. He knew he was losing his temper, and fought to control it. What had gone wrong? It had looked like he'd been establishing a good working rapport with Sargus. "You know that those CBS,Ps are the one vital item on that list. We might as well not have shells or power packs if the human beings in my company carrying them can't function in their armor."

"*Your company*," Sargus said, leaning close and showing the red-veined whites of his eyes, "should have thought of that before. I'm tired of getting all sorts of crap from the reconditioning facility when I send the used units from *your company* back to them to be refurbished. The unauthorized modifications make it almost impossible to tune them up so they can go to another, decent unit who don't screw with the programming of your so-called most vital item! And I don't even want to talk about the extra mess. Now, if you don't mind, Lieutenant, I'd like to get back to what I was doing on my restday before you decided to waste my time."

With a shove, he propelled the infopad back toward Daivid, who caught it just before it fell off his side of the counter. Sargus backed up and stabbed a button with his thumb. The security wall crashed down out of the ceiling, sealing the supply hatch before Daivid could reach over the counter and grab him by the neck. Fuming, Daivid stormed out of the building and marched back toward the transportal.

"*What* unauthorized modifications?" Daivid demanded.

After forty minutes bottled up on the transport where he couldn't even vent his temper because security eyes were all over the tube-train, he had stormed all over the barracks looking for someone, anyone, to explain the last humiliation to him. Having dismissed everyone to enjoy the remainder of their restday meant hunting out the various hiding places in which the Cockroaches could find a little peace and quiet without the brass coming upon them casually with a scut assignment. He had managed to find Thielind practicing tai chi in his swim fins in the mess hall.

"It's not for me to explain, lieutenant," Thielind explained, leading Daivid back to his quarters. "I'm just the ensign. But I have got about a dozen locations where Lieutenant Borden or Chief Lin might be." He held up a small personal tracking device. "They're in the memory." Daivid reached for it, but Thielind held it just out of reach. "Looey, don't let this finder get into range of an infopad. It took us ages to get those spaces the way we like them. If the data hits the base source computer, everyone will know they exist. I mean, they could use our implant tracers to find us in 'em if they really wanted, but—Just don't, sir. These are *our* vacation spots."

Daivid gestured impatiently. "Agreed, ensign," he said. He activated the little device, noticing that its 'eye' had been covered by a strip of duct tape. Thielind was right: that wouldn't stop a handshake transmitter from picking the unit's memory. But Daivid wasn't out to destroy yet another Cockroach tradition. All he wanted was either Lin or Borden, in front of him, immediately.

The screen showed the first nook no more than fifty feet from where he was standing. His feet driven by the memory of the smug look on Chief Sargus's face, he strode toward it, readying a diatribe on not giving him sufficient briefing to handle a situation, and how he felt, personally, about being humiliated.

He missed the entrance three times before he found a gap between two ancient and battered metal tanks feeding the water-purification plant. He squeezed through it and discovered a circular area about four meters across and lined with discarded ship's carpeting. He hastily backed out again.

"...The contemplation of the newfallen snow is less lonely with you beside me, and the stars look down upon us and laugh for joy..." Mose read off an infopad. He lay with his head on Streb's chest at the far end of the enclosure. The muscular petty officer plucked grapes from a bunch in a bowl beside them and fed one to the poet, who continued with his reading, letting his warm baritone voice echo magnificently in the metal tube. "…Cold the future, and cold the past, but warm the present held in your hand fast…." Daivid backed hastily out, hoping Streb and Mose hadn't noticed him. Activating the tracker again, he headed for the next 'vacation spot.'

It amazed him how many dead areas there were on a spaceport where every square centimeter was supposedly in use and under tight surveillance. Adri'Leta was lolling in the sun, reading a book out behind a spent-fuel storage block. She glanced up in surprise when he appeared almost beside her, and he threw her a salute. If not for the silhouettes of the fighter craft behind her, she might have been in a luxury resort, up to and including holoposters adhered to the side of the storage shed.

Daivid didn't really need to use the finder to locate Jones. He found the Cymraeg standing knee deep in waders, fishing in the rocky brook that flowed parallel to the landing pad about a kilometer out and singing light opera in his big voice. Ewanowski and Aaooorru sat slung in a pair of insulation rings sipping out of cocktail glasses festooned with paper umbrellas which they lifted in toast to Daivid as he frowned at them. Funny, corlists and semicats were not species that usually got along well. But he still hadn't found the right person. He strode on, stalking his prey with all the intense concentration of his namesake animal.

Meyers looked up with concern and gathered up the arrangement of Tarot cards she had spread out on a cloth across the bottom of an unused shipping container and snuffed out the candles burning at the corners.

"Sorry, sorry," Daivid kept saying, getting more and more angry in his embarrassment.

Finally, he located one of his two quarries, at the bottom of a gully bounded on three sides by an ox-bow of the ancient river that bounded the spaceport.

"There you are!"

A naked Chief Boland scrambled up and out of the double-recliner chair at the sound of Daivid's furious voice. The big man reached for his discarded breeches and started to tug them on. Lin, similarly unclad, merely shrugged and shifted her eyeshades up onto the top of her head. Her slight but taut body was a criss-crossed network of healing scars and decorated here and there with tattoos. On her knee was a raised area resembling Ambering's do-it-yourself Cockroach.

"So, you went to Supply," she said, her eyes crinkling up at Daivid with amusement. "How far'd you get?"

"What unauthorized modifications?" Daivid exploded. "You set me up."

"Nah," Lin waved a protest. She found a bottle of sunprotectant on the ground and handed it to Boland. Obediently, he opened it and began to rub it on her back and shoulders. "It was worth a try. I thought your background might get the request past him. You're going to have to go through Mason to get replacements after all. Sorry. I was hoping you wouldn't have to."

"You knew he was going to refuse?" Daivid asked, feeling his blood pressure rising.

"Well, maybe 80%." She took the bottle and began to anoint her small breasts with the white lotion.

Daivid lost his patience. He threw his hands in the air. "What unauthorized modifications? What did you do to the CBS,Ps that I am going to have to take the request to the commander instead of just requisitioning them like any other unit?"

"Everybody does it," Boland interjected. Daivid just glared at him. The big chief looked momentarily sheepish. Daivid transferred the glare to Lin.

She looked a little embarrassed, too. "All right, maybe they don't. But they could."

"Do what?" Daivid pressed.

"Well, you know what the CBS,P does," Lin began. "It monitors circulation, and responds to drops or increases in ambient pressure. It keeps up a wave of compression going all over the body."

"Yes, so where does—??"

"Let me explain," Lin pleaded. "So, you know, sometimes transport to the arenas takes so long, and people were getting bored— We adapted it so that maybe it compresses a little harder in some places."

"And a little faster," Boland added. "Okay, a lot faster. Not all the time, just after a while. Then it stops."

Daivid eyed them. "And where does it start this faster, har— Oh, tell me you're kidding!"

The two chiefs had the grace to look ashamed of themselves. "Uh, no."

"So you've turned the space service's main survival garment into an all-over *masturbation* machine? No wonder Supply is furious with you!"

"He's quick on the uptake," Lin told Boland. "Most of 'em don't get it right away."

"Would you like us to adjust yours?" Boland offered. "If you're not interested in the sex thing, it also gives a hell of a good backrub."

"And a footrub," put in Lin. "*Totally* sensual."

"No!" Daivid exclaimed, horrified. "So,you say you turned in the used garments for new ones, and they refurbished the material, and then some poor unsuspecting bastard in another unit puts it on and activates the mechanism, and—" The image in his mind of a body stocking putting intimate moves on its wearer started to form in his mind. The guy had to be squirming in his armor, unable to explain what was happening to him. Daivid tried to remain upset about it, but the more he thought about it, the harder it was not to laugh. The situation struck him as irresistibly funny. "And he's got to explain to his commanding officer that he can't—because he's got— and then he—" He gestured feebly as words failed him. He started laughing. His knees folded under him and he slid down until he was sitting on Lin's deck chair. Tears leaked out of his eyes. He wiped them away with the edge of his hand. In a while he gasped for breath. "Oh, my God! I love it."

"After a while you get used to the effect," Boland explained. "I mean, once I had to do an insertion dive before I…er…finished. It was kind of cool, getting turned on in mid-air. It doesn't interfere with your effectiveness, I swear. We don't run it during the missions themselves. It just keeps us from being bored during the long stretches in the suits."

"So what are the limericks and the other time-fillers for, then?"

"Hey, you can't jerk off all the time!"

"Are you sure you don't want to have the programming installed yourself?" Lin asked.

"*Hell*, no," Daivid said passionately, getting himself under control. "And if anyone does that to my suit without my permission, I'll space them."

Boland made a face. "You gonna make us undo ours?"

"It would help if you deprogrammed the old ones before we turn them in for replacements," Daivid pointed out, reasonably. He stood up. "*If* I can get that tightass in Supply to give us replacements."

Lin waved a hand. "They've got to give them to us anyhow. Just get Mason to sign off on it. She'll do it, no problem. She's done it a bunch of times."

"Fine," Daivid said. He'd had enough, and he had his answer. "I'll leave you alone now. Enjoy the rest of your day. See you at 0600 for PT tomorrow." He boosted himself up the bank.

"Hey, lieutenant?" Lin called. "You passed the test. You were a good sport. Captain Cohen, the CO we had before Scoley, went into a complete snit the first time he found out about the CBS,Ps, and we ended up doing survival evolutions every day for a month. But then he asked Boland to reprogram his, and he never again gave us shit about it."

Daivid smiled down at them, the sun behind him casting his long shadow over their faces. "How do you know I won't?"

Lin gave him a half-smile, soldier to soldier, Family to Family, woman to man. "I just know."

"Don't think you've pegged me as a softy, chief," Wolfe warned her. He waved and walked away.

The soft blue glow of the chronometer on the front of the mess hall read 0200. Two of Treadmill's three moons, tiny gleaming white bubbles, sailed high overhead through a clear, black, star-spangled night. That night, Daivid moved on soft-footed tiptoe to the door of the enlisted barracks. In the red glow of the emergency lighting, he could see humped shapes on each of the bunks and floating in the corlist's tank. He knew they had been over the big room with electronic detectors and other means of investigating whether he had planted some form of discipline upon them.

Sometimes, he mused, low-tech was best. Standing at attention in the doorway, he removed a finger-long silver cylinder from his breast pocket, raised it to his lips, and blew.

The whistle's blast tore the air like a descending tornado. Snatched from sleep, the Cockroaches sprang out of bed. Or tried to. As each of the occupants of the bunk attempted to draw his or her feet out of the covers, the Vortex, a complicated but nearly undetectable folding together of top and bottom bedsheets, twisted together around their lower limbs, immobilizing or significantly hobbling them. As Daivid punched on the overhead lights, he was treated to the morally satisfying sight of nineteen of his twenty enlisted personnel flailing about as they thrashed, fell out of bed, or staggered upright with their sheets clinging to their legs. The corlist swam to the side of his tank and hung there by his upper limbs, watching with bemusement. With a final grin at his troopers, Wolfe pocketed his whistle, spun on his heel, and marched out of the barracks into the night, leaving the confusion behind him.

A touch on the arm nearly made him jump out of his shoes.

"It's me, sir," Borden's voice whispered. She drew forward into the light. Thielind stood at her elbow, his large eyes gleaming. Both of them wore grins that nearly reached their ears. "Very nice, sir. I wouldn't have missed it for anything. The Vortex is— very effective."

Daivid couldn't help sharing their grin. "A shock for a shock," he said succinctly. "Let the punishment fit the crime. Good night, lieutenant, ensign."

"Good night, sir," they chorused.

Daivid marched off to his own quarters, cognizant of a job well done. This might be the start of a battle of practical jokes, but he was ready for it. On the way back from the main base he had had plenty of time to review all those long-dormant tricks he had learned at camp. What with modern technology and the experience of the intervening years, he was pretty sure he could hold his own. If he woke up the next morning with his clothes soaked and tied into knots, he would cope.

The geese woke him two hours later, at false dawn. Wolfe stared at the ceiling for a moment then rolled over, carefully feeling the bed-clothes with his feet. No strings had been tied to his toes, no return Vortex played on him while he was sleeping, but he still had the feeling that someone had been in his quarters. He had no specific reason, no clue to which he could easily point, except for a faint, foreign scent in the air that couldn't be put down to his perambulation of the base nor his personal toiletries. He stretched out a hand to palm the control for the overhead lights. He could see nothing unusual. He eased himself out of bed.

Very gingerly, he stood to one side and activated the doors to the closet and the bathroom. Nothing. No bucket of water tumbled to the floor, no tripwires sprang up from the smooth, synthetic flooring to grab his ankles, no sudden blast of marching band music shocked him into jumping backwards. The contents of his bureau and desk had been left alone. None of the drawers were booby-trapped. His infopad seemed to function correctly, and all his uniforms were dry and properly pressed.

With a sudden attack of panic he felt for the card on his chest. It was intact, with no sign that any attempt had been made to tamper with it. The miniature screen sprang into life when he held the retinal scanner up to his eye. None of the access alarms showed.

A half-hour's search turned up no signs of intrusion. Still feeling a little uneasy, he stepped into the shower and turned on the tap.

The out-rushing torrent from the showerhead knocked him against the back wall. Wolfe flailed for the grab bars and hauled himself upright. He slammed the lever downward and stood panting, water streaming down his body.

A cursory flick of the lever produced another waterfall-power cataract. Wolfe turned it on and off a few times just to make certain that it was ordinary water coming out of the rose, not perfume, paint or a few other less savory liquids that he knew could be loaded into a tank. He laughed until the enamel-walled room rang with the sound. Either the faulty plumbing had healed itself overnight, or the Cockroaches were responsible for the puppy-piddle stream he had bathed with for the first few days of his tenure. They were waiting for a sign that he was worthy of their respect. How many commanding officers had come and gone through here, never knowing that the shower could work properly?

"I wonder which one it was," he said aloud as he adjusted the spray to a comfortable one, halfway between drowning standing up and a fine mist, before stepping in, "facing the supply chief, or the Vortex?"

An hour later he jogged in place on the exercise yard as the chronometer turned over from 0459 to 0500. The door of the barracks zipped open, and every member of the Cockroaches swarmed out, attired in workout gear.

"Morning, lieutenant," Boland greeted him with a snappy salute. "So, what do you want us to do first?"

"As you can see, we have already returned twenty-two units," Wolfe said as Commander Mason read through the supply request he had placed on her desk. "They're ready for refurbishment."

"They are?" Mason asked, glancing up from the infopad. On the tip of her tongue was an unasked question. Wolfe picked up the cue as neatly as he could. He put on a stern expression.

"Yes, ma'am. I think you'll find them to be in as good a condition as CBS,Ps can be when they're so overdue for replacement. I believe they should have been swapped out over 150 days ago. Even standard programming can't stabilize an elastic fabric that gets that much wear in the course of a military task. My troopers might have to rely upon those units to save their lives. Not that I am criticizing a senior officer, ma'am. Just quoting regulations."

"Standard programming, eh?" Mason murmured to herself. "Miraculous. I mean, good." As Lin had predicted, the senior officer read the notation on the infopad, and affixed her signature code. She pushed it toward him.

"Thank you, ma'am," Wolfe said, saluting. "I'll take this directly to Supply. We have only three days until we lift."

"Lieutenant," the commander began tentatively. Wolfe stopped. "I—I have to say how remarkably well you're doing with your new unit. I was very impressed by the results of the inspection the other day. I wouldn't say such strides are unprecedented but, admittedly, they are rare."

"Thank you, ma'am," Daivid said, pleased.

But Mason wasn't finished. "I, uh, you didn't have to put any *unusual pressure* on your company in order to get those results? There's nothing you need to discuss with me?"

Wolfe groaned inwardly. He knew exactly what she meant. Was he threatening the Cockroaches, Family style, to get them to shape up the way they had? He almost opened his mouth to admit to her he had made most of the beds himself.

"No, ma'am," he assured her fervently. "My interaction with X-ray Company is pretty much all within normal parameters. Don't worry, commander. I'm sure it won't all be such smooth sailing in the future."

Mason sagged visibly with relief. Wolfe guessed she felt torn between two reputations, the Cockroaches' and the Wolfe Family.

"Glad to hear it. I mean, please keep me apprised of your progress. And if you have any troubles over the next few days, come to me. That's what I'm here for."

Wolfe saluted briskly. "Thank you, ma'am."

Colonel Inigo Ayala stood before his captain's chair on the bridge of his flagship, the *Dilestro*, as the helm officer prepared to bring the ship out of nonspace transition. The starchart he saw on the three-dimensional viewscreen was a computer-generated projection. What was actually outside the ship in nonspace, that fourth-dimensional jump in between linear points, was nonsense to the human eye since they were traveling faster than light, but people, he mused, could not stand to have nothing to look at. Stars were pictured as streaks, relative to their proximity to the ship, the color dependent upon the Doppler effect of which direction they were moving in the great cosmic dance.

Even if it was an illusion, Ayala rejoiced in it. It was pretty. And each streak out there represented either a star system that humanity had conquered or had yet to conquer. In his opinion, Man was wasting his time not taking over more worlds and making use of their potential. That was why he followed General Sams. She had the same belief he did. Maybe it was a big dream, one that would never be realized in his lifetime, but he still enjoyed picturing the universe as the rightful playground of the hairless, clawless apes from Terra. Not bad for a race that spends its formative years helpless and frightened, eh?

Ever since humanity made the non-linear jump between Sol's star system and another, questions arose, not just "how can we do this again?" but "how far can we go, and what effect does it have on the people who make the jumps and the ones they leave behind?" With nonlinearity, the disruption of lives was minimalized. Transit, while not instantaneous, was greatly reduced in endurance, so that to cross the thousands of light years comprising the Thousand Worlds sector of the Milky Way galaxy along the longest axis took less than two hundred days. Why, travellers had to be fairly hyperactive even to get bored during that short a trip.

Humankind's footprint in the galaxy had increased in size every year since the discovery of faster-than-light travel, and began to overlap those of other intelligent races. The first thing humans discovered was that they could do it—travel faster than light and survive—and the second was that they could do it again. The next thing they learned was that they were not alone in the galaxy, and some of the beings out there could do it, too. The other thing they learned was that people, in their zeal to travel great distances, kept their eyes on the distant prize and less on their immediate surroundings. To a boy who had grown up picking pockets in the capital city of Great Fufford, Bailey's Planet, he hoped that starfarers would never lose that idealistic, billion-light-year vision.

From the trio of worlds that was the Insurgency's base of operations, it was forty days to the central trade routes. The latest gen from his spies gave him copies of the bills of lading about the loads he was interested in: the Tachytalks and millions of credits' worth of other supplies had already set out from their worlds of manufacture on board a fleet of trade ships bound for distributorships in five different destinations. The trick was to catch the ships before they split up.

Ayala's ships were built for chase and conquest. They lacked the comforts of most of TWC ships, such as entertainment centers and holosuites, and were sometimes even devoid of shock padding anywhere but the crash couches, but they had capacious cargo holds and better-than-average shielding. The people who shipped aboard them didn't mind the discomfort. They were zealots. Each had come to the Insurgency with his, her or its own agenda and own particular grudge against the central government, but by and large they managed to operate under a reluctant truce. The first thing was to overthrow the status quo and get rid of the unresponsive, overblown government. How things worked after that was a war for the future.

Not that Ayala had anything against non-humans. Most of the crew of *Dilestro* were bugs. With their hard carapaces, they were more radiation resistant than humans, and cared less for the comforts most humans craved. Ayala, who slept on an unpadded plastic slab, never listened to gripes about soft beds.

The one thing the bugs liked were fresh leaves—a fortunate coincidence, since the cheapest way to recycle carbon dioxide-heavy air was to let plants breathe it in. Every ship had all-shift grow lights beaming down on mosses and vines that clung to every non-essential interior surface. So the wild growth made it a little hard to read door signs and indicators once in a while, and every so often one tripped over a vine seeking more room to grow. So what? Green refreshed the eyes.

Once the Insurgency had succeeded in overthrowing the central government, he intended to lobby for certain resource-poor worlds to be transformed into nature conservancies. No sense in supporting an impoverished industrial complex when there were so many others making a profit in the universe. Specialization—that made for survival. Let predators be predators, and let herbivores be their prey.

The ever-present howl of the drives faded as they slowed. The bright streaks in the navigation tank shortened from dashes to dots. Ayala rode out the rough transition, bending his knees like a surfer at each bump and judder. He would not sit down. To have to hold on to something was a sign of weakness. He cursed his knees, which had forced him to suffer replacement surgery. They did not understand who was master here. Mere joints and cartilage! What were they against neural tissue and its potential for greatness?

Itterim Sol Oostern appeared at his side. "We've cleared nonspace," he chittered.

"Good," Ayala said. "Any fresh info?"

"Awaiting transmissions from shell-brothers. I sent a coded squirt letting them know our vector. It could be up to half a day. Do we want to wait?"

Ayala nodded. "No sense in throwing a surprise party if the guests of honor aren't coming."

He deplored the use of spies, but the other side employed them, so he had to. No sense in refusing to take up a weapon. He felt that the Insurgency had the right on their side. The Thousand Worlds Confederation was outdated, dying under its own weight. What was needed was a simpler outlook: everyone to their purpose, in cooperation with all others, for the greater glory of the galaxy.

Deep inside the bloated bureaucracy, others shared his vision. The identities of some of them would surprise the senators and representatives who purported to speak for the people. They would be amazed to know how many of their so-called constituents felt that government had gone off track and was sticking its nose into places it didn't belong.

An itterim at the communications console signed to Oostern, who checked his battered infopad.

"They have received our coordinates and will arrive shortly, colonel."

"Good," Ayala said. "Tell them we await their news."

CHAPTER 5

CAPTAIN HARAWE OF the TWC destroyer *Eastwood* obviously knew X-ray Company's reputation, and didn't like it. He surveyed the unit as they reported to him at the shuttle landing zone with the distaste one might have upon discovering a freshly coughed-up hairball.

Harawe, a tall man with very dark skin and epicanthic folds over hazel-green eyes, let his gaze travel from one trooper to another. "I just want to get some things clear before you set foot or whatever," he amended, peering at the corlist, "on my ship. I don't take slag, but I give out plenty. There are no easy berths aboard the *Eastwood*. You'll work for your passage. Is that understood?"

"Aye, sir!" X-ray chorused obediently. Daivid distrusted them when they sounded that angelic. He snapped off a salute.

"Lieutenant Daivid Wolfe, Captain!" he barked out. "These are my officers, Lieutenant (jg) Donna Borden, and Ensign Ioan Thielind."

"I saw your names on the manifest," Harawe growled, spinning to face them. "We're not going to get chummy. I'm your ride, and that's all. Your company will work, eat, excrete, recreate, and sleep, and stay the hell out of my way. Is that clear?"

"Yes, sir!" Daivid held himself erect.

A regular Navy type. Someone like Harawe sounded like he hated you, but if you dug down deep enough into his inner psyche and really probed his heart, you would find out that he didn't care enough about you to bother with hate. If your plans didn't coincide with his, then you were the one who had to change, and pronto. Whatever made Mason treat Daivid and the others with such leniency didn't impact upon Harawe at all. All the captain wanted was for them to follow orders, avoid conflict, and make it through the journey so they would get the hell off his ship. Daivid was comfortable with an arm's-length attitude like that. He had given X-ray a lengthy speech on just getting there and back again without attracting notice. With straight faces, every one of them had assured him that peace and quiet was all they wanted.

Daivid was already feeling nervous. He had given strict orders not to bring with them the still or the piece of hull plate, but he had noticed a flash of melon-pink behind a rack of weapons before Nuu Myi had slammed the cargo container shut. When Daivid had demanded she reopen it for his inspection, she pretended to have forgotten the code sequence. So the memorial was traveling with them. When he realized they were not going to listen to him, he had made sure he was the last man out of the enlisted barracks and checked the battered closet at the end of the room. The still was still there, its heating element turned off and sealed. Daivid had felt a surge of relief but, when he kicked the tank, it rang hollow. Groaning, Daivid had made tracks for the depot to do a quick check of the rest of their cargo.

The array of packing containers piled up ready for shipment was daunting, but no one ever told a Wolfe there was a job too big for him. He had taken the manifest out of Thielind's hands and scanned it for potential hiding places Somewhere, they had managed to pack a hundred liters of white lightning. How the hell could anyone conceal that much liquid? He doubted they had sold it all to the spaceport bar. Daivid started opening big carriers, poking through the padding around artillery pieces and lifting up the spacer bars in between weapons. Not a single thing sloshed or burbled that wasn't supposed to. By the time Harawe had landed, Wolfe still hadn't found the liquor. He hoped the captain wouldn't happen upon it by accident.

Harawe eyed the enlisted troopers with distaste. "There's sixty skids of goods coming on board. You people are loading my cargo as well as your own. I'm not bringing anyone down here to help. No one gets a free ride on my ship. Do you hear me?"

"No, sir!" Boland led the rest in a hearty salute. Daivid shot the noncoms a wary glance. They grinned at him.

Harawe nodded curtly. "Then let's get this load of crap moving!"

"Hey, lieutenant," Supply Chief Sargus called, pointing a thick thumb at an army of frontloaders rolling along behind him. "Here's the rest of your ammo. And your suits. I don't believe it! Everything checked out. You must be the luckiest dumb fragger ever to board ship, or the toughest. Good luck!"

I'm going to need it, Daivid thought.

The *Eastwood* must have been well-favored by Central Command, or it had been recently commissioned. Everything *smelled* new, like a flitter straight out of the display room. Daivid oversaw the loading, with Harawe towering over him disapprovingly. X-ray stowed the containers of battle armor, weaponry and personal goods. Daivid hovered around them nervously, listening for that telltale gurgle. The last of X-ray's equipment was loaded, and he was none the wiser, but Harawe hadn't noticed anything unusual, either. Daivid would have to check once they got on board. In the meantime, the rest of the loading job remained to be finished.

"Watch that, there!" the stern captain shouted as Ewanowski guided the first of Supply's frontloaders out of the warehouse, a box over six meters long by two broad. "That's my new flitter. One scratch, and you will all be remelting and mending ceramic bulkhead all the way to your drop site!"

"Aye, sir," Daivid acknowledged. "Er, wouldn't it be easier to take it out of its crate, secure the crate, and drive the flitter inside the hold? That would lessen the possibility of it getting any bumps on the way in."

"Good idea. See to it!" Harawe stalked away to talk with Commander Mason, arriving in the wake of the supplies.

At Borden's direction, Meyers and Boland undid the locks at one end of the long container. Boland stuck his head inside and let out a long whistle.

"What a beauty!" he crowed. Before anyone else could move, he swung inside and dropped into the pilot's seat. "Hot slag! Antigrav displacement emitters, Parkinson positronic drive, Van Clef-Menow MR3 stabilizers, multi-source renewable fuel—this baby will never run out of power, no matter how long you run it!"

"It's not yours," Daivid said firmly, foreseeing a potential incident like the one to which Boland had alluded on Daivid's first day.

"Of course, not, sir," Boland replied as if shocked. He ran his hands over the instrument panel then punched both thumbs into the drive actuators. With a roar, the flitter jumped forward, covering the hundred and ten meters between the warehouse and the shuttle in seconds. Daivid ran after him. The crate trundled behind him at one twentieth the speed of the flitter.

When Daivid got inside the hold, Boland was polishing the traces of oil from his fingertips lovingly off the sides and control panel of the flitter.

"She's fantastic, sir," he said, with genuine affection. Rag still wound around his hand, he patted the vehicle. It bobbed slightly on its magnetic anti-grav lifts as if responding to the caress.

"Well—" Daivid was not immune to the charms of a fast flitter. He leaned over to take a sniff of the smooth upholstery. It smelled newer than the shuttle. It reminded him of the personal craft his uncle had given him for his sixteenth birthday, the one he and his cousins had wrecked dive-racing along updrafts in the mountains. "You leave it alone, chief. It's the captain's personal vehicle. I don't want you to touch it again while we're on that ship."

"Agreed, sir," Boland said. He threw a salute then turned to help Meyers and Okumede recrate the runabout. With deep misgivings, Wolfe returned to the warehouse to oversee the next load. There was something in the chief's assent that struck him as too ready and too smooth. He'd have to think about the exchange and figure out where the hole in his logic had been.

Daivid always got a feeling of stepping off a cliff every time he went on a mission. A faint, undefinable feeling of going off into the unknown. Excitement made up a large part of the elixir, a touch of fear and a large dollop of curiosity. They were going to fight humanity's enemies and make another part of the galaxy safe for civilization.

Almost ready to go now. The loaders and ground transports were all emptied, their burdens tucked into the belly of the gleaming shuttle. The wheeled vehicles and all the base's personnel withdrew behind the ten-meter-high, transparent firescreen at the far edge of the vast polycrete surface of the launch pad. Daivid squinted into the brilliance of the afternoon sun. Supply Master Chief Sargus stood at the edge, back propped against a forklift with his big thumbs hooked into his belt. Commander Mason hovered behind the window like a house pet watching its master departing, except instead of being sad, her shoulders were slumped with relief. She was getting rid of her problem children, possibly forever. A little of Daivid's excited energy abandoned him. He followed his troopers on board the shuttle.

The Cockroaches were directed to impact benches just to the fore of the hold.

"Hey, look at this!" Aaooorru announced, poking his forefeeler to the third joint in the padding. "Comfy!"

The others threw themselves into the couches and wriggled against the cushioning. Petite Lin almost vanished into her seat's depths. They took up a great deal more room than the usual crash-couches, but Daivid thought they'd be worth it, preserving the health of the troopers enveloped in them. And they'd be a lot more tolerable for long transits than the old style seats, which were more like riding on a bench than a safety device designed to deliver soldiers to their deployment in good working order.

Everything—bulkheads, seats, control panels, infoscreens, disposers, dispensers, signage—was perfectly clean and new or in good repair, not a chip, a tear, a stain or a scratch visible anywhere. Daivid experienced deep envy at the newness, the air of prosperity all around him. Why couldn't *his* unit have ships and facilities that weren't sixteen-times hand-me-downs?

The pristine corridors rang with their footsteps as he and his two officers followed the *Eastwood's* executive officer, a narrow-faced man with thin red-brown skin and flaring nostrils, from the enlisted troopers' cabin forward to the bridge. Harawe gave them one sour glance as they strapped in, and never looked at them again.

The shuttle, so pristine that its exterior plating shone like the glass it was, lifted off effortlessly in spite of the heavy containers in her belly. Treadmill's mosaic landscape receded hastily in the star tank. At Harawe's order, the navigator, a plump woman with barley-gold curls, turned the view outward. The *Eastwood* gleamed in the star's light like a planet, its curved arrowhead shape shimmering white as the shuttle. The exterior was studded with laser ports and missile tubes. Since she was not designed to land dirtside, no expanse of her white belly had to be left flat for landing gear. She was defensible from every angle. Daivid counted six gun emplacements angled around the landing bay into which the shuttle flew.

Treadmill was a sleepy little hamlet compared with the bustling complement of the *Eastwood*. Grapples captured the slowing shuttle and eased her into her landing cradle. Hoses and cranes snaked out of the walls and hooked onto the hull with assorted clanks and thumps, followed by technicians and repairbots. Harawe smacked the safety buckle on his impact harness and was up and on his way out off the bridge before Wolfe, Borden and Thielind had undone theirs.

None of the *Eastwood's* officers looked at the three of them. Wolfe shrugged. Even if he hadn't been paying attention when they had boarded, the way to the exit was clearly marked in Standard and eight other languages, and one destroyer was pretty much laid out like another. He had done his initial service on the destroyer *Van Damme*.

What to do when he reached the shuttle bay was another thing. Once they had debarked and passed through decontamination in the vast shining white airlock, they paused, hoping they didn't look as lost as they felt. Fortunately, Harawe had arranged for a welcoming committee.

Bong! A bell-like sound echoed in Daivid's head as the ship's communication system broadcast directly into his mastoid implant. A crisp female voice announced, "Please proceed forward twenty meters to the next set of double blast doors. Then halt. Your escort is waiting for you."

"Did you hear that?" Daivid asked the others.

"Did I ever!" Thielind said, shaking his head. "That computer has one sexy voice."

"You need to go on a date," Borden smirked.

"What's the hurry? It's only been six months since the last one."

A female junior officer, so smartly attired Wolfe thought she must be going to a costume ball instead of on duty, marched up and saluted him. It took him a moment to realize she was dressed normally. Daivid mentally shook himself. Five days among the Cockroaches was ruining his eye for appropriate military bearing. He had better watch it, or he was going to forget what standards were supposed to be like.

"I'm Ensign Coffey," she said, shaking hands with all of them. "I'll take you and your officers to your quarters. When they're finished stowing your gear, the flight deck master chief will show your company where they're bunking. Come with me."

A muted female voice overhead followed them along the corridor, the public-address computer making announcements or paging crew members to locations where they were needed.

"...Volleyball semi-finals will begin at 1600 hours in the forward gymnasium between Team Red and Team Blue. Supporters will only be admitted during their nonduty shift. Highlights can be viewed on in-ship channel 605. Today's birthdays are Midshipman

Vol Pendgarest, who turns twenty-two; Lieutenant Finela Howes, who turns forty; and Mannalenda Vargas, age two, daughter of Lieutenant Commander Juda Sugg Vargas. The main midships ladder between decks 4 and 5 will be closed between the hours of 2300 and 0200 for maintenance due to worn treads. Please use midships lifts or other ladders fore and aft..."

Daivid experienced a feeling of isolation. A healthy, active military community was bustling all around him with purpose and common goals. It was so different from the way the Cockroaches lived, set apart from the other units on a base that was already considered punishment duty. As much as he was coming to like them, they were still pariahs among pariahs. He also had a momentary surge of guilt, then alarm, realizing that they were still back in the landing bay, not currently under his direct supervision.

"I hope they're behaving themselves," he murmured to himself.

Borden cocked her head. She'd caught the comment. "Depends on your definition of behaving themselves, sir."

"Those are fragile, damn you!" the flight deck supervisor howled as Ambering knocked the side of the shuttle door with her frontloader. The chief, a stocky, swarthy-skinned human male with thick curly hair peeking out of the neck of his dark green coveralls, rolled up to her on legs as round as barrels and banged on the first crate with his fist. "Can't you read it? That's power capacitors! You want to set off a major explosion? Watch it!"

The heavyset woman gave him a glare from underneath her eyebrows. "Aye, chief," she muttered.

Lin, watching the rest of the troopers stacking boxes, pursed her lips and gave her a warning look.

"I can't heee-aaar yeeew!" the chief barked.

Ambering wiped the resentful expression off her face. "Aye, chief!" she shouted.

"That's better! When I talk to you, I want you to reply like you mean it! All of you scum get that?"

"Aye, chief!" the Cockroaches bellowed in unison. Lin nodded.

No sense in starting trouble right away. It was inevitable that there would be trouble, of course. No one could exist around these constipated fancy-suited power-trippers without being tempted to burst the balloon of their self-importance, and the Cockroaches were experts at spotting a balloon that was overdue for bursting. She marked the flight deck supervisor on her mental list as someone she wanted to take down a notch or two over the course of the next thirty-five days. She outranked him, which was an advantage, and she bet he didn't know very much about theology. You could never start too early on a preemptive strike.

She signaled to the others to hurry up and finish so they could get up and explore the rest of the ship. They winked or nodded back, sharing the same thought. Ewanowski, the semicat, bared his teeth eagerly. He and Boland eased the captain's new vehicle out of the hold and locked it into a climate-controlled compartment along with a few other smaller containers.

"First blood, first blood!" Jones crowed, emerging from the hold of the shuttle alongside the roboloader.

"No!" Meyers scoffed. "You couldn't have come up with one that quickly."

"I certainly did," Jones stated, polishing his fingernails on his coverall. "Ready?"

"No. You had to have thought it up in advance."

"I certainly did not! I swear by my honor!"

"What honor?" Ewanowski growled, playfully, as he shouldered by. Jones punched him in the arm.

"Chief!" Meyers protested.

Lin interceded. "You know the rules. The first Roach to come up with a limerick on site gets extra points, more if it's good. We'll be able to tell if it's appropriate, or if he's recycling something from another mission."

"I've got one, too," Mose grinned, lifting his eyes from the inventory screen.

"Me, too," Okumede called from across the hold.

"Jones called it first," Lin decided. "Come on, out with it."

"Get on with the job!" the deck chief shouted. "You're wasting our time!"

"Wait a moment, wait a moment," Jones said, gesturing at him to be patient. "Five lines start to finish. 'A grumpy ship captain named Harawe/ Said to Wolfe, as we stowed his new carawe, "You may come on my ship /But you give me the pip / And I wish you and your troop were all farawe!"'" Jones hooked his hands in his belt and turned with pride to the deck master chief. "So, what do you think of that, eh?"

It took Daivid only a few moments to get his gear stowed. Every compartment opened silently to a finger's touch. The sound insulation shut out the sound of footsteps from the corridor beyond. For the duration of the mission, no geese waking him up at daybreak. Maybe he'd get to sleep until 0500. Luxury.

Once again he took inventory of the chamber that was to be his new home for the next thirty-five days. It was all so splendidly ordinary: five hangers, water glass, chair, desk, bed, bedclothes. Yet the difference between this setting and X-ray Company's barracks was extreme. He felt as though he might be home again in his father's mansion. Genuine wooden moldings framed the door. Polished brass knobs indicated the location of controls and communication outlets. Just out of curiosity, he poked his head into the small lavatory he shared with the junior officers' quarters next door. Sonic shower. *Too bad*, he thought, thinking of the delicious deluge he had enjoyed that morning. Even the captain of a star destroyer didn't have it as good as they did dirtside when it came to hygiene. So there were advantages to living in the back end of nowhere after all.

And yet—Was that a personal surround entertainment hookup over desk above the docking station for his infopad? Yes! He flicked it on. Wow—all the newest threedeeos, including the pictures that were still in full crystal ampitheater release.

He jumped guiltily at the sound of his door signal. "Enter," he called. The door slid open to reveal Coffey, back stiff.

She shot him a very formal salute. "You are summoned to the captain's day room, sir."

"What's going on, ensign?" he asked, smiling at her. "A briefing, already?"

No friendly banter or even a return smile. Coffey's small face twisted into a mask of disapproval.

"No, sir. Would you follow me, please?"

"What do you mean, they're already guilty of dereliction of duty?" Wolfe asked hopelessly.

He stood alone on one side of the captain's enormous white marble-topped desk. On the other side the captain sat glowering. At his left elbow, in front of a wall filled with screens and readouts, hovered a clutch of lieutenants and ensigns. A tall itterim in the rear clicked his mandibles at Wolfe, the bug equivalent of sticking out his tongue. At its elbow, a hardfaced woman with short, wavy black hair and commander's flashings on her collar stood with her arms folded. At Harawe's right elbow stood Commander Cleitis, the narrow-faced XO, and a burly man with a chief's insignia on his coverall sleeves. His square face looked as though someone had tried to pound the corners off of it. Dark red bruises decorated the left temple and jaw, the lower orbit of the right eye and the bridge of his nose. He glared at Wolfe.

"And brawling," interjected the XO, unnecessarily.

"And scurrilous verse, too, derogatory to the captain," the flight deck chief said, moving his jaw very gingerly.

Wolfe groaned. "A limerick?"

"What do you know about it?" Harawe growled.

"It's a unit tradition, sir."

The green eyes pinned him in place. "Have you been a party to this?"

"Not yet, sir—I mean, no." He shook his head. "I'm not much of a poet."

"Neither is your crewman, by the sound of it," Harawe said. He waved a hand over a sensor on his desk. A miniature threedeeo image appeared on the white desk, showing one side of the shuttle, half a dozen troopers, and as many coverall-clad members of the Eastwood's crew. Jones's fruity voice rose out of a concealed speaker. Daivid listened, wishing he could drop straight down through the deck.

"...what do you think of that, eh?" the little round figure said, planting its hands on its hips.

What the listener thought of it was more or less confirmed by the brawl that followed. To Wolfe's dismay, Jones had indeed thrown the first punch, though not until after a conversation of steadily-rising acrimony had occurred between him and the chief.

"Naturally, everything in the secured areas is recorded," the XO put in.

"Naturally," Daivid said faintly.

"Of course, the rest of the file will have to be freeze-framed and expanded to see who was responsible for each of the infractions that followed."

"Of course, sir."

"This does not give me a great deal of confidence in your ability to lead these hyenas," Harawe said. "You do realize that you've joined this ship's complement to undertake a mission of great importance?"

"I do, sir, though we have not yet been briefed on just what that mission is," Daivid pointed out.

That seemed to excite one of the female lieutenants enough to raise a faint twitch in her stiff face. "Commander, in light of the present proceedings, I must ask again if this is indeed the unit to undertake such a vital task. It is, as you know, a sensitive matter—"

Cleitis waved a hand. "That is the entire point of their assignment, Varos."

"Sir," Daivid began, "what *is* our as—?"

The captain interrupted him. "I know you are new to the unit. So I will allow you a trifle of leniency, but that is all. I cannot allow your company to damage the workings of my ship. The man who threw the first punch is confined to quarters during off-hours, with no entertainment systems permitted except for the Space Service's book of rules and regulations. I will review his case in ten days."

"Yes, sir," Daivid sighed. Jones wouldn't consider either part of the penalty punishment. If the confinement lasted long enough, he would probably set the entire book to verse, maybe even to music.

"All of the crew who were involved in the altercation will be assigned to Chief Winston down in Sanitation," Executive Officer Cleitis intoned. "Further infractions will be accorded corporal punishment. You keep them out of trouble at all other times. You will report to Commander Iry."

The hard-faced woman nodded.

"She'll expect to see you daily, and at any time she wants your sorry ass in her office. Is that clear?"

"Very clear, sir," Daivid said.

The hard-faced woman gave him one sharp nod.

The XO echoed it. "Good. Dismissed."

"I was declaiming, sir," Jones argued, sitting on his lower bunk in the cramped six-bed quarters. "He could have waited a moment. It was the last load."

"But you ignored his orders," Daivid explained painstakingly for the eighth time, then decided Jones was just keeping the discussion going to see how long he could string the new commander. "Enough is enough. He had instructions for you."

The burly man settled back against the wall with his hands behind his head. "Ah, well, he threw them around a bit too readily."

"That's his job." Daivid punched the door control. "I'll check on you later."

The other Cockroaches were waiting in Gehenna, the day room assigned to them. The *Eastwood* was carrying a full complement of space service troopers and special forces personnel, but somehow X-ray Company had managed to get one small room to itself. Maybe, Daivid thought, it had something to do with its upcoming mission. He intended to ask about a briefing at the XO's earliest convenience.

The room, like all other enlisted messes, was meant to act as a chilling-out area for up to three companies. It was called a 'day room' because of the lighting, the harsh, brilliant glare that was the equivalent of sunlight under atmosphere. Science now millenia old had proved that human beings had to be exposed to a minimum of six hours a day, or they would begin to suffer depression and some deficiencies associated with lack of sunlight. In certain cases they could even be ordered to spend time in this or any other chamber fitted with the correct lamps.

The company would eat at regular times in the commissary, but food synthesizers and a couple of big storage units had been installed in each of the day rooms for their use in between meals. They also did their laundry here, in the big cleaning trunks and presser boxes against one wall, plus a real wash-tub for personal, non-issue items. If troopers wished to socialize with others outside their command, a Hero-class destroyer like this one had bars and common rooms, the sports areas and multi-use cultural venues as points of interaction.

Traditionally, and this habit Daivid knew went back thousands of years, units assigned to messes were allowed to furnish and/or decorate their messes as they saw fit. Seeing the way they kept their barracks back on Treadmill, he guessed that the room would very quickly turn into a mess in truth. The Cockroach banner had already been mounted on the wall, and the battered memorial was propped up in one corner. Debris, in the form of personal readers, discarded clothing and food containers, lay in clusters on countertops and the row of seats that lined three of the walls.

Equally traditional was an officer having to ask permission to enter. The Service, like all military operations from the beginning of time, was a top-down organization, but to give the noncoms a territory they could control themselves went a long way towards keeping morale steady on long missions. If Daivid had had orders to convey, they were transmitted to the receiver in the chamber, or to the communication units of individual troopers involved. (In the case of an emergency or immediate call to duty, the custom naturally was suspended.)

Though the ten-centimeter-thick door stood ajar, Daivid did not enter. He leaned on the door signal and waited. Twelve of the Cockroaches were clustered around the central pedestal table, cards in hand. The rest of X-ray Company sprawled, sat or lay on the floor or the built-in seats, drinking bug juice, eating hand-snacks and sucking on pows. Meyers glanced up from her cards at the chime, then hastily looked away, not making eye contact with him. Mose shifted a nicotine pow from one side of his mouth to the other, grinning broadly.

"Call," he said.

Groans rose from the others. "I'm out," said Boland.

"Me, too," added Streb.

"I'll see you," Lin said, leaning forward, her eyes slitted dangerously.

"Me, too," added Ewanowski.

"I'm out," Thielind announced, tossing his cards on the table. He tossed a wave at the lieutenant and held up a finger. *Wait.* Daivid fumed. They were playing him. He put a bland expression on his face, and watched the game with polite interest.

"All right, all right," said Aaooorru, fanning his antennae. He spread out his hand. A mischievous light was in his bulging eyes. "Full house. Emperors over nines."

"Poop," Boland exploded. "You had a pair of nines last hand, too. You must have palmed them."

The shrimp-spider held out his multiple pairs of arms. His gray-pink ridged body was covered with nothing but a diaper-like garment over his excretory and generative organs and the water-collar over his gills. "And I hid them where?"

"That big hairball kept them for you," Boland said, pointing at Ewanowski.

"As if, ape boy," the semicat yawned, showing long, pointed teeth and a narrow, pink tongue twice as long as a human's.

Aaooorru paid no more attention to the chief's protests. The rest of the players threw in their cards as the shrimp-spider raked in the pot. Now the table turned to look at Daivid.

"Come in, sir," Lin invited him at last.

Daivid stepped through. "I just came from the captain's day room. Jones is confined to quarters during rest periods. You're all—"

"On sanitation duty," the Cockroaches chimed together.

Daivid frowned. "Did the XO send your orders down here already?"

"Hell, no, sir," Boland grinned. "We always get shafted down into waste management. If Jones hadn't given them an excuse, they'd have found a way to assign us down there sooner or later."

"But it's slag duty," Daivid said. "Why do you look so happy?"

"Even a slag cloud," Mose replied philosophically, gathering up the cards and shuffling, "has a silver lining."

Daivid eyed them uneasily. "What kind of silver lining?"

"Oh," Boland offered an unconvincing expression of innocence. "Nothing special."

"Uh-huh."

"Want to jump in, sir?" Aaooorru asked, swiveling his round eyes in the lieutenant's direction. "I've cleaned out most of their money, but they've still got some left."

"No, thanks." Daivd glanced at the chrono on his communication card. "I've got paperwork, then I'm going to check out the officers' wardroom."

The noncoms and the enlisted troopers exchanged grins and knowing looks. "Good luck, sir."

"Wilbury," said a cheerful, brown-skinned man about Daivid's age, sticking out a hand. The wardroom was larger, better appointed and cleaner than the enlisted mess. "Miklis Wilbury, Andromeda unit."

"Daivid Wolfe. Pleased to meet you. Where are you bound?"

Wilbury looked mysterious. "It's all totally hush-hush. Creeps me out, if you want the truth. We're supposed to be preparing. All they'll tell me is that we're fifty days out, and to get everything, especially my troopers, in good order."

"That's what you're supposed to be doing," said a new voice. A dark-haired man with pale skin, dark hair and deeply hooded blue eyes sauntered by to loom over them. Daivid had thought the newcomer was about his height, until he stood up to offer a hand. The dark-haired man was so perfectly in proportion, with his v-shaped torso, muscular legs and arms, and tight waist, that Daivid was surprised to see how high he loomed over him. "They don't trust you loose cannons with the gen, obviously. You'll be told what's going on when the captain thinks you can handle it. Right now, he's probably sorry he took you on board. The rest of us are bound for the Benarli cluster to take out those pipsqueaks who call themselves the Insurgency."

"Bruno, knock it off," a female lieutenant called from her seat near the wall. She got up to join them. "The side missions are all classified on this deployment. Don't let Mr. Big Shot here let you get the impression he's any more in the know than you are."

"Thanks," Daivid said. "Daivid Wolfe."

"I know. Carmel Ti-ya. Personnel. I processed your orders. I'm supposed to connect with your Lieutenant Borden. Is she here?"

Daivid glanced around. "Not yet. I left her checking the manifests against the containers of our gear."

"A little too late for that, isn't it?" asked a female almost as tall as Bruno, who shouldered up to join him. Daivid recognized her as Varos, the disapproving lieutenant who had questioned the Cockroaches' competence in the captain's mast. "We've already left orbit."

Daivid gave her a summing look. Girlfriend? Defender? While he was trying to guess their relationship, a burly man with light brown hair and a creased brow muscled up and took his place at Bruno's other side. A clique. Mentally, Daivid rolled his eyes. How primary-school. Bruno was the boss, and they were his posse.

"You know what they say about the military," he said, cheerfully. "Check the checklists, then check them again, and again, and again. The paperwork never stops."

"I didn't know they said that," the muscular man replied. The tape over his breast pocket read "Rindel." The dark-haired man shot him a dirty look.

"What do you do?" Daivid asked.

"Supply. Facilities scheduling," Bruno said, with just that hint of malice that showed that he had allowed that power to corrupt him. He knew and Daivid knew he knew and Bruno knew Daivid knew he knew that everyone else had to stay on his good side, or end up in the worst possible facility at the most inconvenient time.

"Facilities?" A head perked up at the table beside them. A narrow-faced junior lieutenant with a regulation buzz-cut atop a soft face and a body Daivid couldn't guess was female or male stood up. "I wanted to talk to you. This is one hell of a big ship. Why are five units jammed into one mess? I thought all we took on board at Treadmill was the one platoon, right?"

Bruno frowned. "I didn't change anyone's mess assignment."

"The hell you didn't, sir. I'm with Ophiuchus platoon. My troopers were in Gehenna, back near the cinema, along with Quicksilver company, from Centauri base. The chief that came in today told my chief we were both shifted to Buzzard. Something about having to have space for her religious practices. Buzzard was at capacity already, commander."

Daivid suppressed a groan. Bruno whipped out his infopad and scrolled to a particular screen. His eyebrows went down. "Nothing's changed. You send your troopers back where they came from. There must have been a glitch in the data given to that unit. What was their designation?"

"X-ray," replied the aggrieved jg.

The dark blue eyes swiveled, homing in on Daivid. "Well, you're reassigned as of now. Any questions on that, Lieutenant Wolfe?"

"I don't give a heap of slag, as long as they treat my troopers with respect," Daivid answered in a low, very calm voice. "Maybe you don't know X-ray's reputation."

There was a murmur through the wardroom. Evidently *Bruno's* reputation was such that no one answered back to him, but Daivid wasn't intimidated. What the hell could he do to them?

Bruno gave him a mirthless grin, nodding. "Oh, I know it, all right. I'll give them all the respect they *deserve*. Any questions?"

"No," murmured the lieutenant from Ophiuchus.

"No," Daivid added, diffidently.

"Fine," Bruno snapped then stalked away like a tiger, smug at having gotten the last word. His two cronies—jackals, Daivid thought—followed behind him. The lieutenant retired to his table, shaking his head.

"Ignore Bruno," advised Ti-ya, tilting her hand to invite Daivid to sit down with her and the others at her table. "He once got a good annual report, and it went to his head. Meet Sameia Al-Hadi and Rokke Barikson."

The dark woman with large, liquid, brown eyes and the solid young man with unruly light brown hair and pale, coarse skin both nodded to him. Wilbury squeezed in on the other side. Each bench in the booth had room for three, though Daivid noticed some tables with five or six officers squeezed in on a side, talking with animation. He supposed that once you'd spent any amount of time in a shuttle waiting to drop into an arena you'd have very little left in the way of personal space requirements. An autoserver popped up in the center of the table. Daivid ordered strong coffee.

"I've heard of Treadmill," Barikson said. His collar flashing showed he was a lieutenant (jg). "What's it like with the prison looming over you?"

"I was only assigned there five days before we were deployed," Daivid admitted, slugging back a solid jolt of caffeine. The *Eastwood* got really good coffee. He intended to drink his share while on board.

"Really?" replied Al-Hadi with friendly curiosity. "So, do you suppose it's your unit or you they want so badly on this mission? The rumor mill is burning up, it's running so fast."

Daivid hesitated. Did they have any idea who he was? "No clue," he said. "They haven't even told us what our task is."

Barikson's eyebrows went up. "Having to fix a plan of battle blind? They must have a lot of faith in you."

Daivid shrugged. Al-Hadi grinned. "We're all part of the big push. I'm the tactical officer for Lancer platoon. We came from Alpha Antares station. Half our base is on board with us. This ship can hold ten thousand crew, though you couldn't tell it from walking through the halls. It's the size of a luxury liner."

"You can if you stick your head into the enlisted messes," Barikson said. "Those are jammed pretty tightly. Some of my people are spending their down time in the bunk rooms or the exercise centers just to get a little space to themselves. We'll have companionship enough when we have to spend thirty hours a day in our armor."

"No lie. Lancer just had its first anti-grav training in three months, and we were bumping into each other like popcorn in a popper. The sides of my helmet felt like they were closing in even closer against my skull. I wanted to tear off my suit right there."

"Don't let us stop you now," Barikson said with his ready grin. Daivid grinned, too. Al-Hadi was an attractive woman. She gave them a mock glare.

"In your dreams, guys. Not that the training or the maintenance jobs we're doing aboard ship is putting much of a dent in my troopers' time, of course," she went on. "They're treating the transport phase like one long R&R. I mean, it's not the best vacation—no sightseeing, no nightlife, but at least the toilets flush, so to speak. We had one assignment, border patrol on the Draco Major frontier, on a leaky old tub. Everything started breaking down. The only thing that really worked were the drives and the weapons. Life systems, eh. Hygiene facilities, double eh. Everything stopped working at least twice over the course of the four months we were stopping lizards from crossing into TWC space. We got to know one another by our smells. It's too bad that stink can't cross vacuum. It would have deterred anything with nostrils from coming anywhere near us."

"That's one of the good things about Treadmill," Daivid laughed. "Real showers. Our quarters are next to the launch facility, way the hell away from the rest of the base, and the base is way the hell distant from the nearest town, but we've got plenty of water."

"Working showers," sighed a female commander at the next table. "I can't tell you the last time I had a water bath—yes, I can. It was during my leave on a T-class planet about two years ago. What a luxury. Poteet Corrundum, Xerxes Company," she added, holding out a hand to Daivid.

"Hey, two X's. Daivid Wolfe. X-ray Platoon, Neutron Company."

"Uh-huh," Corrundum said a little more cautiously. "I—uh, I know Commander Mason."

"Oh?" Daivid asked, coldly.

"Uh-huh. We were in OTC together. She's good people. We're in touch as much as we can be, tach mail, the occasional live call. She—mentioned you were being transferred to her command. She thinks you're doing a good job, you know."

"How can she tell in five days?" Barikson asked, curiously.

Corrundum picked up on Daivid's disapproval. She shot Barikson a quick smile. "You can always tell. I once had an enswine that was so stupid, he started thinking 'slag' was his real name. 'Cause that's what I said every time I had to clean up the mistakes he made. There wasn't a position I could leave him in without supervision. The chiefs kept saying, indirectly but where I could hear them, that maybe they should frag him so he could finally do some good, like feeding a carrion-scavenger. But I bet he'd find a way to make them sick. I got him transferred to another unit. He's somebody else's problem."

"My ensign's an amazing fix-it man," Daivid said, and raised his eyebrows back at his fellow officers who gave him surprised looks. Sooner or later someone was going to make him explain his philosophy. "You know how cleanerbots are always flaming out. The barracks bugs we have are still running, and they must be sixteen or eighteen years old. Well past replacement."

Al-Hadi snorted. "Sounds like you have the same procurement prerogative we do: until it crumbles into its component molecules, you don't *need* a new one, do you?"

"No kidding. I've never been on a ship that had all new equipment—until this one—" Daivid looked around enviously.

Wilbury snorted. "Political pork-barrel. When it looks like the Space Service is going to get its budget slashed, they buy something big to suck up the surplus. This probably ate up the total tax money from three or four systems."

"Harawe earned this," Ti-ya corrected him with a frown. "He's an incredible officer. When I had a chance to come on board the *Eastwood,* I jumped at it. The Old Man's going to be an admiral before long. The Benarli war will probably get him his promotion."

"And make a bunch of Senators very happy," Wilbury said.

"You're a cynic," Daivid said. "I like that."

The food in the wardroom was as superior as the setting. Daivid scrolled down the six choices available on the table menu screen, and down into the à la carte menu provided for those who just wanted a snack. Like most ships that ran on full shifts, meals had to be served on a constant rotation. He was sure that the robochefs had thousands of recipes but sharply limited the daily menu for sound psychological reasons. His father, aunts and uncles said much the same when they got together to discuss offerings for the Family's various restaurant chains. If you gave customers too few choices, they got bored. If you gave them too many, they would never make up their minds, and the whole idea was to get the bottoms into the chairs and out again in a reasonable amount of time. The download of the ship's manual into his infopad said meals were served for one hour every five hours, to provide two per shift. If a crew member missed one service, for whatever reason, there were hard rations, balanced-nutrition bars or colloid cups in several locations on every level, and sweet juice drinks—or 'bug juice'—in every mess, wardroom and day room. He hoped the noncommissioned crew got as wide a selection. He only saw one raw-food choice, and that was all the corlist, Aaooorru, could eat. He was still curious as to why one of the shrimp-spider beings had chosen to enlist in the Space Service. According to the corlist's file, he was high-born and well-educated. He shouldn't have been in the Navy any more than, well, Daivid.

Whereas the newcomers were fairly friendly to one another, a number of the assigned crew of the *Eastwood* were, in a word, jerks. As on many other ships, the officers who were supposed to coordinate interaction, such as intramural activities, saw themselves as petty dictators with a realm to protect. If you didn't think their way or admire the things they did, then you were relegated to secondary status. Daivid didn't like to play those games. The best way to win was to stay out of their way and hang out with friendlies. His new acquaintances seemed like good people to spend a month getting to know.

"What do you think?" Carmen asked. "I like the sushi rolls myself. Six different fillings."

"The computer never, never puts enough wasabi on them," Wilbury complained. "I've talked to the cooks, and they just stare at me. 'It's what's in the book,' they say."

"You don't think they can really cook!" Al-Hadi laughed. "You know what the service is like. If you were trained as a cleric, you get put into fire control. If you're rated in navigation, they put you in engineering. If you know how to cook, they make you a drill instructor."

Daivid heard a familiar voice at his back. He turned around to see Borden talking with more animation than he had ever seen before.

"…AI systems the likes of which no one has been able to make for a thousand years," she was saying. Her audience, a handful of serious-faced officers, were nodding in agreement. "Independent decision-making capabilities but still using the Asimov strictures. It has applications for practically anything. Information retrieval could be revolutionized—with an intuitive structure, one of these devices could think like a human brain."

"The first thing they'll use it for is mind-control," said a very thin man as tall as an itterim, just loud enough for Daivid to hear. "They'll install it *in* brains."

"That's illegal!" protested Borden. "They must be contemplating a use in industry."

His mahogany-skinned, chunky companion folded his arms. "Wrong. The first application will be military. Ever and always. They'll find a way to kill people with it. You wait."

"But Asimov—!" the round, dark-faced woman next to Borden protested.

"The most important thing is to use any new technology to preserve life," Borden said fervently.

Hear, hear, Daivid thought. That was his philosophy to a T. He ought to have a good talk with Borden one of these days.

"Besides, the difficulty of the mind-brain interface would make it difficult to produce a true mind analog. It has been known for millenia that though the brain creates the mind, that is by no means a simple explanation of the phenomenon…"

Borden had found like-minded computer-heads. Daivid quickly got lost in the half-heard unfamiliar scientific jargon, and dragged himself back to the conversation going on at his table.

"…Escort duty. The Space Service is really getting their money's worth out of this ship," Ti-ya was saying.

"Where are we going next?" Daivid asked.

"Your clerk got full briefings to add to your infopad but, now that we've got you, we're heading out toward the Benarli cluster. You've probably heard about the Insurgency raids. Our first jump is due in two days, just outside Praetoria."

Daivid nodded. He recognized the name of another stop on the major trade routes. His family had a chain of good restaurants in the space station, a huge rotating spool hanging halfway between the heliopause and the primary.

"Beyond that, they're holding all other information back from us. So we don't need to worry about it. Piece of cake. Just sit back and enjoy the ride. Do you play poker?"

"A little," Daivid admitted, allowing a glint to show in his eyes.

Lin, Boland and D-45 reported to his cabin the next morning before PT for the daily status report.

"We missed your money last night, sir," Boland said.

"Sorry. It was getting to know some other credits in the wardroom," Daivid said, stretching his arms out with every evidence of satisfaction.

"Successful night?" Boland asked with a grin.

"Oh, yes, my money made a lot of friends," Daivid replied blithely. His winnings were locked up in the safe-drawer underneath his bunk, accessible only by a thumbprint scan. "Progress report?"

"All go and on green," said Lin. "No problems, except it was hard getting to sleep without any noises except the troopers snoring. This is the quietest ship I've ever been on."

"Jones all right?"

"Aye, sir," D-45 replied. "I think he's enjoying himself. He's got Thielind running back and forth to bring him goodies from the day room—Well, you didn't say he couldn't have provisions, did you, sir?"

Privately, Daivid admired the Cockroaches' ability to read loopholes into any order. "May I remind you he's supposed to be on punishment? That doesn't include room service. Thielind is supposed to be fetching and carrying for *me*. Never mind, I'll tell him myself. Anything else?"

"Three of us tried to get into the anti-grav gym to work out during off-hours on the late shift," Lin said. "The chief in charge told us we've got to stick to the rota. Sir, I know the ship is crowded, but some of us are rusty on zero-gee skills. It's been three months since we were last in space. We need more than one shift every four days."

She pushed her infopad toward him. He read through the schedule: long-range weapons drill twice a week, and short-range drill three times a week, both using virtual-reality technology so as not to risk damaging the ship. Daivid could attest that the devices attached to the units' weapons and handguns simulated exactly the sensation of firing and kickback. Hand-to-hand twice a week. Refresher lectures on the weapons systems were available over the ship's net, and were required

"I'll see what I can do," Daivid said. That meant dealing with Bruno, but if he brought the matter to Iry, she ought to intercede for him.

CHAPTER 6

"BATTLE STATIONS!" A siren whooped, filling Emmy Lin's dreams. "Battle stations! Report! Report. This *is* a drill. Repeat, this is a drill!" Lin's eyes sprang open. She was already standing beside her bunk, reaching for her web suit.

Every light in the barracks went on at once. The Cockroaches sprang out of bed and snatched their new CBS,Ps off the end of their bunks and shrugged into them, shedding their skivvies on the way. The new webs fit like an outer epidermis, adapting to the temperature of the body against the air. Lin took a moment to glance at the chrono glowing over the door: 0400. Typical. Their unit had been placed on third sleep shift. The drill was coming smack in the middle of it. They had only been aboard the ship three days.

"Never mind the grousing!" she shouted over the usual complaints. "Get the job done."

"The noises!" Gire lay in his bunk with his hands over his ears. "It's too loud!"

The small chief gestured at Meyers, who slipped her arm around the medic's shoulders and helped him up. "What's the matter? Your ear filters not in place?"

The medic felt his head. "The voices are inside!"

Lin sighed. "You left your personal player on again," she said patiently.

She dug under his pillow and came up with his communications card. Yes, it showed that it was switched to a prerecorded program. Gire often needed entertainment to sleep. Not that he slept much; he had nightmares most of the time when he drifted off. In any other unit, he would have been given a medical discharge, but the Cockroaches took care of their own. He was a good field doctor, even though his primary specialty was dentistry, and they all knew he could never make it successfully in civilian life.

"What is it this time? Pretty young girls with cultured accents pretending to be men so they can engage in lesbian sex for the pleasure of older men even though a monkey wouldn't be fooled by their disguises, or a rich family having to deal with skeletons in the closet after the death of a family member they never knew existed?"

Gire favored unbelievable scenarios that were far removed from his own miserable life. He never talked about where he had come from if he could help it. All they knew was that they'd pulled him out of the wreckage of a small cruiser crushed between two lizard flanks, the sole survivor of a thousand trooper push.

"No." Gire blinked. His hands groped for the card and switched off the input. He wrinkled his nose at the blaring noise. "What's all the sirens for?"

"Battle stations exercise," Meyers said, helping him out of his underwear. As soon as she had yanked down his shorts, Gire came to life and started stretching out his CBS,P so it would go on more easily. With practiced hands he drew the body stocking up and on, sealing the front with gloved hands. "Where's our station?"

"Sanitation," Lin said dryly, "as usual."

"Heads up, everyone!" Boland bellowed, his deep voice carrying over the chatter. "Let's move it! Weapons set for exercise. Non-lethality!"

They jogged into the cabin next door, which was where their armor and arms were kept. Lieutenant Wolfe and the other two officers were already there, suiting up.

"Evening," Wolfe said, grinning so that his yellow eyes were slits. The skin around them looked drawn and puffy, making him look older. "Nothing like throwing us in head first, eh?"

"No, sir," Lin said. "You look like you haven't been to bed yet."

"Er, no. Long meet-and-greet session." Wolfe smirked.

"You leave them any money?"

"Enough for tomorrow," the lieutenant said smugly.

He clapped his helmet on at the same moment as Lin, rendering him faceless and almost invisible as the chameleon armor took over, displaying the wall behind him. The heads-up display inside her helmet gave her a solid red outline showing a warm body, overlaid by the blue image of his energy signature, and topped with a gold tag that carried his ID number and a coded dingbat for rank. That marking served to identify him as one of their own in the case of a scrimmage. Telemetry began to spell itself out in the text box across the top of her readout. Their orders were repeated in text and over their mastoid implants.

Wolfe's voice came over her in-suit comm system. "Squad leaders, troopers ready to rally! Shoulder weapons! Duty stations, double time!"

Lin heard a general-purpose groan from the troopers. He sure was new. Any experienced officer would take it as read that a squad that trained even irregularly would know what to do without being told.

At least he was holding back from the door until the point troopers went out it. D-45 and two of the other sharpshooters unshipped their rifles. Crossed on their backs were sword and can-opener, the latter a hooked and flattened metal rod the same length as the sword, with a pointed screw thread at the other end. The can-opener was the space trooper's best friend. It could be used with equal success to crank open hull plating or the suit of an enemy trooper. Pop an opponent's suit in vacuum with the pointy end, and he was no longer a problem. The screw end was to wind into a bulkhead in case of zero-gee conditions. You held onto it with one hand and your shooting buddy with the other while he fought the enemy, anchoring him. Even so-called recoilless weapons caused some kickback. It was hard to fight a successful melee if you were caroming around the room like a ping pong ball in a wind tunnel. The swords were modeled on classic sabers of ancient Terra, though the point was sharpened to a singularity, the better to pierce through one's opponent's armor joints. Since this was an exercise, the nonferrous blades had guards fastened around them. It was bad form to spit your allies like seekh-kebabs, even by mistake.

As soon as the word came over the helmet audio that the hallway was secured, Lin shouldered her way out next, covering Lieutenant Wolfe's exit. He looked around, too, as he slid out into the corridor, drawing that beautiful pistol of his. She sure would have liked to get a close look at it. Unless she was very wrong about the age of the gun, it was a lot older than the boy himself. There was a story behind that, which, she guessed, the Cockroaches were *not* going to hear. The sword was also not strictly standard issue, a thing of beauty. The metal gleamed silver and blue, ripples of color playing up and down the blade's length for the moment that Wolfe had had it exposed. It was almost a pity to quench its cold fire in an exercise guard. He was favored by his family. For a moment Lin felt a twinge of envy, then dismissed it. The Cockroaches were her family. So they never gave her fancy birthday presents. They never forgot it, either.

The others poured out into the hallway behind them. The coast looked clear. No warm bodies were within stated range.

Suddenly, three red forms leaped into their field of view at twenty meters distance. The squad dropped into firing formation then paused, embarrassed, as they paid more attention to the real-view of the 'intruders': three junior ensigns in full dress whites, two males and a female. All three giggled at the sight of an entire platoon in armor in the middle of the night. Lin groaned.

"Sir?" she asked on the private channel that broadcast to his mastoid receiver only. "How many units are participating in this drill?"

"Damned if I know, Top," Wolfe said, over the same channel. "I was not informed this exercise would be taking place. It wasn't on my schedule, or I'd have prepared a plan of battle. It could be just us and the computer. Borden, see if you can raise Commander Iry or her aide. In the meantime, we'd better get down to deck B. B-deck forward, zone 6 muster station! Let's move out!"

"Aye, aye, sir," Lin replied in a dead voice. *Stop micromanaging us!* she wanted to scream. *We know what the hell we're doing!* "Combat names, sir?"

"Er, yes. Yes, of course."

"We don't know yours, sir."

"Blink," Daivid replied.

"That's stupid," Boland commented, "sir. With respect, with your name we should call you 'Big Bad.'"

"Hey, yeah!" Thielind agreed.

"No!" Daivid protested, but he knew it was no use. He'd gotten the tag Blink pinned on him for his speed with his sidearm. He'd wanted to be called something like Lightning or Nuclear, but his senior officers paid no attention then, either.

The Cockroaches jogged toward the lifts in double-time, weapons at the ready. The scouts, led by D-45, fanned out to cover all approaches, including scanning the ceiling and floors with their infrared visors. Daivid let his eyes follow theirs for a moment, seeing an engineer above the false panels wrenching something upwards between his hands and hacking at it with a tool, two more sitting quietly studying the tunnel to their left, and another pair who were busy but weren't engaged in engineering at all.

Daivid chuckled. Over the platoon channel, Daivid heard an echoing laugh from several of the troopers. Normally no one would have noticed a courting couple, officially or otherwise, but the heads-up display played no favorites. It revealed all. If you were alive, you could find yourself on Candid Helmet Camera. At last Borden spoke.

"I've raised Petty Officer Gruen," she said. "He says this is a one-on-one exercise. Just X-ray versus either a virtual reality program or another unit. We won't know until we get there. Our objective is to capture the enemy beacon. Hits will be recorded by tagging. Survival is less important than achieving the objective, but both would be preferable. Naturally, sir. The exercise will last for one hour, unless the beacon is secured or everyone is 'killed.'"

"Laser tag, eh?" Wolfe mused.

The game had descended almost unchanged from their ancestors of five millenia ago and involved running around in dangerous territory with artificial weapons that shone a beam of low-level, visible laser light. If your timed shot hit another player, you scored a point. A kill was worth three. The military had adopted this useful technology as a training exercise from the very beginning of the space service, with adaptations for the more sophisticated weaponry the military carried. It saved wear and tear on the ship, the troops, and the non-combatant 'civilians' who might otherwise be struck by stray live fire in the closed environment.

"Keeps us alert if we can't anticipate whether we're facing AI or live fighters we can psych out. Stay with it, troopers. We don't know who the enemy will be. Everyone else is to be considered a neutral. On stealth. We want to maintain the element of surprise as long as we have to. Is that understood?"

Unable to keep the boredom out of their voices, the Cockroaches chorused, "Aye, sir!" Lin noticed that the red blob that represented Wolfe winced slightly. Good. They were getting through to him. He wasn't the first baby officer they'd nursed into maturity.

Wolfe followed his forward point up the forward ladder toward Deck B. It made him nervous that they had to emerge into the 'war zone' head first. It gave the enemy an advantage. Nothing like being kicked in the head to start off an exercise. Above them, all was dark. The lights had been turned off in zone 6. That way, no one could tell if they were facing AI or live opponents. At first, that is. The readout in the helmet screen would be the same, but a blow from an actual combatant, in identical military-issue armor, was a mule-kick in comparison to the love-tap the suit gave itself when the AI said 'body-slam'. It wasn't a perfect system, but it got troopers used to physical strikes, and didn't put them in the infirmary for what was just a war game. The idea was to train their reactions, not the ability of their bodies to knit.

Every ship, no matter how high technology rose in civilization, had retained the low-tech methods of securing a deck, with heavy-duty latches or wheels to close the door and seals, in case power failed during an emergency. Both physical and electronic locks were easily disabled by Thielind and Aaooorru, the corlist acting as the ensign's assistant, his 'good four right hands,' as Thielind put it. As they exited the ladder, the scouts hesitated against the ceiling, weapons up, before slipping through and crouching on the floor in the dark.

Wolfe read the first bogey signal about fifteen meters ahead. He clicked over to D-45's audio frequency. "I'm seeing five, chief, er, Numbers."

"Me, too, sir." A moment of silence while the noncom checked with his squad. Wolfe could hear Ambering's voice over the other channel responding to a query. "Cuddles says six, but she's at a better angle than me. From 12 o'clock, twelve, one, one-thirty, two at five, seven."

"Got it." Wolfe passed the word, but the others had already seen what he had. "Ready to go?"

"Aye, sir!" twenty-two voices chimed in his ears.

"Go, go, go!"

D-45's squad leaped up through the hole into the dark, laying down cover fire as the rest of the Cockroaches scrambled up into the combat zone. Returning fire cascaded, red streaks lancing out from the dampened laser weapons. The bolts represented the smart-bullets the weapons would normally fire: each explosive projectile had an onboard chip telling it not to detonate when it hit hull plate or other materials that matched certain chemical signatures. That way defenders wouldn't be scuttling their own ship while attempting to defend it.

Daivid and the others returned fire. In his headset he watched the red-in-blue forms duck and come up shooting, over and over.

He wished there was a visual image for his eyes, but the automatic targeting software in his heads-up display helped him track the enemy. He let out a short burst over the head of one opponent behind a square obstacle. As soon as the form raised its head to return fire, Daivid nailed it in the throat. The blue glow around the 'live' body went green, then yellow. A solid kill. In a real combat situation, he would just have put an explosive armor piercing round right into one of the most vulnerable points on an invader's suit.

"Oh, slag!" Somulska wailed. Daivid glanced at him, checking the stats in his heads-up display. The big man's armor had gone green and begun to flash on one side of the upper body. "I'm hit!"

"Where, Talon?" Gire asked.

"Left shoulder. My damned web suit's pinching me. Fraxing computer simulation."

"You're not dead yet," D-45 growled. "Keep fighting. Cockroaches can keep fighting for a week even if you cut off their heads."

"We're fighting for the glory of all the cornflakes under the refrigerator!" Mose cheered. The others joined in.

"Axe?" Wolfe asked his XO. "Are you hearing the beacon yet?"

"No, sir," Borden answered, firing her sidearm with one hand while she ran a scan with her infopad up and down the range of sound waves. "It'll be faint, otherwise it'd be too easy to find in a small environment like this one."

"Sir! Right roll!"

Lin's warning came just in time. Daivid threw himself down and rolled over twice, coming up firing. Two of their hidden foes had chosen that moment to leap straight at him. He shot one of them, a clean hit in the joint between the left shoulder and back. At that angle it ought to have been a killing blow, piercing through the heart, but the fighter scrambled away on hands and knees.

"Cheat!" Boland bellowed. Lin and Corpsman Gire blasted at the retreating body. The corlist, brandishing six miniature sidearms and one two-handed rifle in its small manipulative limbs, blazed away from between their hips. Finally, the suit dropped to the ground, its aura yellow.

"Bad AI," commented Ambering.

A barrage of flashes erupted at three o'clock. Boland's squad spun to return fire. Two of the unfriendlies fell, their suits registering slightly green instead of blue. Wounded, not dead. They elbow-walked behind an obstruction to get out of the line of fire. Meyer's 'bullets' stitched the floor in pursuit, nipping at the heels of the figures' boots. Her suit gave her enhanced targeting abilities, but their suits lent them speed.

"Damn, I missed!"

Daivid scrolled the map of this section of the deck on his side screen. "There are two exits from this room. One leads to two more corridors. Ammo, take the exit at 11 o'clock. Tullamore and Numbers, the one at 3 o'clock. Go!"

D-45's sharpshooters laid down cover fire for the other two units to scramble across the room toward the doors. Three of the remaining unfriendlies rushed to block Lin's way. The petite chief drew her sword and swung out at the hot signature of their weapon barrels, now too close to fire at her. The resulting *clang!* surprised them all.

"Hey! These are real bodies!" Gire exclaimed.

Ewanowski waded forward, grabbing one enemy fighter's gun by the barrel in one huge paw and wrenching the trooper off the ground. It kicked as he picked off its sword and can-opener and threw them across the room before heaving the body after them. Aaooorru started jabbing with his can-opener at the other suit blocking the door, making him dance.

"Go, sir!" Lin shouted. "Find the base!"

Ashamed of himself for temporarily freezing up, Daivid signed to the other two units. One of the scouts at the fore drew a flash grenade from a pouch, triggered it, and sent it flying overhand into the corridor beyond the doorway. Daivid closed his eyes but his mask registered the actinic glare. The enemy on the other side would be temporarily blinded. He hoped.

"Aaaarrgh!" Boland bellowed, as they burst into the hallway. Six bodies faced them, one lying down behind a machine gun. Pencils of hot red light strobed across the floor, each burst representing a bullet. The Cockroaches retreated into the room from which they had just come.   ·

"We've got to take out that machine gun!" Daivid yelled, ducking back.

"Yes, sir!" Boland bellowed. He chambered a round, leaned out the door, pulled the trigger, then leaned back in again. The fléchette beams had stopped. "What now, sir?"

Daivid stared for a moment then pulled himself together. "Go get 'em!" he shouted.

D-45's sharpshooters led the way with flash grenades and short bursts of fire. Daivid and Borden followed in their wake, shooting over their heads. On the other side of the wall, the six had frozen temporarily from the surprise of the second flashbang. Choosing their shots with remarkable speed, D-45's scouts picked off the leader and another trooper. Both suits of armor faded to yellow, and the troopers inside them sat down to play dead. Their fellows, however, returned fire fiercely. Boland took a hit in the knee, which made him hop around and swear, but he kept shooting.

Five more shadows moved in from the rear. Daivid had been aware of them as faint glows beneath the deck, tracking the movement from below. Now they surged upward through another hatch in the floor as the remaining defenders rushed them from the other side.

The Cockroaches were caught in a pincer movement. The door through which they needed to escape was beyond the newcomers, to the right. Still firing, Daivid transferred his pistol to his left hand while drawing his sword up and over his body.

"Duck!" yelled Boland as Party A, the three remaining troopers on the left, opened a barrage on them. The Cockroaches hit the deck. Red light flashed over their heads. A howl came from behind them. Party A realized they had just killed a fellow unfriendly in Party B in the crossfire. Several others were slightly 'wounded.' Daivid snickered. His troopers let out derisive snorts and catcalls. Too bad audio channels weren't open. There were some choice insults being wasted. The enemy drew swords and closed.

The Cockroaches, clustered together, still had the advantage of firepower. The center line came up shooting over the heads of the sword wielders, one squad facing in either direction. They took out two more of the enemy before suits of body armor slammed into them from both sides.

"I've located the beacon, sir," Borden said. Her voice cut through the hollow banging of swords.

"How far?" Daivid asked without turning his head.

"Ten meters, sir. Behind you, second left, then left again, then third left in an equipment cabinet at the rear of the chamber."

"How do you know it's an equipment cabinet?"

Borden sounded hurt. "The platoon is stationed down here during normal shifts, sir. I make it a point to know the department the unit is in."

Once again Daivid couldn't help but be impressed by his XO's precise ways. "I see. Okay, everyone, you heard the lady. Let's clear the bodies and get out of here. Ammo!"

"Aye, sir," the senior chief's voice came. She sounded as if she was enjoying herself.

"Axe is sending you coordinates of the target."

"Aye, sir." There was a pause.

Daivid ducked under a wild swing from the trooper he was facing, and came up with his blade upward, taking a swipe through his opponent's crotch. It counted as a cut to the left femoral artery. The enemy trooper tipped over, and its aura turned pale green. Daivid spun to confront the next fighter in line.

"Dammit, Tullamore, I told you they'd put it there! It's in the sump closet."

"The what?" Daivid asked, parrying a chop from his opponent.

"The sewer head, sir," Lin explained. "Aaaggh! Spidey, that's me!"

"Sorry, Ammo," came the corlist's little voice.

"It's the main valve for the ship's disposal system. If there's a major clog, you open it up and send the bots through from that point. It always stinks in there, sir. Like a dead diplodocus and the forty tons of rotting kelp in which it was buried."

"Well, we're not likely to smell it through the armor, chief," Daivid said sternly. Lin sighed audibly. "Did you say something, chief?"

"No, sir. We'll make our way to you."

Party B realized that they were just getting in the way of Party A and retreated down the long corridor, pursued by Boland's squad toward a linked cluster of rooms. Daivid saw in his heads-up display the color change and slump of another unfriendly as it ran out of hit points. The Cockroaches were doing very well in this battle. He was impressed by the cohesiveness and skills of the unit. They must have pissed off some very high-ranking personnel to be considered outcasts. Or, he reasoned, as he kicked an enemy combatant in the chest, they could be innocent victims, like him, who were too inconvenient to keep around. The skeptics would see he and his unit had value!

His kick had all the force of his powered armor behind it. The enemy flew backwards, crashing into the bulkhead. It slid to the floor, blue aura becoming tinged with green. Daivid grinned. The hard landing wouldn't really hurt the trooper inside, since servos and the CBS,P would absorb most of the force. The officers and D-45's squad continued to hammer away at Party A until they were forced to retreat toward their original position. Daivid sheathed his sword and drew his sidearm.

"Snipers! Take out that machine gun!"

"We've already killed the gunner, sir."

"Not the gunner, the gun!" Daivid said. "Tag it. I want it out of the equation."

D-45 dropped flat to the ground and fired off a shot that went between the legs of the enemy. As they were hopping around trying to figure out who had gotten hit, the sharpshooter bounded to his feet.

"That'll take 'em a minute to realize," he announced.

It took less time than that for the defending force to deduce that their heavy weapon had been disabled but, by their body language, it made them mad. As the Cockroaches bore down upon them, Party A met them squarely, charging their approaching opponents with frenetic force. Coolly, Daivid assessed the big figure who had targeted him. His suit's reaction time had been tuned up to where he could dodge Daivid's laser bolts. Daivid stopped trying to land one on an easy target and began to bracket the fighter, making him dodge from side to side. He might not have been able to hit the other, but he hoped, by the time the red-in-blue figure reached him, that that the faceless trooper would be damned motion-sick. As the trooper closed, Daivid tried one more shot to the neck. The trooper ducked and came forward with amazing speed, wrapping his arms around Daivid's body.

The suit's servos whined as a force equal to its own crushed inward. The exoskeleton was rigid, providing a solid framework but a certain amount of flexion existed in the material in between to help dissipate the force of a missile, much the same way the ancient and time-honored protective material Kevlar did. One quickly learned in hand-to-hand combat training that those softer zones were where sword blades and can opener tines could lodge. The other clearly knew where the vulnerable places lay. He swung one arm up, trying to get it around Daivid's neck. Daivid's hands shot up, breaking the hold of the arm around his chest. He kicked out at his opponent, flinging himself backwards.

An obstruction stopped his flight. Another armored combatant grabbed him by the arms, locking onto his wrists with a death grip. Daivid tried one martial-arts twist after another to make the trooper let go, including mashing him backwards toward the nearest bulkhead. The first would-be crusher picked himself up and charged. In a moment, Daivid would be caught in a suit sandwich. Well, if his hands were not available, he still had his legs. Feinting backwards with his heel for a dirty kick to the crotch, he suddenly threw in every servo and flung a leg forward, upward and over his head. His body protested mightily at the abuse as it was forced to follow the leg, but it was an anti-grav trick that he had used before in a non-zero-gee situation. He ended up more or less sitting on the fighter behind him, who had let him go in surprise. Daivid took a point-blank shot up the gasket at the back of the fighter's head then aimed at the oncoming hulk. Unfortunately, a couple of suits tumbled in between them.

Daivid scrambled up, and a twinge of pain shot up from his knee to his groin. He wished he'd had time to limber up before the exercise began, but it wouldn't have helped much. He wasn't a yogi or a ballet dancer, and he was going to pay for that twist later. Still, it worked. The fighter under him had turned yellow, a casualty.

"Take this one, sir," Trooper Software's voice said in his ear. The red-in-blue blob with the gold tag gestured toward the suit she was facing. "He's almost finished."

"What?"

Instead of replying, Software threw a flying kick at the knees of the approaching suit. It staggered, and drew its weapon over its head. Or tried to.

"I got mine," Thielind's voice said as he leaped onto the enemy's back. The floating gold tag superimposed over the small blob clinging to the hulk identified the ensign. "I can help."

"I don't need anyone to help me!" Wolfe roared. The new opponent at his feet was glowing green. Almost in pique, Wolfe reached down and twisted the helmet until the seals protested and popped. Yellow. "I can take out my own targets!"

"We saw you do that leap," Borden said calmly as she fired precise round after round into the joints of the huge combatant's armor. No chance of an accidental slug impacting a fellow attacker. Wolfe couldn't wait to see her scores on the target range. The last remaining fighter in Party A slumped to the ground. "Can you walk?"

"Of course I can walk!" Daivid raged, and took a step. The pain shooting up the tendons in his inner thighs made him stagger. Tightening up the servos so the suit would carry him instead of relying upon his abused muscles, he strode out ahead of his surviving platoon members toward the beacon location.

"Uh, sir," Borden began as they approached the door with Daivid in the lead.

Fuming with embarrassment, Daivid barked out orders. "Sharpshooter scouts to the fore! Everyone else, draw weapons and cover your piece of the pie!"

"Aye, sir," the squad replied with a sigh. D-45 and the other scouts slipped through then relayed a signal to follow. No unfriendlies within range. Daivid's own display agreed.

"How many does that make, Axe?" Wolfe asked as they scoped out the new chamber. In the darkness, towering red signatures on a deeper blackness indicated the position of the sanitiation plant. Sticking to the edge, the platoon skirted huge booming cabinets from which pipes a meter across ascended to the ceiling. This must be the main pumping station for the sanitation department. In a ship this size, there were auxiliary stations in at least three other locations, but this was where most of his troopers spent their shifts, overseeing the machines that extracted all the water out of the waste material. As he understood it, the solids remaining were dried down to a fine powder that was nearly odorless, stored and offloaded in regulated facilities where it went for uses like fertilizer. The water was purified and went back into circulation throughout the ship. The gas was not so nearly easily dealt with, venting occasionally through escape valves into the sanitation chambers when pressure got too high, as now. His suit took out nearly all of the smell in the air, but a small amount of it made it past the filters.

He coughed then gagged. "God, this is awful," he said.

"You should try it without armor, sir," Mose said. "The pump head's worse. That's the actual interface."

"Sixteen combatants, sir," Borden interjected, after a moment's calculation. "All dead or too wounded to follow us. If the exercise is truly one-on-one, then there are only seven left."

"Squad leaders, report," Daivid said, trying to ignore the fumes. It seemed as though the smell had a cumulative effect. He thought he should be getting used to it as he went, but it seemed to get worse. Deprived substantially of one sense—sight—under the terms set by the exercise, it felt as though his other senses had become heightened. Now was not the time he would have welcomed enhanced senses.

"Two casualties," Lin stated. "Doc and Spidey. No wounded. These guys couldn't hit a starship from the inside."

"Taz is a casualty," Boland announced, lighting up Streb's and Vacarole's stats in Wolfe's helmet display, followed by Nuu Myi's and Haalten's. "Mustache, too. I'm wounded. So are Pearl and Mantis."

"Romeo's out," D-45 added, illuminating Injaru's icon. "Three wounded, all walking."

"Good. Let's get this over with. The hour's almost up."

Instead of hampering his thinking, the hammering of the sewage pumps created a deafening white noise that was surprisingly easy to ignore. If Daivid was designing an exercise like this one, and he had, the squad that was left to defend the objective would be the best troopers he had available, and they would have the most ordnance. They knew the Cockroaches were coming, they were holed up in a small, defensible location, and all they had to do was wait out the time limit. Twelve minutes to go. Daivid didn't have to announce that to the platoon; all of them had chronos in their visor displays.

Lin's voice came through his headset. "We're in the room, sir, seven o'clock off your flank."

Daivid noticed the cluster of faint red smears behind the heat signatures of the engines. "Thanks, chief. You're familiar with the terrain. Any suggestions? Anybody?"

"They're going to sit tight," Boland opined. "That room's about three meters on a side, very cosy. I doubt we can get them to chase us. I vote for flashbangs and a hard push when their eyes are dazzled."

"Anyone got anything they like better?" Daivid asked. "No? Good. Are percussion grenades likely to rupture the sump?"

"Doubt it, sir," Lin said. "It's made to withstand over 6000 kpc."

Six thousand kilos per centimeter. "Right. Grenadiers, load 'em. Sharpshooters, give them cover. Ammo, I want your squad to be in charge of retrieval. You're pretty sure the item is in this sump?"

"It's what I would do, sir," the senior chief replied.

"Right. We'll have to assume they'd play the same."

"Okay," Lin announced to her squad. "I want a volunteer to be dirty bird."

"Aw, chief!" "Peee-yeeew!" "Uh, I just cleaned my armor."

"I'll do it," Jones said amiably. "I've smelled worse."

"Thanks, Songbird. You're elected."

"Troopers ready?" Daivid asked. "Open 'er up!"

Ewanowski and Ambering leaped forward to spin the big wheel. The semicat grunted and the human groaned with the effort.

"Can't move it, sir," Ambering said.

Borden consulted the circuitry behind a panel on the left of the door. "They've got the bolts locked and the electronics jammed."

Daivid turned to his ensign. "Tinker, you speak machine. Can you get it open the easy way, or do we have to blast it?"

He could almost hear the grin. "Sir, I can get that door to understand me. If they haven't changed the emergency codes since last night."

Daivid stopped himself asking why the ensign would have wanted to break into the sump the night before, and decided it would take longer than the eleven minutes they had left. "Then start cracking! Everyone, hold ready until you see the whites—uh—"

"The red of their heat signatures," Borden supplied helpfully.

"Uh, yeah. Hit it!"

There was no way to disguise what they were attempting to do. On the other side of the door, Wolfe picked up the faintest pink traces of body heat as the defenders mustered. One of them had leaped forward and was mirroring Thielind's actions, trying to prevent him from engaging the battery-powered emergency system that would unlock a jammed hatch.

"Got it!" the scrawny ensign crowed, leaping backwards into the ranks of the sharpshooters as the hatch sprang free.

"Go, go, go!"

Ewanowski grabbed the edge of the hatch and swung it open with himself behind it as Parviz and Okumede heaved flash and percussion grenades into the room. They 'exploded,' filling the room with blinding light. Their visors automatically darkened against the blaze, the Cockroaches charged in, firing.

The wave of stink that greeted Wolfe clawed at his nose and throat with sharp fingers, almost halting him in his tracks. He swallowed his gorge with difficulty. Though his web suit kept him at a constant comfortable level, the ambient temperature was almost twenty degrees Centigrade higher than outside the room.

"We should have left them in here until one minute to," he gasped. "They'd have been begging to have us shoot them."

Red lights flashed towards him. He rolled out of the way behind the doors, firing as he went. The defenders must have been expecting flash grenades, because they did not seem to have hesitated a moment before responding. Their shapes, dark pink like rare meat, hunched along the walls, shooting round after hot red round at the invaders. The charging Boland let out a yell then tumbled to the ground as his suit went yellow. His troopers dodged, using the falling body as cover, to press further into the room. Wolfe, Borden and Thielind came in behind, shooting as targets presented themselves. Lin's heavy-weapon squad pushed in behind, then kept going as the rest of the platoon covered them.

"Get the target!" Wolfe shouted.

The defenders were well dug-in. Their pink silhouettes faded behind obstructions invisible in the dark. His visor provided him with a rough topography, but he and the rest of X-ray wasted a lot of rounds on metal cabinets, ceramic-lined objects and pieces of portable equipment on wheels and gurneys.

Almost as soon as he had thought it, his sensors warned him of an inanimate object rushing towards him. He threw out his arms to fend it off but was hit below waist level by a rolling metal table of some kind. It served to distract him for just the moment needed by one of the defenders to leap out of cover and make directly for him, sidearm blazing away.

Without stopping to wonder if the trooper knew he was the CO, and how he could identify him without ident tags, Wolfe ducked behind the convenient rolling table and fired back. Tags floating over red forms in the center of the room showed Lin's squad covering Jones as he belly-crawled toward the fountaining heat source there. Wolfe felt a 'click' that indicated the current magazine in his pistol was spent. The figure was almost upon him. With a twinge, he cast the gun out of reach and drew his sword.

Quick as lightning, his opponent whisked his own saber out of the sheath with the opposite hand, continuing to bracket Wolfe with red flashes until he was close enough to sweep the blade over and around. Damn, this trooper was fast! Wolfe had just enough time to raise his own guard to keep the other's weapon from slamming into the side of his neck. He sprang to his feet, using the momentum to parry and riposte, cutting at the other's neck and shoulder joints. His opponent was several centimeters taller than he. The table still lay between them. Wolfe felt it push to the right as the other tried to get it out of the way. Just as tenaciously, he hung onto it and kept it in place. Anything that prevented the other from closing that distance was good.

Around him, shots bombarded X-ray's troopers as they attempted to enter the chamber. Daivid counted three more fall to keen marksmanship that would have been superior anywhere, though there were few awards given for knocking off a target at three meters. He also counted far more than seven bodies without tags in the room. His onboard computer found fifteen.

"Axe, do you see a discrepancy between what we were told and what you can observe around you?"

"Aye, sir," the voice of his XO sounded cool even though he could see her engaged in a close-range sword fight with a bruiser who would have outweighed her two to one without the armor. She brought her blade down and around in a nasty riposte that slashed into the trooper's knee joint and up again into his groin. The blue aura turned sickly green. "We are outnumbered. That is far more likely in a real-world scenario."

"But not one we're supposed to have to face on our first surprise assault in the middle of the night."

"Captain Harawe has a reputation for testing the mettle of those under his command, sir."

"Bugger Harawe," Daivid said, leaping backwards as the heavy blade of his opponent slashed downward. He felt it nick the surface of his armor. He slashed back, but the other was a much better sword fighter. He was parried almost at every turn. Gradually, he was beaten back to the edge of the room, not a long trip, and held there as a barrier against any more Cockroaches getting in.

The others figured out the ploy and fired around Daivid at the big trooper, who ducked and dodged the bolts, using Daivid as a human shield. Wolfe continued to hack at his opponent, though his own aura was turning green from all the small hits he was sustaining.

"Help the lieutenant!" Lin shouted.

"No!" Wolfe yelled back. "Achieve the objective!"

With renewed energy, he resumed his defense, hacking with the lower half of his blade. It bounced off the other's helmet and shoulder guards, but he used the momentum to keep striking. Few of the hits scored any points, while he continued to lose ground. He heard a yell behind him, and saw on his scopes that a single defender, heretofore hidden on top of the pumping equipment, was shooting his troopers in the back. They hadn't looked up. Fatal mistake.

He was making more fatal mistakes at the moment. His next slash missed his opponent's elbow joint, impacting instead on the upper arm. Not enough to disable. The other took advantage of his arm being out of the way to take a shot of his own. One skilful stroke that started in the upper right quadrant of his body and skirted his guard streaked down to the leg joint on the opposite hip and struck home. He could almost feel the other's glee as the CBS,P tightened around his body, preventing him from moving. He lost his balance and toppled over, his aura reading yellow.

"Lieutenant!" Borden cried.

"Keep fighting," Daivid ordered them. "Get the—ack!" The CBS,P closed firmly over his windpipe. It loosened in a moment. He gulped in air, and tried to speak again. "Use the—gack! Slag—urk!" The web suit, or someone in a control room monitoring him, evidently had ideas about him giving orders from beyond. He took the hint.

So did Lin. All three officers had been taken down, along with several more X-ray troopers. Seven of the fifteen defenders survived. She and the remaining gunners carried on a barrage to protect Jones as he pried open the sump hatch with his can-opener. It let out a pop. Daivid's eyes watered as gas poured out into the small chamber. The rest of X-ray Company, stuck out in the hallway, decided discretion was the better part of breathing and stayed beyond the stench, potting away at the defenders from there. Jones began to feel around in the sump, which was approximately a meter across, swearing colorfully in three or four languages.

Knowing as surely as Daivid did that there was less than two minutes for X-ray to achieve its objective, the seven moved in, blasting out a river of red dashes. The Cockroaches returned fire more slowly. One after another of them fell, suits turning from blue to yellow. It was apparent that, not only were they outnumbered but the defenders had a lot more ammunition than they did. Daivid meant to take the matter up with Commander Iry in the morning, after he'd had some sleep. The smallest figure in the center, who he identified as Lin, took out the biggest defender with a keenly placed shot to the throat, then her gun clicked audibly.

"Oh, damn!" she shouted, feeling through her side pouches for more magazines. There were none. More guns clicked empty. She turned to the four remaining troopers. "We're history, guys! Do your best!" They took individual shots, but Daivid could tell they had fewer and fewer charges left. The defenders crawled towards them, inexorably, until Jones raised a hand on high.

"Hey, you!" Jones shouted at the trooper who had dispatched Daivid. "Kill our commander, will you? Here's my reward to you!" He drew his arm back then flung it forward as if throwing something.

The substance barely registered above room temperature in Daivid's scopes, but the disgusting splat as it struck the trooper in the chest left no doubt as to what it was. The trooper cringed and retreated, batting at its chest. The other Cockroaches, seeing the fantastic reaction, took to Jones' idea at once and began to scoop up handfuls of raw sewage from the bubbling sump.

"Hey, ugly!" Ambering shouted, heaving glob after glob at the nearest defender. "Is it raining slag, or is it just your aftershave?"

"This has got to be yours," Ewanowski said, throwing a headsized dollop of sludge at the largest trooper left. "I recognize the butt print!"

The Cockroaches slung their useless guns aside and began to reach for more material. The stink was overwhelming. The defenders retreated to the walls and covered their heads with their arms as the Cockroaches pelted them with slag. Daivid, lying helplessly beside the door, wished he could crow.

Suddenly, Jones let out a musical yodel of triumph. He raised a blue flashing orb over his head. "I've got it!"

At that moment, the lights came on.

Commander Iry walked into the room, clapping her hands very slowly. "Very good. Very good. That was the ugliest performance I have ever seen in my entire life. Effective, but ugly."

She turned to Daivid as the CBS,P let go of his limbs and let him struggle to his feet. The abused ligament in his thigh erupted into a symphony of pain. He tried to keep the wince off his face as he removed his helmet. He glanced around at the shadows that represented X-ray Company, some of whom were all but scuffing at the deck with their toes.

"You win, son. I wouldn't have believed it if I hadn't seen it. Disgusting, but I can't fault you for resourcefulness. I guess what they say about your unit is true."

The defender who had cut Daivid down strode forward. His chameleon armor dripped with brown sludge that almost radiated visibly with stink. He yanked off his own helmet. It was Bruno. His dark eyes were ablaze with righteous anger. He threw a hand back at the other members of his team. Almost all of them had been liberally decorated with the same substance. "Commander, this is hardly fair. They were supposed to achieve their objective with conventional weaponry."

"Who says?" Iry asked, turning to him. "Results are what count in wartime, son. Just because they weren't afraid to get their hands dirty, they did what they were supposed to do. I believe that I can make a case for your team having started the *caca pelota* rolling, Lieutenant. Whose idea was it to put the beacon into the pipe in the first place?"

"Well—But now we have to clean our armor."

"Inside *and* outside?" Daivid asked innocently, enjoying the memory of the other troopers cringing against the onslaught of the rain of crap.

Iry let out a snort. "Save it, sonny. It could happen to you one day."

"Hey, slag happens," Ewanowski leered. "In this case, it happened to Lieutenant Bruno."

"You should eat some of that," Streb advised Bruno, indicating the mess on his chest. "It'll do you good. Hey, if you eat some, it'll do *us* good, too! With all due respect to your rank, sir."

"Troopers!" Daivid thundered.

"That's insubordination!" Bruno raged.

Iry looked at him impassively. "No, just being sore winners. I've heard you indulge in a little extracurricular trash talk in your time. Let it go. Lieutenant Wolfe, will you please tell your platoon to save their gloating for the day room?"

Wolfe threw himself into the salute. "Aye, aye, ma'am!" The gesture was worth the pain.

"Right. I'll log this one as a successful exercise. Dismissed." The commander turned to the other officer, now seething openly. "Lieutenant Bruno, you were supposed to give them a run for their money, and you did. Though," she added, running a summing eye over the defenders, "I think you might want to send whoever counted your troops back to remedial mathematics. That's all right. You have plenty of personnel available to clean up this site."

"Ma'am!" Bruno protested, looking around at the sickly greenish brown stains running down the bulkheads and equipment in the small chamber. The defenders looked aghast. The Cockroaches tried hard not to grin from ear to ear. Some of them failed. Daivid didn't plan to punish them for it.

Iry was unmoved. "Loser's penalty. You know the custom. By the way, well done. In the end you only left four of them standing. That's why you're an *Eastwood* officer."

"Made *my* day," Wolfe muttered under his breath as they gathered up their weapons and pushed past the other troopers.

CHAPTER 7

"SIR, CAN WE talk?" Lin caught up with Wolfe as he limped back toward their armory.

Daivid glanced back. The other Cockroaches had slowed down until none of them was within earshot. He looked at the nearest chrono. 0515. He could have sworn that exercise had taken all night and part of the next day.

"Sure, Top. Why don't we sit down in the day room, just as soon as we get these suits into the cleaner boxes. I'm damned if I'm going to smell like everyone else's excreta."

Without the helmets on, the powered armor was rendered plain black. The walls were white. Daivid didn't realize how starved for light and color his eyes had been until the exercise had come to an end. Or maybe he was just tired. The mandala on the wall of the day room attracted his gaze, and drew him in until Lin interrupted his thoughts. She slid into a chair on the opposite side of the table.

"Sir, I didn't want to bring this up in front of the others. I'm the closest thing you've got to a best friend in this platoon, and I'm your top noncom."

"So it falls to you to hand me bad news," Wolfe translated. "What is it?"

"It's not strictly bad news," Lin assured him, her small face solemn. "You did an okay job for your first time out. But we've all been together for years now. You don't have to tell us so much. It comes off sounding, well, pretty green."

Wolfe winced. "Chief, I'm not half the idiot that I sound like when I'm giving orders."

"No, sir, but neither are we. Trust us a little more. If we're not doing something, call us on it. If you've got fresh orders, give them. We can change gears pretty quickly. I picked up on your idea, didn't I?"

Wolfe nodded. "Yes, you did."

"We're all still alive, even after some pretty nasty missions, so we haven't made a fatal mistake yet."

Involuntarily, Daivid glanced toward the memorial panel that had been propped against the wall, at the names that had been laboriously punched through the melon-pink cerametal. Lin's eyes followed his.

"They didn't make mistakes, as you think of mistakes," she said, shaking her head. "But there's bad luck, bad planning, inadequate cover, misfires, malfunctions, breaks in the chain of communication. You name it, it's happened. Not just to our unit, but to every unit that's ever marched together since Gilgamesh and Enkidu." She noted Wolfe's smile. "Yeah, I went through the officer training history of warfare course."

"You finished OTS, but you're a noncom? Who'd you piss off?"

Lin smiled wearily. It made her look ten years older. "You want the whole list?"

Wolfe shook his head. "I don't know about you, but I came off four hours of poker, and I'm wiped out. Just tell me what you want."

Lin tilted her head. "Are you really listening? I want you to lay back. Just give the orders you need to, and trust us to do the rest. It's not a one-on-one game, no matter what the recruiting posters say. You're in charge, but you don't do everyone's job. You just do yours. You tell us what you need done, and we will figure out a way. You don't have to paint a picture for us."

Wolfe hung his head. "Sorry. I was just trying to be a good officer."

"A good officer recognizes his or her troop's talents, so he or she can concentrate on achieving the goal and staying alive. In a way you're lucky this was a training exercise. You got killed because you were paying more attention to what we were doing than what was happening right in front of you. You had a good idea, but we would have come up with it eventually. After all, we work down there. We know what everyone else thinks of it. We have the exact same visceral reaction as Bruno's squad every time, and it's got to be eighteen, nineteen times in a row we've been stuck down in sewage management on transit voyages."

Wolfe smacked his hand on the table. "There's got to be something we can do about that."

"Don't worry about it. There are perks. People stay the hell out of our way, mostly. And a couple of other things. We keep everything going, and we get a lot of free time and some actual privacy, which you can tell is not so easy on a starship. But it's good that you care. You're showing promise, really. It's been noticed and appreciated. You've just got a lot to learn. God or Mother Nature or the Powers That Be are letting you have a long learning curve, but it won't last forever."

"I thought I was doing all right," Wolfe frowned.

"You are. You lack experience, that's all. Keep going the way you're going, listen to the people who have been around, and you'll be a good officer."

Her words stung, but Wolfe figured he had them coming. "Uh-huh. And how do I avoid these little talks in the future?"

Lin cocked her head. "That's easy. You can just tell me *not* to tell you when you're screwing up, sir. Or you can admit you've got something to learn, and say what any recruit does when he's getting punishment he doesn't really want but probably deserves?"

"What's that?"

"'Thank you, sir! May I have another?'"

Wolfe laughed. "Thank you, ma'am! May I have another?"

Lin laughed, too. "At least you're teachable. That'll help you survive in the long run."

"I'd better," Daivid Wolfe said wryly. "If I don't come back in one piece, my dad's going to kill me."

Lin snorted. "As long as he doesn't kill *us*."

"No way," Wolfe assured her fervently. "More than any other person you will ever meet, my father knows the difference between people who were around when someone died, and people who were responsible."

"You're so sincere. It's so cute!"

Wolfe grimaced. "Thanks. Not. But may I return the favor while we're having this private little chat?"

Lin raised a suspicious eyebrow. Wolfe felt the walls coming up again. "You're the CO, sir."

"This is just friendly. I know how isolated we are when we're on base. We're the neighborhood lepers; no one wants to associate with us. Being alone throws people together, and sometimes they get— involved. But you know regulations: someone around here won't have the same knowledge, however limited, that I've got, and may even think he's doing one of us a favor by getting him or her transferred out of a unit because he or she is fraternizing with a fellow trooper, maybe even one in the same chain of command. You and I both know that trooper is likely to get transferred back to X-ray again one day, but in the meantime he or she and his or her partner might have to undergo some enforced loneliness waiting for that day to come. So, be—I mean, tell the others to be more discreet, huh? I don't want to lose anyone in my command." He gave a toothy smile, showing all his canines. "It's my first platoon, and I want to keep the whole set."

Lin smiled broadly. "You're a romantic, sir."

Wolfe held out his hands. "No way. And I'll fight to the death anyone who even suggests something like that. Do you have any more whips for my back? No? Then let me go and take my poor bruised body to bed. See you tomorrow morning at PT." He pushed the chair back and limped toward the door.

"Good night, sir."

"Oh, and by the way," Daivid said, pausing in the doorway with one hand on the frame. "I smelled my armor when I got into it."

Lin gulped. "Did you, sir?"

"I certainly did. When I didn't find a single bottle or keg anywhere among our luggage, I wondered how you got all that booze on board. Let me make it clear right now that if I ever find my suit stinking like a fraternity lounge ever again, I'm going to fill the rest of yours with nitrous oxide. Just remember the Vortex."

"I do, sir. Good night, sir."

Daivid grinned. "Good night, Lin. Can't fault you guys for creativity."

The strings of space tied together all existence. Ayala could feel them around him. He felt as if he could draw them in, making planets and suns dance at his order. His puppets. His creation. At his order, suns swelled to supernovae. At his command, microbes evolved into useful societies loyal to him and him alone. Some of them were unworthy, and those he destroyed with a wave of his hand. He pictured a new sense of purpose in the universe, where comfort was not as important as endless productivity. Such a situation had been tried on ancient Earth millennia before, in the Uncertain Century, when workers served unwillingly the exponentially growing demands of their employers. It was followed by the Great Overthrow, resulting in an implosion of the world economy—since it had been based upon too few doing too much work—and lacked a unified goal. That would not be the case in Ayala's Universe. *Everyone* would work. And they'd like it. Or else. Dispassionately he wiped out another system that was not complying and created in its place one that would do its work without complaining. Certainly there was little else to do while they awaited the rest of the fleet to check in.

"Captain Roest calling Colonel Ayala," a chittering voice announced over the main speakers. The communications officer, a human, nodded. Via non-linear space he was able to hear the itterim in real time, and verify his identity as though he was standing and looking at the green-shelled being. Though Ayala experienced the miracle of Tachytalk nearly every day, it still made him marvel at the cleverness and persistence of the human being. If they could conquer transgalactic information-sharing, how long would it be before they owned every parsec?

"Captain Ziil calling."

"Lieutenant Maaren calling, Colonel. The captain cannot come to the communicator. She was eaten."

"A pity," Ayala replied, signing to his aide to change the file. "She was a good officer. You are promoted, Maaren."

"Of course, sir," the voice replied crisply.

The other ships checked in, fifteen of them in all. Two of them were destroyers like the *Dilestro*, but the others were smaller frigates. All carried on board single-pilot fighters, though fewer and in poorer condition than he would have liked. Well, if they could secure the merchandise they sought, the proceeds ought to buy a few hundred more, all new, or a thousand 'previously owned,' though he hated bargaining with used starship salespeople. They were all crooks, and it took a thief to know a thief.

"Good. Our siblings in the cause report that the shipment approaches."

"Unguarded?" the voices asked greedily.

"Yes, unguarded, or so our spy swears," Ayala said. The itterim, Kaarl Veendam, had been almost slavering in vicarious anticipation of conquering such an easy target. He also confirmed the cargo itself. Tachytalks were almost a thousand credits on the open market, and these, which had not yet been assigned to one of the long-distance communication systems, would be nearly priceless to the kind of people who shouldn't get their hands on them—such as Ayala and his cohorts. For the rest, portable power supplies would enable them to make better use of their captured weapons. Plasma guns required new cartridges or constant recharging of the old ones. With those in hand, and carefully reworked for the kind of amperage needed for the task, the insurgency could conquer whole cities, using their own power grids against them. Also on board were letters of credit worth nearly a billion credits. They had to be especially careful to take those intact. One scratch on the confirmation seal, which had to be completely undamaged upon presentation, and even the corrupt bankers who did business with the Insurgency would laugh in their faces.

He sent them the coordinates for the junction of the strings where the cargo ships were expected to emerge. There, and only there, were the ships vulnerable. It was impossible as long as a traveller was in transit along a singularity route to catch up with him. The speed of each was constant. All they could hope to do was find a string capable of propelling them greater distance in a shorter time, intercepting them as they emerged, and taking the captured cargo and vessels back into the transdimensional stream, leaving no evidence but a few spent ions from the vaporized crew that anyone had ever been there.

"Alas, I will not be able to accompany you on this enterprise," he added. "For I am on the way to a remote location for another mission that is of great importance to the cause, and then on to our final destination. Once you have succeeded, you will join me with the goods to be used in the furtherance of our great work of liberating the galaxy! Success or destruction!"

"Success or destruction!" the captains echoed.

Daily reports from the noncommissioned officers were held in Daivid's quarters, clustered around the small desk.

"...And I've been trying to see when we can get into the antigrav chamber," Lin was explaining. "We all need to be recertified in zerogee combat. The ship's complement is so bloated with units on the way to Benarli, they're rotating us in there in shifts. We really need to get in there more than once every five days, sir. Otherwise we stand no chance of getting into the action if the *Eastwood* boards another vessel. No one will sign off on us."

The antigrav chamber lay at the rear of the ship as null-displacement for the circular gravity generator that hung like a gong between the horns of the backward-facing crescent that was the main body of the ship. Along with the rest of the newly arrived visiting officers Daivid had been taken on a tour of every section by Ensign Gruen, Commander Iry's clerk. He longed to get in there and try out the facility, which was newer and more complex than any he had ever seen, including obstacle courses and a padded sphere for practicing close-quarters nongrav combat. He knew the others were itching to try it out, too.

"I went to the officer of the day," Lin continued, "but he said you have to go to Supply to change our whole schedule."

"I'll see what I can do about getting us in there more often, Top," he agreed. "When's our first evolution, Borden?"

Borden consulted her infopad. "1300 hours four days from now," she said. "The next is five days after that."

"Not enough," Wolfe agreed, making a note of his own. "I'll see what I can do."

"Enter!"

Wolfe waited until the hissing door receded into its niche before he strode into Lieutenant Bruno's office. The supply officer stood waiting with his back turned to the doorway, hands clasped behind him, pretending to study a framed document on the wall. Even from there Wolfe could see that it was a certificate of merit, the kind he had a dozen of stored in his infopad. It took some kind of insecurity to print one out and stick it on the wall. He could also see the other's eyes reflected in the perspex.

"How's the leg?" Bruno asked, spinning around suddenly, as Wolfe stood before his desk.

"Fine, thank you," Wolfe answered politely, determined to keep the interview civil. After all, he wanted a favor.

"Your own medic take care of it, or did you go to the infirmary?"

"Just some analgesics and a little hydrotherapy," Wolfe admitted. "A couple of days, and it went away."

"Ah. I got over the same injury in a day because I've been practicing yoga for ten years," Bruno said offhandedly. "Although I strained my thigh during a boarding maneuver against the Lizards. My suit was punctured, too."

Wolfe smiled even more politely. To attempt to win this one-upmanship contest was to lose the objective for which he had come. "I see. That was some attack, by the way. If the swords had been unpadded you might have gotten me with that second thrust."

"With the first," Bruno corrected him. "The neck injury would have been fatal. The monofoil on the edge of my blade is new. I always replace it before a battle." Seeing that he had quashed his opponent thoroughly on at least three counts, he came around to business. "May I ask why you've requested this meeting?"

"X-ray Platoon has been on ground duty for over three months," Wolfe explained. "Many of my people are overdue to recertify for zero-gee combat. My senior chief said that the first time you can get us into the chamber is several days from now, and at fairly long intervals after that until the ship reaches the front. I'd like to request an accelerated program."

Bruno eyed him. "Your platoon, and I say this regardless of its reputation, some of which I experienced the other night, is only a very small unit, and its priority is going to be correspondingly low. You do realize that we are carrying almost ten thousand spacers and troopers."

"Yes, I do. I've made inquiries among the other officers, and most of them come from space stations or have been transferred from active duty to join the push, so they're fresh. I'd say 90% of them have their status current. I would appreciate it very much if you would increase our access to the training module to, say, every three days or every other day, until we certify, then you can increase the interval to whatever you want. The other ten percent of the complement would probably appreciate a speeded-up process, too," Daivid added, trying to make it sound like a win-win arrangement. "That way you would have 100% compliance by the time we get to Benarli. You'd probably have thought of it yourself. I'm only trying to bring it to your attention for your convenience."

Bruno frowned thoughtfully. Daivid had him there. It would make him look good, but a born bureaucrat had to resist somehow.

"We've got a 1300 hour training time in four days. Could you schedule us, say, tomorrow for the same time as we have for our first scheduled workout? 1300 hours?"

"I'll see what I can do." Bruno nodded meaningfully toward the door. The interview was at an end. Daivid retreated.

Ignoring the insults Bruno had managed to work into the conversation, Daivid was pleased with the outcome. Instead of passing it along by way of an infopad link, or asking Thielind to relay it, he decided to take a few moments and drop down to the sanitation department to tell Lin in person. Besides, Borden's quietly competent assertion that she always studied the venues where the platoon was stationed made him feel guilty. He should have known that—should have been doing that. There was a lot to learn about being the CO. It was like piloting a spacecraft. You didn't pay so much attention to how it was done when you were a passenger as when you finally got dumped into the front seat.

Whistling, he swung down to Deck 6 and made his way forward toward the Sanitation Department. Funny how much smaller the corridor looked, now that he could see it in the light. Creeping down it with only his scopes and infrared vision to go on, the transit seemed to have taken forever. The ceramic walls and blue directional signs looked like any other section of the ship. Wolfe knew he had arrived when the air took him by the throat, making him cough. His eyes watered. He tried to clear them, but rubbing only seemed to make the situation worse. He sniffed heavily, trying to drive the tears back. That brought in a fresh lungful of stench, and he hacked it out again.

Streb waved to him from the top of a tank along the huge main array that ran through the pumping room. He swung down, landing nimbly at its base.

"Hi, sir! Great day, isn't it?" ·

"How do you stand it in here?" Wolfe coughed. "It stinks in here—I mean, stinks! How do you breathe? You would have to burn my clothes. Even the box couldn't get the reek out of them."

"This is nothing," Streb assured him, flipping the wrench in his hand up in the air. It turned end over end before he caught it slap in his palm. "Sometimes the fumes are so thick you can't see through them." He clutched Wolfe's arm when the lieutenant looked stricken. "I'm just kidding, sir! This is about as bad as it gets. The valves had to be opened while we replaced some gaskets. The air cleaners only kicked on a minute ago. Pretty soon it'll smell like roses in here. Comparatively, that is."

"Thank God," Wolfe said. "I'm looking for Lin."

"She and her squad are on the firing range, sir. Boland's here…uh, maybe he's not," Streb hesitated.

Wolfe raised an eyebrow. Hesitancy in a Cockroach meant trouble. "*Where* is he?"

"Uh," Streb gulped, realizing he had given something away. He bent his head to study his wrench. "Compartment 64D, sir."

Eyes stinging, Wolfe went in search of whatever trouble his platoon had gotten themselves into. He realized he was not going to find 64D without help, and called up a chart of the deck on his infopad. The 64's were a cluster of small square chambers that housed cooling pipes adjacent to the main plant. No hatch from the big room gave onto them in case of a breach in the pumping system, so he had to wind his way through the labyrinth of linked rooms behind the long wall until he came to doors marked 64B, 64D and 64F. He palmed the lock on the center hatch.

The door slid aside, and a huge, clear, bulging pseudopod lunged toward him from the open door. Wolfe jumped back.

"Dammit, halfway! Only open it halfway!" Boland's voice came. Wolfe heard sloshing noises and found himself face to face with his noncom.

"Chief Boland," Wolfe asked with some gravity. "Why is it every time I come looking for you I find you naked?"

"Uh, sir, I can explain," Boland said, reaching behind him. A dark-skinned hand stretched forward and handed Boland a soggy towel. The noncom wrapped it around his waist, but the towel insisted on floating on the surface of the water which occupied the room from that level downward. Wolfe recognized Ambering, who grinned at him sheepishly. She was naked, too, as were all eight of the Cockroaches in the water with them. Waves of warm air washed out into the corridor.

"I can't wait," Wolfe said, folding his arms. "Explain."

"Uh," Boland glanced over his shoulder at the others as though looking for inspiration. "Did we tell you there were perks in working even the worst jobs?"

"I don't really see you working," Wolfe pointed out. "I ought to report this, you know."

"Not really, sir?" Boland pleaded.

"Give me one reason I shouldn't!"

"Well, we did all our assignments for the time being. We even asked Master Chief Winston if he had any more tasks. He said not at the moment."

"Okay, so within the letter of the law you're not skiving off," Wolfe said. "Though you know if your chief hasn't got anything for you to do you ought to look at the job board on the ship system. But what about the waste of energy?"

"There's no waste, sir," Ambering spoke up. "This water's heated in the process of the purification system. In fact, it has to cool down from vapor to liquid before we can use it. This is about halfway down the cycle."

"What about when it has to be *re*purified after you bathe in it?"

"It uses about one erg more of energy to raise the temperature back to steam, sir." Boland added temptingly, "And I bet that pulled muscle of yours would really respond to moist heat."

"Well," Wolfe thought about it for a moment. He did miss the water-showers on Treadmill. The sonic cleansers did not really provide a satisfactory substitute. "But what the hell's this?" He poked the bulging balloon that held the water.

"Emergency shelter, sir," Boland said. "Practically indestructible, and absolutely weightless."

"Those things only get to be two meters on a side!"

Boland looked proud. "Not if you fill them with water. They can get to be a heck of a lot bigger than this."

Wolfe was agog. "You've done this *before?*"

"This happens all the time, sir. I learned the trick from a CPO I served with when I was a grunt the first time. You get stuck down in plumbing as often as we do, you look for the little creature comforts. Besides, who's going to look? You *have* to check on us, and *you* don't like it."

"You can't really hide something like this in inspection. What about your section chief?"

The chief laughed. "Oh, we showed him how we did it. He's going to keep this in place when we leave. Private facility, you might say. After all, there's no security eyes in here, and the ambient heat of the section keeps the hot water from being readily detected. It's okay with him, sir. How about it?" Boland offered him an ingratiating grin. "You're not really going to make us empty it. After all, they always dump us down here. Nobody cares."

"I care, dammit! I don't want us to be the unit everyone points to as the bad example." No. Wolfe shook his head. What point was there in protesting? If he ordered it taken down, it'd almost certainly go back up the moment he left. And the responsibility for this section really lay with the department chief. He could almost rationalize it, thinking of the seductive roll of hot water running over his sore muscles. "Forget it. You're right. I'll be back with my trunks after shift."

"Hey, we just heard," Lieutenant Ti-Ya said eagerly when Daivid appeared in the wardroom for a late meal.

He eyed her uneasily. Had word spread about the hot tub? "Heard what?"

"The other day, you kicked Bruno's ass."

Daivid looked around. The Supply lieutenant was sitting with his posse at the table at the wall farthest from the door where he could watch everyone. Daivid nodded to him. Bruno returned the nod curtly.

"He's the one who kicked my ass," Daivid said, loud enough to be heard. "I got killed. That was stupid. My senior chief shredded what was left of my posterior afterwards."

"No, really, we heard you slagged them," Ti-Ya grinned. "Literally."

Wilbury came in studying his infopad and glanced up. His face lit up when he saw Daivid. "Hey, I heard you busted up the home team," the lanky man crowed. "It must have been—!" He noticed Bruno and the others glaring at him from the back of the room, and hurried to flop down beside Carmen. "Sorry," he whispered. "I didn't see him back there. Now I'm going to get all my assignments screwed over. I better eat some crow." He picked himself up again and strode to greet the fuming assembly. "Bruno! Big guy!"

"I want to hear all the details," Carmen said, keeping her voice down. "It happened, when, four days ago, and all we knew was the new guys reached the objective within the time frame. That was it! And then today one of the guys on the squad broke silence. We were doing water survival rotations, and she mentioned your *nonstandard* technique. Tell me all."

Daivid glanced towards Wilbury, who was giving a grand-stand-quality clown act for Bruno and his friends. The severe lieu-tenant still hadn't changed his expression, so Daivid doubted that

Wilbury had managed to appease him. "The loss must really have pissed Bruno off."

"He *never* loses," Carmen insisted. "If everyone else on his squad gets killed, he goes and creams the rest of the enemy by himself. This was the first time his hand-picked company ended up in second place."

"Cleaning the battlefield," Daivid recalled, unable to keep a big grin off his face.

"Yeah. Since no one is really killed or hurt in these exercises, Captain Harawe figured that there ought to be some penalty for losing, and he came up with making the unsuccessful squad mop up, or reseal the enamel on the walls, or whatever. That stinky pipe is one of their favorite hiding places. Cleitis likes to sic Bruno's group on newcomers, to see what they're made of."

"I guess we're made of slag," Daivid pointed out, not at all ashamed of himself. "At least, that's what we left all over them."

In an undertone, he began to recount the event, including the uneven odds, the convenient AI that forced X-ray to take all its losses but seemed to let even mortally wounded spacers keep fighting, and the conclusion, which he had to watch from the floor. As he spoke, others dining or reading in the wardroom began to drift over, sitting close so they could hear his low voice. The chortles and outright laughter that erupted from the group as he got to the part about Jones yanking open the sump lid couldn't be ignored, and they weren't. Bruno cut Wilbury off with a curt gesture, rose to his feet, and stalked out of the room with Varos and Rindel on his heels.

"You're going to pay for that," Wilbury said ruefully, coming back to join them. "He's a real son of a bitch when he's embarrassed."

"My fault," Carmen said, with a tilt of the head for apology. "I should have IM'ed you for the details, but voice is a lot more satisfying than text."

Daivid looked after the retreating Bruno with contempt. "I can live with it."

The mayor of a small town seized Daivid's hand and pumped it gratefully. The people behind him, all statuesque women in scanty clothing, looked as though they were close to tears with joy. "Lieutenant, we're all so thankful. Your army saved us from the blobs, and all you had was a crate of bubble gum! Thank you so beep. Beep. Beep! Beep!"

Daivid rolled over as the town faded into the blackness of his cabin. He stared at nothing, until the noise came again. It was the door signal. With a groan he noticed the chrono: 0314. He swung his legs out of the bunk and yanked his robe on over his skivvies. "Come in!" he called.

A skinny female frame stepped hesitantly into the room. Daivid thumbed the lights to reveal the face of a very junior midshipman.

"Yes?" he asked.

"Sorry, sir," the midshipman said, "but Commander Cleitis wants to see you."

"*Now?*"

"Aye, aye, sir. That's what he said. He said not to send a message, but to notify you in person. That's why I'm here."

Uh-oh. What had the Cockroaches done now? They'd been good about running under the radar since he discovered their hot tub and let them keep it. Even Jones had been freed from confinement, after he had promised to make up no more limericks about the captain.

"But you know how it is, sir," the hearty Petty Officer had said. "They tell you not to think about something, and then you can't think of anything else. I've got dozens of good ones—but I'll save them until we're deployed somewhere else."

No point in asking this youngster about the crime of which he or his unit had been accused. Cleitis always preferred to lower the boom himself.

"Thank you, midshipman," Daivid said, reaching for his pants. "I'll be there as soon as I'm dressed."

"Aye, aye, sir, I'll inform him." The junior officer was already taking up her infopad as the door closed behind her. Daivid ran the depilator over his scratchy chin and yanked on the rest of his clothes. What now?

"What *now*, Lieutenant Wolfe?" Commander Cleitis asked, his narrow face looking even more narrow and haggard since it appeared that he, too, had been pulled out of bed. His usually crisp uniform collar sagged a little, and a haze of gray-white whiskers frosted his cheeks. "Isn't a schedule change notation good enough for you? Do you require an engraved invitation? Must we provide an escort for each and every one of your troopers?"

"To attend what?" Daivid asked. He was wide awake now, but his head felt as though it had been filled with insulation.

"Antigrav combat practice," the XO replied, with some asperity. "You must be aware how crowded the ship is, lieutenant. Do you think you can screw up the entire workings of the ship just because something is not convenient for you?"

"What, sir?" Daivid asked, feeling as though plascrete had been poured in to compact the insulation in his skull. "The only thing I've asked for in the last several days is to have us get more rotations in the chamber."

"And you got them," Commander Cleitis snapped. "Your group ought to have been in that very anti-grav chamber as of 0300 hours. Where were they?"

The whole scenario became clear in his mind as if set out on a screen. Ti-Ya had warned him, and he hadn't paid any attention. Daivid stammered. "I—I didn't know we had been given a slot at 0300, sir. I asked Lieutenant Bruno yesterday if we could be assigned for 1300, the same time as our future assignment in three days. I didn't realize—"

"Oh-three-hundred, not one-three-hundred," Cleitis said, exasperatedly, pointing at the screen in his desk. "Did you not check your next thirty hour schedule when you retired, as you were instructed to do all the way back in OTC? You're on evolutions every two days at 0300 until we reach our destination. You were sent details of this change last night."

Wincing, Daivid examined his infopad. His friends in the wardroom during his free shift had been sending messages during the nightly poker game to avoid distracting the other players. By that time word had spread all over the ship about the 'dirty win' the Cockroaches had pulled over the *Eastwood* home squad. A few were jeers from Bruno supporters, but most were brief, and often anonymous, congratulations. There were so many coming in that after a while Daivid couldn't concentrate on his own game, and had stuffed his infopad back into the pouch on his belt. He'd been buoyed on the fun he was getting out of telling the story, and had a lucky night, with, it seemed, one glaringly obvious exception.

Just as he feared, sandwiched among the hundred or so IM's was an official schedule notification from the Supply Department, datelined 2915, informing him that X-ray's first official zero-gee assignment was four hours hence. And now he recalled that Bruno had been in the lounge when he put his infopad away. He had then gone to bed, without clearing the unread message buffer. Bruno had him. Daivid looked up at the XO.

"I—I missed it, sir. I apologize. I did not mean to throw off the schedule of the entire ship. I will get my platoon down to the chamber immediately."

"It's too late for that, wouldn't you think?" Cleitis asked, eyebrows raised. "It's already half past. You'd have less than two hours to complete the course."

"I—Yes, sir. We could do part of the exercise tonight, and start fresh in two days."

"Every part of the module has meaning, lieutenant, meant to train each part of your body to the uttermost skill level. Do you think that the enemy will excuse you if you don't know how to perform a certain defensive move? That he'd give you a pass, and let you kill him out of sympathy?"

"No, sir," Daivid replied.

"No, of course not. And now every unit that follows yours has to be bumped up the line. It throws off the whole day, and it's all your fault."

"It won't happen again, sir."

"Damn right it won't. I've heard about X-ray Platoon, lieutenant. I checked out your service record, too, after the other evening's victory, thinking that perhaps the brass had assigned you to X-ray in hopes of reforming it. I'm beginning to think they put the two of you together to keep both of you in one place, to lessen the damage you can do."

"No, sir, it's not like that," Daivid protested.

"Get out of here," Cleitis said wearily. "I have too much to do in the coming weeks than worry about one sad little scout unit. You go to exercises when you're scheduled, you do them to the best of your ability, and you stay under the radar, do you hear me? Don't let me see you in here again." He flipped a hand toward the door.

"No, sir," Daivid said. "You won't, sir."

With his tail firmly between his legs, he retreated.

"Sir?" Borden asked on the way to PT the next morning. She held her infopad out to him. "I was going to ask you about this entry, but you look terrible."

"I didn't get a lot of sleep, Borden," Daivid admitted, stretching his arms over his head. "I got skunked. We got skunked. It's my fault. We've made an enemy for life, and he won the latest round. The alert came through after you went to bed. I didn't check, so I couldn't notify you. I don't know why I didn't hear the priority alarm."

Thielind pointed at a code in the header of the order. "No alarm, looey," he said. "It was disabled. You can do that, if you want to send a priority message but you don't want to wake someone up. It's just a command in the menu."

"So we missed zero-gee practice?" Lin asked. "Sorry. I don't mean to rub it in."

"Yeah," Daivid said glumly. "And I have some good news and some bad news. The good news is we have zero-gee every other day. The bad news is it's at 0300."

"We saw. It's not your fault. The guy's a prick. 'Scuse me: the *officer's* a prick."

The hatch leading to the gym slid open and Bruno emerged, cheeks pink and with a towel around his neck. Lin's hand shot up in a salute. "Why, sir, we were just talking about you!" The rest of the Cockroaches followed suit, grinning widely.

"Morning, Lieutenant," Wolfe said evenly.

Bruno ignored him. He started to push past the platoon without returning the salute, but the Cockroaches blocked his way, shifting as if to make room for him, then cutting off his retreat. Wolfe cleared his throat meaningfully. Finally, grudgingly, the supply officer tipped his fingers against his forehead. Thielind was the last to lower his hand. He beamed blindingly at Bruno.

"Out of my way, enswine," Bruno growled, shouldering directly at the smaller man. Thielind, not moving quite fast enough, got slammed into the corridor wall.

"That's 'ensign,' sir," Thielind said in a very small voice, to the retreating officer's back. If Bruno heard him, he showed no sign. Daivid vowed that one way or another he was going to make sure the supply lieutenant got the message that no one got the better of a Wolfe, not for long, and no one was going to undo the good work he had started on his platoon's self-esteem.

Endorphins, Daivid reflected, pulling on fresh fatigues after a sonic shower, were amazing things. A good stretch, followed by a brisk run and strength-building exercises, more stretching and a little target practice, did wonders for the brain running on insufficient sleep. He felt ready to dig into his paperwork, ready to ream out every detail and provide the best and most complete report Lieutenant Commander Iry had ever read.

No, he thought, slumping down at his desk and flipping open his infopad, no matter how he tried, he just couldn't convince himself that paperwork was either interesting or vital. Who in hell ever decided that you couldn't run a military operation without fifteen forms having to be filled out for every bolt, every battery and every pair of underwear? You would think, five thousand years after the first electronic computer had been built, that they would have a program that funneled the information from one form into all the others, but they had not. Once he was running things, they would. That pair of shorts would begin in a report from supply as being issued to a spacer, then the data would run fleetly into a report to procurement for replacement, then to the physical base, ship or station where the spacer was assigned to work out parameters on how much space was needed to store it, how much power was needed to clean it, the approximate life after which it needed replacement, and a note to engineering at *that* time on the disposal of that many grams of waste. They'd hail him as the man who set the officers free!

He fed the report on "Laundry, X-ray Platoon, Officers" into the busy slipstream of message traffic that flowed through the ship, followed by "Laundry, X-ray Platoon, Non-Commissioned Officers" and "Laundry, X-ray Platoon, Enlisted." He checked his schedule every time he went out of the word-processing mode, determined that another land mine like the one Bruno had planted under him the other night would not explode again.

Among other duties a visiting officer might be assigned were those small jobs that the ship's officers were too busy to take care of, such as acting as ombudsman to settle a dispute between crew members (and often a stranger was the best person to handle a situation like that: never seen before, and never seen again), acting as a witness at certain traditional marriage rites, refereeing a sports match or appearing at, as Daivid's day list now showed, a "bris." That required a live call to Commander Iry's office.

"What do they need me for?" he asked.

Gruen, Iry's clerk, grinned. "It's an ancient Judaic rite," he explained. "The mother gave birth eight days ago to a boy. The father's not on board. Apparently the ceremony's got to be done today. We've got a rabbi among the chaplain staff, and the mother has found a female sponsor, but the child needs a male sponsor, too, and all the rest of the officers are busy doing something— useful. This is a warship. Sorry, sir. I don't mean to make it sound unimportant, or like you're unimportant."

"No apology needed," Wolfe replied.

"Well," Gruen said. "If you need more information, you can look up the extract in the ship's library."

"I don't have to look it up, " Daivid said, pleased to be in the know. "I'm already a godfather."

Gruen looked uneasy. "Is that supposed to be funny, sir?"

Daivid mentally cudgeled himself. Of course Iry knew all about him, so of course her clerk did, too. "Er, no, ensign. I mean, I was the *kvatter* for a friend's son three years ago. I know the drill."

"Good. Uh, the commander will be pleased to hear that."

It did make a change from umpiring soccer matches, Wolfe reflected, holding the baby, a fine four-kilo boy with caramel skin, black hair and muddy blue eyes, as the *kvatterin* fed it sacramental wine on the end of a folded napkin. It contained, the rabbi pointed out, a mild sedative. The fringed eyelids drooped slowly shut, and the chanting rabbi moved in on the baby's genitals with a contraption that looked like a combination thimble and pencil sharpener.

"Waaaaaaahhhhh!"

Wolfe winced and clenched his own thighs together in sympathy. The other males did the same or looked away. Or both.

"I thought you'd done this before," the *kvatterin* whispered to him, as the rabbi bandaged the baby and tucked him tightly into fresh swaddling clothes.

"The last time it was a girl," Wolfe whispered back. "I only had to hold her while she was given her name."

"Congratulations," he said, shaking hands with the beaming mother. The baby, now named Edward Pierre Jacom Sen-Yu Goldstein Akiya, was fast asleep over her shoulder. "Here." He took an envelope out of his belt pouch. "It's a certificate for baby clothes at the Stellar Stores. They ship. Shipping's included."

"That's very nice of you," Lieutenant (jg) Goldstein said, astonished. "but you didn't have to."

"He did, sort of," the *kvatterin*, Goldstein's best friend, Lieutenant Penny Buchanan. "After all, now you're his…godfather."

Daivid purposely kept his face fixed in a bland expression. "I guess I am." So they did know who he was, or were guessing. He wasn't going to give them a clue. Buchanan shrugged.

"Maybe we were wrong," she commented to the mother. "Maybe it was some other Wolfe."

CHAPTER 8

THE RACKETY INSURGENCY shuttle landed just outside the confines of the Gibson factory dome. The crackling blue curve, just barely visible through a haze of cold nitrogen gas liberally mixed with chlorine, stretched away from the shuttle over a space of almost a thousand acres.

"Not a good place for hatchlings," Itterim Oostern complained, reading the telemetry on atmosphere content and gravity. "Too heavy by half."

Ayala read the gauge himself: 1.53g. Not pleasant, but the added gravity added to the density which was all to the good. Parker Gibson as a settlement existed solely to provide a home for Parker Gibson Electronic Servants Dot Com, a venerable and respected manufacturer of domestic and industrial robots. The planet had a wealth of mineral ores that needed only to be supplemented by a few rare metals and synthetic materials to have everything needed on hand to make its sturdy little cleanerbots and repairbots. For the purpose the Insurgency had in mind, its function and its isolation were ideal.

"We will take this and make it the breeding ground for our future warriors," Ayala said, taking a deep breath. "Pilot brains, tank brains, submarine brains! All capable of following orders with as much intuition as though they were human beings—no offense, my friend."

"Is it not too early to count on success?" Oostern asked, clicking his mandibles together. He did not take Ayala's comment as an insult. He thought of everything in terms of itterim superiority, and assumed that any creature with sufficient pride in its species would do the same. "You do not have the device yet, nor the means to copy it."

"I *will* have it," Ayala said positively, "and copying it will be the work of this factory. It is the perfect employee in and of itself. Give it an order, and it will follow it blindly and obediently until you change the parameters. We can have a thousand, a million warriors! We will not need to train nor risk living beings—they can't really be trusted anyhow. And they are just too fragile."

He signed to the helm officer to deploy the landing bridge.

"How many are in there?" Oostern asked the telemetry officer.

"Only one," the itterim at the scope replied. "A human."

"So we were told the truth," Ayala said, pleased.

Clapping the helmet onto his head, he listened to the hiss of the seals securing it to the neck of the environment suit and entered the tube-shaped airlock, which had been extended to within centimeters of the dome. At the end of the corridor two itterim held the edges of the flexible framework between them. Swiftly, they tossed it toward the heaving blue electrical fire. The edges adhered to the transparent material underneath. Within the door-shaped rectangle, the sparks died away.

"That is the door," Van Yarrow confirmed, eying the black oblong bisected by the airlock. "A little to the left, though."

"Fix it!" Ayala boomed. The itterim leaped to obey, tugging the accordion-pleated material until the ring was framed entirely. "Open it! We must make this place our own."

"It is so clean here," Oostern said. The Insurgency force, all five of them, treaded lightly along the plascrete corridor. He heard a hissing sound and spun, weapon out. Behind them two cleaner bots were busy sweeping up the dust they had tracked in on their walk from the dome's edge to the factory complex.

Ayala laughed aloud. "That is why there is only one person here. Once the robots are made, they maintain the factory and keep it clean. Very intelligent. I wish we could conscript the designer for our cause."

"That you, Linewire?" a man's voice came echoing down the long corridor from the open door at the end.

Except for emergency indicators, the only light on in the place was that yellow rectangle. Ayala strode toward it.

"Look, I said you could be a few days late, but a week is really pushing it. I deserve my leave, too—Oh."

A scruffy man in coveralls, his puffy hair tied into a dozen buff-colored pigtails and tied in one knot behind his head, emerged from the room.

"Who are you?" he asked, shifting a pow from one side of his mouth to the other. As an afterthought he took it out of his mouth and held it behind him.

"I am Colonel Inigo Ayala, Insurgent and rebel," Ayala announced proudly.

"So Linewire didn't send you?" The man scratched his long beard, unimpressed. "Well, if you're not here to take over so I can get out of here for a while, then you and your buggy friends had better hop your butts back out of here. This is private property."

"Oh, we are here to take over, my friend," Ayala said. He tilted his head towards Van Yarrow, who drew a weapon. The man raised his hands and backed away.

"Hey, you don't have to do that!" he exclaimed. "All I want to do is go on my vacation. Look, I shouldn't be here. My co-worker was supposed to take my place."

"Oh," Ayala said, snapping his fingers. Two more itterim came forward and dumped a body on the floor. "Do you mean him? We intercepted him at the edge of the system. In his defense I must tell you he was worried about you, too. I am glad to say that you are both going away from here together, but not as you think."

The bearded man's eyes went wide, and he turned to run. Oostern hesitated, so Ayala drew his own gun and blasted the man. The plasma bolt hit between the shoulder blades, searing a blackened hole through the torso. The body fell forward and kept sliding. Ayala holstered his weapon. The itterim went to pick up the body.

"Leave it," Ayala ordered. "Let the bots take both of them. Now, this facility is ours. Roosen and Deelt, find the controller complex and learn the programming. When we return from our successful mission, we will need to start production at once. We need more intelligent minds working for our cause, and we need them six months ago."

"Yes, colonel!" the two itterim chimed, saluting.

Behind them, clusters of cleaner bots dragged the bodies away.

Daivid looked up from his infopad as the klaxons in his cabin erupted into deafening *a-OOO-gah*.

"The ship is exiting trans-space. Repeat, the ship is exiting trans-space. Please assume braced positions until the all clear. Thank you."

He saved his current material and stuffed the device into the padded drawer of the desk. His chair wasn't rated for crash-worthiness, so he moved to his bunk and strapped himself down. The bed, responding to the tug on the belts, drew him downward into a recess now padded by the thin shockfoam. It was a lot like being in a coffin, he mused, but with better neck support.

He turned on the entertainment screen over his bunk with a verbal command, and clicked his way through the on-ship channels until he got the view from the bridge's main screens. As usual, all he could see was the projected, dashlike images of the stars they would have been passing if they had been visible to the human eye in folded space. The calm voice of the on-duty helm officer carried on in a near monotone.

"Preparing to drop to sublight. Increasing energy envelope to protect hull. Engines prepared to drop."

Harawe's voice came in sharply. "Drop!"

Daivid braced himself, elbows and knees jammed against the padding of his bunk. The means of traveling faster than light meant going through the pipeline, or rather one of thousands, maybe millions, of pipelines available throughout the galaxy. The drive relied upon these 'strings'—mini-wormholes—to penetrate the fourth dimension that bridged the other three, enabling ships to go much faster than light. The speed varied, depending upon not only the width of the rift, but its length. Scientists had hoped these strings might be infinite, enabling humanity to cross the great divide between galaxies, but they petered out unexpectedly, usually within range of the end of one or more others, leading the theoreticians to speculate on whether strings affected one another or originated from common hubs.

Starships transited the strings one at a time. Star maps showed in which direction 'traffic' flowed in each of the known and commonly used lanes. A few reckless captains had ignored the rules and caused collisions that resulted in the destruction of their own ships and the unhappy travelers who met them head on. The accidents also tended to render the string involved unusable for a long time, so even pirates made a point of obeying the right of way. The strictures of physics also meant ships could not travel side by side.

Just throwing a physical object into one of these two-dimensional strings would result in its destruction. Astrophysics engineering had come up with a generator that balanced the forceful pull against itself, creating an egg-shaped envelope in which the ship traveled safely. The footprint did not rely upon mass. In fact, it was the same, whether the ship was a lone scout vessel or a full-throttle dreadnought.

To enter or exit a string, a ship only had to sidestep, which meant that all string-drive vessels had slipstream engines that pulled the ship into or pushed it out of the string. Some slipstream engines moved their vessels slightly, at just enough angle to break out of the singularity. That meant the exit point might not be very precise, but it was a gentler transition. The big ships, with heavy shielding and good shock absorption for the crew and cargo, could drop or shift a virtual 90°, exiting at precisely the point desired, coming out into real-space just in time for the men and women aboard her to throw up. Daivid had prided himself he had pretty good sea legs, but sharp-shift made him queasy. The elite squads chose their members partly on whether or not the applicant tossed his or her or its cookies on exiting wormholes at full speed.

Suddenly, reality lurched sideways. Daivid's skull and heart felt as if though they had been jerked out of his body then restored without so much as an apology. His heart raced, glad to be back where it belonged.

He glanced up at the screen. Twinkling stars dotted the infinite blackness on the screen, refreshing live diamonds after the computer-generated streaks of fourth-dimensional space. He didn't know how he knew what he was seeing was real; he just knew the difference when he saw it. The ship also had companions, silver and black boxes that dwarfed their drive tubes.

"All clear," the helm officer announced. "Move to Level 2 alert, maintain until further notice. That is all."

Daivid hit the release on his restraints. The center of the bed rose up to its normal level, and he rolled off. Keeping one eye on the screen, he reached for the infopad in his desk and sent a message to Borden, Ti-Ya, Wilbury, Barikson, Corrundum and Al-Hadi.

Any idea what's going on? he asked. *There's a line of ships out there, looks like a merchant fleet.*

No one's asked to come on board yet, replied Al-Hadi, whose assigned station was the signal room, *so they're not selling us anything. Must be an escort mission.*

Don't they usually announce it to the crew? Borden inquired. She had become part of the evening poker games at Daivid's initial insistence, and stayed because she liked it. Her ability to count almost anything with no apparent effort meant that she stood a good chance of guessing what combination of cards everyone at the table was holding. Daivid started losing money to her and demanded they switch over to five-card stud, when she couldn't see their discards and work them into her calculations. *It would be a routine mission, wouldn't it?*

Need to know, kid, Wilbury interjected. *And we don't. We'll find out if we need to.*

Rumor spread faster than the official word, but Al-Hadi's guess turned out to be a good one. The ships had requested a silent escort, which meant a security crackdown until the point of interception. Officers and crew, seeing the vessels hanging in the viewtanks in every corridor, speculated on what they were carrying that required such heavy firepower as the *Eastwood* was carrying.

"Need to know," Wilbury kept saying. "Trade ships are always at risk. They're sitting ducks. When they jump out of a string, it could be seconds, minutes or hours before the next ship follows. That leaves plenty of time for pirates to strike."

Al-Hadi let her cronies in the wardroom know that the department head had ordered all communications from the ship be routed directly through him. "Kind of unusual," she said, dealing cards. "I think something's up, but I have no idea what."

"Need to know," Wilbury repeated darkly. He gathered up his five cards and began to arrange them.

A calm voice, belonging to the helm officer on duty, came over the intercom system. "Attention, please, prepare for sideslip. Repeat, prepare for sideslip. Fifteen minutes from—Mark."

Everyone in the wardroom looked at the screen in the rear wall. They noticed for the first time that the coterie of trade ships flying alongside the *Eastwood* had diminished in number to three. As they watched, another one bloomed with light until it was surrounded by a translucent egg glimmering with blue, yellow and red. It seemed to jump violently to the left, and shrank out of sight before they could draw another breath. Within five minutes, the second departed.

"All personnel strap in. Preparing to enter trans-space."

As the third and last trade ship began to glow, the officers cleared the wardroom, heading for the harnesses concealed in the panels behind the walls of the corridor. Wolfe was lucky enough to find one close to the nearest screen tank. The heavens around the dreadnought were empty. It was their turn. The stars took on brilliant color; it was the bubble of protective energy growing around the ship. He hung on as the *Eastwood* lurched sideways, its drives whining audibly. Daivid's intestines twisted. Only the first few moments were rough. Once the ship was part of the slip-stream, it was like traveling in a hot-air balloon, an experience Wolfe had had a few years ago. No matter how rough the wind, if you were travelling with it, you didn't feel it. The stars strobed weirdly, the nearest ones elongating into glowing worms. By the time the order came to stand down, they were a colored bubble, floating through a tunnel of white-hot needles of light after a dozen more colored bubbles.

"Trans-space achieved," the calm voice said.

A meeting of the Engineering Department's officers left Wolfe none the wiser as to their eventual mission. It seemed to him that Harawe and Cleitis were holding back on something. Certainly he was no closer to receiving his orders, and that was beginning to make him and the other troop officers nervous.

"They're waiting for something," Corrundum said definitely, as they came out of the meeting. "I can sense it."

"Maybe the location we're coming out of fourth-space is classified," Ti-Ya suggested.

"If the cargo needed to go to a secure location they'd load it on board the *Eastwood*," Al-Hadi pointed out.

"Okay, so the cargo's commercial," Barikson said. "That means it's got nothing to do with us. That still begs the question of what we're going to do when we get where we're going. How am I supposed to draw up supply requests and order of battle without mission gen?"

"I dunno," Ti-Ya said gloomily. "They must let you know before we arrive. I just cannot guess when."

"Speculation's useless," Daivid said. "See you all later. I'm going to check in on my people, then it's back to reports."

"You and all of us," Wilbury grumbled.

One of the lifts opened at the end of the corridor, and a crewmember got out pushing a hover-cart. Daivid increased the length of his stride to catch the lift.

"Lieutenant!" a voice hailed him.

"Yes?" He turned, and noticed the lift doors shutting. "Dammit." He turned back to the owner of the voice, a lanky man with straw-dry red-blond hair and a long, pointed chin. Lieutenant Commander Arvie Kerlow was a space officer about fifteen years older than Daivid and attached to the *Eastwood* in the Fire Control department.

"Lieutenant, may I have a word?" Kerlow asked, grasping his upper arm firmly with long, spatulate-tip fingers. Daivid noticed the strength in the skinny hands as the other pushed him urgently into a nearby niche and blocked his escape with his body. "Got to talk to you," he whispered. He glanced around at the others approaching then put his arms around Daivid.

Daivid wondered if he'd given the man some signal that he desired intimacy, and decided he had not. He tried to figure out how to extract himself politely. "What about?"

"Booze," the man murmured, standing close so the word barely reached Daivid's ear. "You've got some of that good old-fash-ioned white lightning. The sample your people sent me was *more* than adequate. I loved it. How much?"

So the Cockroaches were selling their liquor on board! Damn them! "I, uh, leave that to my noncoms. I'll have to find out what they're charging." He hoped this wasn't a sting operation, set up by the XO or, worse yet, Bruno. "How much do you want?"

The officer's tongue flicked out of the side of his mouth and drew a slow, sensual line to the other side of his lips. A passing ensign snickered then covered the expression as both men turned to glare at him. "Can I get two liters? I was brought up on good moon-shine. It's been a long time since I was on my granny's farm. You know what that's like?"

Wolfe thought longingly of the cellar full of vintage wines underneath the main house on the family estate, and for a moment forgot that he was in the arms of a fellow officer on a ship hun-dreds of light years from home. "I sure do."

"You, er, won't mention it to Harawe, will you? He's a stickler for rules. If he heard I'd been buying it, well, we'd all be in trouble. Contraband has a corporal-punishment penalty on the *Eastwood*."

"I wouldn't dream of it," Wolfe said, carefully detaching the other's hands from around his waist and putting him at arm's reach. "But, please, don't touch me again. I might have to break your neck."

Kerlow had the grace to look abashed.

"My apologies." He tipped Daivid a wink, and retreated hastily down the corridor in the opposite direction. "Thanks, man. I owe you."

Carmen caught him as he stalked furiously toward the lift. "I hope you've had your shots. Kerlow will screw anything that moves."

"He's not my type," Daivid said in a black humor. "He wanted to talk about my—unit."

"Uh-huh," Carmen leered. "I wouldn't mind asking about your unit, but you just didn't seem interested in any of us. You're just too all business. Al-Hadi was devastated. She's never been so thoroughly ignored before."

Daivid felt his cheeks catch fire with embarrassment. "No, I mean my platoon! Besides, you know the regs on fraternization."

"Ah," Carmen nodded knowingly, her brown eyes sympathetic. "Got in trouble over those before? I know, when you get read out over something, it makes you sensitive to repeat issues. Sorry I brought it up. See you later?"

Daivid let his temper cool off. "Yes. Sorry. Thanks." And *that* wasn't what he'd meant to say, either. Al-Hadi had been interested in him? Dammit! *No*, he chided himself furiously. *Don't get involved. Not again. Don't get involved.*

Covered in confusion, he stormed down to Deck 6, forward, in search of a neck to wring. If the guilty parties were in their hot tub, he was going to puncture it with his bare hands and shrink-wrap them all.

"Uh, lieutenant, what can I do for you?" Chief Boland asked as Daivid stormed into the Sanitation Department. The hot gold light in Wolfe's eyes suggested that clever banter at the moment would backfire like the sidewash from a plasma cannon. He switched off the ceramic melter, set it down on the floor at his side, and waited. Wolfe stopped, folded his arms, and reclined with deliberate casualness against the door frame, incidentally blocking the noncom's escape.

"Lieutenant Commander Kerlow sends his regards," he said, raising one eyebrow. "He would very much like to know how much for two liters of your hootch, bearing in mind that it's a crime to sell unregistered liquor, especially to officers on board a ship where we are considered cargo, and cargo non grata at that?"

"We were going to cut you in, sir, I swear," Boland protested guiltily. The old-timers really hadn't taken their new officer into account, and now he was calculating how much that would cost them. Boland would start the bidding at 30% of profit, ready to go up to 60% if necessary. He was used to paying for miscalculations, and wasn't going to begrudge the extra this time. You couldn't blame fate when you had left an element out of the formula. "We figured you'd run interference for us." He offered an ingratiating grin, but it washed up against the breakwater of Wolfe's stony visage.

"That just makes me an accessory," Daivid said matter-of-factly. "I'd *rather* be able to testify against you."

"Testify!" Boland got flustered. A few of the Cockroaches turned around at the outburst then hastily went back to work when they saw the annoyed look on their commanding officer's face. "Aw, come on, lieutenant! I mean, someone with your family background—" His eyes widened as Daivid advanced on him, burning with fury.

"Don't bring up my family. I am not my family. I love them, but I will never be like my family."

"Sorry, sir, sorry!" Boland exclaimed, backing away. "Wow, I didn't mean to set off nuclear weapons, sir! I just meant, you know, they find a commercial need to fill, and they fill it. Just a little initiative. It worked out for us the other night, sir, didn't it?"

"That's not the only 'initiative' you've taken on this vessel that I've discovered. I'm sure there's more. Isn't there?"

"Well…" He didn't want to lie, but to say that the Cockroaches had taken a flyer on a couple more income-producing enterprises that were not strictly allowed by the rules might set off another explosion. "Depends on your point of view, I guess."

"Are you trying to get us in trouble? I pay for it as much as you, and I'm guessing here, you know the regs. Borden can recite them chapter and verse, and I bet Jones can sing them!"

"No need to get so excited, sir!" Boland exclaimed.

Chief Winston bore down upon them. "Anything wrong here, lieutenant?" he asked. Any invasion into his province Winston saw as a personal attack.

"Just an internal platoon matter, chief," Boland hurried to explain. "The lieutenant here was reminding me of something he wanted me to do."

By the time the chief had been mollified and gone on to the next job on his roster, Wolfe had calmed down. "I apologize for going off on you, Boland. —Just be more discreet, will you? We're going to get our asses reamed on a regular basis as it is. Don't add any screw threads to the reamer, all right?"

"Aye, aye, sir," Boland replied, inwardly jubilant but with a fresh respect for the new CO. He really was trying to understand them, which was a bright change from most of the officers they'd had over the last few years. "I don't need any more rifling either."

The escort run through trans-space was expected to last three more days. The Space Service could always find work for idle hands, but the minds of the officers were free to speculate.

"The lead ship gets in touch with us daily," Al-Hadi told her poker buddies as they took the lift from the wardroom to Deck 3, forward, where most of the entertainment areas were situated, "but the others never communicate with us directly. They talk *a lot* among themselves, though. The transmissions are coded with about 256-bit security, so they show up as gibberish in my readings, but there's lots of them."

"They're talking more strategy than we are," Corrundum said glumly. "I have heard that the Benarli campaign has been in the planning for a year. And they're going to wait until we're almost there to give us the data we need to fight the battle on the front lines? That stinks."

"And my platoon was picked for a special mission," Daivid added. "I still don't know what it is. I bet we're on recon, and they're saving the word until it's too late for me to plan."

"We're supposed to intuit what they want," Wilbury said sourly. "And we're supposed to read their minds right, or we catch slag. That's the Navy for you. Wow, look at the crowd!"

The *Eastwood* had one large auditorium that was used for official briefings and crystal threedeeos. Around it smaller function spaces had taken on their own identities. One of the larger rooms had been set up as a lounge cum pub with pool tables, electronic games and other games of skill. Still another, the object of that evening's interest, had the air of an ancient coffee house, dark inside except for small lamps on the little round tables surrounded by low chairs or big puffy cushions. At one end was a dais for acoustic music, comedy routines or, in this case, a poetry slam. A notice announcing the event flashed in the screen framed alongside the doorway, scrolling up to show a list of names, probably participants in the slam, and ending with an admonition in all capital letters: NO LIMERICKS. Daivid surveyed the sea of shadowy heads and pointed to a corner halfway back from the stage, which seemed more empty than the rest. The six officers eeled their way in between bodies until they squeezed into the small space.

Except for rare exemptions to allow for religious or cultural needs, facial hair was eschewed in the service to lessen the chances of jamming equipment in space or combat helmets, so Daivid guessed that the tiny goatee that adorned the chin of the master of ceremonies had probably been applied for the occasion. His longish black hair might have been a wig or his own, though a CO would have been all over him for the greasy stringiness of its appearance. No one had worn spectacles like that since the invention of genetic vision correction: black wire oval frames 4mm thick clasping lenses that distorted the man's eyes. The costume was also retro in nature: a loose shirt of nondescript color with a tear at one side of the neck, tight black trousers that exposed part of the ankle and wide-strapped sandals.

"Hey, dude, do thou dig the nuclear alert emblem on the chain," Al-Hadi whispered, nudging her companions.

"I don't think you've got the period dialect right," Ti-Ya whispered back. "And it's a 'peace symbol'. I asked last time."

"It's old," Al-Hadi scoffed. "I'll bet you none of them could tell you what century any of those phrases came from."

"I believe," Borden began, "that the first dates from approximately 5200 years ago—"

"Shhh!" Wilbury hushed them. It had been his urging that got them to attend. "It's starting!"

"Brothers and sisters in art," the emcee intoned in a smooth voice, lifting his hands with thumbs and forefingers joined in a big circle, "like, be."

· "Be," the audience intoned. Wilbury breathed out the syllable, his expression rapt.

"Be what?" Daivid whispered.

"Whatever you want," Wilbury whispered back, keeping his eyes on the stage. "There's no pressure to live up to anyone else's expectations. That's what the poetry is about: freedom."

Daivid wondered why he hadn't noticed before that Wilbury was a born follower. He sounded independent, intelligent and creative, then sucked up to bullies, or bought in to pseudopsychological babble from the Stone Age. That guff about freedom was not likely to impact him directly.

"The first artist to light your fire will be Miyeki Hanssen."

"...So I said to him, 'bury me, then, because I'm dead to you. Dead already. Lost and gone. Bury me!' And he turned away. And cried."

The slim woman with long black lashes and a tangle of mixed red, white and black hair stood up from her crosslegged crouch on the stage, inclined her head, and departed, plasheet in hand. The audience remained silent.

"She was right about 'dead,'" Daivid commented to Carmen.

"Yawn," Carmen agreed. "But they often open up with losers and keep the good acts for last. You should be here on vaudeville night."

"Hey, you!" the following poet, a cheerful red-faced man with close-cropped blond hair, saluted them deafeningly. He needed no amplification to fill the room with sound. Daivid suspected that his day job was drill instructor. "Whatcha? What do you know? How do you go? Good day! Great day. Have a nice day. Top of the morning to you! Bright blessings. Good to see you! Well, if it isn't old what's his name! How's your father...?"

Daivid tuned him out and scrolled hastily through the drinks on offer from the server table. Beer. Wine. Tequila. Brandy. It sounded like the litany pounding in his ears.

The next man stood in the middle of the stage and struck a pose with one hand on his chest and the other before him palm up in the air. "Aaoooooo!" he howled. "Aar-aar-aroooooo! Yee-aar-rooooo! Aow! Aow! Aow!"

With her head cradled ruefully in one hand, Corrundum murmured, "I miss my dog." Daivid and Carmen snickered.

Monosyllabic recitation ensued, performed by a woman with her face and naked upper torso painted dark blue, followed by blank verse recited by a poet who accompanied himself on a wooden guitar as old as the hills. Wilbury watched them all with shining eyes, an acolyte in his place of worship. Daivid and his friends watched *him* with more interest than the performers on the stage.

"Hey, wait," Daivid whispered as Mose took the stage. "This is one of my noncoms."

"Really?" Ti-Ya asked. "He looks familiar somehow."

"Well, you went over our records when we came on board," Daivid reasoned.

"No, that's not it—"

"Shh!" Wilbury cautioned them. The slight man strode to the center of the stage. His hands were empty. Either he was going to make it up as he went along, letting the spirit move him, as Wilbury insisted, or was confident enough not to need a script. Daivid was betting on confidence. Mose tilted his head playfully.

"The summer day you learned to play..."

The recitation went on for some time, becoming steadily more lyrical and more intense. Daivid found himself listening, deeply moved by the imagery framed in rhyme. The energy built to a climax then faded gently into silence.

Mose bowed deeply and moved off. Daivid clapped, whistled and stomped his approval for his trooper's performance. Now, here was poetry that sounded like poetry!

Suddenly he realized no one else was applauding. He glanced around. Some of the others were flashing their table lamps, but in total and bewildering silence. He let his hands drop into his lap, and grinned sheepishly at the glaring Wilbury.

"Sorry," he said. "I thought everyone was being quiet because all the others stunk."

"*Their* voices are the only ones who are supposed to be heard tonight," Wilbury explained impatiently. "We came to hear *them*, not each other. Shh. Here's the next one."

Daivid endured the rest of the performance in silence, even setting down his drinks so quietly the glasses didn't click. If he had not admitted it to himself before, he did now: he knew nothing about the arts. His mother would have laughed until she cried.

The slam went on for what seemed like years. Daivid felt wrinkles starting in the skin around his eyes and mouth, his hair turned gray, and his teeth fell out. No, that was just a lump of ice from his drink. The last performer retired from the stage, and the lights went on. Daivid blinked owlishly at the sudden glare then leaped to his feet.

"Did you like it?" Wilbury asked his friends.

"Some parts very much," Carmen said politely. "I liked Daivid's trooper. Look, there he is." She pointed. A door at the side of the stage opened, and all of the evening's performers emerged, Mose among them.

"Come on, let's congratulate him," Daivid said. "If that's allowed?" he asked Wilbury.

"Of course," the other lieutenant said stiffly.

By the time they reached Mose, Streb had joined him and gave him a brief hug with one arm. Daivid's quiet word to Lin about not being seen to 'fraternize' had evidently trickled down to the troopers.

"That was very good," Daivid said, shaking Mose's hand. "I enjoyed it."

"I know you did," Mose said with a wry smile. "I heard you. Everyone did."

Daivid reddened. "Sorry. I didn't know the culture. I'll be more sensitive next time. You're really talented."

The wry smile became more twisted. "How the hell would you know that from one poem?"

"Well, I—er, I heard you reciting before, one day," he admitted lamely. "My, er, second day on the job."

Mose shot him a slantwise look then grinned widely. He elbowed Streb. "I thought I heard footsteps," he said.

"You're really good," Daivid pressed, trying to cover his confusion at having interrupted a private moment and gotten caught at it. "Ever thought of going pro? Publishing what you write?"

Mose glared. Streb grabbed for the collar of his tunic. "Are you making fun of him? Are you? Who the hell do you think you are?"

Daivid twisted his hand inside the arm, took hold of the thumb and turned it upside down with all his strength. The petty officer found himself kneeling on the floor. He brought his face very close to Streb's and hissed, "I don't know what set that off, but unless you want to do some time in the brig on board this bucket, you will never touch me again."

"Sorry, lieutenant," Streb gasped. "It was just an impulse. I'm sorry."

Daivid let him up. To his chagrin, a crowd of officers and enlisted personnel had crowded around. He wondered how much they had heard. He held up his hands.

"Sorry, folks. Just a man who's had a little too much to drink. I'd have pounded them down myself if I'd been smart."

"You need any help?" Al-Hadi asked.

"None," Daivid assured her, over his shoulder. "See you in the wardroom."

"I'd heard his unit was all hard cases," Corrundum whispered as they started away, just loud enough to reach Daivid. She shot him a look that told him she meant him to hear.

He turned back to Streb, standing against the wall in the emptied coffee house, rubbing his wrist. "Now, what the hell brought that on?"

The petty officer glanced at his lover.

"Oh, well," Mose said offhandedly. "I thought you had all our files."

"I do. So?"

Mose and Streb shared a puzzled glance. "Then they gave you the edited version."

Wolfe raised an eyebrow. "So, what's the unedited version?"

Mose pursed his lips. "Are you ordering me to tell you my life story, *sir?*"

"Well, no, not *ordering* you," Daivid began. Mose interrupted him.

"Then, with all due respect to your rank, sir," Mose spat out the word, "I decline to further your education. Are we dismissed, *sir?*"

"Yes. Dismissed." Puzzled, Daivid watched them go. Both Lin and Borden had told him to take a close look at the troopers in X-ray Platoon, but they weren't making it easy for him, and the brass was offering him no additional data in spite of his requests for information. He was going to have to come up with a way to wrangle the truth some other way.

CHAPTER 9

"BATTLE STATIONS! BATTLE stations!"

The lurch that returned the *Eastwood* to normal space brought with it not only the normal blanket of stars, but also the red tracers of laser-guided, warp-assisted missiles and the gray-white bloom of depressurizing explosions half seen by distant starlight. Daivid's eyes stayed glued to the nearest screen tank as he ran past it toward the armory. The trade ships were under attack!

"Where the hell were you?" the captain of the lead trader howled as the communication system linked into the ship's intercom system. "They were waiting for us!"

"Stand by laser cannon," Harawe's voice barked over the speakers. "Battle stations. Repeat: battle stations."

Wolfe detached himself from the wall and ran to the nearest ship's ladder and all but slid down the spiral bannisters six decks to his crew's quarters. By the time he got there, the Cockroaches had heard the alert and had skinned out of their uniforms. Lin threw a CBS,P web at him and continued to put hers on. The beige, skin-tight suit felt warm for a moment, until the little brain sensed his body temperature and lowered its own to match his. Wearing a web felt like going naked except for the faint pulsing that began as soon as he sealed the front panel. A gentle squeeze around the biceps told him the peristalsis was working. The compression action on some of the modified suits was more obvious. D-45 looked as though his arms were being swallowed by boa constrictors. Daivid did not want to look too closely at anyone's front.

Daivid grabbed his communication bar out of his uniform sleeve and the infopad out of its holster at his side, pushed his way into the armory, looking for his battle gear hung with the others along the walls. Since he was tall, his suit was easy to spot, being one of the longest and the only one with red first-lieutenant insignia on the chest, which would become invisible as soon as the suit was operational. He slapped the thin card into its slot in the neck of the suit. The tiny lights inside the helmet glowed into life. He shoved the infopad into a rigid envelope at the left side of his ribcage. Its computer functions, including data storage, hooked directly into the suit's computer system. He hoisted ammunition cases and clicked them into their slots along the sides of his legs and the small of his back.

The others were bumping into one another as they pulled the semi-flexible armored suits on like snug trousers. Aaooorru calmly clicked his way up the wall and onto the ceiling to get his on, the only one of the Cockroaches able to avoid the scrimmage. The semicat Ewanowski kept half a protective eye on the corlist as he smacked his weapons into place. Wolfe wondered about the relationship between the two, who seemed to have so little in common. Software and her pal Somulska braced against one another's backs to gear up, then they checked one another's weapons and ammunition. With a friendly smack, platoon armorer Jones sent Thielind sprawling, indicating he was ready to go. The burly Cymraeg finished by clapping the helmet on his own head and lining up in front of Lin. The three squad chiefs stood by the door, counting off their troopers.

"Hop to it, X-ray!" Daivid called over the in-helmet channel, watching the seconds tick by on his heads-up display.

"Aye, aye, sir!" He heard none of the false ennui or backtalk. Screw around they might on every other available occasion, but when it came to the real thing, they were all business. Three tidy lines of heavily armed shadows stood ready to be deployed. Less than three minutes had elapsed since the platoon had hit the armory.

"Let's move out!"

With smooth precision, the sharpshooter scouts slipped out the door and into the corridor. All around them red-in-blue figures jog-marched toward their battle stations. X-ray fell in with several other units headed for Deck 6, forward. Each unit peeled off in turn, leaving the Cockroaches and Engineering's own personnel moving to defensive stations in the forward compartments.

"Stand by," Iry's voice came. The stocky commander and her officers appeared in the midst of the squads. "You are designated companies one, two and three!" Daivid saw the number 2 appear in his view. Immediately it was superimposed on the gold tags that identified each one of his troopers. "Company 1, emergency bay 6. Company 2, main pumping chamber. Company 3, lifting chamber and all ship's ladders. Stations!"

"Aye, aye, ma'am!" Daivid joined in the chorus. He relayed the order to his chiefs, but everyone had heard the command and was on their way to their assigned posts.

"Don't any of you clowns mess up my plumbing," Chief Winston growled over the in-helmet channel.

"Stow it, Winston," Iry barked. "Get into position, now!"

X-ray Platoon spread out through the huge chamber, identifying entry points. Squads broke up into pairs who flanked the vulnerable areas under cover and trained their weapons, ready to take out intruders. Ewanowski and Ambering hit the floor behind heavy guns, one aimed at each main door. Daivid took up a sheltered position where he could see both entrances. Borden and Thielind had spread out from there, each overseeing one point. Telemetry was good: he had a reading on every one of the *Eastwood's* defenders throughout the ship.

All during their deployment, voices had been giving orders over both the ship's system and the helmet channels, "...Pilots to their ships. Squadrons one through eight?"

"Aye, aye, sir!"

"Launch!"

"Goddammit, there's hundreds of fighters hammering the traders!"

"One hundred forty three," Borden's quiet voice murmured to herself.

"Emergency systems all green. Fire control all green."

"Gunners at the ready. Fire at will!"

In his heads-up display Daivid brought up telemetry from the bridge. He saw the besieged ships pinpointed on a star map. The pirate cruisers which had deposited the one- or two-man fighters stood off at a considerable distance from their prey. Tiny blue dots shot from their torpedo ports: computer-directed missiles targeting drives, weaponry and life-support systems that would have to be destroyed in flight. The fighters themselves were depicted as dark red dots, harrying the traders like gnats around a hiker. Clusters of tiny gold dots jetted out from the *Eastwood*. Blue-white missiles issued around them, seeking the enemy's projectiles and ships. With their NLS drives, the missiles sped up visibly then seemed to vanish. Some of the enemy's blue fire appeared to hesitate, change direction and disappear. The only way Daivid or the others knew if they had cancelled one another out was if a blossom of white fire appeared suddenly in the midst of the arena.

Seeing the *Eastwood* emerge, the pirates began to take evasive action. Though it did little good to try and outwit missiles with computer brains, the marauders put the traders between themselves and the dreadnought. The action served to prevent the *Eastwood's* plasma cannon from having line-of-sight in which to fire. The distances involved were so great that if Daivid had been able to watch the battle from the cockpit of a fighter alongside one of the traders, both of the other parties might be invisible. It was only in scale they appeared to be close enough to see one another.

"This is not crystal threedeeo!" Iry snapped. "Get your eyes back on your station!"

Guiltily, Daivid ordered the heads-up display to show him Deck 6 and his troopers. He was certain he wasn't the only one who wanted to see what was happening, but he did know his duty was there and then. Hands clutching his machine gun, he waited.

And waited. And waited. His eyes remained fixed on the doorframe, though his vision began to swim. He blinked then turned to the other doorway, holding it tightly in his sight until it, too, began to dance and turn white. To counter boredom, he counted how long it took for his eyes to recover then covered his other target, back and forth.

"Got one!" crowed a voice Daivid identified as Thielind's. "Uh, sorry, ma'am. Aye, ma'am."

Under their feet the Cockroaches felt the ship's drives kick in suddenly. Daivid could only guess that they were going in pursuit of one of the ships, perhaps the destroyer that stood off to starboard at an even greater remove than the cruisers.

"First blood!"

"Not *now*, Mose," Daivid snapped.

A slight juddering vibrated the *Eastwood* from port.

"Were we hit?" he asked aloud.

"Shields holding," Iry announced. "The bastards are swarming us. Are they stupid, or what?"

"Maybe their telemetry's not very good," one of the others laughed. "They're looking at us through the wrong end of the telescope." The others joined in. Their nerves were getting stretched, waiting for an attack that might never come.

Boom! The deck shook, jarring some of Wolfe's troopers out of their perches. They picked themselves up, swearing. Adri'Leta retrieved her rifle, which had spun out of her hands.

"Come on," Daivid chided them. "Hang on harder. Pretend it's a beer mug."

"Wish I *had* a beer," Boland grumbled, but he clambered back into his vantage point, nestled in between a lifter and the neck of a tank.

"Me, too," Lin said.

"Me, three," said D-45.

"No, you 45," Okumede said.

A chorus of groans erupted from the rest of the Cockroaches. "Oh, don't start that again!"

"Sorry," Okumede replied meekly. "It was automatic."

"Well, get back on manual," Ambering chided him.

"Can it," Iry stated. "They're making another pass. Oh, hell's bells!"

The words had barely hit the air when the ship shook again, more violently than before. Sirens and shouting erupted beyond the pumping station. Wolfe checked his telemetry to see dozens of red bodies rushing around. Had the pirates managed to board?

"They've holed us," Iry shouted. "Lanyard mines! Man your stations! Get that under control!"

Lanyard mines took magnetic hull-piercing explosives and tied them into a chain that went off in a rapid sequence like holiday firecrackers when it managed to cling to a ship's side. A long chain, up to half a kilometer, could cut a section off a vessel. Every TWC ship carried patching materials that could be rapidly deployed, as now.

Another explosion rocked the *Eastwood*, this time so close to Daivid it jarred his heart. A black line thinner than his finger appeared in the bulkhead beside him, hissing furiously. They'd been breached! Loose tools and testing gear went flying toward the breach. Light-boned Software, in spite of the weight of her suit, went flying toward the gap. Parviz and Nuu Myi made a flying tackle and brought her down, Parviz activating the magnetic clamps in his boots. The hatches automatically slammed shut and locked.

Daivid turned down his audio pickups and bellowed into his microphone. "Commander, we've got another hole in here."

"Handle it," Iry snapped. "We've got our hands full out here."

Inside the double-walled hull, cells of thick resin were punctured by the pressure of the explosion. Hydraulics pushed the goo toward the break. It was too slow. The chamber was depressurizing.

"Get the patch!" Daivid shouted, triggering his boot clamps. His troopers were already on the move toward the emergency repair station. He struggled to join them. The klaxons howled the warning. Implosion could follow at any moment. "Hurry!"

"We're hurrying," Lin growled back. Having to pick up one foot and place it carefully meant they moved like robots. The ship continued to judder as the tail of mines detonated. Their progress only seemed slow. They yanked the emergency release on the repair kit. A red plastic parcel the size of a large human rolled out into their arms. Even with the enhanced strength the armor gave them, the pull of the vacuum tilted them toward the breach. They fought to hold on to the kit.

"Six!" Borden announced as the explosions finally stopped. "We're sliced about ten meters."

Daivid read the instructions, which were printed in white on the container. "That's about all we've got. Let's get this spread out!"

Lin drew her knife and slit the seals. The parcel unrolled into a sheet ten meters long by three wide by approximately ten centimeters thick. Getting it toward the break in the hull was no problem. Fighting the vacuum to get it placed where they wanted it took the combined strength of everyone in X-ray. Daivid hung on to his corner, wrestling it up the wall with the help of Meyers, Somulska and Aaooorru. Meyers wrapped her legs around a plumbing fixture and wrenched the far bottom corner into place. Ambering held it up so it didn't drop too soon. High up the bulkhead, Boland, Vacarole and Gire draped the remainder over their heads, working it over the biggest part of the gap.

"Okay, sir!" Borden said, peering underneath the folds. "That'll do it. Let 'er go."

The ten of them let the fabric slide out of their fingers. It slapped against the bulkhead, sealing tightly. Daivid staggered backward, as the fierce pull of vacuum was cut off. They watched as the sheet began to change color from red to white, indicating that the cold of space was causing the gel inside to set.

"All clear, Commander," he called to Iry.

"Well done," she replied. "Stand by—They're making another pass, damn them. They must be insane! There's only half a dozen fighters left. Hold tight!"

Wolfe and the others braced themselves and counted. No booms resounded through the hull. Sixty, sixty-one, sixty-two...Daivid almost let himself relax, when a loud clank echoed from outside the wall he was standing on. He jumped back just in time. With a *BANG!* the hull imploded, spraying molten metal, then air whooshed out again. The alarms, just recently stilled, began to howl again. Another explosion came, perpendicular to the first one, widening the gap.

"Get another patch!" Wolfe yelled.

"We don't have another one," Lin replied. "That one was intended to cover a *number* of small breaches."

Daivid looked around frantically. Improvise! They had to improvise. What could they use to cover the gap? Think, he gritted. Think like a Cockroach!

"The hot tub," he said.

"What, sir?"

"Go get the hot tub. The survival shelter. We can cover the gap with the membrane. It's big enough."

"Oh, no, sir," Boland moaned.

"Yes! Get it!"

Lin let out a little croon that sounded like a noise of approval, and clanked out of sight, followed by Gire and Ewanowski.

"But, sir, it'll spill thousands of liters of water everywhere," Boland pointed out. Another mine detonated, opening the slit in the bulkhead still further.

"Water, or our guts?" Daivid asked.

An audible *POP* issued in the distance. Lin's return was heralded by a gush of water that instantly began to flow up the wall and freeze. The senior chief and her helpers carried in the clear plastic sheeting, which was already beginning to contract to its normal size. He seized an edge of the flexible membrane and hauled it upward, spreading it over the long black gash. The slick footing made his boots slip.

"Duck, sir!" Borden cried.

Daivid detached his magnetic boots and leaped towards the floor just as a fourth explosion shot through, leaving a hole the size of his head. Repair resin dribbled in, sealing most of the break, but it left a pinhole that slurped at the running water like a thirsty camel. The ship shifted hard, making Daivid sway. Harawe must have ordered a hard turn. Daivid and Aaooorru, who still clung to the wall overhead, tugged at the clear sheet until it dropped over and into the gap. The pinhole, temporarily deprived of its drink, sucked the plastic outward, creating a bubble. The rest of the plastic began to creep slowly into the gap.

"It's not thick enough," Daivid said. "It's going to pop in a moment. We need something to bulk it up. Is there anything? Firefighting foam?"

"Not thick enough," Borden said, doing a rapid mental calculation.

"We've got plenty of material," Jones began in a speculative voice.

Daivid followed the direction the Cymraeg's mask was pointing. Toward the sump room. "Oh, no, Jones, not that again."

"We've got lots of it, sir, and it's thick. I had my hands in it enough the other night to testify to that. It'll freeze in place, and keep the survival tent from bursting. We can't go out in search of anything else, sir. The hatches are sealed."

Daivid groaned, but he had to bow to the inevitable. "All right!" he said. "Hurry up. Get...some. Move it!"

Chuckling evilly to themselves, a handful of the Cockroaches stalked out of the main pump room. In short order they returned pulling a hover-cart laden with sloshing canisters.

"Just heave it up there," Jones advised. "It'll stick."

The largest troopers—Ewanowski, Okumede and Boland—grabbed a canister apiece and walked up the wall, pouring out the thick sludge along the gap. The heavy brown muck started to flow, then halted in place. Daivid didn't realize he was holding his breath until the creeping edges of the survival shelter slowed, then lay flat. It worked! The little corlist scuttled forward, grasping the loose edges of the tent in his many hands to fold over the heavy sludge. It adhered then froze in place.

"Make cleanup more easy," he chittered. The others leaped to help him, turning their improvised patch into a neat package.

"Very tidy," Jones opined. "You'd hardly guess what was in it."

"Excuse me," Lin retorted, "but the color does show through."

"You know what they say," Mose pointed out. "When life hands you slag, make a slag sandwich."

"With ice on the side," Streb added.

"Is that in your limerick?" Lin asked.

"And have someone say my poems are full of slag? Not a chance."

Daivid had to snicker as he keyed his communications channel open to Iry. "All under control, commander."

A siren sounded the All Clear. "Stand down," a female voice ordered. "All hands, stand down from battle stations."

"Thank God for that," Iry's voice came through with relief. "Any casualties?"

"None, ma'am."

"You're sure?"

Daivid glanced at his platoon, doing a quick headcount. "Yes, ma'am."

"Let me in there," Iry ordered. "I want to see for myself."

"Retreat!" Itterim Captain Maren ordered her cruiser, the *Tchtchtch*. "All fighters on board!" Her green clawed feet clung to the deck as she stared in dismay at the navigation screen. Where had that monster of a ship come from? How had they not known it was coming?

She wished to pursue the merchants—the Insurgency was counting upon their cargo—but she could see no way to maneuver past the gigantic ship, which had appeared out of nowhere like a huge gray ghost. Small craft had swarmed out of its bowels like the hatching of a gigantic litter, and engaged all of their fighters, sometimes two or three to a ship. Though the Insurgency ships outnumbered their original prey, they were vastly outgunned by the new and unexpected opponent.

One by one, the trade ships had escaped from the battle, diving into the nearest entrance to nonspace. To follow was impossible. If they did, the TWC dreadnought could notify the Space Service to have a full-scale navy meet them at the other end of the string.

Once the last merchant had disappeared, the gigantic ship began to attack in earnest, now that no vulnerable civilians could be hurt. One after another the Insurgency ships were blown into ragged shards. Maren made the decision to flee to save the lives of the other rebels.

The giant ship chased them as far as the entry point of another string. Once the scanty remains of her fighters were on board she let the singularity take the *Tchtchtch*. She could only hope that the TWC ship would not send messages ahead of them now, but it was a faint hope. They wished to destroy the rebellion and all who fought the good fight against the oppressors.

"What *was* that?" Ziil howled over the ship-to-ship video channel, heedless of whether the signal was being scrambled or not. His forelimbs rasped against one another in extreme agitation.

"A full-scale TWC dreadnought," replied Roest, safely aboard the destroyer *Chittatin*. "We were duped. The ships were not unprotected, as we had been assured. Prepare for their weapons only, the report said. It was a lie!"

"But it was my own hatching brother who sent the report," Ziil said.

"Then he was corrupted," Roest said, flatly, "and should be eaten. Has he a mate?"

"You're a fine one to talk about eating," Maren hissed. "I have heard your crew agitating for your giblets. Do you feel so safe accusing Ziil's hatching brother?"

"He must have been lied to," Ziil insisted.

"Did he not threaten adequately?" Roest countered. "Did he not offer sufficient bribes for accurate information?"

"I am sure that he did," Ziil replied sulkily. "It must be that his sources did not have accurate information for sale."

"Colonel Ayala will need to be notified of that," Maren stated.

"He will need to be notified of our failure as soon as we emerge," Roest said, with sudden misgivings. "We may all need to be wary of who is looking hungry around us."

"Three ships," Ziil wailed. "We only have three ships left!"

The Cockroaches stood at attention in the captain's day room. Daivid angled his chin to loosen the formal collar around his neck. His troopers were arrayed in new dress whites, wrenched out of Supply's clutches for the occasion by special order of Commander Iry. The troopers didn't clean up half badly, he mused, surveying them with pride. He wondered why they had been summoned. It was probably so the Captain could chew them out personally for messing up the pumping station again. Once the repair bots had sealed the hull from the outside, the chamber had heated up again, and the water had sloshed everywhere, shorting out components and running under the floor plates. And the improvised patch itself had started to warm up and soften enough to slide down the wall. Aaooorru's attempt to package up the slag only worked to a point. It had been a stinking disaster to dispose of.

The captain peered at them down his aristocratic nose as he paced up and back.

"I don't usually single out units after a battle," he said. "I expect every crew member to do the job without expectation of special thanks. That's why you join the Space Service, to give your all in defense of the Confederation."

So, why bring us in? Daivid thought. He glanced curiously at the captain, who caught him looking. He snapped his eyes back to straight ahead.

"Once in a while, however, a unique situation comes along that requires recognition. Your unit handled not one, but two hull breaches while the ship was under attack. You did it speedily and well, with no loss of life. You saved a vital section of the *Eastwood*. But I am told that there was only one repair kit in the department accessible to you, and that you had to improvise with what you had at hand: a survival shelter and—material present in the department." Harawe's eyes were a mixture of amusement and outrage. "I will *not* have an official report filed that my ship was saved by a load of dung! Over my dead and desiccated remains will a reference to such a substance be used. There will be no dung in my records. Therefore the report will be amended."

"Er, you can say we made use of 'alternate materials,' sir," Borden suggested.

"So noted," Harawe snapped, approvingly. "Good choice. Coffey! Take that down."

"Aye, sir." The young ensign recorded the change in her infopad.

"And you, troopers of X-ray," Harawe said, turning to Daivid's platoon, "should also make use of the term when referring to the incident."

"You can count on us, sir!" Daivid said heartily. "Alternate materials it is. Right, X-ray?"

"Aye, aye, sir!" the Cockroaches chimed in.

Harawe nodded sharply. "Then get out of here. Good job. Dismissed!"

Ayala was as upset as Maren had predicted. When they finally shot out of the nonspace string, they waited for the next window to make contact. The three remaining fleet captains were dreading it. He trusted them, and they had failed.

"I shall kill Veendam with my own hands," Ayala growled, miming the strangling of the unhappy itterim spy. "How dare he send me false information. He lied to my face!"

"I am sure he was lied to," Ziil insisted. "He would never conceal the information if he knew the traders had requested Space Service protection."

"I am cutting off his payments," Ayala said. "And you may warn him he has two days before I send an anonymous message that he is a mole."

"Colonel!" Ziil protested. "That will condemn him to death!"

"We lost twelve ships!" the colonel shouted. "Damn you! I need allies who can forward our cause, not set it back five paces for every step forward."

"Yes, colonel," the itterim captains chorused obediently.

Ayala turned to stare directly into the screen, as if he could see the eyes of each of the captains watching him. "We will rendezvous at our final destination. I expect your full support."

"But, sir," Maren began, "we have had to travel three days in the wrong direction. It will take us time to find strings to carry us back towards you."

"Be on time or don't come back," Ayala said, snapping a hand toward his communications officer to close the link. He paced back and forth on the juddering bridge. "You would think I could attract more quality people to our cause! I'll do it myself, if I have to."

CHAPTER 10

"HEY, DAI," CARMEN called at the beginning of second shift, "are you heading for the wardroom? The rest of us are going to the crystal ampitheater showing of "Peristalsis III: The Devouring"."

Daivid didn't halt in his businesslike trot down the corridor, but he turned and jogged backwards. "No, I've got to take care of something. Tell me about it later."

"Will do!"

Daivid hummed to himself as he went. A little praise went a long way. During his stop in to visit the platoon on duty in the pumping station that day, they all seemed to be in good spirits. Success, however unconventionally achieved, was a great morale booster. He figured now was the best time to pry open a few of the troopers' shells and find out what they were really like underneath.

"Permission to enter?" he asked at the door of the day room.

Lin glanced over. The platoon was still settling in. Vacarole was scrolling impatiently through the snack menu of the food dispenser set in the wall. Boland was pouring purple-red bug juice from a pitcher half-and-half with the clear liquid Daivid recognized as the Cockroaches' proprietary white lightning.

"Come on in, sir. Want a drink?"

Daivid sidled in casually, knowing they were all looking at him. "I thought I'd spend the evening with you, if you didn't mind. I've got a proposition for you."

Lin's left eyebrow rose high on her forehead. The others looked as curious, and as wary.

"We thought this'd come sooner or later," Boland said. "Aren't you happy with the way we've been working? We're heroes! The whole ship knows about it. Even the captain likes us today."

"It's not that," Daivid said, settling down in a chair and tilting it backward until his shoulders touched the wall. "It's what happened after the poetry slam. And back on Treadmill. There are a dozen other land mines that I am tired of stumbling over. I keep pissing all of you off over things I don't know existed or ever happened, and

I'm sick of it. Break out some of the white lightning. I want to hear your stories."

Somulska crossed her arms. "I don't think I want to talk about mine."

"Or mine," Software chimed in.

"Then I'll play you for them," Wolfe said, the gold glint in his eyes. He picked the deck of cards off the big table and shuffled it from one hand to the other like an accordion. "Any game you want. If you can beat me, you can take my money."

"Or we can hear *your* story," Mose said. "There's no good reason for you to be here, either, or so you say. Give us a chance to find out."

"All right," Wolfe said slowly, calculating. "For that, *all* of you have to beat me once. You're entitled to one question per winning hand. I will consider it a debt of honor and, if you know about my family, that means more to me than life itself. I swear by anything I hold dear that I will tell you the truth, however painful it is. Is that worth it to you?"

"Fair enough," agreed Boland.

"But if you throw in your marker and I take it, you owe me the truth. The *whole* story. How about it?"

"Our whole lives against one question to him? That doesn't sound like an even exchange," Ewanowski rumbled.

"It's a game," Mose said flippantly. "He can't possibly beat us all."

"I dunno," Streb ruminated. "Anyone who marches in and makes a claim like that is either stupid or really clever."

Vacarole's eyes twinkled. "Like a fox."

"Like a Wolfe," Daivid corrected him. "Is it a deal?"

"Okay, why not?" Gire said. "It's not like we have anything to do. This adds some spice to the nightly game. It sounds like fun. What'll we use for markers?"

"Plastic'll have to be good enough tonight," Jones said. "I'll whip something together in the machine shop tomorrow."

"Do you need mine?" Lin asked. "I already told you about me."

"Just to be fair," Wolfe said. "Maybe I can think of something really nosy to ask you. And if you're really uneasy about letting me hear what you've got to say, you can redeem your marker, cash only. But then don't jump me if I step over invisible lines."

"How much should the buy-back be?" Aaooorru asked.

"A hundred?" Injaru asked.

"Too cheap," Wolfe dismissed the suggestion. "I've seen pots bigger than that on a single-card hand in our own barracks. I know you've been shafting the local talent out of that much."

"Five hundred?" Nuu Myi asked.

"Too much!" Boland growled. "When was the last time you saw five hundred credits?"

"Three hundred," Lin suggested.

"Okay, Top," Gire agreed. "Three hundred, sir?"

"Yeah, that sounds fair," said Meyers. "It's a couple of high stakes hands' worth at the worst."

"You'll enjoy the challenge," Wolfe said, looking at each of them in turn. "This is for your benefit as much as mine."

D-45 snorted. "I've heard that before, mostly from people who were about to beat the crap out of me."

"I am," Wolfe said pleasantly.

Now was the time to show off the lessons that Randy had beaten into him from the age of eight. *Fingers, don't fail me now!* He riffled the cards, built a neat little castle in the air, and tucked all the cards into a tidy block again. Jaws all around the room dropped.

Boland whistled admiringly. "We've been had. He's a sharper. We should have known."

Wolfe smiled ferally. "What'll it be? Seven card draw? Five card stud? Bridge? Crazy eights? War?"

"How do we know you won't cheat?"

Wolfe raised an eyebrow. "You don't. How do I know *you* won't cheat? You're the ones with the reputation."

"Yeah, but you're the one with the family background," Okumede said.

Wolfe waved the deck enticingly. "Come and find out. *Try* and find out."

"I'm in," Lin said at once.

"Me, too," said D-45. "What's the worst thing that could happen?"

Wolfe took the deck, divided it into two parts, divided those into two parts then shuffled the pairs separately with one hand each.

"*He* is," Ambering groaned.

There wasn't room at the table for all the people clamoring to take their first shot against Daivid and his personal markers. They finally drew cards for six seats, and the rest agreed to take turns on successive evenings. Jones elected to sit out. The burly armorer took a seat with a good view of the proceedings, cutting a sheet of discarded viewscreen into strips.

He dumped the first half dozen on the table. "I've cut your names into them so there's no mistake," he said.

"Thanks," Mose said, shuffling his chip to the bottom of his stake. "My underwear goes into the pot before this does."

"Not the leather thong," Streb teased him, seated behind the taciturn petty officer's shoulder. "Anything but that."

"No, that I keep," Mose said with a dry twinkle. "The melody may be ended, but the thong will linger on."

"What?" Daivid asked, thoroughly bewildered.

"Ancient literary allusion," Mose said. "I don't expect anyone to recognize it. Deal, big cheese." He tapped the table.

Daivid stopped the card pyrotechnics, let Haalten on his right cut the deck, then shot cards around the table clockwise. Aaooorru, Ewanowski, Mose, Lin, Meyers and the itterim had all won places. They picked up their cards and arranged them, shoving their ante into the kitty.

The corlist put his hand face down on the table and shoved a credit chit forward with a delicate claw. "Fifty."

"Fifty," the semicat added, "and fifty more."

"Give me two," Mose said, sliding discards toward the dealer. Daivid dealt him fresh cards. "I'll see your hundred credits."

"I'm out," Lin grunted.

"Me, too," Meyers said.

"See you," Haalten chittered.

"Raise a hundred," Daivid said. He held a safe three sevens and a queen. His hand could only get better. It was good to be handy with cards; it was better to be lucky, and he was lucky. His nanny had always told him so. "Trust it," Randy said. "Trust it and it will never let you down." The bidding went around twice more, until Ewanowski called.

"Let's see 'em," the semicat said. Obligingly, the others laid out their cards.

"A pair of queens!" Meyers announced.

"Ace high nothing," Mose said, with the gambler's air of 'win some, lose some.'

"Three threes," Haalten hissed with pleasure.

"Three sevens," Daivid said, pulling the pot towards him.

The semicat looked him straight in the eye. "You stacked the cards."

"Prove it," the lieutenant said. "I'm just lucky. I don't have to be dishonest."

"Or the cards are marked."

"Which he did while you watched?" Mose asked scornfully. "Forget it, Puss in Boots."

"I want to deal," Ewanowski insisted.

Daivid pushed his cards into the center. The semicat gathered the deck with his eyes fixed on the lieutenant as he shuffled and dealt. Daivid almost crowed as he gathered up his cards. *Trust luck, and it will never let you down.* He set the cards face down and raised every time the bid went past him. The others dropped out in turn, leaving only him and Ewanowski in the round.

"Okay, sir," the semicat said. He spread out his hand. "Three aces."

"Three twos," Daivid said. Ewanowski started to reach for the pot. "And two threes."

"A natural full house!" Lin gasped as he flipped the hand over. "Damn!"

"The fate gods love you, sir," Ewanowski said with respect. "I dunno what yet, but they're keeping you for something."

Not every hand went his way. He lost seven hundred credits on one big hand, including a chance at two markers, when his two pairs of queens and jacks were beaten out by Lin's straight.

"Ha HA," Mose said, taking his turn dealing a couple of hours later. "Aces for me, and garbage for the rest of you." He looked at his cards, then at his stakes, which were growing meager. "Er, ten."

"Raise you twenty," Lin said.

"Me, too," Meyers added, with a fat look of satisfaction on her face. "Twenty more."

"Fold," Aaooorru bubbled.

"Fold," Ewanowski echoed.

"Fold," Daivid made it three.

Mose glanced at his bank. "Twenty." Nothing was left but his marker. Lin and Meyers looked at one another.

"Raise fifty," the chief said, with a mischievous expression.

"Fifty more," Meyers said.

With a disgusted look, Mose threw in the marker. Lin folded. Meyers pounced. "Call."

Mose put his cards down. "A straight."

Meyers laid hers out in a tidy line. "A flush. Mine!" She gathered the chips in and stacked them, placing the plastic marker on top of her own.

"Well, I'm out," Mose said, pushing back slightly. "Anyone want to take my place?"

"No, thanks," Boland said, speaking for the rest of the Cockroaches. They had their eyes fixed on that marker on Meyers's bank.

Meyers did not have a poker face. When her hand was good, it showed in her eyes. The next deal made them light up. She threw in fifty to start. The corlist folded at once. His fortune had not been good that evening, and he was nearly stripped. Ewanowski stayed in. Daivid watched the other players and peeked at his own cards. Three threes! He made sure his face didn't twitch. The other two cards were a two and a four. He threw in the fifty and twenty more. Meyers matched him, and raised. One by one the others dropped out. When the bet came around to him again Daivid signed for two cards. The first was an eight. The second was the fourth three. Holding his breath he put in a hundred then turned to Meyers.

She drew two, too. Her expression still said she was holding a terrific hand. She looked at the lone fifty-credit chit to the left of her smaller change, then at the two plastic tags. Suddenly, she tossed Mose's chip into the center. Daivid held his breath as the bidding went around to him again.

"Call," he said.

"Full house," Meyers said.

Daivid didn't say a word, but set down the cards one at a time.

"Goddammit!" Boland howled.

"I'll take that," Daivid said, raking in the pot. He picked up the marker. "Unless you want to redeem it?" he asked Mose. "Three hundred."

Mose grimaced. "I don't have it. You can see that."

"Then, pay up, trooper," Wolfe said, making himself comfortable with hands folded behind his head. "Tell me all about yourself. How'd you get here?"

"I don't want to tell you my life story," Mose said, settling back as Lin cut the cards and Aaooorru began to deal.

"No fair, no fair!" the others shouted.

"That's not the deal," Boland boomed. "You agreed, like the rest of us."

"Now, now," Mose raised his voice over all of theirs. He held up his drink and twisted the glass from side to side to admire the warm gold of the contents. "I'd rather tell you a hypothetical tale of things that can happen to an innocent person. The traditional way to begin a tale is 'once upon a time.' Once upon a time there was a meek little lieutenant who worked in the Central Command intelligence service. He was an observant little lieutenant, who did his job and went home at night to his quiet little hobbies and his quiet little friends. But along the way, the meek little lieutenant observed," Mose stressed the word, "that security procedures in the CenCom intelligence service were laughably ineffective. He went to his superiors, who were big bad bureaucrats, and explained to them what he had seen, and gave them some practical suggestions on how to solve the problems for little money and with very little fuss. But the big bad bureaucrats decided in their experience and wisdom that to change things was to suggest that they were being done wrong to start with. Other people might notice that the big bad bureaucrats were not perfect, and make fun of them in public. So nothing changed. And bad things happened to lots and lots of innocent people, all of which could have been prevented if only they had listened to the meek little lieutenant.

"Now, even meek persons can become outraged. This lieutenant sat down one day while he was on his meager annual leave, and wrote a tell-all book about the intelligence service. The very first publisher who read it was just as outraged as he, bought it, and brought out millions of copies, with royalties being paid to a blind trust, because one thing the meek little lieutenant had observed was that the bureaucrats knew how to follow the money, so he made sure none of it ever appeared to reach his hands. So, the one thing that the service cannot prove is that he did it. He'd been with them long enough to know how to cover his tracks. If they can prove he wrote this naughty book, he will go to prison for a long time for blabbing state secrets, even though the book helped to spur the system to change. But so far they can't prove it, and they can't get him to confess, not even with drugs or mind control, because they themselves taught him how to resist those.

They hope that a stretch in a punishment detail will change his mind, or he might get himself killed, thereby taking the problem out of their hands forever. Either way he has nothing to lose by keeping his mouth shut." Mose swished his drink and took a swig. "But that's just a story. That little lieutenant and I have nothing in common except a literary bent and an outraged sense of justice."

Wolfe was silent for a moment. "That was a good story," he said. "I think we all agree it was just a story, don't we?"

"Always have," Boland agreed.

The room seemed to take a deep breath, then exhaled as a unit. Daivid felt a measure of triumph that had less to do with his winning over three hundred credits of his troopers' money and more to beginning to crack the wall of silence that kept him from understanding the people themselves.

"I've got a new name for Sourpuss Cleitis," Jones declared, over his minitorch from across the room, as the cards went around again. "I think we should call him Love and Kisses. For XO, get it? If there was ever a man who was less likely to get either, I think he's it."

The others chuckled. "He's got to file forms to have an orgasm," Okumede laughed. "You wouldn't believe the paperwork, like form OOHBABY-435. In triplicate."

"Him? Three in a row?" Ambering asked with a hearty chuckle that went all the way to her ample midsection. "Not even with me on top of him, honey."

Aaooorru didn't join in the laughter. In order to stay in the current hand, he had to throw in his personal chip or fold. The dilemma showed in the way his round black eyes rolled and his antennae waved. Daivid waited patiently, like a cat about to pounce. His hand was weak, a pair of queens, but he sensed no one else had much, either. Now that he had won one life story, he was playing mostly for fun. Lin, now out of the running, browsed around the table. She glanced at his hand then looked him in the eye with a wry squint. Daivid shrugged playfully.

He stayed with the bidding to the bitter end, fixing his companions with a confident stare. One by one they dropped out.

"Mine, then," he said, slapping his cards on the table face down. He reached for his winnings.

"Wait a minute," Ewanowski said, reaching for his hand. "I want to see what you had that was so hot. One lousy pair of queens! I had *two* pair." Disgusted, he threw the cards away.

"He psyched all of you out," D-45 snorted.

Daivid chuckled. "Psychology is a big part of poker. Trooper, pay up."

"No." Aaooorru's eyes lowered and drew close together. He pushed back from the table, hopped down from his chair and tottered toward the door on his delicate little feet.

"Hey, you can't refuse," Meyers said. "It's a debt of honor."

"I care nothing for debts of honor," he bubbled angrily. "What good has honor ever done me?"

"I'll tell you. For free," Ewanowski halted the corlist before he could get to the door. "People make all sorts of rotten comments about the two of us, even saying we're perverts, crossing species. I'm his bodyguard. I used to be a bouncer in a bar in the capital city on Vom on the dry side of Mishagui, the trading area. His folks got in touch with me when he went into the service. Aaooorru's royalty."

The corlist protested, his round eyes bobbing in alarm.

"Shut up. These are the best friends you ever had in the universe, and I'm including those so-called buddies you had back at the palace. You're a hell of a lot safer here than there. He's like the two hundredth offspring, not real close to the throne, but still in the succession. Corlists have big families, but only a few make it to adulthood because of disease and lots of natural predators, and they don't have real long lifespans."

He strong-armed the protesting Aaooorru back into his chair and pushed a drink toward him. "Think. Don't go off like that. Anyhow, he was head of a regiment. I was his ADC. I dunno if you know anything about the politics going on, but Vom's fallen out of favor in the TWC senate. The system's close to the lizards, and there are people who want to make nice, not fight back. If you know anything about the lizards, you know they don't make nice, they make lunch. His family's on the wrong side of the argument. Every one of them's a target for assassination, and about fifty of them have already gone down. So, his folks thought it'd be safer if he got transferred to a unit where he would be out of the way until the tide changes. Hah! If they knew the crap they assign us to do, they'd yank him out of here and pack him in bubble wrap!" Ewanowski showed all of his impressive teeth in a mirthless grin.

"You make me sound like a weakling," the corlist murmured, his words muffled in his water collar.

"Hell you are," the semicat growled. "Do you know how easy it would have been to get sucked down that gap in the hull the other day? At your size? And that's only the most recent example. He jumps right in there like any other trooper, sir. His unit loved him. I bet they're still wondering what happened to him."

"Is there anyone in this unit who wasn't busted down from officer?" Daivid asked in astonishment. "I knew I was the most junior crew member, but I had no idea everyone outranked me."

"Just most of us," Lin smiled.

"I didn't," Streb said shortly. "But you're gonna have to win my marker to hear."

"I look forward to it," Daivid said. He stood up and stretched his back. "I might take you up on reprogramming my CBS,P—for therapeutic backrubs only."

"Sure thing," Boland said. "Just leave it here with us any time."

"I'll do that. I'd better get back to my endless paperwork. I left half a dozen queries beeping at me on my infopad. Everyone wants their reports now. Thanks," he said to Mose and Aaooorru.

"You won it, fair and square," the poet replied with a half grin. "You are a hell of a player."

"Don't tell anyone," the corlist added.

"License to republish," Daivid said, "was not included in the original purchase price. Don't worry. I'd never snitch on a fellow-in-arms."

Aaooorru nodded. Ewanowski offered him another toothy grin.

"Come on back tomorrow," Meyers called as he headed out the door. "We want a chance to get our money back."

CHAPTER 11

WOLFE HAD ANSWERED the summons with alacrity. The executive officer wished to see all of the unit commanders at 1100 hours in the briefing room. Wolfe had gulped his lunch without tasting it, and arrived more than fifteen minutes early out of sheer excitement. All of his wardroom colleagues were present, all spring-loaded with the energy that went with the anticipation of action. At last they were going to receive their assignments. Wilbury caught Daivid's eye and gave him a fierce grin. This was what they were all there for. The ship's officers sat in a row against the front wall. Behind the podium, Executive Officer Cleitis cleared his throat.

"I know all of you have been waiting a long time for gen on the upcoming missions. Captain Harawe and the command staff of the *Eastwood* have been acting under sealed orders until now."

A few of the officers glanced at one another. The Captain's voice came from the back of the room.

"We have had suspicions that there is a leak somewhere in the operation." All heads turned to track Harawe as he stalked forward towards the lighted dais. "To that end, there has been a controlled release of information, including misinformation on the subject of the trade ships and our escort service. In other words, we let it out that those ships were going naked. Since it panned out that there was an Insurgency attack on the flotilla, word is coming from somewhere, but since you all knew about it and the Surgies came anyhow, you're all in the clear."

Wolfe raised his eyebrow. Harawe couldn't be as naïve as that. He personally knew twenty-three ways to extract data while appearing to be in another place. It had been part of his upbringing in the Family. At the time he'd thought it was cool. He suspected that his unit could amass another twenty-three hundred among them, if it interested them at all. He also knew half a dozen historical examples to prove that it was possible for one side of a war to sit on a piece of information in order not to give away the fact they had spies on the other side. Harawe seemed to divine his thoughts.

"The actual info was never on this ship, Mister New-in-town," he said, biting off each syllable. "I received my briefing in person at a remote location. The test message released aboard the *Eastwood* has not been transmitted or recorded, but the break showed through elsewhere. It could not have come from one of you. The spy has been identified. So it is time to give you your assignments. Cleitis?"

Subdued, Daivid sat back. Harawe had his number. He wasn't seeing the bigger picture. Lieutenant Ti-Ya was right about the captain being a careful man.

The ascetic XO took his place behind the desk. "Commander Christophle."

"Sir!" A tan-skinned woman of thirty or so with very dark lips responded alertly, turning interesting caramel-colored eyes forward. Wolfe admired the length of her black lashes. On the screen behind Cleitis, a star map appeared. The point of focus zoomed in on a small primary star, red-orange, with orbits marked out for five planets, two of them gas giants, and two of them small rocky worlds spaced out in between.

"When we break into normal space, you will take the number six auxiliary. Admiral Banks awaits you. She is reestablishing TWC control of the Nonnen system, now that she's driven the damned Insurgents out of there. Because of the diversion, we're a couple of days later than she was expecting, but that's war. You're relieving Commander Harris Boone, who's going back to Central Command for debriefing."

"Sir!" Christophle's eyes shone. He signed to her to turn her infopad toward his aide, who would beam her site maps and more detailed orders.

Wolfe envied her. He'd heard of the siege of Harrim, Nonnen's capital city, a domelike space station orbiting a gas giant at 2 a.u. from the Nonnen primary. The pirates had taken over several of the smaller city-domes and were holding them hostage, trying to force the Nonnen government into surrendering. Banks had managed to stretch the navy forces she had brought with her to attack on several fronts until other Space Service ships had arrived to assist. It had been said there wasn't one trooper on board who hadn't been decorated. The pirates, somehow not getting the message, had kept trying to retake Nonnen. Someone, maybe the legendary General Sams herself, had decided it was too important to lose, so there continued to be plenty of action.

Daivid gave an imaginary one-two punch to Sams, thinking what he would do if he had been in Banks's place.

"Lieutenant Wolfe! There's no need to dance about it. You'll get your own assignment."

Harawe's voice brought him sharply back to reality. He felt his cheeks burn as the other officers chortled to themselves. Daivid shrugged. Couldn't blame a guy for dreaming.

"Taith," Harawe turned to an itterim sitting at the end of the briefing table. "Your force and Cosimi's," he nodded to a human male with short-cropped blue hair, "are going to be dropped off on Belmont Station. You are relieving two units who are due for leave. You'll carry on with resettling the refugees who are returning, now that the eruptions have ceased. You won't find it onerous. It's mostly traffic control at this point."

"Ossum," Itterim Taith enunciated with a click. Belmont boasted a T-class world with gravity .85 that of Earth. Daivid had friends who had gone there on vacation. The dramatically rocky terrain was a climber's dream, and the lighter gravity meant their muscles could take them that much farther. He listened as Cleitis doled out assignment after assignment, each sounding worthy as well as exciting. He tried to hold out hope for a mission with similar promise of glory, but every one of the commanders around him had far more experience than he did. Nor did their units suffer from the reputation of being the worst in the Space Service. His heart had sunk deep into his boots by the time the XO turned to him, last and least.

"As for you, Lieutenant Wolfe," Cleitis began, a saccharinely sweet smile on his face, "we've got a nice, easy little mission for you. It's a cream puff. I am informed by your CO that you have only been in command of X-ray Company for about twenty days now. This will be a mild breaking-in exercise for you."

"Aye, sir?" Daivid asked, suddenly wary. This was when they told him that the Cockroaches were being sent into the heart of a high-radiation zone to extract the 1% remaining useful ore from the bottom of a seventeen-kilometer-deep shaft. He hoped he'd have a chance to send one last missive to his mother before his skin began to peel off in strips.

"Yes, my boy. You're going to thank CenCom for this from the bottom of your green little heart. Your unit has been especially chosen for the job because of your—low profile. You are tasked with going into a small town on a well-to-do world in a non-combat zone and retrieve a single piece of technology and the data to run it. Then you will be extracted. Three days, start to finish. The *Eastwood* will drop you, hang off-world in concealment in the heliopause, then come and get you and your objective. Is that clear? Even your unit should find that hard to screw up."

"Aye, sir," Daivid replied, puzzled. Where was the part about mortal danger? Where were the enemy forces? "I'll need maps and briefings on the site, and the intel on the unfriendlies." He started to extend his infopad toward the XO, when Harawe held up a hand.

"He hasn't got anything for you, Wolfe," the captain said, with bleak satisfaction. "I do. Here's your target information. Enjoy."

He dropped a sheet of plastic on Daivid's desk. As soon as it hit the surface, the video data printed into the plastic gathered enough static electricity to activate. A miniature Ferris wheel erected itself and began to turn. Roller coasters lined the perimeter. In the center a crenellated keep of bright orange towered over all. Tiny figures in astonishingly colorful detail joined hands and danced around the brochure's perimeter. Tinny voices broke into song. The other officers stared at it then at the captain, then at Daivid, who was gawking at the images with his mouth open. The officers present all protested at once.

"He gets to go to *Wingle World*?" Taith squawked, his mandibles opened wide in outrage.

"Sir, does CenCom know about this unit's reputation?" Varos broke in. "I—this—Couldn't this be considered a mismatch of mission and, er, resources?"

"Hey, we'll do it," Cosimi said. "X-ray can go rappel down cliff-faces. We'll take the amusement park."

Heedless of the heated protests around him, Daivid gazed in pleased astonishment at the animation. Wingle World! He hadn't been there since he was nine years old, over half his lifetime ago. Wow. He had always been a big fan of the Bizarro Twins, a couple of happy-go-lucky wolves or foxes or something of wild canine descent with purple fur who were always getting into amusing trouble. During games of make-believe, he had tried in vain to convince one or another of his sisters to be the other Bizarro Twin so that they could act out the capers he saw on threedeeo animations. It had been a happy day when his father had packed off the four children in the care of an army of minions to go for a jaunt to Wingle World. They had been there almost a month, staying in the on-site luxury hotel, dining on room service or having special meals with the characters (who were threedeeo animations, people dressed up in anthropomorphic-animal costumes or AEROs, Animated Electronic RObots, a Wingle trademark), watching shows and parades and fireworks displays. He had been the envy of his schoolmates when he returned.

He knew he was grinning like an idiot, but he couldn't help himself. Wingle World!

His classmates had nothing on the rest of the unit commanders aboard the *Eastwood* when it came to envy and resentment. Pulling himself back to the present, he glanced around at his fellows. With few exceptions, they all wore glares or puzzled frowns. If they'd been school children, he might have been looking for a fight behind the gym after the bell rang. He admitted to some puzzlement himself.

"Sir," he said, clearing his throat, "could this be right? This is a courier job, not a military mission. We're a scout force. Do you really need us to do something this—easy?"

Cleitis frowned, but Harawe nodded. "Fair question. We'd send a courier, but this piece of hardware is of interest to many more than Central Command. We can't look too obvious going in for it, because we don't want to attract too much attention."

Daivid raised a finger tentatively. "Er, isn't a whole platoon of uniformed troopers going to look a trifle obvious and attract that attention?"

"Service personnel visit Wingle World all the time, lieutenant," Cleitis said impatiently. "Special discount for the armed forces. If any of those other interests show up, Central Command wants the escort to be capable of defending the item until the ship can return to orbit. A small force with a reputation like yours," he cleared his throat meaningfully, "is intended to be an extra piece of misdirection. You'll just look as if you're on a weekend pass. No one will figure you're there to protect a sensitive piece of hardware."

"But, sir—"

Harawe spun to glare at him. "Are you questioning Central Command's judgement, lieutenant?"

"No, sir," Daivid said with a sigh, trying not to look as pleased as he felt. "Just trying to clarify our assignment."

"Clarification: you're tasked with getting one single item. You drop outside of town. Don't damage anything. Don't draw attention to yourselves. You walk in, get the item, walk out and wait for retrieval in three days. Got it? And be inconspicuous. That's the most important thing. Your group showed itself to be resourceful during our battle with the Surgies. Keep your eyes open."

"Aye, sir."

Commander Iry stood up and pinned him with her stare. "This is an easy one, son. Be grateful. Do it right, get back here without incident, and your unit will be a part of the big push in the Benarli cluster."

"Aye, ma'am." Daivid did a little mental math. "Er, Commander, if we have any time to spare after we secure our objective, may we use it as personal leave?"

Iry let out a bark of laughter. "If there's any extra time, you can do whatever you want, as long as it isn't going to get you killed or thrown in the local slammer. If your troopers get arrested, you'll wait for retrieval until after the mission to Benarli. Now, shut up and let us get on with his briefing."

"Aye, aye, Commander." Daivid had to take that as the final word.

Iry reminded him a little of his mother. Not in any physical sense: Iry was a square, hard-assed woman who had come out of the commando units and Daivid's mother was willowy and elegant, and cultivated an air of gentle delicacy, but both Iry and Daivid's mother had seen thousands of young people in their diverse professions hung out to dry over the years, and had occasionally done the hanging themselves.

The dissatisfaction among the other officers grew palpably, but Daivid didn't hear a word. He found himself reading over the brochure again, losing track of the rest of the assignments the XO was handing out while he reveled in the moment. Wingle World!

"Hey, Wolfe," Bruno hailed him from the doorway as the meeting broke up. "Come on back to the mess with us. We ought to drink to your unit's good fortune."

Lieutenant Rindel seconded it. "Yeah. Come and tell us what's this secret that gives X-ray the inside edge on this mission. I'd heard they were a bunch of screw-ups." Not very surreptitiously, Bruno elbowed his jackal hard in the ribs. "Hey!"

Sensing a covert wedgie in his future, Daivid excused himself. "Thanks, guys, maybe later. I've got to go brief my noncoms and get an order of battle running."

A few of the other junior officers gave him a gesture that showed they didn't begrudge him his good fortune. Wilbury gave him a wry grin, but accompanied it with a thumbs-up. Daivid mentally noted the names of others he would have to watch out for for a few days. After that, everyone would be too involved in the job at hand to take time for petty grievances, though he would be the first to admit that it wasn't uncommon for payback to come around years after the initial event. All he could do was handle the assignment with efficiency, and deal with consequences later.

And what an assignment!

Daivid all but fled back toward his company's day room. He couldn't wait to tell the good news. For once, X-ray Platoon wasn't being given the scut assignment. No garbage, no hazardous materials, no inadequate numbers against overwhelming odds. Three days! They'd have plenty of time to pick up the item—Cleitis said it was small—then spend the rest of the time just enjoying themselves before lifting the shuttle to rendezvous with the *Eastwood*. He glanced up at the nearest screen and read the chrono. It was just before shift change. He spoke into his wrist-mounted communication link. "Lieutenant Borden, Ensign Thielind, Chief Lin, Chief Boland and Chief D-45, please report."

"Here." "Here, sir." "Aye." "Yes, lieutenant."

"Yo, what it is, lieutenant." Boland had a taste for archaic expressions. This one dated from a Terran period in between the seasons of courtly verbalizations and the precise compuspeak that heralded humankind's first space colonization efforts.

"We've got our assignment," Daivid said, hardly able to contain the gloating in his voice. "Meet me in the day room."

To his surprise, by the time he had arrived there, the entire platoon had assembled in the brilliantly-lit chamber, some of them still clutching cleaning tools and wearing their coveralls, face masks and boot covers. Of course, the enlisted troopers would have been with their squad leaders in the bowels of the ship. They were all curious where they were going. A normal unit would have stayed on station, waiting to be informed by their immediate superiors, but the Cockroaches was not a normal unit. Daivid was concerned that they might be coming to think of him as a chum, not a commander, a mindset that could prove fatal in a battle scenario. He decided not to make an issue of it then—in spite of the overpowering aroma of sewage. He was too wired.

"Sir?" asked Master Chief Lin as Daivid hesitated on the threshold.

He came in, waving the brochure. "It's a pickup and delivery mission," he said, knowing his eyes were glowing. "We are to make an insertion into a civilian location. Three days. Easy in, easy out."

"What's the location?"

"Dudley," Daivid gloated. "The item's in *Wingle World*. We have three days. Once we achieve our objective, the rest of the time's our own. They want to remove the *Eastwood* from sight while we're there, to avoid attracting attention. The XO assured me it would be a *minimum* of three days." He deployed the brochure, and the Ferris wheel rose in a welter of music. The Cockroaches stared at it.

"Wow!" Streb crowed. "Wingle World!"

"I spent my fifteenth birthday there!" Meyers exclaimed, her face pink with pleasure.

"I did my master's dissertation on its economics," Borden said, looking as excited as she ever did.

"I always wanted to go," Lin said. "It's nice of the Space Service to send us."

"The other officers are all jealous as hell," Daivid said, enjoying the looks on his troopers' faces.

"What's the catch?" Mose asked.

Everyone stopped talking. Daivid opened his mouth then closed it. The poet was right. It did sound too juicy.

"C'mon," the wiry trooper said, tilting his head skeptically to one side. "Mama didn't raise no fools, and I am pretty sure yours didn't either, for all you're as green as an emerald. What's the hangup? There has to be one. Never in a million years would they hand something like this to us if it wasn't a clusterfrax. Something's tricky about this. What is it?"

"I have no idea," Daivid had to admit, plopping himself down at the poker table. "I called you all here for your input, and it sounds like I need it. Let's sit down and figure this one out."

Daivid transmitted the briefing to all the units' infopads, and they started scrutinizing the brochure.

"Atmosphere is pretty normal," Lin said, reading through the meteorology reports encrypted in the 'travel agent' information section. "The planet's got a four-season year, like Earth, except that it's longer. Bigger orbit, but bigger sun, therefore closer in proportion. As a result, the part of Dudley where the park is situated has only about a one-month winter, but they get real snow."

"Gravity'll be nice," Ambering said. "It's .97 of Earth's, or just a little lighter than Treadmill. It'll be easy on the feet. Maybe that's why people enjoy going there. Muscles have less to haul around, so humans get a little extra spring in their step."

"Meaarow is a heavy world," Ewanowski pointed out. "I remember the first time I hit Earth grav in a ship. My buddies and I were bouncing all over the place. Now I hate going back, because my *grandmother* can jump farther than I can." He slapped his muscular thigh with a clawed hand. "It'd be a nice place to visit, but if I stayed too long I could never go home again."

"Oxygen mix is 1.025% higher than fleet standard," Borden added. "There are other trace elements, but the air remains pretty well scrubbed. I have read papers on the environmental strides that the Wingles have put into place. The park recycles not only its own water, but also that of the region for eighty kilometers in every direction, right up to the mountain ridges that surround the plain. Very impressive. I hope I can take a little time to ask the park engineers how they handle disposal of the effluent."

"What did you say about winter?" Mose interrupted, holding up a finger for attention.

"I said it's pretty short," Lin said, highlighting the section for everyone to read. "About a month."

"Have you ever known anyone who was there when it snowed?"

"Well—" Everyone thought about that for a moment.

"No, huh? Because no one ever is. Wingle World is closed during Dudley's winter, the whole month of Fimbul, local calendar."

Daivid pulled his infopad closer and stared down at the listing. "When is Fimbul, on the TWC calendar?"

Mose looked him solemnly in the eye. "It starts in about thirteen days."

"The whole damned park is going to be *closed* when we're there?" Boland asked.

"Slag, that figures," Ewanowski hissed, showing his fangs. "We're gonna spend three days slogging around in the snow looking at stuff that doesn't work. No midway games. No shows. No girls. Dammit."

Mose crossed his arms. "I told you nothing is as easy as it sounds in the Space Service."

Daivid felt as though he'd been hit over the head with a tank. The assignment had sounded so good. But it was time to face reality. "Okay, Cockroaches, would you rather be envied or laughed at?"

"Envied, to be sure," Jones said, collecting nods from the others. "We're almost always laughed at."

"Fine. Then no word of this little piece of information goes beyond the walls of this day room. Got it? We can take slag if they think we're getting something good, but we have a whole battle to fight alongside these units at Benarli. We can confess that the park was closed when we're back on board with Harawe's gizmo in hand, mission accomplished."

"Aye, aye, sir." Lin eyed him with respect. "You're smarter than you look."

"Sometimes it's useful for appearances to be deceiving," Daivid pointed out. "We'll catch less crap if they don't know what's really in store for us."

"You hear about them Cockroaches?" Supply clerk Milton Edgerton asked Bruno, slapping the lieutenant familiarly on the arm when he stopped into the main office.

Not only was the quartermaster's office an important hub for the spacers' equipment, but a central clearing house of ship gossip. Bruno had been known to drop in frequently to hear the latest or to start a rumor of his own. While he didn't rise to the level of the powerful lieutenant's circle of friends, Edgerton was an important link in his circle of power, and worth cultivating for that reason. For his own part, Bruno despised the pot-bellied spacer. Regretfully, Edgerton was not a short-timer, having at least twelve years left on his thirty, and had openly vowed to make them all, but he was useful. Bruno intended to keep him on board the *Eastwood* until he became too much of a pain in the ass to tolerate. Then, a quiet word in the ear here and there on circuits to which Edgerton did not have access, then no more hearty whacks or breathy wheezes that left speckles of nicotine pow stain on Bruno's pristine uniforms.

"I heard about them," Bruno said peevishly. "I can't believe it. Anyone with sense would have assigned a courier from the ranks of the *Eastwood's* crew. Why should they have taken on this bunch of dirtballers to do something any one of us spacers could do, and do better?"

"Ah, well, you know, don't ever risk a spacer when you can risk a trooper," Edgerton said, with a wise wink. "You and me is too valuable. Couldn't run the ship without either one of us, huh?"

Watch me, thought Bruno. "But this wouldn't be a risk. It's a piece of cake. Besides, rewarding them with three-day pass to Wingle World! You must have heard what those sick bastards did!"

"Everybody heard, lieutenant," the clerk replied, leering at him. "Played you dirty."

"It took me sixteen cycles to get the stink out of my armor. Giving them a walkover assignment like this is like telling the universe it's all right to make fools of your fellow spacers."

Edgerton shook his head. "It's not like they get the whole experience, lieutenant. It's the same as if they was on duty. No park hotel, with hot-and-cold running licensed characters. They still has to live in regulation quarters and eat regulation meals."

Bruno grinned evilly. "Yes. That, in fact, is why I came down to have a little talk with you, personally. They have pissed me off, and nobody pisses me off. You're in charge of dispensing those regulation meals."

Edgerton eyed him. "I can't short them, lieutenant. You know the rules: three weeks' rations for three days' assignment. Redundancy saves lives. They all get 21 days' worth of food, or I'm in trouble, and the mission might be scrubbed. It's not worth it."

"That isn't what I mean at all," Bruno groaned. Edgerton was more obtuse than usual. "The mission must succeed. Don't jeopardize the mission. I just want you to make their lives a little more— the same. Be *selective*." He leaned to whisper to the clerk, holding his hand so the security cameras couldn't read his lips. Edgerton listened, then guffawed out loud.

"Sure, lieutenant," he cackled, pounding a hand on the counter in merriment. "That won't hurt 'em a bit. Whatever you say. Always happy to help out a fellow spacer."

"I know I can count on you, Edgerton." Bruno swaggered out of the supply room with a big smile on his face. He was in such a good mood he didn't even call his aides on the carpet for imagined screwups for the remainder of his duty shift.

CHAPTER 12

"THREE DAYS," COMMANDER Iry had said as the shuttle eased out of the *Eastwood's* landing bay and fell in a gentle arc toward Dudley. Iry's voice was still ringing in Daivid's ears as sharp as the taste of Cockroach liquor on his tongue. Borden had explained the unit tradition of drinking half a glass of rotgut and leaving the glasses waiting on the table until they returned.

"That's the first part of the tradition," she had said. "It is superstition, I know, but it helps us come back."

"Is there a second part to this tradition?" he had asked.

"We don't do that until we get back on board," Borden said shortly, and Daivid knew he wasn't going to get any more information out of her.

Like Treadmill, Dudley looked pretty from space, but more like a watercolor painting than a mosaic. True, the wide brush-strokes of green were various kinds of marshlands, and the purple-blues decorated liberally with the whipped-cream white of cumulonimbus clouds betokened high mountain escarpments that slashed the continental masses into individual ecospheres surmountable only by VTOLs or hardy all-terrain ground vehicles, but it was much more interesting to look at. Daivid strained his eyes to see if he could pick out the province that contained Wingle World. The last time he had been fending off a water-gun attack by his younger sister at the time the family ship made orbit, and missed seeing what he saw now. Presumably nothing had changed, though that wasn't a sure thing any longer, not with current terraforming techniques and the amount of money that poured into Dudley's economy during the vacation season.

Lieutenant Borden piloted the shuttle. That was to say, she sat at the controls, ready to take over manually if the autopilot happened to fail. Like everything else aboard the *Eastwood* this craft, the *Carferry*, a smaller version of the one that had picked them up on Treadmill, was new and in perfect condition. Borden literally sat on her hands because there was nothing else she had to do with them. Beside her,

Adri'Leta acted as navigator. Both of them were clad in full armor. Daivid sat behind them in the jump seat, normally occupied by weapons control. The shuttle was fully loaded with a plasma cannon, lasers and a couple of missiles that could achieve string-drive speeds, though none of these were likely to be needed on this mission. The laser emplacements, to either side of the passenger compartment, were unmanned.

The rest of the Cockroaches had taken their places in the cushy crash seats behind the bulkhead that separated the bridge from the passenger compartment. In their armor, they blended in perfectly with the beige high-test upholstery as the chameleon camouflage pixels on the surface identified the objects behind each trooper and changed to match. It was like being the only person alive on a ghost ship.

Act inconspicuous, the commander had told them. Daivid's combat armor was in the cargo hold, but he wore a uniform made of microinfinitesimal impact-resistant plates that would spread the impact of a bullet or a blow, with a matte dark blue surface that gave some protection against laser weapons. He wore a clear helmet over a field officer's cap. One of them had to be able to do the talking without disappearing into the scenery and scaring the locals. He just hoped no one would ambush them and blow his head off. Some of the troopers had instantly gone to sleep, napping away the three-hour orbit-and-drop. A few of the others were playing games with the palmsized controllers that a clever military contracter had back-engineered to work with the suits' heads-up display, watching video, reading, or just shooting the breeze. Jones, Daivid felt certain, was making up a limerick he could deliver upon landing. If they were making use of the secondary function of their CBS,P webs, he didn't want to know about it. Their personal gear was stowed in packs that hung from hooks all across the ceiling like overweight khaki-clad vampires. *Carferry* was made to hold twenty-five passengers, so there were five extra crash seats, occupied by duffels full of gear.

The capacious cargo hold also contained little but 21 days' worth of MERDs (the mission was three days, but redundancy was the military's middle name), 23 one-being tents, the inevitable portabiffy and a frame-mount sonic cleaner, plus a box containing a portable big-screen crystal threedeeo unit with full surround-sound earbands for all, and a download of the latest cinematic extravaganzas. Now that they knew they had three days to kill beside a closed amusement park, the Cockroaches had argued for and gotten an entertainment center. Better that, Daivid reasoned with his superior, than subjecting the people of Dudley to a band of bored, heavily armed, visiting troopers. Everyone had chosen at least one vid for the collection. Besides the usual hardcore pornography, horror movies and action adventures, there were at least two unashamed classic sentimental weepers, half a dozen animated children's videos, some ancient Terran documentaries on dinosaurs, and the opera *Lucia di Lammermoor* performed in itter. Daivid wouldn't give extra points for guessing who had asked for that recording, but he would never have figured that the itterim liked opera. It just showed you couldn't guess someone else's tastes by talking to them. But it was clear that one trooper's favorite would make another one heave. That, Daivid decided firmly, just made it simple as to who would be on guard duty during which shifts. The number of selections in hours far outnumbered the amount of time they would actually be spending on Dudley. Chick-flick fans could march during the documentaries, porn fans could skip the weepers, opera haters had the option of listening to the sounds of the night sky while the itterim enjoyed his favorite 'mad scene.' He might or might not take a walk during that one himself. His mother liked opera, but his father always said it sounded like a family argument set to music.

"Why did dey say we couldn't land directly in de park, lieutenant?" Adri'Leta asked. He looked toward her, only certain of her location because of the signal sent by her implant to his heads-up display showing her ident number and the red heat signature of her body through the pilot's seat. "Begging your pardon, sir, but I dink it's a reasonable question."

"Security," Daivid shrugged. "No flyovers. It isn't allowed even by their commercial atmospheric craft."

"I think dey just don't want people dropping into de park ond gettin' in wit'out payin'. It cost too much. My friends came here wit' eight kids, dey practically needed a second mortgage to buy admissions."

"Eight!"

Adri'Leta shrugged. "Subsistence world. I tell 'em it's overpopulation, but dey tell me it's survival."

Dudley was anything but a subsistence world. In between the marshlands was higher ground. Daivid leaned over the external scopes and zoomed in tightly to the fields. The crops had evidently been reaped already. Only wisps of golden straw remained on the rich, black earth. You could grow anything in soil like that. Gravity was .97 Terran standard, the atmospheric mix was .1% greater in oxygen, and the two moons, one large and one a captured asteroid, rotated around at the rate of one Dudleian month, or 27 days of 27 hours each, providing slightly irregular tides. Daivid was grateful for Space Service timepieces, which displayed ambient ship's time, calculated local planetary time for their landing zone, and Terran time, which was the dateline for all official activities. On the ship's 30-hour day clock, it was 2800, the middle of the night; at Wingle World, it was three minutes past two in the afternoon; and on Earth zero meridian, it was five past four Tuesday morning.

"Automated landing instructions being received," Borden said. Daivid tuned his implant to the control frequency.

"…Please follow global positioning coordinates 30°15'27" north by 45°02'16" west from magnetic north," the mechanical female voice recited. Daivid glanced at the nav tank, which showed a rotating graphic of the globe passing underneath them with a grid overlaid. As they approached, the squares of the grid grew larger and larger. A blue dot flashed urgently from a spot in the curve of a mountain ridge as they crested the dayside of the planet. Daivid increased magnification of the light. It became a circle with the words "LAND HERE" inside.

"Duh," Borden verbalized through the mastoid implant, the better not to be overheard by the mission recorder.

"Remember," Daivid said, "they deal with tourists most of the year."

"That's right. I forgot, sir."

The ports darkened protectively as the shuttle dipped into the atmosphere. Skin temperature rose to over 1,500°, and the little craft juddered and bucked as it descended. Daivid leaned back and the seat's straps tightened around him.

"Dis is de only roller-coaster ride we get," Adri'Leta observed.

Daivid waited until the vehicle had come to a rolling stop before lifting his head out of the protective padding.

"Nice job," he said.

"Thanks, sir," Borden's voice said from the seemingly empty pilot's position. "I wish I could take credit for it."

He peered through the forward port, clear once again. Daivid saw neatly-manicured lawns, flower-filled gardens and rows of single-family dwellings. "It looks—suburban—out there."

"This is where the computer told us to land, sir," Borden replied.

"Not very rural, is it? I thought we were going to be out of town. Well, let's get this done."

"Aye, sir." A pair of faint outlines rose from the seats, shifting in color as the chameleonics compensated to conceal the two women's figures. Daivid opened the general headset channel.

"Open hatches. Troopers, rally at the bottom of the ramp," he ordered.

"Aye, aye, sir!" twenty-two voices echoed all at once in his helmet speakers. He winced slightly and lowered the volume of his audio pickup. The floor of the lightweight vehicle shook as the heavily-laden company jogged to the hatch. He followed the shifting forms of Borden and Adri'Leta. Thanks to the chameleon armor, he could see all the way to the hatch 'through' his troopers' bodies. The lights went green as the ramp unfolded itself and descended.

Bright sunshine and the song of a distant bird met them. The houses along the broad, shaded avenue had been painted or sided in bizarrely bright colors, jade green in between petunia pink and interstellar distress orange, across the street from cobalt blue, copper orange and grape purple. They were brighter than the gardens around them, which had been planted with autumn flowers of more somber cream, bronze and gold in dark green foliage.

To the immediate right of the shuttle was a drinking fountain, its arcing spray sparkling merrily. About fifteen meters away stood a slide, swings and a climbing frame in a sea of red-brown wood chips. They had landed in the local park. On the other side of the small ship a bronze statue of a man with a large moustache raised a benevolent hand in benediction from his stone plinth. A plaque at the base read, to Daivid's magnified vision, "Oscar Wingle, Visionary and Humanitarian." It was the only human figure around. The street and the park were deserted. It looked like an image in *Ideal Home* magazine.

"Nice," Lin's voice murmured over the main channel. "Reminds me of where I'll retire someday, if I ever turn into an accountant with three children."

Daivid took a deep breath and let it out slowly. This was it, his first mission with a company under his command. Now, to accomplish his objective and make his superiors and his platoon proud. "Fine. Squad leaders, squads into parade formation, weapons at low port. Audio frequency one, change to odds every ten minutes, up to nine and down. The number is fifteen."

"Aye, sir." The meager numbers formed into three rectangles of six or seven beings each, who blended in with the scenery as soon as they stopped moving. The one thing the suits couldn't do was conceal the shadows the troopers cast, so Daivid found himself inspecting twenty two black streaks coming in from one o'clock low.

He glanced back at the shuttle, squatting like a gigantic white pigeon in the middle of the park. "We can't leave that here. Commander Iry was more than specific about us keeping a low profile."

"What do you suggest, sir?"

Daivid racked his brain for any situation that he had ever heard of in officer training, in briefing sessions, or any time afterward about landing a shuttle in a suburban location in peacetime. There was none.

"We'll have to take it with us."

"Sir?" He couldn't see Borden's lifted eyebrow, but he could hear it. "What was that about low profile?"

"Well, er, we're going to have to bivouac somewhere for three days. We'll bring it to wherever we are assigned space to sleep."

"But, sir, the ship is a little hard to conceal. We can't take off and land it again. That will attract *more* attention, besides defying planetary government and Captain Harawe's instructions."

"We could just drive it where we're going."

"People are going to notice, sir."

"True—"

"Sir, permission to speak, sir!" The slender outline snapping a limb to the faint bulge in the air that must be its forehead had to be Thielind. Yes, there was his keycode on Daivid's display. "I can help, sir!"

"How, ensign?"

Thielind jogged over to the nearest tree. Daivid saw the flash of metal as the ensign drew his knife. With one resounding *whack!* Thielind chopped a dead branch and came back carrying it.

"Watch this, sir!" The branch began to twirl in the blurring hands. Almost of its own volition, it flew up into the air, turning end over end. Daivid saw out of the corner of his eye the shadowy figure before him turning a cartwheel and ending up on one knee just as the branch came down. Thielind grabbed for the stick, but missed. It hit the ground and bounced with a clatter. The hands picked it up and started twirling it again. The next throw the hands caught, and resumed spinning. A sheepish voice muttered in his ear. "Well, that's kind of what it's supposed to look like. This baton is heavier on one end than the other. I can lead us there, sir. This place is used to all kinds of parades. We'll just be another one, even the shuttle. Inconspicuous, see?"

"Very impressive, ensign," Daivid said, sincerely. "Keep up the good thinking. Let's do it."

"Hey, yeah," Boland's deep voice came over the link. More noises of approbation followed.

"You can't be serious, sir," Borden interjected, aghast.

Daivid turned to the ghostly outline of his second-in-command. "Why not? He's right. We couldn't look any more ridiculous if we tried. Why not shame the devil and bull it out by looking as though we're here on purpose? Where's Wingle World?"

A faint hand, shifting in color all the way, rose in front of his nose and pointed a ghostly finger. "That way, sir." At the same time, an indicator popped into place on the headset overlay inside Daivid's helmet. "I hope we don't need a permit to conduct a public display."

"We'll plead ignorance, lieutenant. If they fine us, we'll charge it to the Space Service. Right. Light burners and follow us. Trooper Adri'Leta, assist Lieutenant Borden. Boland, get a few of your troopers and unload the vid box. We may as well have music. Company right face! Forward, march!"

"Sir, aye, sir!"

With Thielind capering before them to the deafening strains of a march played by the entertainment center, which Boland's squad towed behind them on a hoverloader, Daivid led his platoon up the small street. The town wasn't actually deserted. As they passed each house, he glimpsed figures behind the huge front windows staring out at them. He turned and flapped a gloved hand at them.

"We've got an audience," he told the Cockroaches. "Wave to the nice people." The troopers followed suit, some with more enthusiasm than others.

According to the map, the town was called Welcome. It had been constructed in reclaimed swampland on a peninsula at the southmost edge of a major land mass. In the distant west was the expected massif of purple-blue with white glaciers frosting the top edge. A breeze was blowing from that direction, carrying a bit of the snow's chill with it. His temperature indicators showed 15°.

"Funny, I don't recall it being this chilly."

"It wouldn't be during season, sir," Lin pointed out, blowing kisses to a man who gaped at them from his porch. "This is what passes for winter in this part of Dudley. We might get rain or snow while we're here. You should ask Adri'Leta for telemetry readings on the current atmospherics."

At the sight of a trooper in dark blue leading three squads of ghosts and a movieola up the street, followed by a star shuttle hovering just off the ground, the man leaped up out of his chair, ran into his house and sealed the door, the front wall closing around it like a zipper.

"Hey, act inconspicuous," Boland chided her.

"Yeah?" asked Amberling, raising her voice unnecessarily over the blaring brass band music. "How?"

"This is the cleanest place I've ever been," said Mose, his head turning from side to side. "Next to this, the *Eastwood's* a slum. No offense, captain!" he added hastily. "I forgot we're being recorded for the mission report."

Daivid grinned. "I'll attest that you were overwhelmed by the pristine quality of our destination, Petty Officer Mose, and that in your efforts to be respectful of the locale, it momentarily robbed you of tact."

"Thank you, sir," Mose said, his voice filled with relief. A snort, probably from Streb, echoed in Daivid's other ear.

In spite of their initial protests, the Cockroaches loved being in a parade. They all shouldered their weapons and marched proudly, their occasionally visible silhouettes straight as a plumb line. The man who fled from the sight of them was a notable exception. Dudleyites were as curious as anyone else in the galaxy and not much more jaded. Out of the gaudy houses came parents carrying children who pointed at the invisible troopers and cheered when the Cockroaches waved.

At the sound of approbation, Thielind increased the complexity of his shenanigans. The stick soared into the air frequently, spinning end over end, and hit the ground only occasionally as Thielind's moves came back to him. Daivid could see the ensign's outline as the nimble little man turned cartwheels and did back flips up the street. Later Daivid would have to ask where he had learned to tumble like that. The crowd loved all of it.

"Well, Jones, I'm waiting," Daivid said. "You've got a rep to protect. Where's your limerick?"

"I'm thinking, I'm thinking," the hearty Cymraeg assured him. "Just working out the last syllables."

"I've got you now," said Okumede, cackling. "I'm ready now."

"Go for it, Oku," Lin told him.

Okumede recited. "'We're wandering around down on Dudley, For reasons best defined as muddly, We'll find out what gives, From the fellow who lives, With the critters who look cute and cuddly.'"

"Not bad, not bad," Mose said. "You've got messy scansion in line two, but you could say 'The orders they gave us were muddly.'"

"I suppose," Okumede replied, not sounding pleased to be corrected.

"Well, I've got one, too," Daivid said.

"*You*, sir?" Jones asked. Daivid could feel the eyes of the entire troop on his back.

"Me. Ahem." He cleared his throat, raised his hand, and declaimed. "To be stuck at this park out of season, Is a crime that equates with high treason. We'll go visit Wingle, And give him a jingle, And ask him what could be the reason?"

The platoon fell silent with respect.

"It scans perfectly," Mose observed. "Well done, sir."

"You get the points, sir," Lin said.

"Congratulations, sir," Okumede said, grudgingly. "It is better than mine."

"Three cheers for the lieutenant!" Jones shouted. "Oggy oggy oggy!"

"Oi oi oi!" chorused the rest of the platoon.

"Yes, sir," Daivid said with deep satisfaction. "It's times like this that I'm proud to be a Cockroach."

Borden indicated a change of direction, and placed an arrow to the right on the map in their visors. With a flourish of his makeshift baton, Thielind steered the parade around the next corner. The shuttle continued to float along behind them a meter off the ground, never getting a millimeter closer than it had been to start with. Daivid felt deep respect for the junior lieutenant's talent. Everything Borden did, she did with precision. He wondered what sin she had committed that would compel some commander to transfer that kind of talent out of a command. And he knew he wasn't going to find out until he won her marker. She was also a precise and careful poker player, who never bet more than she could afford to lose.

Word had spread of the impromptu parade. People were waiting for them on the approach road to Wingle World, crowding the curbs, standing on the roofs of houses and personal flitters, perched on fence posts and hanging from tree branches. One had to know they were used to spectacles of every kind, living next to one of the most famous amusement parks in the galaxy, yet they seemed to enjoy themselves as much as if they had one special event a year. Daivid wondered if this mood of innocence persisted at the other Wingle parks. He knew there were Wingle World outlets with a hundred rides or so on other worlds, but this was the original, the biggest, the most impressive of them all. A thousand rides! A dozen theaters! A live zoo! Three petting zoos! Restaurants that could serve a hundred thousand meals a day! Oscar Wingle VII had added to the wonder of the heritage left him by his eponymous ancestors by improving the cinema production facility here to the state of the art. Live threedeeo broadcast from here often made the Infonet entertainment channels. And yet the people who lived there were happy to show up to watch a parade consisting of one marching company and one float. Hundreds filled both sides of the road before the Cockroaches reached the gates of Wingle World. Which were shut.

Thielind caught his baton and waited for Daivid at the entrance. Intricately curled ironwork barriers ten meters tall and twenty meters wide filled a drive that was meant to accommodate dozens of vehicles at a time through the pink-painted walls embossed with the medallions featuring the face of Bunny Hug, Wingle World's most famous denizen. Daivid peered through the steel lace. Beyond it was a parking lot large enough to set down the *Eastwood* with room around it for every spacecraft parked at Treadmill. And unlike the town, Wingle World really was deserted.

"Halt!" Daivid called.

The crowd melted away as swiftly as it had gathered.

"Now, what?" Wolfe asked.

"Ring the bell?" suggested Thielind. He pointed to an oversized button mounted in an ornate brass plate to the left of the gates.

Daivid examined it with the scopes in his helmet. "I don't see any current running to it, but give it a try."

"Ewanowski," Lin ordered.

The semicat, huge in his armor, glided forward. He stretched up on his extended hind feet and pushed the button with one hand. They waited. And waited. Fifteen minutes passed. Twenty.

"Hail them, Borden."

Over the helmet pickup, Daivid listened to the pilot attempting to communicate on every frequency except the emergency channels. He stared through the gray lace over the vast pastel plascrete field to a distant fringe of color at the far end of unmagnified vision. No signs of life.

"Nothing," Ewanowski said. "No one's home."

Chief D-45 examined the big doors. "Has anyone tried them to see if they're actually locked?" Before Daivid could respond, the Egalitarian pulled at the right gate. Silently, it swung open.

"How about that?" Daivid said. "They must really trust the locals." Streb leaped forward to take the left gate. As they neared the walls the gates seemed to swing slower until they halted in place a meter away from the twinned faces of Bunny Hug.

"Magnetic clamps," Jones said. "Don't run your computers over those two zones."

"Or telemetry equipment," Lin added. "Those'd screw it blue."

"And plasma gun shielding," Boland added, cradling his big gun protectively. "If that magnet's strong enough it could rupture the protective envelope. Ka-boom!"

"Like the doctor said, don't do it," Daivid said reasonably. "Deploy point. Keep an eye out for anything unusual. Platoon, forward!"

Daivid almost laughed at his own order. What was an amusement park but a collection of unusual artifacts and activities?

Keeping well away from the outer doors, the Cockroaches shouldered their way in. Chief D-45 and the other sharpshooters fanned out in front of the marching troopers.

It took thirty minutes to march all the way from the gates to the entrance. Almost four kilometers, and the parking lot stretched more than double that in width. Once you calculated in the mass-transit arrivals and charter vehicles, you were talking about a significant number of beings arriving to take advantage of Wingle's legendary hospitality. A major hassle that none of it was in evidence at the moment.

Ten meters from the scarlet-roofed open-air building sheltering the turnstyles, Wolfe signaled with the flat of his hand to Borden to halt the shuttle. The hover drives shut down with a windy sigh, and the white craft extended landing feet and settled down on the pavement. Borden and Adri'Leta emerged and joined the others.

D-45's voice erupted in his ear. "We don't see anything, sir. No heat signatures, no movement, no nothing. Whoa!"

Daivid drew his weapon and spun. All of them found themselves covering a bright blue vehicle with the pink bunny logo on the side that appeared almost in their midst. It rolled up to the shuttle and threw a yellow-enameled hook around the landing gear. From old-fashioned looking conical loudspeakers on top of the car, a nasal voice blared.

"Attention, please, occupants of this vehicle. You cannot park here. It is designated for differently-abled beings only. Please show your DA license or move the vehicle. Repeat. Only differently-abled beings may place their vehicles in this location. It would be a grave discourtesy to leave it here. Please comply. Wingle World appreciates your cooperation. Attention, please, occupants of this vehicle...." The message continued to repeat, in full, growing slightly louder with each repetition, and the little car attempted in vain to tug the shuttle with its hook arm.

D-45 peered inside the dark glass of the windshield. "It's a drone, sir."

"Where the hell did it come from? This parking lot's empty!"

The Egalitarian pointed to a hatch that Ambering was covering. "It rose out of the ground, sir. There's a dozen more trap doors like that one. They're pretty well camouflaged and *very* well shielded. Sorry, sir. We'll be more careful."

"Attention, please, occupants…!"

Wolfe rapped on the top. "Listen, we just want to leave our craft here for a short time. We have an appointment with Mr. Wingle. I'm Lieutenant Wolfe with the Confederation Space Service. He's expecting us. Hey!" He pounded on the top. "Listen to me!"

"It doesn't have the facility for interaction, sir," Borden informed him. "Limited function only. We need to do something, or we'll have park security on our hands in a moment. That will be even less cooperative."

Daivid took his hand off the holster of his laser pistol. "Oh. True. I suppose those will be mechanized, like this drone."

"Robotic and efficient. It won't hurt you, but we'd probably have to blow them up to get them to let go of us, and that wouldn't fit in with Commander Iry's version of inconspicuous."

Daivid grinned. "What about the Cockroach version?"

"We'd strip it and sell it for parts," Boland said. "I could make a hell of a go-cart out of this baby."

"Attention, please, occupants…" The voice had reached rock concert volume.

"All right!" Daivid shouted. "Borden, move the damned thing. If this little noisebox has been sending a signal to the central office, we may finally find someone to talk to."

Snapping off a salute, Borden stalked up the ramp. In a moment the engines started up again. The shuttle, robot drone clinging to it, floated backwards until the automatic announcement ceased. The resulting silence was such an abrupt contrast that Daivid had to shake his head to clear the ringing in his ears. As soon as it set down again, the blue car dropped off like a sated tick, rolled back to the hatch, and sank rapidly out of sight.

"Hi, there!"

Daivid literally jumped. He looked down in amazement as a little girl appeared at his side. The platoon wheeled to cover her. She looked at all the heavily-armed shapes and smiled politely.

"D-45, I thought you were watching for intruders!"

The squad leader sounded chagrined. "Sorry, sir. My telemetry doesn't even pick up movement from underground. We'd have to punch holes in the shielding just to get an echo."

"Uncle Oscar wouldn't like that," the little girl opined. About eight years of age, she had fluffy pigtails of dark, rusty red hair and freckles across her nose. Her eyes were large, brown and twinkling with mischief. Her red dress was very old-fashioned, even antique, in design, with a round, little white collar and a big sash around her middle and petticoats to hold out the circle skirt. She reached up and took his hand. "You're here to see Uncle Oscar. I know. Come in and meet him. He's waiting for us."

"I know who you are," Daivid said, memory dawning. "You're Naughty Emma. You know I shouldn't do anything you say."

"Right!" the child laughed. "Welcome to Wingle World."

"How did she get here?" Borden demanded.

"Same way as the parking drone," Wolfe said. "Through a secret door in the ground. She's not real. She's a robot."

Naughty Emma wrinkled her nose. "You're not supposed to say things like that. I'm real. Well, sort of real. Come with me. It's safe. You're in Wingle World."

CHAPTER 13

THE COMPANY PASSED through the turnstyles, huge brass wheels that looked ornate and friendly, but were calculated to allow one-way passage only. Daivid tried pausing in the center and nudging his wheel back the other way, but it locked into place. It was in, or nothing. In the ceiling of the pylon, square sensor arrays scanned every person entering. They ignored Naughty Emma, but as soon as D-45 tried to enter with his plasma rifle, the turnstyle wheel halted, trapping him, and a discreet but urgent bonging began.

The android put her hands on her hips and pouted at the ceiling. "It's all right!" she scolded it. "Uncle Oscar said they could come!"

The noise died away with a disappointed moan, and the wheel came free. D-45 shoved out of the barrier and stood looking back at it with suspicion.

"Why didn't it stop me?" Daivid asked.

"Oh, you've only got a bullet gun and a knife. I scanned you. You could only shoot or stab one person before the protectors stopped you."

"Why wouldn't it want me to get rid of my weapons before entering the park?"

Emma beamed at him. "Well, you might not use them at all. We like to think the best of people. But *his* gun," she pointed accusingly at D-45, "is a Richards 203H model shoulder-mounted plasma cannon. It could clear a swath a meter wide and a hundred meters long. And the backwash might kill more people right around him. That would make just too much of a mess. Uncle Oscar wouldn't like that."

Daivid's eyebrows went up.

"I think the space service could take some lessons in security from your Uncle Oscar. Take me to him."

"All right," Emma said, taking his hand again. "Come with me."

They followed their little guide up the center street of Anyville. Though seldom featured in the many broadcasts and specials that originated from Wingle World, Anyville was the heart of the park. It had been the first part constructed by Oscar Wingle the First to give settlers on this world so distant from Terra a taste of home, though it was a home that no one living, even at that time, had ever seen. The cosy, warmly-colored buildings with their gingerbread cutouts lining the gables of the peaked roofs betokened a well-established, warm, peaceful town that stretched far back into humanity's origins. It seemed to strike a chord with other species as well. The sound coming over the open helmet channel from Ewanowski made it sound like the big semicat was purring.

Underfoot, the red-brown cobblestones made for unsteady walking, but Daivid could see how they were calculated to make one stroll leisurely up the lane instead of striding briskly and going too quickly past the attractions and, more importantly, the gift shops. Hoverchairs were available for small children and the handicapped, obviating the need for personal vehicles that ran on wheels or rollers.

The shop windows were empty, and the showrooms behind them were dark, but the street was exactly as Daivid remembered it. As if he had never left, he recalled every single detail of his previous visit to Wingle World. He looked around, summoning up memories of parades full of colorful floats, loud music, and the faces of rapt children looking up at the familiar characters who waved and joked with the spectators. If he glanced up he could see the big façade on the upper level of City Hall that featured Bunny Hug, the famous spokes-rabbit, looking down at them, the huge blue eyes in the pink and white face. When he was a little boy it made him feel safe and loved. Now, it was—

"Creepy," stated Meyers, interrupting his thoughts. "Look at that thing looming over you. Makes me think of the CO."

"Yeah. Same blank expression," said D-45 with a boyish grin.

"Why aren't there any people here?" Daivid asked their escort, who towed him along firmly, refusing to let him pause to glance at any of the rides.

They passed an interactive map that displayed every attraction in the park, scrolling the list so that every one of the thousand-plus items could be seen. As Daivid drew within a meter of the standard, it called out to him in a comforting female voice. "Hello. What is your name? May I suggest some things you would enjoy seeing, based upon your age and interests?"

"No, thanks," Emma said nastily, pulling him away before he could get a good glimpse. He ordered his helmet recorder to take a full image of it to peruse later. Might as well see what he would be missing. Surely Oscar Wingle would let them look around the place even if wasn't operating.

How oddly exposed it felt walking through the streets with no one else in sight. Even as a child he'd had the distinct impression that he was being watched. At least with fifty thousand people surrounding him he had the anonymity of the crowd. But what with face-recognition software he was sure that the security force could find him any time it liked. Wingle World had a reputation for reuniting lost children with their parents faster than almost any other facility in the TWC. Perhaps faster than the children might like, considering where they were, but no successful abduction had ever been carried out within the Cheerful Community. Children who had been momentarily separated from their families usually returned with an icepop or corn treats and tales of an underground city with nice people who reassured them, washed their faces and let them use the bathroom. Daivid longed to get a look at the security system for professional reasons. There must be a thousand spy-eyes either implanted in the facades and ceilings of buildings, or hovering around in the air disguised as balloons or other merrymaking impedimenta. But no people. Daivid waved a hand in front of Emma's face to get her attention.

"Why is it so empty here? Where is everyone? I would have thought this was the time that the park underwent maintenance. I'd have expected to see hundreds of people."

"In Fimbul? Oh, no," Emma scoffed. "Everyone on the planet goes on holiday all at once. The only ones who don't go are the ones who can't. Or don't like to," she added, thoughtfully.

Daivid looked around longingly as they left Anyville and moved into Future Land. Rollercoasters. Water rides. Parachute drops. Holoadventures. All of them temptingly near, and all of them closed for the season. Even more desirable, the food concessions hadn't turned off their threedeeo displays. Visions of meter-high sundaes and sauce-soaked sandwiches danced along the marquees of booths that were, disappointingly, also shuttered. He stared at a vision of steak-on-a-stick, trying to decide if he would have liked the selection with extra onions or not, when Emma poked him in the side.

"There's Uncle Oscar's place. Go right in."

Daivid brought his attention to the building she pointed at. Stuck into the perfectly green grass was a rustic wooden sign that read "The Old Inventor's Workshoppe." He *sort of* remembered the cottage, or he had seen it in crystal-threedeeo features about Wingle World. It was a tiny, plaster-walled bungalow with a roof made of fibrous bundles like sticks. The shutter-framed windows were very small, set deeply into the walls. They didn't look as though they'd let in very much light.

"That can't really be it," Daivid said. "He wouldn't really have his lab right in the middle of the park for everyone to see. It looks like straw and plaster."

"Don't let appearances fool you," Emma chided him. "That kitschy cottage is made of a supertough polymer. Resists wear, scratches, graffiti, even bullets. Uncle Oscar invented it himself."

"But he couldn't just leave the door open like that."

"Why not?" Emma asked. "No one bothers him."

"But you could just walk right in," Daivid protested, gesturing toward the open door.

On either side of the path, clay pots full of bright flowers perked up at the sudden movement and began to sing.

"Welcome, we bid you welcome! Welcome to Wingle World! Welcome, come one, come all! You'll get your turn to see it all, you'll sing and play and have a ball, So when you leave our gates we'll miss you lots, but we will keep you in our hearts. You'll want to come back...to Wingle World!"

Jones groaned. "That's terrible."

"Children like it," Emma said, imperturbably. "But it keeps any over about ten from wanting to go inside and visit, which is the way Uncle Oscar likes it." She opened the door and stood to one side. "Go right in. There's room for everyone."

Daivid glanced at the little cottage doubtfully. It looked as though it could only hold eight or nine people, which didn't leave much room for the Inventor. He had to bend over slightly to go under the lintel, but Emma was right: the room would hold them all. The sense of smallness was an optical illusion, a Wingle specialty. One by one the Cockroaches joined him, Lin and D-45 having to ship their plasma guns to make it inside. The inside was much like the outside, plaster walls and flower pots, a primitive fireplace with black andirons and a kettle on the fire. But the wooden floor was bare of furniture, let alone the presence of their host.

"So, where's Uncle Oscar—", Daivid began to ask, when the floor dropped out from underneath them. The entire platoon found themselves hurtling through a titanium-lined tube.

"You knew you shouldn't do anything I say!" Emma's voice echoed above them.

"Oh, slaaaaaagggg!" was all Daivid had time to say before he and all of his troopers landed heavily in a swimming pool-sized tub full of pads. Thanks to the armor, no one was hurt. Their highly trained reflexes got them out of the container and back onto their feet in seconds, weapons out and on guard. Daivid had his sidearm drawn in a flash as he surveyed the dimly lit room. There was nothing in it but the landing tub, and one furious company of space troopers.

"Goddammit!" Boland growled. "Now I remember that little fraxer from the kiddie shows! She was always getting people in trouble. And we fell for it! Literally! It's a good thing we're not fighting the lizards, or that goddamn Insurgency. We'd have been toast!"

"Serves you right," said a cranky voice from behind the tub. The lights brightened as Oscar Wingle the Seventh entered the room. The lined, sharp-chinned face with the wild gray hair, eyebrows and mustache would have been familiar to trillions of children throughout the galaxy. He and his many-times forefathers had delighted the young with their calm warm speeches, and their own pleasure in the entertainments they seemed happy to offer their viewing and park-going public. None of that placid hospitality was evident on this face. The deepset gray eyes with the avuncular crinkles at the corners were amused, all right, but definitely inclined to laugh at, not with, his current audience. Wingle was dressed in a coverall made of slightly shiny fabric Daivid recognized as being proof against fire and most known kinds of caustic fluids. He pointed a wrenchlike tool at them. "You said you knew not to trust her, and what do you do? You obey the first thing she tells you to do. Hah! Grown men and women falling for a trick like that. Literally, falling! I loved it! A kid wouldn't have listened to her. He'd have remembered the rule. You grownups, you just believe whatever you hear last. And what's all this about cockroaches? I don't stand for bugs in my park."

"That's, er, that's the nickname of our unit, sir," Daivid said, recovering his wits. "Lieutenant Daivid Wolfe, X-ray Platoon. My unit. The Cockroaches." He nodded briefly toward the immobile ghosts arrayed behind him. Wingle was unimpressed.

Wingle gestured with his wrench. "What in hellfire are all of you doing here in my park in the middle of the off season? Go away at once."

Daivid was faintly shocked. Wingles didn't swear. They told children it was bad manners to use bad language. There was even a song about it.

"Sir, I have orders from my commanding officer to receive an item from you, a controller chip. I have, er, no other description, but I am sure you know what I'm talking about. If you will just give it to us, we will return to our ship."

Wingle's eyebrows went up then down. "So, they didn't listen to me after all. Hear me now, you young scoundrel: *the chip is not ready yet.* I told your admirals that they could have it when it's ready. It'll be ready when it's ready! Did they try and hurry Michaelangelo? Did they try to hurry Leonardo da Vinci? Did they try to rush Paine Fitzwallace?"

In fact, their patrons *had* tried to hurry the first two in their endeavors, but the third was a stranger to Wolfe. "Paine Fitz—?"

"Inventor of the shields for string-drive starships," Borden murmured in his ear, using the implant channel. Wingle's eyebrows went up again.

"Right you are! Bright girl. And without even an electronically enhanced memory. Don't like thost things anyhow. But you shouldn't mumble. I can hear you fine, just fine. Technology's a wonderful thing."

Borden made a quiet noise of astonishment. Wolfe stared. Wingle shouldn't have been able to hear a secure channel.

The brows dropped once again. "Now, can you hear *me* fine? I told you to scoot. Come back when it's ready. I'll send a message."

Daivid opened his mouth to say that it wasn't so easy to get back there, that their ship was on its way to a war they didn't want to be late for, and Harawe would cut off his personal parts if he returned with a message like that. "Sir, I will have to check with my superiors."

Wingle watched the changes in his expression, no doubt reading his mind. "Never mind, then, boy. I'll do it. This way."

Weapons still at the ready, the Cockroaches fell in behind the old man. Wingle heard the click as D-45 automatically thumbed off the safety on his plasma, and glared back. "You don't need that here. Nothing happens here and nobody comes here without my say-so. You're safer here than you were in your mother's womb."

"Didn't have a mother," Adri'Leta growled under her breath.

D-45's head swiveled toward Wolfe, who nodded. The safety clicked back on, and the squad chief slung the gun strap over his shoulder. His squad, and the other two, followed suit.

The shiny steel walls of the corridor were strongly lit not only from above, but also from the tops of the walls. Triple shadows caused the chameleon coating of the Cockroaches' assault armor to go crazy trying to disguise itself. Daivid watched the play of light and dark on the backs of the squad ahead of him, though he kept his eyes on their host, who stumped along at the head of the parade. In his humble opinion, Thielind made a much better drum major.

The ensign, walking at his side, kept turning his head to stare at each new detail, overwhelmed with awe as each new wonder revealed itself.

"Look at that," he said over the private channel as they passed through a set of blast doors that opened without a single sound. "They didn't have anything that good on the *Eastwood!* Triple-shielded, hardened deuteronium layered with semiliquid dampening resin. They could stop a plasma missile."

"But it makes a hell of a mess of the floor," Wingle agreed. "Smart kid, aren't you?"

Thielind fell silent. "I forgot he could hear me."

"Tight-band transmissions," Wingle said. "I didn't invent it, but I perfected it. It's my technology you're carrying around in your head, and in your helmets, so of course I can pick it up just about anywhere. You think I wouldn't keep the master codes?"

Wolfe frowned. "Are you sure you ought to be telling us this, sir? If you're in possession of top secret technology, you're vulnerable to the enemy."

"They're not gonna hurt me," Wingle assured him, turning to look at him with the bushy brows on high. "Both sides want me to keep on doing what I'm doing, inventing things for them to use against one another. Me, I'm just having fun. Sit down, shut up, and don't touch anything."

This last was delivered as they crowded behind him into the room at the end of the long corridor. *Crowded* was the operative word. Though the space was over twenty meters on a side, it was jammed with tables, boxes, racks, scientific apparatuses, glass cases, cabinets, partial figures of some of the park's most famous characters (and some Wolfe didn't recognize) on stands, on tables and on the floor, and so much more that he was gawking just trying to take it all in. Wingle plopped himself down in a rolling armchair of ancient design in front of an old wooden desk covered with the most modern of communications equipment.

"Sit!" Wingle ordered. Concealed within the fascinating jumble were several dozen chairs. Most of the platoon followed Daivid's gesture to sit down, but Thielind began to wander, looking at some of the cases. Wolfe could hear him crooning to himself in the soft voice he used to talk to machines. This had to be his idea of heaven. The slender ensign came to a wooden cabinet with hundreds of small drawers in it and pulled one out at random. A hand came around the side of the cabinet and slapped him on the wrist.

"Hey!" Thielind exclaimed. Naturally such a blow couldn't hurt him through his armor, but the sudden movement surprised all of them. A pink-cheeked youth appeared from an alcove beside the cabinet and leered at the ensign.

"Good boy, Sparky," Wingle said over his shoulder. "Don't any of you fools touch anything! And take off those goddam helmets. I like to see who I'm yelling at. Why, look there. A bug. And a spider!" he exclaimed as Haalten and Aaooorru removed their masks. "I wondered about you, shorty," he said to the corlist. "Didn't know whether those were prosthetics or limbs. Don't see too many of your people lately. We get all kinds here. Gives the humans and non-humans a weird sense of belonging together when they interact with my critters. Big load of nonsense, if you ask me. Hello, kitty," he said to Ewanowski. "I always liked cats, but I'd hate to have your vet bills."

Daivid was flatly astonished. "This is the beloved Oscar Wingle, who makes all those appearances for charity? Who loves children? Who's known to have the patience of the saints?"

Wingle let out a bark of laughter. "Me? Hell, no. I had my fill of appearances when I was in my twenties. Marching in parades six times a day in the hot sun. People shaking your hand when all they

want is to shake your wallet. Kids puking on your leg, and having
their moms shout at you that it's your fault. Getting hammered from
the moral majority minority every damned generation that you're
corrupting the minds of the innocents when it's them that ought to
be legislated out of existence. *There's* the Oscar Wingle everyone
knows. Dudley!"

A light went on across the room, illuminating yet another niche.
Inside it, an exact duplicate of Oscar Wingle, to the last hair and
wrinkle, smiled and raised a hand to wave at the troop. He lowered
his hand and the light went out.

Wingle grunted. "He can put up with any amount of bull. I
made him that way. He's more advanced than any synthetic creature
that humankind or anyotherkind has come up with in over three
thousand years."

"He's an android?" Borden asked.

"A puppet, miss lieutenant. The jolly marionette that dances to
my whim. Didn't you ever visit my overblown establishment up
there? Hell's bells. Maria!"

From yet another dark recess that Wolfe now noticed were
cut into the heavy stone or plascrete walls came a silver-skinned
being. She was beautiful and terrible at the same time, a creature that made Wolfe think of a higher chord of humankind,
something they would evolve into in another hundred thousand
generations. Her longlegged figure stalked past him, drawing his
eyes to the gentle sway of her hips. The slender lines of back and
arms undulated like silk sheets hanging in a light breeze, her breasts
softly rounded, just waiting to be cupped by eager hands. And yet
above the delicate features of her face she had huge blank eyes,
plain silver with no whites, irises or pupils, like the ancient statues
of gods ten thousand years old that were still preserved in the
museums on Terra, and there were coin-shaped protruberances at
the sides of her knees and elbows, as if to remind the viewer that
what he was looking at was not human, but was she something
more or something less?

"Mmm-*mm!*" Injaru hummed.

"No lie," Parviz agreed, his round brown eyes fixed on the
swaying figure.

Wingle glanced over at her as though she was no more beautiful
than the battered and timeworn desk his elbows rested upon.

"Get these youngsters something to drink, Maria. Tea, or whatever the hell they want. Liquor closet has about anything you've ever heard of, and probably hundreds you have never heard of but are good at giving you a hangover. I like a little brandy, but it's too early for me. Help yourselves."

The silver goddess undulated over to the big wooden cabinet at the side of the room opposite the desk. Wolfe couldn't keep his eyes off the grace of her movements. Neither, he noticed, could most of his crew, but Thielind had the most avid gaze.

"She's amazing," he breathed.

"Prototype," Wingle said shortly, his long, gnarled fingers punching buttons on a communications console that looked old-fashioned, with its ornamented wooden case, but responded with the blinding speed of the newest units. He leaned close to the screen, peering at the logos that flashed by almost too quickly for the brain to acknowledge having seen them. "I invent all kinds of things the military wants to have. No one here knows about it, which is just fine. When I come up with something, I run the stats through my database to see if it has any military implications or uses, then I get in touch with the central government. If they want it, they buy it. If not, I sell it to someone else. I don't care. I've got plenty of money. Much too much money. Takes all the sport out of life."

"Do you play poker?" Boland asked hopefully.

"Shut up," Daivid and Wingle said at the same time.

The inventor leaned into the screen. "Hello? Is this the commander of that dreadnought up there? What's your name?"

In the three-dimensional display, the head and shoulders of a very young female lieutenant with her black hair in a complicated braid stammered. "Lieutenant Parr, sir. How may I help you? Er, how did you get on this frequency?"

"I damned well dialed it up," Wingle said, raising his bushy eyebrows. "Now, who's in charge up there? I want to talk to him, her or it, *mach schnell.*"

A plain blue and gray image of the Space Service emblem appeared in place of Lieutenant Parr's worried face, the graphic Daivid referred to as the "One moment, please" image. Bland music floated out of the speakers for approximately three seconds.

"Silence! Voice only."

The troopers' shoulders relaxed slightly. They all disliked the computer-generated music. A bureaucrat's favorite use was to keep an unwanted caller listening to it endlessly until he felt like getting around to responding.

Wingle must have had exactly the favored status he claimed, because Captain Harawe's face replaced the Space Service logo in under a minute.

"Yes, Mr. Wingle?"

"Now, you look like an intelligent being," Wingle began, settling back in his chair and fixing the captain's face with a gimlet eye, "so maybe you can tell me what part of 'it's not ready yet' your high-ups cannot understand? I've got this house party full of armored soldiers here to take it away, and I just told your superior officers not two days ago that I would let them know when they could come. And here you are, circling around this planet like a vulture ready for one of us to drop dead, scaring the hell out of the locals, and sending in a whole fighting force when all it would take is one single solitary messenger on an unpowered bicycle to pick this up?"

Harawe's dark complexion deepened further. If Daivid and X-ray Platoon could see him, he could see Daivid and X-ray. The goofy expressions on the faces of most of the Cockroaches except for Borden indicated that they were listening with deep and abiding pleasure to their stern captain getting a dressing-down, the likes of which none of them would ever in their careers be in a position to deliver or even to listen to under most circumstances. After a brief moment in which Daivid knew their eyes met, Harawe focused on Wingle, absorbing the diatribe without changing expression at all. They were going to catch hell for the liberty, Wolfe didn't know where or when, but Harawe was going to inflict some kind of punishment on them for getting to overhear.

At considerable length, Wingle ran down. "Maria!" he barked. The silver automaton was at his elbow in a moment with a cut crystal glass containing an inch of amber liquid. He took a sip. "Well, Captain, what are you going to do about this band of unwelcome visitors, eh?"

Harawe's face softened into an ingratiating but not obsequious smile. "Sir, I extend the apologies of the Thousand Worlds Confederation Space Service for inconveniencing you. I trust that you know how much we value your input..."

"Hah! Costs you enough," Wingle agreed.

"Monetary compensation is only a small part of the apprecia-
tion and esteem which we owe you," Harawe purred. "The galaxy
is that much safer because you choose to put your considerable
talents to work in its service. I know I never forget that. I am
equally certain that my superiors also know it. If you would put
down the premature arrival of my troopers as overconfidence on
the part of CenCom, I would be in your debt."

Wingle's face started to soften visibly under the rain of endless
praise. Daivid listened with growing admiration to the captain's
smooth patter. He had only seen the hardassed side of the *Eastwood's*
captain. No wonder Carmen Ti-Ya worshiped him. He was *good.*

"Well, there's no harm in thinking that might be the case," Wingle
began, in a calmer voice.

"There is also the matter that my ship is on its way to another
mission. Space is vast, and our route brought us here to Dudley at this
moment in our journey. I am sorry that it was inconvenient to you to
appear now, before you were ready. Do you think that you could
give us a better estimate on when the device might be available?"

Now Wingle was almost purring. "Well—the tests are beginning
to show some promise. I'd have to think about it."

In the tridimensional screen, Harawe looked patient but hopeful, not pushing the inventor a micron.

"Hmm—Get a few more of the tests finished, run the stats up,
knock out another prototype—Three weeks. No sooner. But I'll put
my reputation on an outside limit of three weeks."

"My ship is expected at our final destination within nine days,"
Harawe said. "This is a tricky time, sir. We know that other parties
are interested in this technology."

"Darned right they are," Wingle said with pride.

"With that in mind, I would like to leave my troopers on site,
to receive the item from you when you are satisfied as to its
completion."

"Do what you want. No one is going to bother me while
I'm working."

"Very well, sir. I appreciate your forbearance and your consid-
eration. May I speak to my officer?"

"Suit yourself, captain." Wingle slid away from the console. "You
heard the man."

Uneasily, Daivid sat down in the chair, facing the captain.

"You heard all of that, didn't you? Enjoyed hearing The Old Man handed a rocket?"

"No, sir!" Daivid exclaimed.

"Don't lie to me. I never trust a liar. You enjoyed it, didn't you?" The olive green eyes bored into his. Daivid hesitated. The captain thundered out, "I asked you a question, trooper! Answer me."

"Aye, aye, sir!"

Harawe's eyes narrowed, but one corner of his mouth went up. "Let's hear it from the rest of your platoon."

Daivid threw a wide-eyed look of exasperation over his shoulder at the others. "You heard the captain!"

"Aye, aye, sir!"

Harawe widened his field of view, staring at each of the Cockroaches in turn. "And you laughed, didn't you? Let's hear you laugh at The Old Man."

"Heh heh heh," was all Daivid could muster.

"*Do you call yourself a Space Service trooper?*" Harawe bellowed. "Let's hear some real laughter. Now!"

"Hah! Hah! Hah!" Daivid exclaimed, pushing every syllable up from his gut. The others joined in, every bit as insincerely, but the captain had them where he wanted them. He was all too keenly aware of Wingle's sharp eyes on him. Harawe's mouth quirked again and he nodded, his eyes hooded with amusement.

"*That's* better. I'd have laughed myself if I'd heard my captain chewed out like a schoolboy who blew up the chem lab. But as of now, the conversation I had with Mr. Wingle is classified at the highest level. You are not to discuss it with anyone outside of the platoon except for me. Understood?"

"Aye, sir!" Daivid said, snapping his hand up in a salute.

"Good. You are to wait for Mr. Wingle to complete his work, then secure the item and hold it for our return. Your objective is to prevent it from falling into anyone else's hands."

"As you say, sir."

"Good. Ask Mr. Wingle if I may have another moment of his time."

"I'm right here, captain," the inventor said. "I see we have the same ideas about keeping our emotions honest. What can I do for you?"

"My troopers will remain on Dudley while we complete our other mission. They are at your service in the meantime."

"Well, that's very nice of you, captain," Wingle said. "All I want is peace and quiet to finish my work. Not another thing. Oh, except for my remuneration. That, of course."

"Of course," Harawe agreed, politely. "Then I will wish you a good afternoon. Thank you very much, sir."

"Fine, fine," Wingle said, clearly bored with the conversation. "Have a nice war. See you later."

Harawe opened his mouth slightly as though searching for the correct reply, and decided none was necessary. The screen returned to its blue and gray graphic.

"Off!" Wingle ordered. The unit shut down, all its colored lights dying. "Well, that's that."

Daivid cleared his throat. "As our captain said, we'd be happy to help you in any way we can."

"Good," the inventor said, turning to face him. "Push off."

"What, sir?"

"Push off. Leave. Vamoose. I don't like people underfoot while I'm working. They ask questions, they get in the way, and they *touch things*. Sparky!"

The freckled youth snatched a small box out from under Thielind's curious hand. He shook a finger in the ensign's face. "Naughty, naughty."

"That's exactly what I meant," Wingle said, his brows drawn right down over his eyes. "Take a walk. All of you. I'll call you when I want you."

"Er, well, sir, you heard our captain."

Wingle turned to him, raising the shaggy brows high. "Yes, I did, but it's not a gift if I can't turn it down. I don't need your help, I don't want your help, and I would not like your help. Go away."

Daivid fumbled for words. "But what are we to do in the meantime?"

"Whatever the hell comes to your feeble little minds," Wingle said, waving a hand. "So long as it isn't around here. Sparky, show them out."

"Follow me," the young man said with a saucy wink. "I'll show you the short cut. Not the short-short one you took in. That's only one way."

With a final glance at the beautiful Maria, Daivid turned to go. Wingle sat down at a worktable lit by blazing blue-white lights at each corner, pulled a micromagnifier over his head and bent over a silver-blue apparatus the size of his palm. The silver automaton brought his crystal glass to his side.

"These tunnels run all over the park," Sparky said, gesturing at the echoing square metal tube in which the group found itself. "Oh, too bad, your sensors won't work in here," he said as Borden consulted his infopad. "The shielding won't let you use global positioning."

"How about proportional benchmarking?" Borden inquired.

Sparky gave her a brilliant smile not unlike Thielind's. "Smart lady. So you'll be able to figure out where *one* of the tunnels is. Or was. They move, you know."

Daivid put on his helmet to see if the young man was telling the truth. Sparky was right about sensors not being able to penetrate the walls. All he could detect was the section of corridor in which they were presently walking, along with twenty-two organisms, now that the heavy-duty blast doors had closed between him and Wingle's laboratory. Daivid did a double-take and counted again. Twenty-two?

He consulted the infrared scan, and confirmed the count. Of red bodies in blue armor aura, twenty-two. Of one blond, freckled youth with a cracked-coconut grin, none. He took the helmet off again.

Sparky was as quick in his movements as he was on the uptake. He sprang to Daivid and put his arm around his shoulder. "Don't tell anyone my secret," he said in a stage whisper. "My mother would be so distraught."

"What?" Lin asked, missing the point of the interchange.

"He's an android or something," Daivid said, gently peeling Sparky's arm off his shoulders. "Not a living being at all."

"Really?" the senior chief said, eyeing their guide. "He looks so real."

"So do you, sugar," Sparky said insouciantly, plastering himself on the petite chief's arm. "Supernova hot, if you ask me."

"I didn't," Lin said, extricating herself and putting her own helmet on to check Daivid's statement. "Not an android, sir. No onboard brain or motivator."

"Of course I'm not an android," Sparky insisted, showing all his teeth. "Androids are dull. Did you see Maria? Brain the size of a planet, and she's fetching drinks for the old man? How boring is that?"

"Well," Daivid admitted, "pretty boring, I suppose. Then what are you?"

"Puppet. The Old Man told you himself. In a long and honored line of Wingle puppets. I belonged to Oscar Seven's grandfather. There's the way out."

The corridor ended at a flat, featureless wall. Instead of opening a door in it, Sparky turned to the right and pressed both hands against a panel. A section slid away, revealing another tunnel that sloped upwards to the bleak sunshine.

"There you go," Sparky said. "See you guys in three weeks." He put an arm around Daivid and led him toward the top. Daivid tried to free himself, but the puppet was astonishly strong. Probably made of some of the same polymer as the cutesy cottage upstairs. He let himself be guided up and found himself five meters from the ticket kiosks outside the park.

"And you'd better take your shuttle with you. The parking droid has already figured out you came in without paying. Bye!" Sparky waved to them from the ramp. A panel of the parking lot closed over the tunnel and set seamlessly into place. Wolfe admired the precise construction. If he hadn't known the door was there, he would never have seen it.

"Well, sir," Borden began. "What do we do now?"

Wolfe glanced around. He fastened on his helmet for warmth. The sun had retreated behind stratus clouds, leaving the sky a sheet of dull silver. Somewhere far beyond that, the *Eastwood* was on its way to the Benarli cluster and a glorious pitched battle. The shuttle was surrounded by a cluster of blue and pink parking droids, all shouting unintelligibly at it.

"Well, first, we move the ship."

CHAPTER 14

HARAWE'S ORDERS HAD been very specific: they were not to let Oscar Wingle out of their sight. They had failed in that first objective.

"Then we need to stay within sight of the park," Daivid reasoned. "If Mr. Wingle needs us, we'll be able to respond within moments."

The map Daivid had been provided in Harawe's brochure showed only the interior of the park, with every ride indicated as an interactive touch spot for further information (and appropriate sound effects). As for the perimeter of the park itself, information was provided only as it pertained to entering and leaving a vehicle. It omitted dead areas like the narrow side paths through thick shrubbery to nondescript doors the employees used, and the recycling center at the rear of the thousand-acre enclosure. Access was provided by a wide road and a very utilitarian-looking gate. All the rest of the walls were separated from the surrounding residential neighborhoods by a broad moat ten meters deep.

"And the top of the walls are electrified," Injaru pointed out, sharing a reading from his scopes on their heads-up displays.

"Nice," Daivid said, admiring the safety measures, as aboveground security kiosks lit up in red along the perimeter and in several places within the park. "I think Adri'Leta's friend was right about the Wingles not wanting any nonpaying guests."

"It looks as though there are only six ways in or out of the park, except for by air," Borden concluded. "Only two of those entrances are obvious, and this is the other one. It seems like the best alternative to staying on site, and the old bastard won't let us."

"Garbage again," D-45 grumbled. "Just when I was getting used to the fresh air."

The air became fresher still as they set up camp. Three of the Cockroaches stayed in their armor to patrol the perimeter, but the others changed into fatigues to pitch shelters and set up the entertainment center, and noticed the change in temperature.

"Brrr!" Thielind said, emerging from the shuttle bay in his string vest and swim fins. He looked up at the steadily graying sky. "I smell snow."

"That would suck," Boland said.

"I noticed a bar about three blocks from here," Jones said hopefully, unrolling another personal shelter. He kicked the valve, and the tent inflated in seconds, creating a double-walled hut two meters high. "We could get warm, have a nice drink and get to know the locals."

"No," Wolfe said, picturing the platoon let loose upon a world that was accustomed only to clueless tourists and endless children. He dreaded to think what kind of trouble the Cockroaches could get into. "We're on deployment. It's only three weeks, people. We can entertain ourselves for that short a time."

"I should have brought more booze," Boland muttered.

As if on cue, the wind whipped up. It had the sting of ice crystals in it.

"You're not going to make us sit out in that, sir?" Parviz asked. "Do we have to set up the field disposer or the sonic shower out here? I'm not crazy about baring my ass in this wind."

"No," Daivid decided. "The shuttle has plenty of capacity and power. We'll sleep out here, but use the facilities inside. Let's move the stuff around in the cargo bay. If we pile up the supply boxes two deep it makes a pretty good table. After we eat, we can play cards and watch threedeeo. If we secure the unit to the wall in the seating area of the shuttle, it'll make a very comfortable theater."

"I can do that," Thielind spoke up at once. "I need two volunteers to help me."

"I will," Ambering said. "First dibs on picking the movie."

"I'll help, too," Nuu Myi grinned, showing her big square teeth. "Second dibs."

"We'll take care of this, lieutenant," Boland offered as they surveyed the heaps and stacks of code-stamped military-issue containers full of food.

"No, we'll all help," Daivid said. Noises coming from the forward compartment told him Thielind and his assistants were having a hard time maneuvering the heavy crystal ampitheater box onto their makeshift brackets. He scanned the room, picking out the two "dragon" armed scout vehicles, the heavy artillery weapons, and other things he couldn't recognize under tarpaulins. If they pushed most of the equipment toward the back of the bay, there might be a fair amount of dead space. "Won't we, Borden? The sooner we get this place rearranged, the sooner we can eat."

"It's okay, sir, really," the noncom insisted. "Officers don't have to haul ass like the grunts. It's our job."

"We all have to pull together, Boland," Daivid pulled one of the handlifts off the wall and shoved the lip under the edge of a stack of black crates each containing twelve boxes of caseless ammunition for the direct-fire infantry machine guns. Borden took down the other on that wall. Boland stood in the middle, looking a little helpless. "Well, don't just stand there. Snap to it!"

"Aye, aye, sir," the chief said. He clicked a control on the side of a tripod-mounted grenade launcher. The weapon heaved itself up five centimeters onto wheels that would allow it to be steered with a fingertip. He did the same with the slightly larger artillery weapon known as the 'twinkie gun' because it shot yellow brass-cased cartridges that burned off, sending a white core of depleted uranium at its target. Daivid shifted his load of boxes all the way to the wall. Boland steered the guns into the gap where the boxes had been.

"Chief, what are you doing?" Daivid asked.

After two evasions and a direct roadblock, he definitely smelled a deceased rodent. He tried to see around the chief, who dodged the same way he did. Daivid finally feinted to the right and ducked under the big man's arm.

There was a draped shape that he couldn't identify as any kind of military vehicle at all.

"No, sir!" Boland protested as Daivid swept off the tarpaulin.

The lieutenant stared down at the machine revealed. It took his brain a moment to slot into place what he was seeing and the last place he had seen it. His heart sank, and he sat down on the nearest packing crate.

"Oh, no. Not the captain's flitter!"

"I can explain, sir," the chief said hastily. "I mean, they were going to set us here for three days without any transportation except the dragons, sir, and we were going to have all this time to kill— Civilians don't want us driving tanks into town, sir. Remember, we're supposed to keep a low profile?"

Daivid regarded him bleakly. "Which we can do with a stolen flitter? What did you plan to say when Harawe noticed it was missing?"

"Oh, he won't be using it for a long time, sir! He's on his way to the battle zone. By the time he's ready to go on leave, we'll be back on board. I can…break in the engine for him," Boland added hopefully.

"I'm sure he wanted to break it in himself," Daivid sighed. "I'll try to explain it when we're back aboard, once we've completed the mission and everything's gone well, but it does not leave this hold. Do you understand?"

Boland echoed the sigh. "Aye, sir."

"Let's clear a space," Daivid said, looking around at the others. "What are you all doing, eavesdropping on a private conversation? Come on, I'm hungry!"

"This is pretty good," Lin said around a mouthful of mixed noodles, proteinoids and vegetables. "What did the label say?"

"Chop suey," Meyers read off the label. "Very nice."

"The fellow in Supply said it was the newest meal in the system," Daivid said, slurping down pleasantly salty bean sprouts and bamboo shoots. Fluffy golden and white grains provided a bed that soaked up the brown sauce.

"Millet," Borden identified the round grains. "Rice. Barley. High protein, high lysine, and low glycemic index."

"It's good. I could eat this again."

"Me, too," Streb said. "And I don't even like vegetables."

Military Entrees, Rapid Deployment, had a bad name among troopers on long assignments. Whereas the square black plastic packages took only ten minutes to reconstitute, heat, cool and serve a complex and nutritious meal suitable for lunch or dinner, the menu choices were frequently less than edible. Somewhere along the line it had become more important to the manufacturers that the MERDs packed well and kept, often for years at a time, than to make sure the end user, a month or a decade after it was made, ate it or threw it away and subsisted on local vegetation instead. Students of ancient language often brought up the similarity of the acronym to an ancient Terran swear word, and commented that it couldn't be coincidental. A great deal of political pressure by senators whose constituents sent them samples of MERDs had caused a shakeup in the last few years, resulting in food that was not only recognizable but tasty. Daivid was fond of the vindaloo meal, a hot and spicy entree, and teriyaki, a sweet dish. They were also great combined, a tactic troopers frequently used in the field when the available varieties began to pall.

All of the protein-heavy entrees came with a healthy serving of a low-glycemic carbohydrate that would sustain a trooper through a long day's fighting. To satisfy a military that comprised hundreds of cultures and many different dietary needs, the proteins were vegetable-based, but still fulfilled all the nutritional needs of carnivores. An adjustment before deployment pureed the contents for the use of such creatures as corlists, who subsisted on plankton in their home environment. Aaooorru signalled his approval of the meal with eight thumbs up. Hot and cold drinks were also provided. The hot containers, which could be set to dissolve one of a variety of tablets that reconstituted as one's choice of teas, coffees, or grain beverages, drew water from the surrounding atmosphere, purifying it if necessary. The cold beverage container did the same thing with fruit juice. A side packet featured utensils, spices, condiments, sweetener, creamer, hot sauce, nicotine and theobromine pows, and an after-dinner mint, all of which, except for the utensils, could be combined in a pinch to produce a palatable soup. Breakfast entrees were in smaller, green plastic containers.

When the MERD bowls had been scraped empty, two of the troopers hauled them outside into the recycling area. Thielind led the way with a field light. He had spotted an external access hatch that would enable them to use Wingle World's system.

"He knows we're here," the ensign had reasoned. "Instead of making us pack it out, we can get rid of our trash here. Does it really matter if it's recycled on board ship or down here?"

Daivid removed a deck of cards from his duffle and began shuffling it.

"So, who wants to try their luck?" he asked invitingly.

"I'm on second patrol," Ewanowski said. "I'll watch a show. Anyone else?"

"I'm with you," Boland said. His face still went red every time he glanced at Wolfe. "How about *Creeptown: The Ravaging*? I hear it's got lots of blood and gore."

"I'll try Lady Luck," Jones said.

"Me, too," Lin said. "I don't feel like sitting still, but I don't want to go out in that snow. What's it look like?"

Borden consulted her infopad, which was tied to the telemetry systems of the shuttle. "Over five centimeters already. The atmospheric pressure is dropping. It will probably snow all night."

"Slag," Vacarole spat. "My people live in a desert. I never slept in ice until I joined the service. I'm in."

"Me, too," Nuu Myi said, sitting down at the makeshift table. She held an amulet that hung on a string around her neck under her uniform. "Good luck to us all. Amen."

"Do you know how much it suck being a clone?" Adri'Leta asked bitterly, as the cards went around again. She had lost her marker to Daivid in the eighth hand. With good grace, she didn't wait to be prompted to pay it off. In fact, it seemed as though she had been dying to tell her story. "Everybody in de galaxy expect you to know everything your predecessors know. Bull. When Fifteen died, I wasn't born yet."

"Do you get anything for being next in line?" Lin asked. "An inheritance?"

The trooper tossed back her thick red hair and blew out her lips in disgust. "Hah! No. I'm more like a thing den a person. I'm a legacy. Dere's a foundation to maintain the genetic pattern. It don't matter what I look like, 'cause I don't look nothing like de ones who came before. Dere's so many genes in de cells, de variations just happen, you know? When I die someone supposed to send a piece of me back to dem. *Dat someone* get a reward. Dey don't care what I do, or what happen to me, so long as de genes of Adrian and Leta Krumbacher keep marching through de galaxy." She appealed to the others at the table. "Do me a favor? Don't do it. Just bury me or burn my body. I think it too stupid to go on. I always say I joined the service to die. Why didn't dey just have children de old way?"

Daivid cleared his throat. He handed the cards over to Jones to shuffle. "Well, you know the regs, trooper. If your wishes are set down in your official records, the service has to follow them. After all, the foundation's not enlisted in the space service. You are. They will follow your instructions for the disposal of your remains, if it's at all possible, along with any religious service you want performed. *I'll* follow your instructions."

The clone's face brightened. "Really? No one ever told me dat. De brass just see de number after my name, and end of discussion. You're de first one who say he'd do what I want. Thank you, sir. I follow you anywhere if you promise dat. Twenty bid."

"Well," Daivid said, with some embarrassment, "no one knows better than me, and Lin," he included the senior chief in his nod, "about having to deal with being descended from a notable family. But the law is on your side, I'm almost certain. See and raise thirty more."

Borden cleared her throat as she arranged her cards precisely in her long fingers. "You are correct, sir. Except for ancephalic genetic simulacra who were engendered for organ replacement—and it still happens in spite of the penalties—the wishes of the living being supersede those of a nonliving entity, such as a corporation. Raise sixty."

Daivid threw a hand toward Borden. "There you have it. I wouldn't argue with her."

"Fifty more," Lin said.

"And twenty," Vacarole said, tossing in the cash. Nuu Myi dropped out.

The others waited. Daivid glanced at his cards. Three threes was a medium-good hand. The others were bidding pretty heavily. The odds were against all of them having hands superior to his. They couldn't be so bored that they were risking all of their poker money on a single game when they had three weeks or more ahead of them to kill. They were setting him up to lose! They had obviously arranged among themselves to up the bidding until he had to drop out or risk a marker. *We'll show 'em, won't we, Lady Luck?* he thought.

But Lady Luck must have wanted him to lose a marker that night. Lin won the hand, but only by a squeak, three fours against his threes. The hands that followed were little better and sometimes much worse. Even when he shuffled or dealt the cards himself, he got hands that were mediocre at best. And when the others noticed he was bidding a hot hand, they dropped out. They supported the bidding on one another's hands, forcing him to drop out or pay too much to call poor hands. With a sigh, he resigned himself to fate.

Vacarole clutched his cards, spitting out a spent nicotine pow onto the floor. "Two hundred," he said with a gleam in his eye.

The others seemed to hold their breath as Daivid looked over his bank. With a blank expression, he tossed in a marker. The bidding got more hot and heavy. Daivid's hand was good, but Vacarole held onto his cards with tight fingers. He might win one of the lieutenant's secrets, and he was going to go to the bitter end. Daivid was afraid his hand—good but not great—wouldn't beat it. He felt fortune deserting him away. He tried to believe in it, but he had a vision of the shining lady in green lace patting him on the head.

Not every hand's a winner, she whispered to him before settling down on Vacarole's lap with an arm around his head, playing with the dark hair that curled over his ears. When the bidding returned to Wolfe, he threw in his hand. "Fold," he said.

The big man clapped his hands together in pleasure. He pulled the chips toward him, and held up the marker. The others applauded.

"I didn't think it would be you, my friend," the Cymraeg chuckled. "What'll you ask him?

"Ask him, why did you join the army?" Adri'Leta suggested.

"Where'd you get that pistol?" Jones asked.

"No, I want to know how rich his family is," Streb said.

"Have you ever killed anyone yourself?" Nuu Myi asked, her straight black brows pulled intently down over her eyes. "I mean, not in the line of duty?"

"Does your family really knock off rivals like targets on a wall?" Meyers asked, only half kidding.

Vacarole nodded his head firmly, a question finally taken shape in his mind. He opened his mouth to speak. Quick as lightning, Lin leaned over the table, threw three hundred credits onto his stake, and grabbed the plastic marker.

"Hey, chief!" Vacarole exclaimed.

Lin paid no attention. She held out the marker to Wolfe and stared him straight in the eye.

"What's the card stuck to your chest?"

"What?" Daivid asked, feeling as though he'd been shot. His hands trembled suddenly, and he pressed them hard into the tabletop.

Lin kept the intent stare drilling through him. "We all saw it when we suited up during the pirate raid. I've never seen it before.

You know we've been through everything else you own, so you have been pretty careful about keeping it where we can't find it. It's got to be something special, and my curiosity is killing me. What is it?"

Daivid's mouth was dry as salt. He'd forgotten all about the database in the heat of battle, and since no one had mentioned seeing it at the time when he had stripped off to put on his websuit, he had assumed no one had noticed it. He took a swig of liquor, which burned his throat. "Is that what you're asking me? It's really Vacarole's chip. My debt is to him."

Lin shifted the stare to the trooper. He shrugged. "What she said, lieutenant. I think I'd like to know, too. I mean, it's kind of strange. You know, people usually just keep valuable stuff in a safe."

Daivid flattened his hands out on the table and pushed himself upright. "Well, I won't tell you what that card is. It's personal. And if anyone tries to meddle with it, I'll show you some of what I showed today. You leave it the hell alone."

"You can't say that," Lin argued, her eyes alight. "You swore on your honor that if we won one of your markers you would tell the truth. That was the grounds you gave us for trusting you with our own histories, and you can tell how painful it's been for some of us to talk about those. We have told you the truth. I demand that same truth from you."

"All right," Daivid said, knowing he'd just been strangled with his own tongue. He slumped into his seat. With unsteady fingers he undid the front of his tunic and peeled the card loose. His hand was extremely reluctant to let go of it, but he set it down on the table. "There it is. My father gave it to me before I left home. He wouldn't let me leave unless I took it. It's a database of—some favors that people owe my family."

"Holy crap," Boland breathed, staring at the little card. "That's power. *Big* power. You can get people to do anything you want. I mean, anything! How's it work?"

"I don't use it," Daivid said. "I've been in the service for three years, and I have never called in a single favor. I don't *want* to use it."

"You're kidding!" Streb said, his fingers arching as he gazed at the database. "I wouldn't be able to resist it. Do you know how easy you can make life with that?"

"It's *not* easy," Daivid retorted, regarding Streb with horror. "You don't know what those favors cost. Sometimes just a person's pride, but sometimes the lives of some very good people are lost."

"We won't mess with it," Lin hurried to assure him. "But you've got to realize that you've already lived with us a month, and we thought we'd scoped out all we could discover about you. You're a surprise, sir. That's a compliment."

"Holy crap," Boland repeated, his voice gravelly. "You better put that away, sir. You don't want that falling into the hands of unscrupulous people."

Daivid gave him a wry grin. "There are those who would lump all of you into that category, chief."

"Back at you, sir. You're not with us just because they want you to reform us. But we do have scruples. They just might not align perfectly with the rigid mores of the jerks who've messed up our lives. They're a whole more like yours. You believe in debts of honor. So do we. Ask those politicians if they've ever let anyone down who really needs them."

Daivid lay on the temperature-control mattress in his tent, staring at the inflated fabric shell, listening to the hissing of heavy snowflakes hitting the roof and the crunch-crunch-crunch of the feet of the troopers on perimeter watch. Borland warned him that, since the axial tilt of the planet was so extreme and the season was so short, winter was going to be very intense. They were going to be up to their bellies in snow.

He shifted and crossed his arms behind his head. Boland's little speech had touched him. He *hoped* he was getting through to the Cockroaches. He wanted them to believe he supported them, that if he ever had to lead them into a dangerous situation they should know they could count on him to get them out again. This unwanted unit, which had proved over and over again that appearances could be deceiving, was not unwanted by him. He hoped that the evening's revelations meant they were opening up to him. He had never felt so vulnerable in his life.

A twanging sound and a muttered curse interrupted his meditations. He wrapped a blanket around himself, stuck his feet into his boots, and pushed open the self-sealing tent flap. The sentry, a wavering outline against the acid yellow street light, shifted slightly as if turning to look at him.

"It's the streetcleaning 'bots," the ghostly figure said. Daivid recognized the voice as Meyers's. "We're on their assigned route, so they keep running into our protective perimeter, sir."

Daivid came closer to see a low rectangular mechanical with its front scoop stubbornly pressed against the invisible energy barrier. Meyers pointed around the plascrete square at three other 'bots also determined to push their way through the unseen obstruction. A six-limbed shadow that had to be Haalten regarded one of them. Daivid couldn't see the third sentry, who was probably behind the shuttle.

"Well, regulations say we have to leave that in place," Daivid shrugged. "If we open it up every time a cleaner comes through, what good is it?"

"If we don't do something, it'll go on all night, sir. It sets off the alarm in my helmet and on board the shuttle. Can't we set up a signal or a beacon or something that tells them to ignore this zone until we leave?"

Daivid snapped his fingers. "Good idea, Meyers. I'll get Thielind."

The ensign's tent was on the right side of Daivid's, opposite Borden's shelter. He popped out into the winter night to see the problem.

"Poor little things!" the ensign exclaimed. "Sure, sir! Piece of pastry. They look like the bigger version of the ones in our barracks. If they respond to the same set of signals as the 'bots the service buys, no problem. The encoding's password protected," he explained as Meyers opened the perimeter. "Come here, little one." He popped open the back hatch and started to work the controls "But you can program it by using the factory specs, which no one *ever* resets."

"Cold enough for you?" Wolfe asked the ensign, who was wearing his usual string vest and a pair of shorts. Daivid was freezing, even in the sensor blanket, whose fibers read the body temperature underneath and thickened or thinned accordingly.

"A bit chilly. Not as cold as my homeworld." The slender ensign smiled brilliantly up at Wolfe, who had settled himself to listen intently. "I think what you're doing with the others is smart. I have no problem telling you about my life, so ask any time. We live right on the tundra. That kind of wilderness you can't keep flesh-and-blood pets, so I got to like machines. They like me, too. I have parents and one sister. We're happy."

"I've got three sisters," Wolfe said. He glanced out into the darkened street beyond the yellow square of the recycling center. "It's so quiet here. You would never think that we're in the middle of a resort town. In season there would be a million people or more having a good time."

Too quiet, he realized, standing up. At least half a dozen of the troopers snored, as he knew from sessions in the day room. Troopers who weren't playing cards or watching vids or pursuing other hobbies usually slept, and a few of them rocked the room with their somnolent vocalizations. He tiptoed over to one of the tents, peered in through the flap. The tent was empty.

Well, Daivid reasoned, the trooper had probably gone to use the disposer in the shuttle, or just couldn't sleep and wanted to watch a video. He checked another tent. Then another. They were *all* empty. It was then he observed the footprints in the gradually accumulating snow around the dark gray shelters. The prints didn't lead toward the ship, they led away, towards town.

Suddenly, he remembered earlier in the day that Jones had mentioned a bar a few blocks away. Damn them, he gave an order to stay by the shuttle! Or, he mused, stalking back towards his own tent, whipping his blanket around him more tightly against the wind, he didn't give an order, he had just made a statement without giving it the force of an official order. With the Cockroaches, that omission gave them all the leeway they wanted to bend a rule. They'd waited until he fell asleep then went off to the bar. It was clear the tender speech Boland had made had been meant to soften him up. Well, it didn't work. Wait until he got his hands on them! He *knew* he was letting them get too familiar with him. The instructors at OTS had been absolutely right. That was going to stop at once.

Loud humming approached from over a building. A brilliant light glared down at him, spotlighting him like a lounge headliner. Heedless of the snow, Daivid dropped and rolled out of the beam, belly-crawling toward his tent. He was just reaching for his sidearm when the craft dropped, and a peeved male voice called out to him.

"Are these yours?"

Daivid stood up, skin, underwear and boots crusted in snow, his blanket hanging over one shoulder. The craft touched down beside him, and a large man in a dark blue uniform jumped out, holding Streb by the elbow. "You Sergeant Wolfe?"

"Lieutenant Wolfe. Lieutenant Daivid Wolfe, X-ray Platoon."

"Yes, that's what this boy said," the large man said, shoving the trooper towards him. The newcomer had thick black eyebrows turning gray, deepset dark eyes, a large nose and fleshy red lips. "Sorry to disturb you, Lieutenant. I'm Sergeant Perkin Rivera of the Welcome PD. I got called out to the riot. Come on out, all of you."

Looking abashed, the remainder of the missing Cockroaches emerged from the hovercraft. None of them could look Daivid straight in the eye. Their fatigues were wet, torn or both.

"They were busting up the bar on Bizarro Street. Kind of unexpected to see anybody from the Space Service, since this is off-season. A little surprised no one notified us you were on leave here."

Daivid shook his head. "We didn't mean to cause a disturbance, Sergeant. We were supposed to be in and out on a three-day mission, but it looks as though we've got a delay. My troopers," he glared at them, "were anticipating the long wait by scoping out the local entertainment."

"A *long* delay?" Rivera asked pointedly.

"—It could be three weeks, or possibly longer," Daivid admitted. "Our ship is on—an irregular schedule."

"I see. Well, I was a trooper once. I'd like to help you out, but it looks as though some of your people don't play well with others. The bar owner was plenty pissed when this boy here put one of his best customers through the mirror on the back wall. The guy was only bruised, luckily."

Daivid sighed. "We'll pay for damages, of course, Sergeant. How much?"

"Not too much. Tennie will only ask you for the wholesale value, seeing as you're service personnel. The tourists have to pay retail. May I ask the nature of your mission?"

"I'm sorry, that's classified."

Rivera shrugged. "Had to ask. Listen, we welcome military, really, but under the circumstances, Tennie's not going to let your people back in the bar…"

"Awwww!" issued from every Cockroach throat at once.

"…Unless you or one of your officers is there with them. And maximum ten at a time. You're personally liable for any damage, but my officers and I will return your troopers to you for discipline if there's a complaint but they don't actually kill anyone."

"Come on, sir, what do you say?" Boland wheedled.

Daivid was in no mood to negotiate with the sinners. "I'll think about it. Please give me your contact information, Sergeant," Wolfe said pleasantly. "And the name and number of the bar proprietor."

Rivera gave him a couple of codes, which he entered into his infopad. The big police craft lifted off into the night. Daivid turned to his platoon.

"Drop and give me fifty," he said.

"What?" Boland asked.

"Insubordination," Wolfe said simply. "You can do a hundred. Now. Hit the pavement."

"But there's six inches of snow, sir," Aaooorru said.

"There won't be by the time you finish. Hit it. I won't say it again."

Lin cleared her throat meaningfully. She dropped to the ground and started pumping up and down. Very reluctantly, the Cockroaches got down on hands and toes, or claws or whatever served them as upper and lower digits, and began counting off. Wolfe gradually let go of his anger, and felt a little smug. They thought they'd gotten the better of him, but he had taken control at last.

A cold breeze went up his back. Wolfe suddenly remembered he was standing in an alley in the middle of a winter night in his shorts and a blanket.

CHAPTER 15

"REMEMBER," WOLFE CAUTIONED the first group of Cockroaches as they approached Tennie's Place. The bar, a double storefront in the middle of a trendy-looking block of cheerful-looking shops, all with signs reading "CLOSED FOR THE SEASON," had a façade of Bavarian blue matte enamel highly decorated and gilded, and the name etched on the flexglass window in gold. "You're ambassadors of the Space Service. If you can't hold it together, stand up and head out to the shuttle. Under no circumstances are you to throw a punch, a glass, a bottle, a piece of furniture or a fellow guest of this establishment. If we all get tossed out of here, you will have queered it with me for yourself and all your fellow Cockroaches, and I, personally, will whale the tar out of you in the cargo hold, and you will spend the rest of the time we are on this planet in the shuttle. Is that understood?"

"Aye, aye, sir," the ten troopers behind him agreed. They were all wearing their impact suits instead of armor or fatigues. A few complained about putting on the microplate light armor, but Wolfe was adamant.

"We are still on duty," he had pointed out. "I know this is not hostile territory, but we are on a mission, and as long as we are, we take precautions. And maybe having your uniform on will remind you of whom you're supposed to be. I'm still not sure I should be doing this, after you sneaked out behind my back, but I can't lock you all up for a month, and I don't really want to. See if you can earn my trust again."

"Aye, aye, sir," they had responded glumly, but donned the dark blue outfits as ordered.

The Cockroaches were surprised that he had even allowed them to return to town. Once they had completed their punishment pushups, Wolfe had taken Boland aside.

"What in hell were you thinking?" he had asked the chief.

Boland looked sheepish. "Well, sir, we coulda put up with three days of being sequestered, but with three weeks or more just stretching out endlessly in front of us, well, we just couldn't stand it."

"Don't snow me," Wolfe said, all the more apropos because he was standing ankle deep in some. "You couldn't even wait those three days!"

"I guess it was the anticipation," Boland offered hopefully. "I mean, the genie's out of the bottle now, huh? You just can't keep us from going out."

Wolfe couldn't stand it any longer. He invited Boland to step into the hold with him for a little humility lesson—long overdue, in his mind. He had to make an example of someone, and he suspected Boland, more than Lin, had taken the lead on disobeying his 'suggestion.' He threw his blanket aside.

"Come on, chief," he said, gesturing to Boland with both hands. "You've had this coming for a while."

Boland shrugged then, without telegraphing the move, charged at him. Wolfe was just quick enough to jump aside and grab a passing arm.

He was in pretty good condition, had gotten high marks in five different martial arts, but after twenty minutes of throwing one another into the walls, Wolfe had hardly made a dent in either the big man's psyche or body. It wasn't until he managed to take Boland down with a leg hook and trapped him with the heel of his hand to the chief's throat that Boland had signalled surrender. Panting, Wolfe backed off and wiped his face with the edge of his blanket. Boland had sprung up and retrieved his fatigue cap. To Wolfe's annoyance, he wasn't sweating or even breathing hard.

"I'm the one you had to make an example of to get respect. I can take that." Wolfe felt chagrined, but the chief patted him on the back. "You tried. That's all we're looking for. If you're too delicate to give us both barrels sometimes, then you'll never last in the Cockroaches. I'll tell 'em you whomped me. That'll help you keep order in the future. Night, lieutenant."

In fact, Boland had been at his side to enforce the microplate armor order, and had a few choice words of his own.

"Your best behavior isn't good enough," he warned. "If you don't act like perfect little ladies and gentlemen, I'll give you some of what the lieutenant gave me."

There were a few wolf whistles from the back of the troop, and when Wolfe looked for the culprit, they all pointed to one another.

"On your best behavior, then. Forward!" Wolfe stepped on the threshold of Tennie's Place and paused. A slight hum rose as the security system scanned them. Finding no weapons and detecting personal identification that said they were all old enough to enter an establishment that served adult refreshments, the double doors slid open. Twenty-seven heads turned to look at them. To Daivid's surprise, the scopes in his clear helmet detected that some of them had body temperatures the same as the ambient room, showing no red signature. More puppets, he thought. Well, why not. It's their vacation, too. He unclipped his helmet and approached the bartender with a pleasant smile.

"Evening, sir. What kinds of beer do you have?"

Tennie's establishment served a pretty decent menu as well as having a truly impressive wine cellar and liquor collection. The luck of the draw on the MERDs had given them another serving of chop suey. Daivid could still taste the garlic and soy on his breath as he glanced over the bill of fare. A pity he wasn't hungry. Some of his favorite foods were in Tennie's food comp's repertory: sag gosht, protein (choice of four! the menu bragged) piccata, manicotti, and matzoh ball soup.

The bar was much larger inside than it had looked. Daivid noticed a corridor that ran off both ways from the main room. An open door along the left revealed a large party room. Several similar doors could be seen down the hallway. An electronic bandstand stood at one side of the room. There was a dais for live acts, but at the moment it featured a three-dimensional crystal ampitheater performance by Lindy Aud, a pretty, twenty-something crooner currently in the pop charts. Daivid sat down at a long table near the bar where he could keep an eye on his troopers. Somulska and Software took over one of the eletronic games. Three of the others offered to play the locals at one of the five pool tables on a platform at one side of the room set apart from the table-seating area by a wooden rail. The other five picked up drinks from the bar, and went over to dance to the music with the handful of customers already on the floor.

An attractive woman, whom he had noticed sitting with a group near the bandstand, came over and slid into one of the chairs at his table.

"Hi, there," she said. She had medium red-brown hair and blue eyes under very straight brows in a heart-shaped face. "Want some company?"

"I'm not looking for a date, thanks," Daivid said sharply.

"Ooh, tough guy," she teased. "I didn't offer you a date. I said company."

Daivid was ashamed of himself, for his tone and his assumption. "I am very sorry. I didn't mean to offend you. My mind was elsewhere, and that's inexcusable. May I buy you a drink in apology?"

"No, thank you," the blue eyes twinkled. "But you can buy me a drink out of courtesy. I'd like that."

Daivid allowed her to program her choice into the table's server, and paid with his credit chit. "May I know the name of my guest?"

"Connie," she said, accepting a clear rose-colored liquid in a tall goblet festooned with a paper umbrella.

"I—Is there a last name?"

Her eyes widened. "All I ever go by is Connie. Is that all right?"

"Sure," Daivid said. "I only want to be polite. Are you a singer? You have a pretty voice."

"Well, you're making up very nicely for starting off badly," Connie said with a half-smile that exposed a dimple in her cheek. "I sing a little, but not professionally. I'm a greeter in Wingle World. It helps if you have a pleasant voice. What shall I call you?"

"Daivid," he replied. "Daivid Wolfe. Some people call me Dai, but whichever you like."

"Daivid's nice. So what do you think of Welcome?"

"Well, most of it seems to be closed," Daivid said wryly. "It looks like a fine town. We're here on official business."

"So I've heard. Oh, don't get upset," Connie put her hand on his arm when he frowned. "It's a small town, really. There are few real secrets. It means I don't have to bore you with all the questions you've already answered. I can ask about you. How long have you been in the Space Service?"

"Three years."

He answered absently, watching a little drama going on. Lin got up from the table and had taken a seat at the bar, away from the others. She selected a nicotine pow out of the box as the bartender brought her a scotch on the rocks. He noticed Boland glaring as an unattached man further down the bar changed seats to be beside her. Lin smiled at the newcomer. They started chatting.

On the dance floor, a very tall man swung Meyers into a wild dance. Her shoulder-length hair swept around in a flirty wave, and she laughed vivaciously. He pulled her back, his hand running down her ample curves. She nestled close as they twitched and bumped all around the floor. On the sidelines, Gire stood tapping his foot. Daivid hoped it was in time to the music, and not a precursor to another attack. The medic had been in good shape so far.

"No one at home waiting for you?" Connie asked. Daivid dragged his attention back to her.

"I'm a Seventh-Day Varietist," Lin said, just loud enough for Wolfe to hear, "but I'd love to hear about *your* faith. I support *any* true believer."

Boland's glare increased to actinic brightness.

"...You don't have a wife or girlfriend?" Connie must have asked again, because her voice was louder.

"I'm sorry," Wolfe said. "No, no one."

"But you had one, didn't you?" Connie said, more a statement than a question. "I saw you flinch when I asked if you had one at home."

"That was a long time ago," Daivid replied sharply. "And good riddance, too."

"So bitter still, after how long? Three years? What happened?" Her blue eyes were very sympathetic as she leaned toward him.

"I was engaged," Daivid said, staring down into his drink. "Look, I don't want to burden you. It's my business, and it's old."

"You really ought to burden someone other than yourself," Connie said gently. "It's been eating away at you all this time, hasn't it?"

"I haven't really thought about her in three years."

"Really?"

"No." Daivid scowled. "No, I think about Sesi all the time. I think about what a fool I was. I was so much in love with her I couldn't even see straight. Everyone was trying in the nicest possible way to tell me that she was—dishonest. Deceitful. Rotten." He sighed and knocked back half of his beer.

"She was a thief? She stole from you?"

"Only my trust," Daivid said with a sigh. "Sesi ran every program, matched every possible interface to make sure that I fell for her. She was very beautiful."

"Like me?" The dimple showed again.

Daivid regarded her. "Not like you, thank heavens. You're a warm beauty. You look—welcoming. I'm sorry, I'm being obnoxious."

"It's really kind of poetic," Connie corrected him. "So she was cold?"

"Inwardly, and I didn't know that for over two years. She was dangerous. She was ambitious."

"For what? Your family?"

Daivid groaned. "Not my family—not the part of it you're thinking of. And why everyone always picks up on that! No, she wanted to use me to get to my mother. Mom is famous in her own right, nothing to do with Dad or anyone else."

"Really? Who is she?"

"I—People don't know who she's married to."

"Tell me," Connie begged, her eyes twinkling. "I will not tell anyone, I promise."

"Why not?" Daivid said. "If this is a full confession." He leaned over. Connie was wearing a delicate cologne, something with vanilla in it. He whispered his mother's name. Her eyes widened.

"Really? So, Sesi wanted to get into show business?"

"Yes," Daivid said dejectedly, putting both elbows on the table with a thump. "So she put the full-court press on stupid son in hopes of wiggling her way into mother's life, and maybe getting a chance at galaxy-wide exposure. When I finally figured out what everyone was trying to tell me, I broke it off, but not before she embarrassed me in public. Dad was furious. I felt like an idiot. Mom was very understanding. She's used to people doing that, and she already knew I was being used. She had no intentions of giving Sesi a break based on her relationship with me. But I used up a lot of people's patience, and I ruined my own life."

"It's not your fault," Connie said. She put her hand on his, her long, square-tipped fingers cool and light. "So that's why you joined the service?"

"Yeah. Dumbest reason in the universe, isn't it? But Sesi did me a favor, really. I think I have a vocation to serve humanity—all the races in the TWC. Maybe it was all for the best."

"Sir?"

Daivid looked up to see Lin and Boland standing beside him. They'd obviously patched up their spat. The arm Boland had wrapped around the small woman's shoulders was positively adhesive. The good-looking man was nowhere to be seen.

"What is it, Top?"

Lin looked a little sheepish. "Er, sir, is the prohibition against fraternization still in force? I mean, we're on deployment, after all."

Daivid stifled his grin. If he had had his infrared scopes on, the heat between the two noncoms would have been off the scales. "No, chief, I wouldn't have the heart."

Lin's small face split in a smile. "Thank you, sir! Come on," she said, grabbing Boland by the hand. The two of them headed out the door. Daivid allowed himself to grin when he watched them remember to put on their helmets only after they'd gotten snowed on. They ran off into the night. He turned back to Connie, who was watching him sympathetically.

"You're lonely," she said. "There are a lot of nice people in this town. You could get to know some of us."

"No, thanks," Daivid said firmly. "But I'd enjoy getting to know you more, if you don't mind."

"I would be honored," Connie said. "And I'm honored you trusted me with your secrets. I keep my promises, and I'm perfectly happy the way I am. I had better go home, now."

Daivid stood up. "Would you like me to escort you back? The snow is coming down hard now."

"I never feel the cold," Connie said. She touched two fingers to his cheek as she rose. "I'll see you again."

Daivid watched as she took her coat off the rack near the door, a trendy but not foolish red fuzzy coat with a matching hat, just as cute as she was, and departed. He missed her almost as soon as she was out of sight. She was right. It had been a long time since he'd talked to a nice, intelligent girl with no secret agenda. And it had felt good to get all of that off his chest. He hadn't felt that relaxed in years.

Daivid applied himself to his lunch. Luck of the draw among the coded but not labeled entrees meant he had selected chop suey again by accident. Fifth time in a row. He didn't mind too much, but he was already beginning to dislike their assignment. First annoyance was the delay. The second was the Cockroaches' insubordination. Third was the cold.

The platoon had put up with sleeping in the tents for three nights, then in the wee hours it had begun to snow very hard. When half a meter of thick, wet snow had accumulated within an hour, Borden had suggested that they move into the shuttle, except for the pickets, who had to continue freezing their butts off. When a gale began to howl and cause the little ship to vibrate, it made sleep difficult. Daivid had suffered worse; they all had, but they didn't have to like it. He was going to have to come up with ways to keep the troopers' minds occupied.

A crash interrupted his thoughts. Gire sat at the table, pointing at a MERD that lay against the wall, its contents oozing out onto the floor.

"Aliens," he wailed. "They want to get inside my body. They know I can't operate on myself. I would have to feel them crawling through my intestines, tearing me apart!" His hands clasped at his sides, tearing at his tunic. Meyers flew to the medic's side and wound her arms around him.

"Calm down, honey. It's okay."

Boland walked over and kicked the bowl. "It's just chop suey again. Hey, Gire, don't get nuts. I'll get you something else. I'm kind of sick of it myself."

The chief flipped open the crate containing the MERDs, and started taking out packages. "Ensign, what's the code number for the chop suey?"

"A38-41018," Thielind replied promptly. He was sitting on the floor, recoding one of the emitters for the perimeter barrier. He had suggested to Daivid that he could incorporate the local codes to keep the street cleaners away permanently.

"Oh-one-eight," Boland muttered, flinging one of the indestructible cartons after another out of the half-empty container. "Oh-one-eight. Oh-one-eight. Lieutenant, these are all chop suey! Forty more!"

"Well, no wonder we keep getting the same thing," Daivid said. "Supply gave us whole cases. We're carrying over 900 MERDs. Try the one underneath."

Boland tugged the top crate off and went through the next one. "These are all chop suey, too, sir. A hundred and twenty."

"What?" Daivid asked, going over to help. "You're kidding."

The other Cockroaches who had been thinking about their next meal, too, helped uncrate all of the food supplies.

"Well, damn that fool!" Boland cursed. "*All* of it's chop suey! What a clusterfrax. He must have hit the wrong code."

"It's an automatic program," Borden commented, working on her infopad. "If it glitched, then the autorecover ought to have corrected the problem."

"Guess our supplies were packed in between the glitch and the repair," Lin said. "Oh, well, never mind. I asked the clerk for some extra rations."

"Me, too," D-45 said.

"So did I," Mose admitted. "You never know when you're going to be stuck even longer than the backup supplies will last. It's happened to it more than once."

"Good," Daivid said, with relief. "Well, trot them out, and we'll see what we can put together. If we have to, we'll mix some other flavors in with the chop suey to change it a little."

All twenty-three of them went to their personal packs. Daivid was glad not to be the only one who had asked for a few extra meals. He had learned the trick from his first commander, who had described having to hold out in a hole in the ground while waiting for extraction when his unit had gotten ambushed by the Lizards. A friendly word with the Supply clerk and a few credits or something of nominal value, like a bottle of wine or a crystal threedeeo cube, was often enough to ensure one had an extra week's worth of food. Being entirely dehydrated, the MERDs added no extra weight that was perceptible to a trooper wearing powered armor.

"Okay," Streb said, rubbing his hands together as the Cockroaches dumped their packs out on the makeshift table. "Let's see what we've got."

Daivid turned over his eight cartons, and began to stack them by code number. It became evident after the third one that they all had the same code number. "These are chop suey, too."

"So are mine," Lin said.

"All of them are," Boland said in exasperation. "When I get my hands on that Edgerton, I'm going to make chop suey out of him!"

"Edgerton!" Daivid exclaimed. "That's the same clerk I spoke to."

"And me," Adri'Leta added. "He was the one on duty when I was down there."

"I think we've all had a practical joke played on us by the same man," Daivid realized. "But why? What did he have against us?"

"That man had no imagination at all," Jones scoffed. "He couldn't have thought this up by himself."

"That Lieutenant Bruno," Thielind suggested with a knowing nod. He pursed his lips. "I bet he did it."

"That's it," Daivid said, feeling his temper rise. He shoved aside a pile of chop suey packs. "When I get back, he and I are going to have a private discussion, posse or no posse."

"I'll hold your coat, sir," Borden promised.

"I'll act as lookout," Meyers added.

"I'll help you beat the crap out of him," Streb said. The others all looked at him. "He didn't play fair with us. Why should we give him a chance?"

"The new flavor, they said," Injaru groaned. "We'd love it, they said."

Boland looked at the huge pile of identical boxes in front of him. "How long did Wingle say we'd be waiting?"

"Well, it isn't so much him, now that we're missing the push to Benarli," Wolfe pointed out. "We have to wait until the *Eastwood* comes back for us. Could be weeks."

"A month of chop suey?" Ambering groaned.

"We could eat at Tennie's," Okumede suggested. "Their food looked good."

"They were kind of expensive," Somulska pointed out. "Multiply out fourteen credits a night times, call it thirty nights, and we're out of poker money pretty quickly."

"Could we trade with someone?" Thielind asked.

Meyers, the procurement officer, snorted. "Who'd want nine hundred identical entrees in military containers?"

"We need to put this in perspective," Wolfe said, raising his hands to hush the grumbling. "There's nothing wrong with the chop suey. Now that we know that's what we've got to eat, then we live with it. We've all sure had worse meals. Meyers, will you find where the locals shop and see what you can pick up in the way of spices and sauces we can use to vary the flavor?"

"Will do, sir," Meyers said, looking relieved.

"In the meantime, what do we do about Gire?" Lin asked, aiming a thumb at the medic still staring at the mess on the floor.

"I'll take care of it," Daivid promised. "Doc, come over here." He helped the corpsman over to the spilled entrée. "Those aliens don't stand a chance against us. You figured it out—they couldn't fool you. Their cover is broken. Their chance to infiltrate our unit is over. Now, we'll stomp them out of existence!" And, suiting the deed to the word, he brought his foot down on the noodles and sprouts, pounding away with the sole of his boot until the threatening entrée had been reduced to a paste. "Is that better?"

Gire looked up at him with a beatific smile. "That's it! You defeated them, lieutenant! Now, what happened to my dinner?" he demanded, looking around. "I'm hungry!"

"Good," Daivid said, limping down the ramp to wipe his boot in the snow.

"Nice job," Lin murmured, sitting next to Wolfe as they ate their meals and watched Gire tear through a hot-sauce-laced MERD. "Why did you think that would work?"

"I've got a delusional aunt," Daivid whispered back. "My uncle has to 'kill' things for her once in a while. It always seems to snap her out of it."

The food situation definitely impacted against morale. Regulations, never a long suit in the Cockroaches, began to slide day after day, in spite of Daivid's efforts to sustain them. He continued to insist on PT every morning to keep their reactions sharp. He and Borden suggested plans of study so the troopers could apply for qualifications when they were finally back aboard ship. The two senior officers switched off accompanying the troopers whose turn it was to go to Tennie's in the evenings, spending upwards of six hours at a time at the bar. As for the ones left behind, fistfights began to break out about which video would be shown on the entertainment system. Everyone could see the tall shape of the Carrot Palace over the wall of the empty park in the nav tank, and cursed the dumb luck that had brought them to Dudley in the wrong season.

"Now I know what Moses thought about when he couldn't go into the promised land," Lin said wistfully. "By the way, I'm Jewish this week."

"Uh, to be Jewish you have to have been confirmed," Daivid pointed out.

"Oh, I was, years ago," Lin said blithely. "I go back to it once in a while. Along with Siberian shamanism, it's one of my favorite rites."

Daivid shrugged. Who was he to tell anyone what faith they could follow? Especially Lin, who was among the best at helping to keep the peace in the ranks.

"Boredom's your worst enemy," his CO had told them in OTS. "Keep them moving, keep them occupied, and keep them alive."

The biggest problem was their forced isolation. Except for Tennie's, few of the Welcome businesses were open during the off season. The few people they saw when they went on runs through the city seemed friendly enough, but kept their distance.

I would, too, Daivid thought, *seeing a military unit with full packs jogging through my neighborhood.*

He had Aaooorru, the tactical officer, hang around the park in which they had originally landed, to find out when it was empty, and organized a two-team exercise in unarmed combat.

"All right," he announced to the two eleven-person teams as they jogged in place in the waist-deep snow to keep warm in their fatigues. The sky above them was gray, but Borden assured him that no extra precipitation was forecast for at least two hours. "You won't be cold in a minute. You see that platform over there?"

He pointed to a roofed picnic area among the trees by an iced-over lake. The platform, made of plascrete and raised on pilings to make it level on the gently sloping ground, was the only thing in the park not covered with snow.

"Your objective is to capture it! One or more of your team members needs to be standing on it when I blow this whistle, and none of the opposite team! Ready? Go!"

"Come on!" Borden shrieked, high-stepping through the clinging white, her long legs threshing like pistons. "Let's take that objective!"

"Run!" yelled Thielind, the other captain. "Who takes it first holds it!"

The others, shouting threats at one another, heaved their way towards the platform. On Borden's team, Ewanowski was able to leap up onto the surface of the snow by virtue of his oversized back feet. He grabbed up Aaooorru, and flatfooted like a snow-shoer meters ahead of the next closest combatant. He tossed the corlist onto the plascrete. Aaooorru tucked his many limbs into a ball and came up on all ten, braced and ready for action.

"Come on, you suckers!" Ewanowski howled, baring his claws.

Jones, on the opposite team, had the next greatest advantage in terms of bulk combined with strength. Forcing the snow out of his path as though he was a plow, he bounded up to face Ewanowski, who let out a gleeful war cry that echoed down the glistening slopes of the park. Thielind crowded into the trench carved out by Jones, following into the fray.

Within moments, the rest of the Cockroaches were on the platform, wrestling and shouting. A whoop went up as Ambering picked Thielind up over her head and heaved him into the snow, only to be tackled by Haalten, who rolled her off after him.

Daivid stood at the edge of the field, grinning. Everyone got to work off frustrations, no one would get seriously injured, and as the park was empty at this hour, it wasn't disturbing anybody else. The sun parted the clouds, lighting up the snow to white brilliance. He felt his spirits lifting. He could handle this situation after all.

"Lieutenant Wolfe?" A strange voice.

Wolfe spun on his heel to see three civilians, two men and a woman, slogging towards him along the slushy street.

"May we talk to you?" the woman asked. She seemed to be in late middle age, with a thread or two of white showing in her light brown hair, and a few wrinkles at the corners of her mouth and eyes.

"Of course," he said. "Would you mind if I faced this way? I need to keep an eye on my troopers."

"Yes, well," replied the older of the two men, stout, tall and red-faced, as they came to stand side-by-side with him, their eyes fixed on the melee. "They are why we have come to see you. Oooh."

That was in response to Boland barrelling forward with not one, but three troopers in his mighty arms, and plowing them over the side. All of them were laughing like school children as they packed snowballs and hurled them at his retreating back.

"Unarmed combat only!" Wolfe shouted at them. "What about my troopers?" he asked his guests.

"We represent the Welcome town council," the other man, younger and with arched black eyebrows that gave him a puzzled expression. "We are certain that you are not aware of the laws and regulations that govern our fine city."

"I would have to admit that is true," Wolfe replied, cringing a little as Nuu Myi and Haalten knocked Borden on her back, took her by arms and legs, and swung her off the platform. The junior lieutenant landed directly on top of Lin, who was just pulling herself out of a snowbank. The two women helped one another up, shook hands, and dove back into the fray. "I know the general rules governing a TWC community, but not specific ordinances. Are there any specific ones you want me to know about?"

"Er, several," the woman said, uneasily.

"The first," said the man with black eyebrows, "is that no organized activity may be held in any park without obtaining a permit in advance."

You call this organized? Daivid wanted to ask them as Boland leaped off the platform and hooked Okumede's thick leg as he went down. The two men tumbled together and disappeared into a snowdrift.

"I see," he said. "We just wanted to get some fresh air, councillors. We've been cooped up in our shuttle for several days. Everyone was starting to get a little cabin fever. I thought anyone could make use of a public park. We made certain no one else was here to be disturbed by our activity."

"But they are disturbed," the woman pointed out. "You're worrying people by being here. Mothers are too nervous to let their children play outside!"

"I apologize, ma'am," Daivid said politely, "but we are on a mission. And, I have to point out, our ship has left us behind. We can't depart at present, so I regret to say you'll have to put up with us."

"The most important problem," the florid-faced man burst out, "is that you are not permitted to camp in unauthorized locations. Such as the refuse area behind Wingle World. It is illegal. It is not allowed."

"I see," Daivid said with an agreeable smile. "Very well, we don't want to break the law. Direct me to an authorized campground. Nearby is preferable. We have orders to remain close to Wingle World."

The dark-eyebrowed man waffled. "Er, no can do, Lieutenant. They're all closed for the season."

"Then where can we go? I am afraid we must stay within the town limits."

"I'm sorry, sir. We really don't have provisions for out-of-season guests. You could try one of the wilderness areas outside of the province," the woman suggested hopefully.

"No can do," Wolfe echoed. "I've got to keep within view of the park, at least within reach of it, for the duration. My orders. I can't say more than that. We are here for the common defense. Can't something be worked out?"

The red-faced man sputtered, "I'm afraid not, lieutenant. This is a peace-loving world. We have no standing army. If it were known we let a military unit camp on the very doorstep of our most important landmark—Well, it would invite repercussions. Other military groups might demand a presence. Our peaceful ambience would be ruined!"

This was true. Borden had reminded him that they didn't have a standing army of any kind. Once in a great while, a Dudleyite would join up in the space service to serve the Confederation, but they had no force of their own. Don't have an army, don't invite invasion. That was their philosophy.

"I am very sorry to inform you that if you don't move your force from the refuse area, which is on city property, we will have to..." His voice died away on a mumble.

"What?" Daivid asked, leaning closer.

"Arrest you."

For the first time Daivid noticed that though the temperature was below freezing, no vapor was coming from the councillors' mouths. He no longer felt cold, and he was sure they could see steam starting to come out of his ears.

"Arrest us? We are members of the TWC armed forces, whose duty it is to protect you and your townsfolk," Daivid said sternly. "I could have *you* arrested, and tried by a military court! I could demand, under Section 7C, subsection 49PWN of the Confederation constitution, that you give us such aid and assistance that we require, and that might include housing and feeding for twenty-three for an indefinite period. You're not human beings, or rather, what is here in front of me isn't. You don't even have the courage to come and evict us in person. Did you think that I would attack galactic citizens for giving me an honest quotation of the local laws? I must tell you I am very unimpressed by Welcome hospitality. You wouldn't want me to give my opinion to a public poll on courtesy and hospitality on one of the galaxy's most famous vacation spots, would you?" He raised a skeptical eyebrow at them.

The puppets did not react. He didn't expect them to. After a moment, during which he estimated that the operators were conferring together, probably in their little room under the floor or wherever, the black-eyebrowed man spoke.

"We can let you have three days to find another accomodation, then we must act. Our people are demanding it, lieutenant. Please understand we have to have their best interests in mind. This is not a personal attack on you. Welcomers are not accustomed to seeing billeted soldiers under their noses. It unnerves them."

Daivid was beginning to feel desperate himself. "I sympathize with you, councillors, but we have to live somewhere."

"You have a ship," the big man pointed out. "Can't you stay in orbit until you have to do what you came to do?"

"It's a short-hop transport, sir," Wolfe said. "See here, if there are no campgrounds available, can you give me the addresses of hostels, guest houses or hotels in town that are open this month?"

The woman smiled with relief. "Yes, of course." She produced an infopad, called up a list and held it out to him. He touched the dataport of his pad to hers, and noted the transfer time. It was very rapid, indicating that the list was short.

"We'll do our best," Wolfe assured the puppets.

"By the way," the florid-faced man said with a hint of a smile. "There is no subsection 49PWN. I just looked it up. You're right: we should be more understanding of your situation. Sergeant Rivera brought me up to date. But we have to uphold the law. This month of the year it doesn't matter as much, since no one comes here, but during season if we made an exception and let anyone camp in an unauthorized location, and word got out, very soon the streets would be littered with campers. It would become nightmarish for the park and the town."

"That's true," Daivid agreed. "However, we're not merely an exception. We are your armed forces." But the simulacra were finished listening. They turned and began to walk away.

"Three days," the black-eyebrowed man said imperturbably over his shoulder, not letting Daivid get a last word in.

Daivid had to hand it to the Welcomers: they made their simulacra move exactly like human beings. Very impressive. It would fool a lot of people. Small wonder they were reluctant to meet him in person. They had left him with a knotty problem he didn't really know how to solve. He didn't know if he would feel comfortable having a wild group of troopers on his front doorstep if he didn't know them.

The troopers! He turned back to the melee in progress.

"Hey, lieutenant!" Boland yelled. He was sitting on top of four other people as Streb climbed over his head to claim the now empty platform. "Are you ever going to blow that whistle?"

CHAPTER 16

THE COMMUNICATIONS OFFICER routed the cheerful soprano voice so that it could be heard all through the *Dilestro's* bridge. A sweet-faced human woman with large brown eyes and long, soft sable hair piled on her head in a complicated hairstyle looked out at them from the screen. Behind her was the image of a vast complex of oddly shaped buildings with a huge pink rabbit superimposed over it, waving happily.

"We are so sorry to have missed you!" she said warmly. "Wingle World is closed for the season. We look forward to welcoming you in only—" A perceptible pause followed, as the woman's face froze in a smile. "—Sixteen days! Please come back then. Here is an upload of all the attractions that will be waiting for you here at Wingle World!" A small icon shaped like a star appeared in the upper right hand corner of the screen, and the rabbit pointed to it.

"That's Bunny Hug," one of the human crew members whispered to the itterim next to him.

"I know," the green crewbeing chittered back. "I have loved him since I was a hatchling."

Ayala ignored them. "Where is he?" he demanded of the cheerful woman. "I need Oscar Wingle. I want to speak with him. Put me through!"

The woman's mouth opened, and her eyes looked kindly into Ayala's. "We are so sorry to have missed you! Wingle World is closed..."

"She is a recording," Oostern commented.

"I guessed that! Find me a living being who can lead us to Oscar Wingle!" Ayala slammed his hand down on the rail that separated his seat from the navigation bay. "Find him! Send a shuttle to Wingle World and get him. I want that chip!"

Though it was still mid-afternoon, the sky darkened to smoky gray, and snow started falling in heavy clumps. The sentries were coming in crusted with snow to a depth of five centimeters or more. Meyers trudged in behind Vacarole, who had just been relieved by Haalten.

"I'm sorry, sir," she said as she took off her clear helmet and brushed the snow off of it. "I've been to every single hostelry on the list, and a few I found on my own on the local communication channels, and not one of them is willing to host us."

"You told them we're here on official business," Wolfe said. It wasn't really a question. Meyers was intelligent and would have used every means to reason with the owners. He was becoming worried. So much for Harawe's insistence that he keep a low profile and not attract notice. Everyone in Dudley must know by now that they were there.

She nodded. "I told all of them we could get by on thirteen rooms, or even eight in a pinch, but I guess word has spread. Most of them are short on staff: everyone is on vacation, either off-planet or taking it easy. The ones that are open don't want troopers. What are we going to do?"

Full of nervous energy, Daivid flung himself up out of his chair and went over to change from his fatigues into his dark blue light armor.

"I'm going to talk to them myself," he said as he shoved one leg into the trousers. "No offense to you, Meyers. I have to try. I just want to see if a second time asking makes any difference."

"No!" snapped the rosy-cheeked little old woman who answered the door of the Friendly Welcome Inn. She punched the control to close it in Wolfe's face. He jumped back just before it slid shut on his foot. Not that it would have hurt him, but if he broke the mechanism it would be one more point against them in the eyes of the city council. This was the fifth refusal out of five. Some of them had not even bothered to open the door. He tilted his head to Borden, Meyers, and Adri'Leta, who followed him down the walk to Harawe's flitter, where Boland sat at the controls.

"I told you it'd come in handy," he had informed Wolfe unabashedly when it became obvious that the only other vehicles they had were scout tanks. Against his better judgement, the lieutenant realized that they needed to use the white car to avoid enraging the townsfolk further.

"Sorry, can't help you," said the cheerful-looking man who met them *outside* the Wonder Inn Fly-In-Fly-Out Motel. "Would you excuse me? I was just going to, er—I was just going!" As Daivid and Borden watched in amazement, he dashed down the walk, heedless of the snow, and ran across the way into the heavily-wooded yard opposite.

"That leaves only Wingle Deluxe," Daivid said, checking off Wonder Inn on the meager list.

"That's the grand hotel adjacent to the park," Meyers said. "It would be the ideal choice, sir, but I bet it's hundreds of credits a night per person, even if the proprietor hadn't hustled me out the door so fast I just barely had time to grab a brochure."

She offered the chip to Wolfe, who applied it to his infopad. "It's got everything: water park, game room, casino, entertainment, petting zoo, holosuite. All closed during off-season, of course, but it's a lovely place."

"We can't get our hopes up," Wolfe said glumly. "Most likely we're going to end up in the mountains, spying on Wingle through distance scopes."

Nuthang Codwall III agreed to see Wolfe and his party, but made it clear his time was precious, and he resented the small amount he had earmarked for them.

"You can see that the hotel is closed, Lieutenant Wolfe," Codwall said, tapping his fingertips together behind his desk.

It was made of a gorgeous, exotic red wood banded with gold and black that went perfectly with the rest of the décor in the lushly appointed office. He gestured Wolfe to a gold-leafed, upholstered armchair that only appeared to be an antique. When Wolfe sat down in it, the foam molded itself around his back, seat and thighs for maximum comfort. His escort seated themselves at the hotelier's insistence on a pair of priceless matching couches of rich, dark wood and gold damask cushioning that didn't even squeak under the weight of the troopers' light armor.

"I am sorry, but I really can't help you. No one is here to help *me*. They are all on hiatus until just before the park reopens. You have to allow us our brief period of rest. We deal with tourists all the year round."

"Why didn't you go on vacation, then, Mr. Codwall?" Boland asked curiously.

Codwall pursed his lips. He was a small man with a very round head, across which two finger-thick strands of gray hair stretched from ear to ear. "When you do deal with tourists, chief, the very best vacation you can have is not to have to face other people. I often go wilderness camping this time of year, but even I could not get a reservation. Me! Nuthang Codwall! But," he sighed, "first come, first served. That's Wingle World's motto, too, you know."

"This hotel sleeps over six thousand people," Wolfe offered persuasively, though he was beginning to feel hopeless. "All we wish to do is occupy a very tiny percentage of these rooms. We'll keep them clean on our own. We will take care of our own meals."

He heard Adri'Leta and Meyers groan behind him.

"Three hundred credits a night per person in season," Codwall said matter-of-factly. "This is the finest hotel in Welcome. You can actually enter the park from our rear door! Can you pay that much? I might consider it for our usual rates. Minus ten percent for the military, of course."

"We could pay that for about two nights each," Adri'Leta said. "Mr. Codwall, dey want us off de street. We have nowhere we can go. We've been sleeping in de snow. Right now we're jammed into a shuttle dat is inadequate as living quarters for dis many people."

"That, my dear lady, is not my problem. Codwall has his own problems, but does anyone care? No, I'm afraid you have to leave now."

Very reluctantly and entirely of its own volition, Wolfe felt his hand reaching into his uniform tunic. Nuthang Codwall was such an unusual name, and yet he thought that he had heard it somewhere before, fairly recently, at least within the last couple of years. He was quite certain he had never met the man. He was good with faces, and Codwall was a stranger. So, the only source he could conceive of was the little card given him by his father. He detached the small database with a small but painful tug, brought it up to his eye and touched his thumb to the panel. When he took it down, he saw the astonished looks on the faces of his troopers. He ignored them as he scrolled through the list of thousands of names, looking for surnames beginning with C.

"I believe you are wrong, Mr. Codwall," Wolfe said slowly, with confidence he did not feel comfortable exuding. "We are *not* leaving. We'll stay here until we are finished with our mission. We'll require twenty-three rooms. And meals. Complimentary, of course. We'd appreciate the use of your fitness center during the day. There might be a few other little things, but I'll think of them later, as soon as I've had a chance to confer with my officers. We're staying."

"The black hole you are," Codwall snarled, turning to him, his little round face turning red.

Wolfe sighed. He felt as though he *was* taking an inexorable step toward a black hole he had managed to avoid all his life, but he had no choice. The town councillors had left him with none, and this recalcitrant man with the strange name had pushed him to do something he had never, ever wanted to do.

"Yes, we are," Wolfe insisted. He turned the little card so Codwall could see it. "You owe my father a Class 5 favor."

"Wolfe," Codwall said faintly, falling back in his chair. His face had drained from red to gray in one second flat. "You're one of *those* Wolfes? I mean, that one? He's your *father?*"

"Yes, sir."

"Oh." With both hands pressed against the top of his lovely desk, Codwall rose as if a string was pulling him from the top of his head. His complexion rippled, as though it couldn't decide whether to be pale or red. His face dropped, bowing to the inexorable. "Then—I suppose you are staying. Er. Welcome to the Wingle Deluxe?"

"Hey!" Boland said heartily, wrapping his arm around the nervous hotelier. "Say it like you mean it! That's customer service!"

"Freedom One calling *Dilestro*," the shuttle pilot called.

"Well?" Ayala asked impatiently.

"We have scanned the entire park twice. There are no signs of life anywhere in the complex, not even vermin. This place is sanitary."

"I am not doing surgery there, I want to find the inventor. Did you locate his whereabouts?"

"No, sir. The place is empty. I even set down, in case my sensors were being thrown off by stray emissions from the broadcast system or the power complex. The only thing that came to life were the alarms."

Ayala swore. "Were you seen?"

"Maybe, since we were accosted by a mechanical sentry on wheels, but we took off very swiftly. Nothing pursued us, sir."

"Come back," Ayala ordered. He turned away from the screen. "If he is not there, then we must locate where he goes in the off season. There must be something in the news archives. Access them. A man that famous does not disappear like a shadow."

Ayala waited impatiently as Oostern scrolled through the communications net database.

"All the news reports say that Wingle never goes off planet," the itterim said. "I have heard this myself."

"So he must be on Dudley somewhere. Where would he go in the off season?"

The communications officer clacked her mandibles nervously. "His home?" she suggested. Both the senior officers turned to stare at her.

"It has a listed address," she said, pointing to her screen.

"Cushy!" Jones said, throwing himself onto the big bed in his room. He hailed Lin as she passed his open door carrying her duffle. He brandished one of the six pillows at her. "And did you look at the baths? Positively senatorial!"

"Mine has yellow marble tubs," she said, grinning widely. "Two! And the mattresses give pressure-point massages. Boland, I'm in 2366."

"I'm in 2368," Boland's voice came back. "You have got to see the number of channels on the crystal screens!"

"I will sleep in the tub," Aaooorru put in happily from down the corridor. "The blue-green reminds me of home."

"Hypoallergenic everything," Borden noted approvingly, un-packing her uniforms into one twentieth of the opulent closet in her chamber, which adjoined Daivid's. Daivid had given permission to open the mastoid-bone channel for casual chitchat. "This is all very beautiful."

"We stayed here when I was a boy," Daivid told Codwall as he checked on his troopers. Most of them had immediately made their beds and crawled on top of them to watch the in-room entertainment system, one of the few systems that was still running even though the hotel was closed. Unsurprisingly, most of them turned to the pornography channels, a fact that became evident even though he couldn't see the screen by the cheesy music pouring out of the hidden surround-speakers.

"I hope it is—to your liking again, Mr. Wolfe," the hotelier offered uneasily. "I—I am very proud of this facility. It is the pride of

Welcome. Mr. Wingle himself praised our décor. Um. I hope he will still have reason to—speak well of it."

"I know you're concerned," Wolfe reassured him, striding along, enjoying the beauties of the place and, above all, warm air, "but all we want is a decent place out of the snow. This is palatial, and I assure you that my father will appreciate it. Let me send out a little warning. Now hear this," he cautioned the troopers, broadcasting it over the implanted receivers in their skulls, "no trashing this place. Anyone Mr. Codwall complains about goes back to the shuttle, and you don't so much as breathe planetary air again until the mission takes place. Is that clear? Respond. Borden, take a list."

"Aye, sir," the junior lieutenant said as 'ayes' began to come in from up and down the corridor.

"Is that better?" Wolfe asked Codwall.

Streb threw them a salute as he hauled a heavy gun on its hovercart down the hall in the direction of the fitness center. Codwall looked at the gigantic weapon on the sled and swallowed hard.

"I—I think so, Mr. Wolfe."

"It's Lieutenant," Wolfe reminded him, looking down fondly on the shorter man's head. "I'm here to serve you and everyone in the Thousand Worlds Confederation."

"That's very comforting. I think."

Wolfe beamed at him. In spite of feeling guilty about making use of his father's gift, he was relieved how easily it had taken care of all of their problems. They had rooms, spacious, individual rooms. The shuttle, which had made the neighbors so nervous, was out of the recycling area and stowed in the vast indoor parking hangar at one side of the enormous hotel, off the streets at last. They were going to have a comfortable place to wait out their enforced idleness. They were responsible for maintenance on any facilities they used, but they were accustomed to that. If Codwall had any plumbing problems, they were at his service.

"Excuse me one more time," he said, tapping his implant. "Now hear this. Meeting in thirty minutes in the fitness center. All hands report at that time, in person, to set some rules and make up an agenda for the upcoming week. That will be 1700 local time. That is all."

Daivid looked around at the ornately carved gold-leafed lintels above every door, the thick carpet that reduced every footstep to an whisper, the wooden paneled walls and hanging crystal globe lights, like a gaudier version of his family mansion. He felt inexplicably at home.

"Yes," he told Mr. Codwall. "This is a very nice place."

"Nice place," said Ayala as he stepped into the foyer of the Wingle mansion. The elderly human male who had admitted them lay dead behind the fancy black door. The Insurgency colonel put his hands on his hips and turned in a full circle. He looked up at the swaying crystal drops of the lighting fixture that had been slightly damaged when they burst into the house. "Yes, indeed. That chandelier could pay for a single-being fighter. Mr. Wingle's inventions have made him a great deal of money. All of these furnishings are worth a fortune."

"Should we take them down?" a human private asked him. "They could be sold to support the Insurgency."

Ayala swept out an imperious hand. "No. Not yet. Not until we have the chip. This is the one invention for which he will not be paid in cash. If he gives it up to us without a fight, I will not kill him. If he refuses, *sllllcht!*" He drew a sharp forefinger across his bearded throat. "How many life forms in the house?"

"Twenty," Van Yarrow replied, checking the much-repaired infopad. He smacked it with a claw, and the screen resolved. "Twenty-one. No, that must be a pet. It is too small to be one of the known sentient races."

"It could be lunch," grinned one of the human soldiers, showing cracked teeth.

"Then we are evenly matched in numbers," Ayala laughed. "Not that they are any match for us."

"Voices! Who's here?" A plump woman with soft gray curls emerged from an upstairs room and came gliding down the stairs. She stopped short when she saw the intruders. "Who are you?" she cried.

Ayala doffed his hat and swept it in a deep bow. "Colonel Inigo Ayala. We are here to see Mr. Wingle. Will you bring us to him?"

"I—er—Is he expecting you?" she asked, backing away up the stairs.

"Do not stall, madam," Ayala said, signing to two of his guards to advance and take the woman by the arms. They lifted her up and carried her down to the main landing. "Take us to him. Madam," he continued, as he approached her and gazed down into her eyes. She squirmed in the guards' grasp, whimpering with fear. "I have just arranged for the assassination of one of my own spies. Do not think I will spare you if you trifle with me. Take us to Oscar Wingle."

"I can't!" she wailed.

"You will," Ayala insisted. "I have two hundred soldiers surrounding this house. Three more of my ships are on the way to this planet. In a very short time we will begin destroying things to get what we came for, and I will start with this house and everyone in it, including you."

"I can't do that! You must not disturb Mr. Wingle. He is *inventing*. Please let me go. Please! Don't hurt me."

Ayala signalled impatiently for the soldiers to take her away. He turned to the remaining eighteen who had followed him in. "Find Wingle. Tear the place apart if you have to."

The Wingle Deluxe's fitness center would have made a good landing bay, Daivid mused. His tiny platoon was almost swallowed up in its magnificence. Over five hundred cardio-fitness machines that became treadmills, stairclimbers, rower, recumbent cycle, cross-country ski simulators or any of a host of other configurations, were ranged in front of a full-sized crystal ampitheater screen. A receiver band hung jauntily on the handlebars of each machine. Every other kind of fitness machine, weight machine, floor-exercise equipment Wolfe had ever heard of or seen in a catalog was set up in a station of its own around the walls. Rings, ropes and trapezes hung from the ceiling. Beyond those lay two lap pools, empty (Wolfe meant to ask Codwall to fill one of them later), and on the other side a virtual field of robotic exermassage therapy tables. Drapes for privacy hung on filaments had been hauled up to within two meters of the ceiling during off-season. The pleasure lagoon water park was on the floor above under a gigantic skylight, out of sight of the serious exercisers who considered merely playing in water to be frivolous.

Sitting on the edge of the platform that Daivid recalled was used for exercise classes led by a live fitness instructor (this was a luxury facility, after all) were all twenty-two Cockroaches. The group looked so small amid the forest of equipment he had to count them twice to realize they were all there. As he approached, Thielind snapped upright.

"Tenn—hutt!" he barked out. The others bounded to their feet. "Three cheers for the looey!"

"Wurra! Wurra! Wurra!" the Cockroaches howled. They were all grinning, including the taciturn Borden.

"What's this about?" Wolfe asked.

"You're great, sir," Thielind said. "Boland told us all about what happened. I mean, you could have ordered us to lift the shuttle and camp out in the trees somewhere, or commandeered the ship for yourself and let us sleep in the snow—it's happened to us, believe me—"

Daivid interrupted. "What in hell *hasn't* happened to you?"

They all looked at one another. "We've never been drowned in hot marshmallow cream," the ensign said, "but that's probably because the situation never came up. But you can be sure the brass would dump us in it if it would keep one lousy captain from getting dust on his shoes. I mean, we've had some good officers, but you are the best! You got us into a *luxury hotel*. For free!"

Daivid turned to glare at Boland. "You told them."

"Aye, sir," the hefty chief said, unperturbed. "You had four other witnesses. Don't worry about the safety of your little card, sir. We wouldn't think of telling anyone else. Or boosting it. You're one of us, and your secret is our secret."

"That's what I'm afraid of," Daivid sighed. "Thank you for the tribute. Any good officer would do whatever he or she could for the sake of the troops. Now, since you're so appreciative, let's line out a program of keeping our temporary domicile in the best possible condition. As of this moment we are in garrison for the duration. PT: everyone gets up at the same time every morning unless you were on late sentry shift. Sentry rotation: Borden will give you your assignments. We'll carry out exercises right here in this amazing room. Cleaning: I haven't seen cleanerbots around yet, but whatever they don't clean, you do. You make your beds, just as if we were back on Treadmill. You clean up after meals."

"Speaking of which, sir," Lin asked. "we were beginning to wonder: what are we going to eat?"

"Absolutely not," Codwall said, crossing his arms.

Wolfe gave him a disapproving look. "Mr. Codwall, we have an arrangement. Can't the kitchen cook food for us?"

The little man was adamant. "Meals you can have, but I refuse to start up the whole catering system. In season my restaurants produce over twenty thousand meals and snacks a day, not to mention drinks, pastries and coffee. This system does not work on a small scale. There would be too much waste. You can't get *twenty* dinners out of it. The smallest number it could make is two hundred. That is, unless you would like to have ten nights all the same?"

"No, thanks," Wolfe told him with an uncomfortable glance towards the Cockroaches, whose shoulders slumped at the idea of the same food day after day. "We've already done that. But what do you eat?"

"I cook for myself," Codwall said. "The storehouses and freezers are full. I have thousands of ingredients of every kind, kilos of every spice in existence. You can go through them if you want. There are eight six-burner stoves and twenty-five ovens. Help yourself."

"All right," Wolfe said, turning to the platoon. "Who can make dinner for us?"

"Uh, we don't cook," Boland said uneasily. "I mean, what comes out when I try has been compared to criminal assault. I don't want sixty days in the brig for poisoning my comrades."

"Don't look at me," Gire said apologetically. "I eat anything. I'm not sure I know good food from bad."

"He doesn't," Thielind said. "Good doctor, but better with live tissue than dead."

"I can cook a little," Adri'Leta admitted, "but I burn anyding on a big scale. I try dinner for more dan four, bang. Carbon."

"I can try, sir," Borden offered.

"No!" the rest of the Cockroaches protested at once. Borden reddened.

"Sorry, sir," Jones said hastily. "She's an officer. She shouldn't have to cook for grunts like us."

Wolfe's eyebrows went up. From the junior lieutenant's expression, something else was going on, something none of them wanted to talk about, especially Borden. He'd have to win her poker chip and get the story from her.

"I could do it, looey," Thielind offered. "Look, either we get something out of a can, like beans—anything's better than chop suey again—or whatever one of us throws into a reconstitutor. I mean, I could figure out how to put together a meal, but how late do we want to eat?"

"I'm hungry now," Parviz said, rolling his large eyes.

"So am I," admitted D-45. "It's already past when we'd have eaten in the shuttle."

"All right!" Wolfe shouted over the protests. "Just so we don't go on arguing about it until midnight, I'*ll* cook, but I will do it tonight only. Tomorrow we work out something else, even if I have to teach every one of you myself. And if there's any complaints, the complainer will make meals for the next six days straight. Consider this a logging camp. Moose-turd-pie rules apply."

"You, sir?" Injaru asked, astonished. "You can cook?"

"Yes, me," Wolfe said, almost as embarrassed as Borden had been. "All Wolfes can cook. But don't you apes get the idea I'm going to serve you. I will put it together. You help, you serve, and you clean up. Got it?"

"Got it?" Mose echoed. "If it's edible, we'll kiss you after dinner."

"Save it for Streb," Wolfe said. "Mr. Codwall, show us the storehouse."

The storerooms were as extensive as the health club, which lay directly above, according to Borden's chart of the hotel. Daivid designated Vacarole and Ewanowski to push hovercarts along the aisles as he chose ingredients. The racks of containers, cans, boxes and envelopes stretched up to the ten-meter ceiling. Thielind, agile as a lizard, and Haalten, who could climb with four limbs and gather items with two, eschewed the ladders and clambered along the shelves overhead. Daivid felt as though he had gone back to his early teens, when his father had sent him and his eldest sister to start learning the family's most famous business. They had started at the ground level, bussing tables, and moved up to waiting on them, managing the floor of a restaurant, ordering, hiring (and firing), designing logos, menus and the restaurants themselves. Daivid had opened his first restaurant before he was sixteen. It was still running, a merchant-friendly diner specializing in comfort foods on board a space station along one of the minor shipping routes.

"We're looking for speed here," Daivid said, searching his memory for dishes he could throw together. "So there really isn't time to make dumplings for chicken, but a good stew and quick biscuits will whip up in under an hour. Anyone a vegan? I know Meyers and Nuu Myi are vegetarians. I can substitute bean patties in a portion of the gravy."

"No vegans," Lin said. "Scoley was, but we haven't had one since."

Daivid stopped beside a case full of aseptic square containers of broth. "Hey, Paxton Products! That's a good brand. Three of those," he told Ewanowski.

"That's our highest grade chicken broth," Codwall protested.

"That's good," Daivid said then turned to Nuu Myi, "unless you are against using the meat juices as well."

"One makes many sacrifices for the military," the coffee-skinned woman said. "I have dispensation from my high priest for such things, as long as I do not consume flesh. I will be making due sacrifice when I return home after my time in the service is over."

"Broth's okay with me," Meyers agreed.

"Good. It tastes better than vegetable. In my opinion."

Codwall pointed urgently at another shelf. "Why not try that one instead, lieutenant? That's mulcta broth."

Daivid wrinkled his nose. "Lizard? No, thanks."

"Well," said the manager with dashed hopes. "It tastes like chicken. And it costs half of the other."

"How much do you pay?" Daivid asked out of curiosity.

"Five credits a food-service container. The chicken is ten."

Daivid lowered his eyebrows. "In case you're forgetting, Mr. Codwall, I cut my teeth on ordering bulk supplies for food service. Those containers are three and a half credits."

"But I have to replace them, and they'll slap me with a surcharge for rush delivery. That comes to more than three and a half!"

"For what customers, Mr. Codwall?" Daivid asked, surprised how cool he felt, but this was negotiation, something that was bred into hundreds of generations of his family. He towered over the hotel proprietor, the light of battle in his eyes. "Isn't the hotel closed?

"Er, yes—"

"Didn't you also tell me that the entire staff is on vacation?

"Um, yeah—"

"Isn't it true that it will be almost three weeks before anyone else but you sets foot in here?"

"Uh-huh."

"So for whom do you have to replace them?" Daivid concluded.

"Nice use of a preposition, sir," Lin added, at his elbow.

"Thank you, chief," Daivid said, holding out his palm. Lin slapped it.

The proprietor knew when he was beaten. He stepped back against a pile of crates as Daivid ordered the troopers to load a floating cart from the shelves he indicated.

Daivid ran through the recipes in his head, trying to get the quantities right for a French country ragout. About forty servings, he estimated, since troopers ate far more than ordinary diners. If he stuck his database card in a communicator later on, his mother, or better yet, his grandmother, would transmit him selections from one of the family cookbooks. He'd transmit a request for easy recipes that any one of his troopers could make. This was a special effort, and one to make up for day after day of chop suey. Frozen onions, carrots and celery would be in the freezers—pot herbs, the old cookbooks called them, the basis of any good mirepoix. Tarragon. Thyme. Biscuits—no, batter bread; it was faster. As Codwall followed, wringing his hands, Daivid marched, head held high, deeper into the stacks. A brown package caught his eye, just in time for him to glare at Meyers, whose hand was sneaking towards it.

"Thank you, trooper," he said, brushing her fingers off it and passing it off to Lin. "I can use this for Avenging Angel, for dessert."

"Huh?" Codwall asked. "Avenging Angel? I've never heard of it."

"A little something I came up with when I was growing up," Daivid said. "Join us for dinner, Mr. Codwall. You're probably tired of cooking for yourself. You can try it then. Now, where are the wines?

"That was better than edible," Mose said contentedly, pushing back from the table to make room for a full belly. "That was *incredible*."

"Kiss me, and you'll be looking for your teeth, Petty Officer," Daivid said.

"Kiss you? I'd like to marry you!"

"Hey!" Streb protested, hurt. "Cooking's not everything."

Daivid chuckled. At his signal the troopers cleared the long table, taking the now empty, beautiful gold-rimmed plates from the glowing white damask linen cloth. He sat at the head of his own party, a glass of fine white wine at his elbow, king of an island of elegance. The remaining dining room chairs were stacked five meters high, and the rest of the tables, stripped of their lovely napery, had been pushed against the walls. Crystal ampitheater screens three meters square were set five meters apart all the way around the dining room. They were draped with fabric dust sheets. But on the ceiling, eighteen gigantic chandeliers with thousands of cut-glass drops, glistened and glimmered like suns. Daivid basked in their glow, conscious of a task well done. The manager, looking much more content, even comfortable, raised his own glass to Daivid in a toast.

"You've got a real talent, lieutenant. I'd give you a job in a flash. Master chef. What do you say?"

"No, thanks," Daivid replied, enjoying a leisurely sip.

Codwall leaned forward temptingly. "What if I gave you my best dining room? You'd have the high-class customers only. As a friend of your father's, I'd pay you top wages, of course."

"No, cooking at Wingle World isn't how I see saving the universe for good," Daivid said in a leisurely voice. "Thanks anyhow."

Codwall sighed. "So, what's this Avenging Angel you were talking about?"

Daivid glanced over his shoulder. "Here it comes now."

Holding it like an unexploded bomb, Adri'Leta came out of the kitchen with a vast silver bowl between her hands. Behind her, with an avid expression on his face, Thielind brandished a huge serving spoon. Vacarole brought up the rear with a stack of dessert dishes. The clone woman set the bowl down before Daivid and grinned at him.

"The scent alone almost gives you the will to live, sir."

Codwall was up and out of his seat as the bittersweet aroma wafted toward him. "What the hell is that?"

Daivid brandished the ladle at him. "I told you, Mr. Codwall: Avenging Angel. Killer chocolate mousse from heaven. Pretty appropriate for a fighting force, isn't it? Try some."

At the sound of the word 'chocolate,' even sated troopers who'd had three servings of Ragout au Poulet de Loupe Jeune sat up straight. They watched as Thielind served the hotelier a small bowl.

The grin that popped out on Codwall's face after he tried a spoonful couldn't have been wiped off with high explosives. "Are you sure you don't want to give up the military? Come work for me. You'll make thousands of people happy."

"I'd rather see to the security of trillions, thanks." Smugly, Daivid turned to Thielind. "Dish up. Everyone gets firsts. We'll see about seconds later."

The bowls scooted down the table, propelled by the ensign's deft hand. The troopers seized them as though they were water in a 150° desert, and tucked in, spoons flying.

"More chocolate, please, sir!" Ambering announced, surfacing with a rim of unlicked mousse all around her mouth. She sprang from her chair and headed toward the bowl, spoon raised like a spear.

"Me, too!" D-45 announced.

"Me, too!" Streb said, grinning. "Hey, I'm more addicted than you are!"

"Since when?" Ambering demanded.

Streb, who was only three seats from Daivid, snatched the serving bowl in both hands.

"Hey!"

Streb faking left and right, sliding his prize out of her reach. Giggling like a schoolgirl, the big tactical officer flung herself over Aaooorru's head, trying to capture the disputed chocolate mousse. She ended up, belly down, on the bread platter.

"You big asshole! Give me that! I mean, with your permission, sir!" she added, turning her head for Daivid's permission. While her attention was distracted, Ewanowski leaned over her head and picked the bowl out of Streb's hands.

"Hey!"

Ewanowski, all his fangs showing, tossed the leftover Avenging Angel into Parviz's waiting hands. Daivid just leaned back in his chair to enjoy the pyrotechnics as the tactical officer wriggled off the table and dashed toward Parviz, who was helping himself to a big mouthful of mousse with the serving spoon. The dessert stained his big yellow mustache dark brown.

"This is good!" he called. "You should try some."

Both Ambering and Streb made for him, laughing like idiots. "Gimme that!" Streb yelled.

"You want some?" Parviz asked. "Here!" He scooped up another ladleful and flung it at the muscular noncom. It hit Streb square in the face. "Whoa! Looks good on you, man!"

"You gonna lick it off?" Okumede asked Mose.

Mose hoisted the remains of the pound of butter that lay softening in the heat of the warm room from the dish in front of him on the table.

"Hold on! I said, hold—glub!" Okumede's words were stifled in a fist-sized slushball of butter. Okumede promptly peeled it off and heaved it back. Mose ducked.

The butter missed him, but hit Lin in the ear. With the outraged dignity of an Avenging Angel herself, the diminutive chief rose to her feet. She grabbed the nearest weapon, half a loaf of bread, and marched around the table towards her assailant. In anyone else's hands Okumede was in for a crumbing he wouldn't forget, but Lin was trained to kill with anything, and she looked like she was thinking up a special technique.

Grinning, Okumede scrambled up to avoid her, hands out. "Hey, chief, I'm sorry. Really. Honest. I didn't mean it. Really, chief!"

Lin stalked toward him inexorably. Okumede began to grab things off the table to throw at her: spoons, baskets, even knives. Lin batted them aside with her bread.

Boland must have decided things were getting too serious. Okumede dodged right past him, with his pursuer only a meter or two behind. As Lin passed Boland, he plucked an ice cube out of his glass and slit it down the collar of her tunic. With a squawk, she turned and began to belabor him with her loaf.

"Save me!" he yelped, fending her off weakly.

"Help him!" Borden howled, laughing. To succor the popular chief, a rain of leftover Brussels sprouts pelted Lin from all around the table. Cheese sauce splashed everywhere, followed by a volley of potato croquettes and salad.

"Food fight!" Aaooorru caroled happily, grabbing up missiles with all of his pincers. He picked up a bottle by the neck and prepared to heave it.

"Not the wine!" Meyers yelped, diving for him. Ewanowski took the opportunity to mash a serving bowl of stew over her head. Sputtering, she turned, blood (and gravy) in her eye.

Daivid decided now was a good time to retire from the arena. That book he had started two nights ago wasn't going to finish reading itself, and he felt like taking a jog through Magic Quarter before bed. No, better still, he was going down to Tennie's. Perhaps Connie was there.

Codwall ran after him as he headed for the door.

"Stop them!" the manager pleaded. "Please! They'll destroy the place. That carpet cost forty credits a meter!"

"Really?" Daivid asked, patting him on the cheek with a palm. "You got cheated. Don't worry. They're just having some fun."

"Fun?" Codwall's voice rose to a squeak.

"Yup. Don't worry about it. Good night." Daivid kept walking.

Behind him, Codwall kept chirping out threats. "I'll report you to your commanding officer! I'll—I'll call your father!"

Daivid waved without looking back. "Fine! Tell him I said hello!"

CHAPTER 17

"SO YOU LEFT them there smearing the walls with chocolate mousse?" Connie laughed, swirling the drink around in her glass. Daivid looked smug.

"Borden has my orders. As soon as they calm down they are to scrub that dining room clean, using toothbrushes if they have to. I need to keep them busy until our mission is finished, and you had better believe they are imaginative enough to get into trouble that I could never imagine in my entire life if they have a spare minute. I'm more in danger from my troopers than from the Insurgency or any other enemy of the TWC. Tomorrow morning I'll get them up early for maneuvers." He smiled. "An ancient philosopher said, 'Under conditions of peace the warlike man attacks himself.' I am simply trying to keep that from happening. He also said, 'Out of chaos comes order,' but beyond that I don't agree with anything else the man said or did. I have faith in Borden getting them to take care of their mess when they're through having fun. They're proud of being iconoclasts."

"I think you are very creative," Connie said, showing the dimple in her cheek. "They're lucky to have you. You could just bear down on them and make them behave."

"No, I couldn't," Daivid corrected her. "I've tried simply giving them orders. They judge them on merit and whether I've earned the trust to push them around like that."

Connie's eyes were wide. "But the military isn't a democracy. How can they behave like that under battle conditions?"

"That's why I am proud to serve with the Cockroaches," Daivid said. "They never mess around in a real emergency. They are all business, from the moment the word is given. It's their independent thinking that gives me more flexibility with them than I'd have with a company full of grunts who *need* me to do their thinking for them. The Space Service doesn't realize it, but the platoon they treat as a joke is their *real* secret weapon."

"So, you're here to pick up a weapon?" Connie asked quickly.

Daivid reddened. "I didn't say that. I can't say what I'm here to do. I know rumor is flying. I can't stop that, but please don't ask me to confirm anything."

"I won't," Connie said, taking his hand in hers. "I'm sorry. It's been so nice sitting here with you. I am really enjoying just getting to know you." Her eyes met his.

Daivid felt a spark of something warm to life inside him, something that had been dead for three years or longer. He closed his hand around her fingers and leaned towards her. She let her eyes close halfway and leaned toward him.

"The Old Man wants to see you."

Daivid and Connie jumped apart. He looked up. Sparky was beside him, his freckled face alive with mischief. "Did I scare you?" he grinned.

"Please go away," Daivid said peevishly. "This is a private conversation."

"You're not here to canoodle," the puppet chided him. "Right? Mr. Wingle wants you in his lab right now. Come on. On your feet. I've already spent half an hour finding you."

They trudged along infinite steel corridors. The puppet's feet made almost no noise on the floor as he led the way, almost flying ahead. By comparison, Daivid's boots beating out double-time echoed like thunder.

"Hurry!" Sparky commanded.

Wingle stood to face them as the wall ahead slid away to reveal the messy laboratory. "About damned time," he said. His eyes were red-rimmed and angry. Sparky slumped against the nearest wall.

Daivid felt his spine tingle in anticipation. "Are you finished with the chip, sir?" he asked eagerly.

"Shut up!" The inventor shoved a rolling stool toward him with one foot. "Sit there. I want you to see something. From the security eyes in my country house."

He pointed toward the communications console then walked away, his hand over his eyes. Daivid scooted close to see what was in the screen. He could tell it was security footage, because the point of view covered one 360° view of a room, taking about five seconds for the circuit, then hopped to the next. Almost every scene was one of carnage and ruin. Mottled shadows yanked open doors or pulled down pictures, punched through wall panels, and overturned furniture. Humans, most of them elderly, were held fast in the hands of more shadows, or itterim or human soldiers who had taken off their helmets and were clad in bulky black armor from the neck down. Here, there and everywhere, Daivid saw the same man, a shaggy-bearded, swarthy skinned individual with a long stride and a hard eye, overseeing the inspection. He must be the commander. Daivid studied the face, trying to place it.

"What are they looking for?" he asked.

"Me," Wingle snapped, his voice thick with emotion.

The scenes turned more ugly still. When the raiders, who seemed infinite in number, couldn't find what they sought, they started to torture their prisoners for information. Daivid had seen plenty of carnage, both before and after joining the Space Service, but this was deliberate, shocking cruelty. An elderly woman in the claws of two itterim had her hands—long, graceful hands—broken, a finger at a time, while she shrieked for mercy. The man in the beard continued to ask her questions, as she sank whimpering to the floor cradling her wounded hands. When she didn't answer, he drew a plasma pistol from his side and fired it at point blank range. What remained was no longer recognizable. Daivid shuddered. He was only grateful that the death had been instantaneous.

"The staff has been with us since my father's day," Wingle said, his voice shaking with fury. "Anjanette was always the bravest woman I ever knew, would face down a lion to protect me. She was a hundred and twenty-nine years old. She was going to retire next year, dammit! Why didn't she tell them where I was and save her life?"

Daivid stood up to face him. "It wouldn't have saved her. They would have killed her even if she told them where you are. These are ruthless beings."

Wingle flung a hand at the screen. "Who the hell are they?"

"I recognize the man in the beard," Daivid said. "That's Ayala, one of the highest ranking officers in the Insurgency. I thought he'd be defending Benarli. The Space Service is on its way to liberate the system. He must be here after the same thing we are."

"God damn him! God damn him to hell!" Wingle snarled.

The video was almost at an end. A wrinkled hand crawled into the view and cupped the spy eye, dragging it down and around.

Daivid got a glimpse of forest green velvet uphostery. One watery blue eye and a gray eyebrow became visible.

"I hope you can see me, sir," a quavery voice whispered. "I'll try to send this. They want you. None of us will tell, I promise. Be safe, Mr. Wingle."

"That was Orlo Khazen. We were best friends when I was a boy. I've been trying for an hour to raise him on the comm circuit. They must have gotten him, too. I'm so close, boy! One of the greatest triumphs of my career! But it's not worth the lives of my friends, dammit!" Wingle straightened his shoulders and pulled himself together. "It's time for you to do your job. Get them. Kill them."

"I'll do my best, sir," Daivid promised. "Our first priority is to protect you and your device."

"Never mind that, goddamit!" Wingle shouted. "Never mind *me*. Get *them*!"

"How?"

"That's for you to figure out. You're the military man, aren't you?"

"Yes, sir, I am," Daivid replied, his heart sinking. "Excuse me a moment." He tapped on his communication card. "Borden, come in, please."

A hand covered his miniature screen, and the junior officer's face swam sleepily into view. "Sir? What's going on?"

"We've got a situation, Borden," Wolfe said. "Can you raise the *Eastwood* and get me Commander Iry? Stay on the circuit. You'll need to hear this. The whole unit will need to hear it. And patch through to the planet's telemetry grid. I want to see what's orbiting out there."

"Aye, sir," Borden said. "I'll have to connect with the shuttle's communications station." Her face was replaced by a "Waiting" logo. Daivid drummed his fingers on the chair arm.

Before Borden returned, she had connected him to the local network of satellites showing the topography of the planet and everything in orbit out to Dudley's three moons. Daivid zoomed in on a dot Dudley's ATC system identified as a stranger. He recorded the code numbers its black box broadcast to retransmit to Iry. He was already certain it belonged to the invaders. Who else would go to the trouble of remaining anonymous to the flight computers? He zoomed in further until he got a silhouette of the ship. A destroyer!

Iry's square face appeared suddenly. "What is it, Wolfe?"

He sent the information he had just been examining. "We've got a problem, commander. There's an Insurgent ship in orbit. Colonel Ayala."

"Ayala!" Iry looked grave. "What's he doing *there*?"

"He's after Wingle's device. They have already destroyed his country house, but it appears they do not know he is here. Can you help us?"

"Nonsense, lieutenant. We can't break off from a war to run back to a sideshow."

"Then can CenCom send a ship to protect Dudley?"

Iry disappeared for a short time then reappeared. "I've got some good news and some bad news, lieutenant. The good news is that the destroyer *Orion* is on its way towards you. It's about seven days out."

"Whew!" Wolfe breathed.

"The bad news is that they are currently in pursuit of three more Insurgent vessels."

"What? Where did they come from?"

Iry grinned. "You've actually seen them before. Those three remaining pirates we chased away from those merchants came off a string right into the lap of the *Orion* while it was on its way to join the push out here. They turned tail when they saw him, faked him out, and ducked into a string leading in the general direction of Dudley. The *Orion's* signal room picked up communications indicating they're Insurgents. That attack on the merchant fleet was obviously an attempt to subvert supplies for their cause. We have no guarantee that they are going to Dudley, but if they are, it makes it pretty convenient for the *Orion*. She'll blast them to pieces then come to your aid. Keep Wingle safe in the meantime."

"Ma'am, the Insurgents already here outnumber us at least ten to one! We don't know what kind of armaments they're carrying. This planet has no militia. We have only two armed vehicles and our weaponry."

Iry looked genuinely sympathetic and actually worried. "I'll get on the horn to CenCom, lieutenant. In the meantime, do your best. You're an officer in the TWC Space Service! Protect Wingle and his invention. Do whatever you have to. I will authorize any action short of atrocity, and defend it to Harawe on your behalf. Don't let the Service down."

Wolfe felt proud even as he sensed a shipload of collapsed uranium's worth of responsibility descending on his back. "Aye, commander. Send me any gen that might help me, ma'am."

"I will. Keep me posted, lieutenant." Iry's eyes met his. "Good luck." She broke the connection.

"Are you still there, Borden?"

"Aye, sir. Oh, my God."

"I hope your God is listening," Wolfe said. He clicked in to the aural implants of all the Cockroaches.

"Rise and shine! Report to the hotel dining room at once! I repeat, this is an order! Priority Alpha Emergency! Chief D-45 and Petty Officer Meyers, take some caffeine pows, suit up and meet me at the entrance of Wingle World. Full arms and armor. I'll be there in ten minutes, at the hotel in twenty."

Loud groans reached Daivid's ears through the link. He turned to Wingle.

"I'm having a couple of my people come here to stand guard over you, sir. They are crack shots and trained in hand-to-hand combat. Is there any planetary authority I can contact, to inform them of the situation? A head of government?"

Wingle's bushy eyebrows rose. "That'd be me, you young simpleton. This entire settlement was founded to support my family's amusement park. Every town on this planet has a council to control day-to-day operations, but they all check back with me. We Wingles pretty much own Dudley. I'll tell the councils what happened. You tell me how they can help, and they will."

"Good," Daivid said. "I'll be back to bring you up to date a little later."

"You're not leaving me out of the loop like that," Wingle said. He turned to gesture to Sparky, who rose from his stance of holding up the wall and minced over to Daivid. "You're taking him with you. He'll be my eyes and ears."

The puppet elbowed Daivid playfully in the ribs. "Buddies!"

"Just guide me out to the gate," Daivid snapped. "We haven't got much time."

The puppet babbled out a line of cheerful nonsense that echoed off the corridor walls. Daivid wasn't even listening. How could this happen to him? A month ago he was a brand-new first lieutenant, assigned his first command, a platoon consisting of twenty-two 'difficult personalities,' and now he was the highest military authority on a planet facing one of the deadliest enemies the Confederation knew!

Daivid cringed as he walked toward the automatic-opening double doors that led to the huge dining room. He expected to see chocolate streaks up to the ceiling, and a broken lamp or two shining over a field of brown-stained carpeting. To his amazement, the room was pristine and tidy, every hanging crystal prism agleam. Not one of the carpet, walls, curtains, chandeliers, chairs or pieces of artwork was smeared with chocolate. The Avenging Angel had vanished without a trace.

"Sir, I've been monitoring the orbiting ship," Borden said as she came into the room and spotted him. "Four shuttles just docked with her. I'm reading two hundred and twenty bodies on board now. There's no way to tell how many they left behind on the surface."

"We'll just have to assume that two-twenty is most or part of her complement," Daivid said. "Be grateful for small miracles. If the *Orion* hadn't interrupted those other three ships, we could be facing thousands! By the way," he said, looking around again in wonder, "Good job cleaning up."

"It was easier than we thought, sir," the lieutenant replied, though she looked gratified. "The walls are made of a much tougher material than they appear, and the stain resistance of the carpet minimized the damage so much that the platoon was almost ashamed that they hadn't put a real dent in it."

"I can't believe *nothing* was ruined."

Borden raised her eyebrows. "Only a couple lengths of carpet, and there is a warehouse full of spares. Everything is modular. Mr. Codwall told us you don't deal with tourists unless you can make things look good cheaply, and repair it without breaking the bank, because he says they will find a way to destroy things we couldn't blow up with plasma grenandes."

"I'm relieved," Wolfe said. "I didn't want to have to turn in a report asking for reimbursement for a room's worth of silk carpet, and I don't have a fortune to pay him back."

"I doubt there's a shred of silk in the place," Borden said, "outside of Mr. Codwall's personal rooms. Everything around here resists damage."

Sparky came over to drape a familiar arm over her shoulders. "Hey, pretty lady, you look great!"

"Thank you," Borden replied stiffly. She glanced at Daivid. "Mr. Wingle insisted he come with me to hear our plans."

Borden nodded without another word.

The door opened wide to admit the remaining Cockroaches. Those with visible eye-sockets had deep shadows in them. Those without had drooping antennae or whiskers to show how tired they were.

"What is it, looey?" Ensign Theilind looked bleary. "We only got to bed a little while ago. We're all pooped. This another test? We cleaned up!"

"We've got a situation, ensign," Daivid said sternly.

Borden pulled down the drape from the nearest crystal screen. She flipped through the channels until she came to the local 27-hour news channel. A perky young woman was speaking sincerely to the video pickup.

"A mysterious fire has destroyed the mansion belonging to Oscar Wingle, the beloved owner of Wingle World. Firefighters were alerted only after the nearest neighbor, who lives twelve kilometers away, saw smoke rising. No word yet on why the alarm system failed to go off. Officials are saying that there must have been an explosion or some other catastrophe, since the entire house staff appears to have been killed in the blaze."

"That wasn't a plain old house fire," Boland guessed.

"No. One of Wingle's employees relayed security video just before he was killed." Wolfe sent the file to the screen, and spoke as it ran. "Insurgents have landed on Dudley, under the command of Colonel Inigo Ayala. They murdered a houseful of innocent people then set it on fire, and they're after *our* objective. They will keep searching for Mr. Wingle and his invention until they find him. We are not going to let that happen! Now, pull it together. I just told a lady that you never fail in real crises. Don't make me a liar."

"No, *sir!*" The Cockroaches chorused. Now that they realized what was going on, none of them looked sleepy.

"So what are you going to do?" Sparky asked.

Daivid ignored him. "We've got to get together a battle plan. The biggest advantage we have is that the Insurgents don't know we're here. But no matter how much of the element of surprise helps, there are still only twenty-three against ten times that many. We're going to need help. *Everyone's* help."

"Who's everyone?" Lin asked.

"Everyone in every town on the planet," Daivid said. "They are all in danger until the Insurgents find what they're looking for. Once we convince them of that, we should get some cooperation."

"*Ten* Wingles," Ayala growled as the Insurgency shuttles arrowed toward the first indicated address. "You would think the man had nothing to do but reproduce! Is he not busy enough working on my invention?"

"Only two more Oscars," his adjutant pointed out.

The shuttles set down around the wide, low building. A few life forms showed up on the scopes near the windows then moved swiftly away. The Insurgent vessels had been spotted. Not a moment to be lost.

Ayala gave the signal. Two hundred armed soldiers burst out of the shuttles and into the building, herding all of the inhabitants into a single blue-tiled corridor. The uniformed nurses and aides were terrified into silence. Most of the elderly men and women in hoverchairs looked up at him in confusion.

"Where is Oscar Wingle?" he demanded.

All of the prisoners pointed to the left. Ayala left them there under guard and stormed toward the indicated door.

He burst into the room. Two men looked up at him. One of them sat hunched in a hoverchair, the other on a rolling stool beside the elevated single bed that lay underneath the window. The one in the hoverchair—a very thin, wrinkled individual with wisps of wavy gray hair clinging to his scalp in a monk's tonsure—frowned at the intruder then flung down one of the cards in his hand.

"Gin," he said.

The aide didn't say a word. He was frozen in place by the sight of the armed soldiers crowding the doorway behind Ayala.

"You are Oscar Wingle?" Ayala asked.

"That's the name, sonny," the old man said, taking the cards out of his companion's hand and adding them to the deck so he could shuffle them again. He turned to peer at his visitor, and gave him an unexpectedly sweet smile. "Seen you somewhere before. Or maybe not. Met a lot of people in my day. Deal," he told the aide.

"I know the human is supposed to be old, but not this old," Oostern chittered.

"Turn the place over," Ayala said disgustedly. "The laboratory must be here somewhere."

"Quiet, please!"

Dozens of males and females, mostly human, shouted at one another, making the hotel dining room chandeliers ring with their voices. Knots of people formed, broke, formed again, waving their fists or pounding on chair backs. Some just cried and wrung their hands. They were the town councillors of the major population centers on Dudley. Adri'Leta had brought them all to Welcome from cities all over the planet, representing the six major towns and twenty smaller communities. They had come in answer to Mr. Wingle's direct orders. While they were relieved to know he was safe, the news report of the destruction of his house had frightened them.

"We're being invaded!" a woman cried.

A man demanded gruffly, "Why now? Why off season?"

"Please, would everyone calm down!" Daivid called from the dais. He had chosen to hold the meeting in the dining room because it had the best acoustics. He used his communications link to cut into the music system so that his voice reached everyone present without deafening anyone or distorting the sound. They paid no attention to him.

"Quiet, dammit!" Oscar Wingle shouted, without need for amplification. "Be quiet! Sit down. Now!"

The councillors stared at him, open-mouthed, then dropped into the nearest chairs.

"I can't waste a lot of time here," Wingle said. "I'm working. You all know what that means: it pays your salaries." No one seemed put off by his gruff manner. They must all be used to it. "You listen to this youngster, and you cooperate. Any problems, take it up with me when the crisis is past. Not now. There isn't time. Got that?"

"Of course, sir!" "Yes, sir." "Right you are, Mr. Wingle!"

"Good. Let's get this over with so I can get back to my workshop. He marched past Borden, Sparky and Wolfe, and sat down at a chair at the end of the long table. The councillors didn't let out a peep.

"Wow. I wish I could command that kind of respect," Daivid murmured to Borden. Wingle turned to look squarely at him, the keen eyes underneath the bushy brows amused.

Sparky laughed. "Don't forget, he hears what I hear."

Daivid reddened, but stepped forward. "Dudley is currently under invasion by a small force of armed soldiers. At present we don't believe that the general public is under threat, but I asked to meet with you today to discuss the problem and ask for your support."

"Who are these people?" asked a hoarse-voiced man with bulging eyes in the front row.

Daivid nodded to Borden. "Will you give us a quick briefing?"

Borden was prepared, as always. She indicated the nearest crystal screen, and fed it information from her infopad.

"These are the Insurgents," she said, flicking a finger over a control to display a soldier in the brown and gray rebel uniform. "Their exact number is unknown, but their stated aim is to overthrow the government of the Thousand Worlds Confederation. They are bloodthirsty, brutal and cruel. They seldom take prisoners, and they don't like to leave living witnesses behind who can identify them."

"What are they here for?" asked a tall man in the back.

"They want something I'm working on," Wingle said shortly. "I don't intend to give it to them. They'd misuse it, and make a mess out of the galaxy in the process."

"But they'll come here to get it from you!" the hoarse man exclaimed.

Daivid held up his hands, and raised the volume to overpower the outburst of fear from the audience. "They don't know Mr. Wingle is here. They don't know where he is at present. That's one of our advantages."

Thielind, who sat in a chair in the row behind Borden, signalled to Wolfe. "Bad news, looey," he said, through the mastoid link. "The Insurgents just gutted a retirement facility about three thousand miles from here. The old people are okay, but the help is all dead. One old guy who still seems to have all his circuits firing just called the lab in Wingle World. D-45 took the call and routed the information to us."

A disturbed hubbub arose in the room.

"There's already been another raid," Daivid announced, then realized most of them had heard the report, too. He was going to have to demand an explanation of how. "We need to prepare a defense."

"But what can we do?" a woman cried.

"I'm not sure yet," Daivid replied. He and his officers had been brainstorming with the chief petty officers throughout the night, and had not come up with a single viable solution. "The Insurgents *will* come to this town as soon as someone informs them that Mr. Wingle is here. We have to anticipate that it will happen. There's little time to lose. I have informed my superior officer of the situation, but no one can come to our assistance for at least seven days, perhaps longer. Does the planet have a defense grid of any kind?"

"No, sir! We've never needed it before."

Daivid groaned. If those other three ships did come to Dudley to supplement the one already here, the locals *would* be overrun. "Do you have an army of any kind? Continental Guard? Space Service Reserve? ROTC? A military school?" The audience shook its collective head. "No? Is there *any* kind of organized authority?"

"We have a police force," one of the councillors spoke up. "But there are only about twenty per town. Most of the time they deal with tourists, putting people, er, under the influence in protective custody to regain their senses."

"Gotta love those euphemisms," Boland chuckled from the third row of seats on the dais.

"Or rescuing people who overestimated their ability to deal with wilderness camping," put in another woman very tactfully.

"That's a good one, too," Lin murmured. Daivid gestured impatiently at them to be quiet.

"What do you do to defend yourselves?" he asked.

"We have never needed an army," the hoarse-voiced man said. "This is a resort community. There's nothing to steal. The only real valuable we have to offer is fun. Fun and relaxation."

Daivid forbore to remind them that there *was* an item of value here, however incomplete, and that was the subject of the Insurgents' interest.

"I know how quickly word spreads around here. The people of Welcome already know we are a single unit. There are only twenty-three of us. We will do what we can to draw fire, but we are going to need the help of each and every one of you. The enemy is too large to take on directly."

"I'll destroy what I'm working on," Wingle offered, raising his brows.

"No," Daivid cautioned him. "*We* still want it, and they'll never believe it isn't here. They'll destroy this city, this planet, in revenge. They have killed plenty of people already. We have to kill or capture them, or force them to surrender, or drive them away."

"How can we possibly do that?" the councillors demanded.

"Ideally, we have to convince them that they are overwhelmed by superior numbers."

"But we can't fight," a young woman explained, wringing her hands. "We're not violent people. We're entertainers. This is a tourist attraction. We bring joy to the hearts of young and old. That's what we do."

"But your lives are in danger," Wolfe urged, wondering why they couldn't understand. Time was slipping away, and the Insurgents could be upon them at any time. "If you don't aid in your defense, you may all die!"

"We couldn't face armed soldiers," a small-boned man exclaimed from one side of the audience. "We can't defend ourselves against *weapons*. We're puppeteers!"

Wolfe felt inspiration dawn upon him with the blaze of the rising sun. "Puppeteers?" He felt his face curve into a wide grin. That could be the answer!

"Oh, no, sir," Borden began, divining instantly where his mind was heading. "You can't possibly think—"

He spun to face her. "Well, why not? Can you think of a better way to conjure a fighting force out of the air? The mind is the most devastating weapon of war. Is it more important to overwhelm an enemy, or *persuade* him he is overwhelmed?"

"Well—"

"Think about it!" Daivid said, sketching his idea on the air with both hands. "We could put all of the people puppets in uniforms like ours. An instant army, thousands strong, that puts no living being in danger? And what about the others? Wouldn't it be devastating to have a host of heavily armed giant squirrels, lobsters and dogs marching towards you? You couldn't read their body language—they don't have any if the puppeteers don't want them to."

"I like it," Wingle declared, a wicked gleam in his sharp eyes. "That's a funny idea. We'll do it."

Many of the Dudleyites looked concerned, but at a glance from Wingle they all nodded agreement.

"But we will need time," Borden argued. "Time to organize. Time to, er, make uniforms. And weapons!"

"Time is our problem," Thielind agreed. "The Insurgents are looking for Mr. Wingle, and they won't stop until they find him. Pretty soon they will run out of leads, or someone will tell them where to find him."

"What can we do?" Borden asked.

Wolfe thought hard for a moment. "We'd better give them someone else to follow," he said. "I have something in mind for that. What about volunteers for my plan?"

"You can ask them directly," Wingle said. "Puppeteers," he announced in a different voice, which Daivid heard echoed in his own head, "come to the Wingle Deluxe, tomorrow at noon, park time, for a special meeting. Tell the costumers and prop makers to come with you. The rest of you, get out of here! Keep your mouths shut, and the Insurgents might pass you by."

"Who are you going to get the Insurgents to chase instead of Mr. Wingle?" Borden asked Wolfe as soon as the ballroom had emptied. The only people who remained behind were the Cockroaches and Oscar Wingle.

The park owner snorted. "I'd like to know that myself. Those fools harassed my father. They're probably bothering every other Wingle on the planet."

"Can we use Dudley as a diversion?" Daivid asked. "You say he doesn't mind parades and other public appearances. Well, what if we have him make surprise visits all around the world? We'll lead the Insurgents from place to place until we are ready for them."

Wingle looked at him oddly. "Did you forget that Dudley is a puppet, just like all of the others? I'll have to operate him, and that will eat into my work."

"I—" Daivid hesitated, abashed. "Yes, I did forget. I thought you were only operating Sparky. I thought Dudley was an android at the time, and I filed the impression away without thinking. You made him move like a real being."

"Thank you," Wingle said, a pleased expression on his usually dour face. "That's my real art. Inventing is a sideline. I can handle more than one at a time, boy. I've been doing this all my life."

"Do you use hand signals or light beams?" Borden asked curiously. "I didn't see you palm a controller."

"A controller!" Wingle let out a bark of laughter. "I am the controller! Look here," he said, holding out his hands. "What do you see?"

"Nothing," Daivid replied.

"Good. That's what you're meant to see. The manipulation of a puppet is a behind-the-scenes art form. My family has been in puppetry for centuries. Over the last twelve or thirteen generations, six of them on my many-times-great-grandmother's side, the inventors and innovators in my line have been developing complex technology that becomes a part of you, even as the characters come from within you. Neural implants in the hands and in some cases, feet as well. Aural implants that allow us to communicate—you already knew those were there, when I eavesdropped on you. It's the same technology my grandfather sold to the military. We'd already developed far better systems. You've got our rejects. I can update yours so you can hear each other in and out of my tunnel system. I've got eye implants so I can see what my characters do, and a neural switch," he pointed to the corner of his jaw near his ear, "lets me move between characters. They've got vocal synthesizers to keep a canary from sounding like a lion, but their speech comes from your mouth and out of theirs. When you get good at this, they acquire their own personalities, their own quirks, that just get embedded in your memory, so they don't talk the same. They don't 'think' the same. I can keep up to twenty moving independently, forty or more if they're all doing the same thing." He moved his hands as though he was playing a piano, and Sparky broke into a dance, twirling and leaping.

"I've got boogie fever!" the puppet cried. "Come and join me!" None of the Cockroaches saw Wingle's lips move.

"Amazing!" Thielind beamed at Wingle. "Can I see the schematics?"

The thicket of brows drew down. "Certainly not! Those are trade secrets!"

"Twenty to forty characters per person," Daivid echoed, raptly. That meant if he could get ten volunteers, he could have an army of puppets equal to the invading force. Twenty, and he'd outnumber the Insurgents two to one!

Borden's normally impassive face twisted, dealing with a troubling thought. "Sir, I don't know if we can be a party to this.

Implanted cerebral technology has been outlawed for centuries, since the overthrow of the Mind Control era at the end of the Second Human Empire."

"It's outlawed if it controls or compels the human brain in any way," Wingle pointed out. "We do this willingly. Real puppeteers dedicate themselves to their art for a lifetime. Only the best come to work at Wingle World, and only the best of the best are invited to stay. They never leave. I have manipulators over a hundred years old, and a few younger than ten. It's a vocation. You know the first time you make a hand puppet out of a sock whether or not it's going to be your life. But I still don't like having to play while I'm trying to work."

"Sir, we will only need Dudley operational for ten or twenty minutes at a time," Daivid argued. "He'll make an appearance, then we will scoop him up and sweep him off to the next place we want him sighted. The media will pick it up, and we'll lead the Insurgents on a wild goose chase all around the world. When we want them to come here, we'll have Dudley make a speech at the gates of Wingle World itself."

Wingle let out a long laugh. "I like it. You have a nasty sense of humor."

The next day at noon the dining room was packed to the walls with people. Daivid scanned the crowd and tried to guess which of those present were puppeteers and which were support staff. He thought the ones with animated body language who talked a lot with their hands might be performers, but one never knew. A trained puppeteer might have learned to keep his or her hands still except when needed.

Jones came up to him, and aimed a thumb over his shoulder at a cluster of men and women in the corner. "I've been talking to the folks who run the machine shop, sir," the platoon armorer said. "They tell me they can copy our can openers and swords out of high-grade plastic or wood, no trouble, but they haven't got the quality metal to make replicas of our machine guns for a multitude. Only a few will be able to shoot."

"We may not have a multitude yet, Jones," Wolfe reminded him. "Let's get a head count on our volunteers first." He cleared his throat and activated the link to the sound system. "Can you all hear me?"

Most of the audience nodded, and they settled down to listen. At the back of the room Daivid caught a glimpse of a familiar face and smiled. Connie smiled back and waved to him. He felt a rush of warm contentment to have her there. "Thank you for coming. I am Lieutenant Daivid Wolfe of the Thousand Worlds Confederation Space Service. Mr. Wingle asked you to come here today on a matter that is important to all of us—to all of you.

"An enemy has landed on Dudley. Everyone's heard that Mr. Wingle's house on the other side Dudley was burned down. There have also been attacks on a retirement community and a resort neighborhood near the equator. Those are all the work of a group called the Insurgency. I'm sure you've seen reports of them in the media—"

"Isn't the Space Service battling them right now?" a tall man raised a very long hand to ask. "They've got them on the run out in a star cluster—Benadryl, is it?"

"Benarli. Yes, sir, but it appears they have split their forces. They're here now, and we have to deal with that." Daivid let his gaze pass over his listeners. "You're afraid of the enemy, and you ought to be. They are ruthless, desperate beings. They want power so they can take over the Confederation. Now you're asking, 'Why is this our business? You're the Space Service—*you* handle it.' Ladies and gentlemen, we would if we could. Even though only two or three hundred Insurgents have landed, there are enough of them here to take over this world without even trying hard. Think of it! Two more weeks would go by, and the town will be a smouldering ruin, with everyone dead or enslaved, because you decided that twenty-three Space Service troopers were enough to face them down alone. The park wouldn't be able to open!"

"No!" the crowd cried, horrified. "Not that!"

"Of course we'll help," Connie announced. "Tell us what we have to do."

"I want them to believe that they've stumbled in on a gigantic army," Daivid said, sketching the size with his arms. "A huge military force, *thousands* of troopers, all well-trained and well-armed, ready to defend Wingle World and Oscar Wingle from the invader—but not human, or itterim, or semicat, or corlist. *Puppets.* I'm not asking you to do anything you haven't been doing for years. We're going to *perform* this war. But I need volunteers to operate my army. Puppets, any puppets, as long as they're large enough to be a credible trooper, no smaller than Aaooorru here." He indicated the corlist, who scrambled up the wall of the dining room so he could be seen by everyone present. He waved a foreleg, and the puppeteers nodded.

"How *big* can they get?" one of the men asked. "I perform Ginophant. He's six meters long."

"And I'm Dimmius Grebs!" piped up a black-haired boy of ten. He looked enthusiastic at the prospect of playing soldier. "He's two stories tall!"

Daivid grinned. "Great! The more confusion we can generate, the better. I want to throw off the Insurgents' perception of a fighting force between a meter and two meters tall. I'll be grateful for anyone who wishes to volunteer his or her services. But I can't *guarantee* your safety. Anyone who stays can still be hurt or killed. I understand from Mr. Wingle that the underground rooms in which you perform are shielded and soundproofed. These people have air-to-surface bombs and bunker-killer charges. Anyone who isn't part of the movement against the Insurgents has to be evacuated, and fast. Please make your decision and let me know within the hour. They could be on us any time."

The pretty, redheaded media reporter was so excited she could hardly contain herself. "And there he is emerging from the town hall with the mayor! Oscar Wingle himself! As you viewers know, Mr. Wingle is the galaxy-famous owner of the marvelous Wingle World, the very best entertainment venue in the entire Thousand Worlds Confederation. This surprise visit has thrown the whole of Rembert into a tizzy. Here's the mayor, shaking hands with Mr. Wingle. Mr. Wingle is going to make a speech..." The camera eye zoomed in close on the old man's face.

"Where is Rembert?" Ayala demanded, turning away from the viewscreen.

The navigation officer pointed a pincer at her map. "There, sir. On the southern coast of the east continent, 24° south of the equator."

"How long will it take us to get there?"

"Thirty minutes, sir!"

"Then what are you waiting for!" Ayala spun around again, his eyes fixed avidly on the mustachioed face in the screen. "Top speed! He has something that belongs to me."

CHAPTER 18

"YOU COULD LAND a destroyer in here," Boland said admiringly, surveying the giant underground warehouse. The officers and noncoms stood on a balcony about halfway up the wall. The ceiling was a solid expanse of light, allowing Wolfe to oversee the preparations already under way. Thousands upon thousands of puppets stood in ranks before them. All of them were at his service. All the puppeteers, costumers and prop makers had volunteered to stay in Welcome and help battle the Insurgents to save their beloved Oscar Wingle. Daivid felt a proprietary pride as he counted up his forces. The 'local color' marionettes, resembling the normal races who might visit Wingle World, were the most numerous. Wingle had explained to him that they wandered the park as friendly fellow tourists, or helped frightened children find the parents from whom they had been separated, in a comforting way that the gigantic yellow chick, Beak-Beak, being prepped just beyond, never could. Like Beak-Beak, the remaining puppets weren't based upon real creatures, but licensed characters in the Wingle Company stable instantly recognizable to anyone who had ever grown up in range of a family entertainment center or a crystal ampitheater. Nanny Goat and her kids occupied a mob brushing their hair and tidying their beards. Ginophant's trunk needed to be repleated, and the big hind feet were shifting from side to side with impatience at its groomers. The giant Dimmius Grebs hulked in a far corner, his round blue eyes on a level with the troopers.

"Look!" Lin said pointing. "There he is!"

In the center of the enormous room, as his Carrot Palace stood in the center of Wingle World above them, was Bunny Hug himself. Daivid drew in a breath in admiration. The huge pink rabbit stood almost three meters in height, yet his face would never scare a small child. His big blue eyes were gentle and curious as though they asked the perpetual question, "Why?" Two or three workers clustered around him, grooming his coat with brushes, straightening out his whiskers, which in the animated programs were always getting crumpled when

he stuck his twitching nose into a situation. Daivid envied those workers, remembering how honored he had felt when Bunny Hug had
singled his nine-year-old self out of the entire crowd watching the
nightly parade for a handshake and a big, all-enveloping hug. He
almost sighed, until he caught his fellow troopers looking at him. He
gave them an exasperated look back.

"What are you staring at?" he demanded.

"Nothing," Lin insisted. "Nothing at all."

Daivid resumed his study of the Wingle 'cast.' About a third
were familiar characters, beloved for generations, but more were
new to him, like the silver-horned unicorn with the insane gleam in
its eye, and the gorgeously striped tropical fish, two meters in diam-
eter, who hovered just above the floor to have their tails and fins
fluffed up.

"Ow!"

Daivid peered over the edge of the balcony. Naughty Emma
was having her hair rebraided by a patient-looking woman who put
a firm hand on her head and made her stand still, out of kicking
range of any of the other characters.

"Well, Vingit poked me first!" the girl puppet complained.

"Did not," protested a crocodile-child. He batted aside the hand
of the prop worker trying to polish his teeth. "She started it."

"The puppeteers are in their stations," Borden informed him,
referring to her infopad. "They have supplies and bedding, and are
all prepared to remain on site as long as we need them."

"Good," Daivid said. "I want to check on Jones and Meyers."

The armorer was in the Properties Room, a modest title for a supply
house that would have put any Space Service repair facility to shame.
Daivid counted at least twenty each of lathes, presses and injection
molders all operating at full blast, with the thick-legged figure of
Jones striding among the people, working them like an ancient Terran
master smith. Jones spotted Wolfe and came up to him.

"Going good, sir!" he shouted over the deafening whine of the
drill presses. "We've got a few real guns from locals who go target-
shooting, about two or three hundred rounds each. A couple of the
fellows over there came up with a clever design for a fake grenade
launcher that shoots fireworks—they've got plenty of those! They'll
be *really* annoying!"

"Good!" Wolfe shouted back. "We want to drive the Insurgents into a central location, not get them running all over the park chasing the puppets!"

"Everyone else's going to be carrying cutout guns," Jones continued. He picked one up from beside a lathe operator's table. The woman grinned at them from inside her clear safety helmet. "They based the design around my Dockery 650 machine gun. They look so real, it's a pity they don't shoot!"

"Safer that way," Wolfe yelled, admiring the detail of the mock gun. Made of a lightweight dark gray plastic, it echoed the real thing, including the hundred-round magazine and the underbarrel 3-round grenade launcher. At even a short distance, it would look deadly. "Wingle said the puppets aren't sophisticated enough to shoot accurately. The worst they can do is set fire to the rides!"

"They'll have bayonets, too, if there's time," Jones added. "The swords are going to be the real triumph. We have over two rolls of molecular foil. We've been pasting slices of it into a slot along the edge of the plastic blades. They can really lop some arms or legs off, until the damned things bend or melt, of course. Still, we ought to get in one good strike per hanger."

"Good work!" Daivid said, slapping the big man on the shoulder. "How's the booby trap coming?"

Jones made a face. "Your freckled shadow was around giving me a hard time. He's not convinced that creating piles of rubble with explosives under them is vicious enough. I told him if he had some good strategy to trot it out and tell Lin. I know what kind of reception she'll give him."

"Pay no attention to him, Jones," Daivid said, annoyed. "He hasn't said anything useful yet."

Piles of cutout guns were growing on the floor, but not fast enough. Daivid began to worry that they wouldn't have time to make up a convincing army to face the Insurgents. He tried not to think of the price of failure as he went to inspect the next phase of his operation.

The next workroom was occupied by tailors bent over the screens of sewing machines. The elaborate Seamster 9200s, latest sewing technology of the line, took raw bolts of fabric, cut them according to patterns stored in their capacious memories, then sewed, hemmed and finished them, almost entirely without living hands having to be laid upon them. The only input necessary from the operators was to ensure the measurements were accurate. Even though the process was entirely automated, it was slower than Daivid would have liked. Assistants ran from machine to machine, taking the completed uniforms down and hanging them on racks. Like the weaponry, the dark blue suits had the right thickness and pliability of the light armor, though they couldn't stand up to a single bullet or plasma blast. Meyers, infopad in hand, stood in a corner with D-45 and one of the tailors, shouting over the whine of the machines.

"Sir!" she yelled, catching sight of him. "Glad you're here! I had an idea I wanted to run past you."

"Certainly, Meyers," Daivid replied. "What do you have in mind?"

She tapped the side of her head with the infopad stylus. "Thinking like a Cockroach, sir. Disguise. You've got all those puppets disguising themselves as troopers, right?"

"Right."

Her caramel-colored eyes shone. "Well, then, if you're letting them dress up in our uniforms, then you have got to let us dress up as characters."

Daivid's mouth opened as his brain tried to compute the input it had just received. He shook his head. "Meyers, that's silly."

The procurement officer's face lit up. "No, sir, it's great! The enemy won't know who's a trooper and who's not. Glaijet here says he can fit me out with one of the shells the puppet mechanisms haven't been installed in yet. He thinks I'll make a slagging great bear. I love bears!"

"More slag than bear," D-45 grinned. "My squad's been agitating for the same thing. I thought we'd come up with it first, but Meyers had already brought it to the costumers. It's a terrific idea, sir. How better to hide trees than in a forest?"

"Trees don't carry arms," Meyers argued, laughing.

"They've got limbs; why not?"

The tailor made a note on a pad of his own. "Aqua fur, right?"

"Hold on!" Daivid said, hands out to halt the headlong tumble toward insanity. "I haven't okayed the requisition yet."

"Oh, you have to, sir," Meyers pleaded. "It's good strategy, and besides," she added shyly, "I've always wanted to be a Wingle character."

Daivid looked at D-45, who was looking sheepish. "I suppose you have a childhood fantasy you want to live out, too."

The sharpshooter grinned. "Well, sir, I wouldn't admit it where Boland could hear me—"

"Boland?" asked Glaijet, and scrolled hastily through his notes. "Wants to be a yellow lion. Already talked to him. My people and I could stitch them up in no time, a lot faster than we can make those uniforms of yours."

Daivid raised an eyebrow. "You know," he said, "the more I hear the idea, the more I'm beginning to like it. Thinking like a Cockroach, of course. That would really throw the Insurgents' minds off track. Yes, I like it." He turned eagerly to the tailor. "Sew, Mr. Glaijet! Sew as though your life depended on it."

"How could we have missed him in Rembert?" Ayala snarled, not for the first time, pacing the deck of the shuttle. The crew looked down at the controls. No one wanted to take the blame for having missed the multibillionaire inventor's craft.

"Several ships took off from there at once, sir," Oostern replied impassively, as he had often over the last two days. "We chose the one from which transmissions containing Wingle's voice were issuing. You approved the pursuit."

"It was a media ship!" Ayala shouted, his usually untidy hair in a complete whirlwind. "How could you not tell the difference between live broadcast and recorded data?"

The itterim on the bridge exchanged glances. The normally cold-blooded colonel was losing his composure and becoming more irrational with every disappointment. He had not eaten much, or slept at all since losing track of the inventor. If he had been one of them, he'd be a candidate for eating. A pity human flesh was so unpalatable.

"The signals are identical, sir," Oostern pointed out. "They are all digital transmissions. We traced all the other ships leaving the area."

"Well, what was he traveling in?" Ayala demanded. "We never found him!"

The communications officer raised a foreleg. "I've got him, sir," he said, pointing at his small screen. "The transmissions all emanate from one village. He's less than two thousand miles from here, just inside the arctic circle. Look!"

He touched a control, and the video appeared on the main screen. The familiar gray-moustached face smiled into the threedeeo pickup.

"...Glad to come and say hello to the good people of Coombly Halt. Say, it's cold up here!"

The crowd around him laughed. A hearty, red-faced man in a puffy hood moved close to take Wingle's gloved hand and pose for the cameras.

Ayala smiled. "He is still broadcasting. Get there. Now!"

The shuttle descended out of orbit so quickly that the skin shimmered with the heat of reentry. Ayala waited on the ramp until it touched down. He dashed out and began to push his way through the huge crowd gathered around the steps of the ice-covered building. When he reached them, they were empty.

"Where is Wingle?" he demanded. He caught the arm of the closest person. "Where did he go?"

"He shook my hand!" the middle-aged woman said, her eyes starry. "He is *so* nice!"

"He was here only a minute ago," Ayala said, scanning the crowd. "Where did he go?"

"He said he's on a goodwill tour," the woman said, hugging herself. "It was such a surprise. He said he wants to thank everyone on Dudley for all we've done. It's going to be a good season!"

"It's going to be no season," Ayala growled then asked again, as patiently as he could. "Where did he say he was going from here?"

"Oh! I don't know. But he was here!"

Ayala grunted and thrust himself away from her in disgust. He called Oostern on his communicator as he pushed his way back through the crowd toward the shuttle.

"Listen to the airwaves again. Find out where he is! I must have that device!"

Borden checked off the fourth list of names as the people boarded the red municipal transport vehicle. A big crowd had gathered around the gate of Wingle World

"We will contact you to return to Welcome just as soon as we can," she assured the travellers, mostly children, who clutched suitcases and bags and wore woeful expressions. "You are bound for Rembert. The town council is expecting you. They have quarters prepared."

"What if the Insurgents go back there?" a worried woman asked, herding two small children before her.

Borden gave her a thin smile. "They won't, ma'am. Now that Mr. Wingle has departed from there, they won't pay any attention to it. They won't even have left sentries. They can't waste time watching over what they consider a dry hole. You'll be safe."

Shaking her head, the woman boarded the big red hoverbus.

"You do realize the park is supposed to open in twelve days," asked an elderly man with shaking hands.

"Yes, sir, I do," Borden replied, meeting his watery brown eyes seriously. "We're doing our best to make sure that will happen. Please find your seat." A couple of the troopers came to assist him up the short ramp into the vehicle. Thielind came over to Borden and touched his infopad to hers.

"The fifth 'bus ready to go?" she asked.

"As soon as we're sure Coombly Halt is clear," he said. "What about the special ship?"

"That's not going until the last minute," Borden reminded him. "Not if we want it to be spotted."

"It will be," Thielind said, giving her his brilliant smile. "Streb and Parviz gave it a special paint job. That's all part of thinking ahead. Thinking like a Cockroach." He tapped the side of his head. "Lieutenant Wolfe has a way with words."

"Do cockroaches think?" one of the Welcomers asked, his face screwed up in disgust, lugging his duffle bag with difficulty past the officers.

"We sure do," Thielind stated proudly.

The teenaged boy looked from one officer to the other. "*You're* Cockroaches? What's the matter? Were all the good nicknames taken?"

"Sir, that is a very old joke," Borden began.

"Listen, friend," Thielind interrupted, tapping the boy on the chest, "those bugs are resistant to radiation. They're hard to kill. They seem to be smart. They're strong. They have good survival instincts. Maybe they make people sick to look at them, but you wait until after humanity and itterimity and all the others have blown themselves to hell. The next intelligent species to take over the spacelanes is gonna have six legs."

"Please get on board, sir," Borden said as he stood gawking at them. She took his arm to turn him. "This transport leaves in two minutes."

Daivid entered Wingle's laboratory with trepidation. The inventor sat peering down into a sterile table that had the elbows of dozens of micromanipulators sticking out of it from every direction.

"He doesn't want you here," Sparky warned him for the six hundredth time. Since being assigned to Daivid as a sort of aide-de-camp, the blond puppet had been a gadfly, a nuisance and an imposition, all of which he was being now.

"I need Mr. Wingle's help," Daivid said, turning to face the puppet with exasperation.

"Well, then?" Wingle's voice came from behind him. "If you won't take it from him, then you'd better take it directly from me. Go away."

Daivid spun back to face the inventor with respect. "Sir, we have a strategic problem that we need to solve."

The thicket of eyebrows drew down. "What is it?"

"The snow," Daivid said tersely, determined not to waste any of the man's valuable time. "My plan calls for making use of the underground tunnels. Your engineers are laying them out in a pattern for us. The entrances are all well hidden, but they won't stay that way if the enemy can follow our footsteps." He held out his infopad, showing a chart on the screen. "I have plotted out the minimum number of paths, with a group of dead ends to keep the Insurgents confused. Your staff seemed baffled when I asked them if they could get the plows out today."

The big brows rose on the forehead, and Wingle actually laughed. "Plows? Get with the century, young man." Wingle took him by the elbow and led him to a control panel next to his communications console. "Do you think the snow obediently goes away at the start of season every year? He pulled open a small gray door and clapped a knife-switch down. Daivid heard a violent crackling sound come from overhead.

"That's ice melting," Wingle said. "You can hear it through the ventilation ducts. In another hour or two, it'll be dry out there. Good enough?"

Daivid was filled with admiration. "More than good enough, sir. You think of everything."

The crotchety old man seemed pleased with the praise but still exasperated at the interruption. "Yes, well, we've had seven generations to work out the bugs. Any one of my people could have told you that they'd take care of it, if you asked them the right question. Now, get out of here. If I never see you again, it'll be too soon."

"This place is huge!" Lin exclaimed.

Her voice echoed off the textured orange walls that stretched up three stories to the golden vaulted ceiling decorated with bosses shaped like clusters of carrot greens. Arched doorways over five meters high in each of the four walls let in the winter sunshine to illuminate the uneven plascrete cobbles of the floor. A three-tiered round dais rose in the center of the space. Every wall had brackets for hanging tapestries. Bunny Hug's friendly face was carved into the walls above the doors and the pairs of arched windows above them, the ends of the exposed beams, even the finials on the long, burnished gold brackets intended to support tapestries on the high walls during season.

Beyond each of the four doors were plascrete outlines a meter high that since the snow had vanished were revealed as garden planters shaped like Wingle characters. Lin supposed that they would be filled with flowers and plants from the immense greenhouses underground, just before the park opened. She was very impressed by the park. It was vast but, like an iceberg, only ten percent of its mass stood above ground. The support facilities had to reach nearly ten stories underground. The tourists would be blown away if they knew how much was there beneath their feet.

"We hold afternoon concerts in here," said the grounds manager, Tomario Wassett. "It'll hold fifteen thousand people standing, or six thousand seated. It's big enough for almost any function."

"Well, it's too big for our purposes," the senior chief said, hands on her hips. "If we're going to blast the Insurgents into a black hole, we've got to contain them in one fairly small place. I haven't got enough explosives to seed this entire pavement."

"Ma'am, you're not going to blow up the *Carrot Palace!*" Wassett said in a hushed voice.

"I'm sure as hell going to try," Lin said, scanning the structure with a practiced eye. She smiled patiently at the expression of horror on his face. "C'mon, we couldn't possibly do as much damage as the tourists do. Now, show me where the support beams are located."

"Awright, you scum!" Boland howled, standing tall at the head of a hundred Wingle Irregulars, as the troopers were coming to call their made-from-scratch bridgade. "You, green elephant! Yeah, you!" he shouted as a furry jade-colored pachyderm pointed an innocent trunk toward himself. "Yeah! Ginophant! You call that standing in line? The idea is that there's someone in front of *you*, and you are in front of someone *else*. That way you're not all walking side by side when I tell you to march!"

"Pretend you're on parade," Mose yelled from the head of the second wave. "Do it for the audience!"

"Oh!" the puppets all exclaimed in unison, as though they had just figured out what the big, fat trooper was trying to tell them. Obediently, they formed into two long files, and promenaded through the now-dry main street of Wonder Pavilion, waving at an imaginary cheering crowd.

"You guys suck," Boland grinned.

"Don't say such things, you naughty man," a pretty twenty-something female chided him, slapping his hand as she sashayed by. Her dark blue uniform fit snugly over a pert bottom. Boland grinned, and stretched out to pinch.

"Careful," Mose said, coming to stand beside his squad leader, "remember they're not real people. She could be an elderly man with a squint."

Boland sighed. "You sure know how to take the pith out of a guy's reed."

"You hear that, lieutenant?" Mose asked as Wolfe approached them with Sparky at his heels. "I take the pith out of him."

"Not in public, please, Mose," the lieutenant said with an eyebrow on high. "What you guys do in private is, thank God, none of my business."

"Sir, you are like cold water upon the hot glass of my wit," the poet said with a theatrical sigh.

"Glad to be of service. How's it going?"

"To be honest, they look weirder than we do," Boland admitted, watching half a dozen pink flamingoes preening as they presented arms. They flaunted their skinny necks and fluttered long black eyelashes at Wolfe. "Almost terrifyingly weird, in my opinion. They'd scare hell out of any sane opponent, and it'll be worse when they're all dressed up. You can see they haven't all got uniforms yet." He gestured at a host of costumers on the sideline, who at the moment were fitting out Bunny Hug in his custom-made blues. The boots that went on over his enormous feet would have made good pontoons, and the clear helmet had to be made extra-extra large to accommodate his floppy ears.

"I'm not sure that's going to matter," Wolfe said, watching curiously. "The idea is to confuse the Insurgents as to how many ordinary soldiers we have, and then confuse them with a few of the special characters." He did a quick count. "You've got about a hundred."

"Only a few weapons, though," Boland said. "Besides our own armaments, we've got ten real guns, a few target pistols, about thirty fireworks guns, and two spare grenade launchers. I think that's all I'm going to get."

"You'll have to make do," Wolfe replied. "I'm leaving the largest contingent, along with the greatest number of Cockroaches, concealed around the Inventor's Workshoppe with Aaooorru. The tunnels have been moved so there is only one access to Wingle's workshop, the slide under the floor. He's still our primary focus. Are you going to be able to keep the Insurgents busy until they get to our little surprise?"

"Does this uniform make my tail look big?" one of the flamingoes asked as they marched past the officers again.

Boland groaned. "That one's the complainer," he said. "They really do have their own personalities. And quirks. Yes, sir, we'll do what you need us to do, if it kills all of us."

Bunny Hug straightened his uniform and made straight for the small group of humans. "Little Daivid!" he cried in the deep, friendly voice. "The last time I saw you you were just this high!" The enormous pink paw flattened the air about a meter off the ground. "You've grown!" He threw his arms around Daivid and enveloped him in a huge hug.

Privately, Daivid was charmed. To think that Bunny Hug would remember him after all those years, but then he and his sisters *had* been there a month—There was a loud snicker from the other Cockroaches. Daivid turned to glare at Boland and Mose. "Any other objections?"

"No, sir," Mose assured him.

"I'm ready," Bunny Hug said, and turned cheerfully to the assembled puppets with one big paw on high. "Everybody, into formation!"

Obediently, all the puppets lined up in perfect rows, without a single mistake or complaint. Boland and Mose looked at each other. "What's he got that we haven't got?"

"Respect," Daivid said. "Earn it."

The discipline problems were absent in the corlist's contingent. He and Ewanowski had their two hundred and ten puppets, many of them armed with real machine guns, running complex maneuvers through the Little Village around the Inventor's Workshoppe as if they had been doing it for years. Wolfe watched for a while as Aaooorru drilled his ten 'officers' in short-burst fire. His was the final defense, the last resistance. Wolfe had made sure to assign him puppets operated by the most skilled operators with the best motor control.

"Don't waste ammunition," the corlist instructed them, ticking off the three-count with his extra limbs as he fired bursts of three laser-tag light rounds at his target, a cutout of an Insurgent soldier that had been set up in one of the empty gardens. The red light hit the neck or heart in rapid-fire, flashflashflash, over and over again. He turned his stalklike eyes toward the humanoid puppets staring at him impassively, though Daivid knew the operators in their soundproof bunkers deep below were absorbing the lesson. "These guns can fire six hundred fifty rounds per minute of caseless ammunition. The magazines only hold a hundred bullets, and we can't spare you more than one each. Now, all of you try it."

The semicat was demonstrating a guerilla maneuver. He led a squad of chickens, cats and the Bizarro Twins over the green lawn, pretending to shoot at a target coming up the path, then diving and rolling down behind the food stand on the other side.

"Welcome! We bid you welcome…!" the colorful flowers sang from their pots along the path and on the windowsills. Ewanowski stood up with his paws clapped over his furry ears.

"Can we please turn those damned things off?" Ewanowski roared over the tinny voices. "They're gonna drive me insane."

As though an invisible hand clicked off a switch, the voices ceased. "Thanks," the semicat said to the air.

"Looking good," Wolfe told Aaooorru as the corlist left the target practice to join him. "The—Uh, it was a great loss to the service when they transferred you to the Cockroaches."

The corlist made a wry face. "I miss it sometimes, but not when I had to put lives on the line. With no real troopers in harm's way, this may almost be fun. Almost."

"There you are, sir!" Meyers called, coming around the corner of the Slalom Slope Flume Ride early the next morning.

"Meyers!" Wolfe greeted her. "How's your bear suit coming?"

"Sir!" the procurement officer exclaimed, shocked. "Sir, we've got a problem."

"A problem!" a squeaky voice declared. It belonged to a long-legged stork who stalked over to see if he could help.

"A problem," declaimed a deep-voiced frog. "We have to help!" It hopped alongside until Daivid and Meyers were surrounded by puppets.

"Do you mind?" he said, batting them away. "Go on, Meyers."

"Well, sir, it came up when Boland just tried out a maneuver in his, er, disguise."

"The lion suit," Daivid said, indulgently. "I thought so."

"Er, yes, sir. Well, sir, we're not bulletproof, so while some of the puppets are wearing our blue armor, we're wearing the hard suits under our costumes?"

"That's right. Go on."

"Well, some of the Insurgents have got the same kind of armor we do. We saw it in the video from the Wingle mansion. I mean, it's an older version, looks more like ancient camouflage than invisibility?"

"I've seen it, Meyers. I've even worn it. What about it?"

"Well, it may be old armor, but it has the same kind of heads-up infrared displays as our new suits. Sir, they're going to know that the puppets are not living beings!"

"Awww!" the puppets protested.

"We're alive," an owl insisted, "if you believe in us."

Daivid shushed them again. No, they weren't. His heart sank. In seconds, the enemy would find the few real combatants among the hordes of dressed-up mannequins, and ignore all the others. They would concentrate all their firepower on the Cockroaches. The park would fall in minutes. His plan was about to fail before it was launched. He was devastated. "I do see the problem, Meyers. Any infrared sensor isn't going to be fooled, no matter how realistic the uniforms are. I can't believe I didn't

think about that. We have got to do something about it, immediately. Any ideas?"

"No, sir," Meyers said, "but I've got a meeting with the engineers in about ten minutes. I'll let you know what we come up with."

Aaooorru caught the dismayed look on Daivid's face. "Should
we go on drilling anyhow, sir?" he asked.

Daivid snapped out of his funk and looked down at the corlist.
"Yes, Aaooorru, carry on. We'll solve this. We have to."

The Carrot Palace didn't look at all the way it had only two days
before. Daivid walked through the echoing vault, admiring the
changes. Lin and her squad, plus every able-bodied volunteer who
had not been sewing costumes or making fake guns had been there
to help her haul flitter-sized chunks of plascrete into the vast chamber. Bags of broken glass and shards of metal had been dumped all
along the walls and inward to within two meters of the glass chunks.
Such debris created an obstacle course carefully calculated to put the
Insurgents where Daivid wanted them when he wanted them there.
The glass and metal would present no danger whatsoever to enemy
fighters wearing heavy-duty armor, but it would keep the less protected herded into the center of the big chamber. Deadfalls of more
weighty debris had been tied up in green nets that were camouflaged against the ceiling bosses to delay the escape of the Insurgents
once they were inside.

"We're about out of charges," Lin said. "I've had to substitute
propellant from the fireworks in the storehouse—though we can
make one hell of a big blast out of those, and we spent the last few
hours making demolition charges out of fireworks and boxes of
ammo. They're nasty, but they work. Everything is set to go off
from the control panel aboard my dragon, or from Adri'Leta's if I
get hit."

Daivid toured the placements, admiring the neat work of the
artillery squad and their conscripts. "If I didn't know this place was
full of high explosive, I would never be able to tell."

"Oh, you'll be able to tell, all right," the petite woman grinned.
"You'd better turn off your audio pickup when this place blows,
because your ears are going to ring for a year."

Daivid's communication link sounded. He looked down at
his wrist.

"Sir, it's Meyers," the procurement officer said. "I've got some good news and some bad news. We found the perfect item. It's a little generator that the park employees use to help keep warm during early spring and late fall. It'll give each of the puppets an internal body temperature of about 38°—a little high, but if those helmet sensors read approximately correct body heat, the enemy won't look any closer."

"I concur, Meyers. What's the problem?"

The brown-haired woman shrugged. "There's only about thirty of them. We need about a thousand. The man who makes them is here in town, but he won't donate any units. He wants to sell them to us for twenty credits each! I tried, sir. I'm good at negotiating, but this man was too much for me. Would you like to talk with him?"

Wolfe saw no point in chewing her ass. If she said she'd tried, she had. She wasn't setting him up for a joke. The fraternity initiation he'd gone through was over, and every soldier in his troop was serious about the mission. Daivid got the information from her and borrowed Boland and Captain Harawe's flitter to pay a visit to the workshop at the north end of town.

"Mr. Trewer, maybe you don't understand what is at stake here," Daivid said, trying again to explain.

Lachlan Trewer paid no attention to him. He lay back on his upholstered rocker-couch in front of his entertainment wall, and hiked up the volume again. Daivid nodded to Boland, who went over to the crystal threedeeo unit and pulled the power cell out of the core.

"Hey!" Trewer gestured as the three-dimensional images of two naked women wrestling in hot-pink slime vanished. "Put that back."

"Not until we've talked," Daivid said, sitting down heavily on the end of the couch. His weight raised the other end enough so Trewer had to sit up to keep from rolling off. "Do you have the capacity to produce more of those little heating units?"

"Sure I do, but I won't. The way I understand it, the only person who's in any kind of danger is Oscar Wingle. He's got all the money in the world, and he's got you guys to look after him. If I just sit tight, nothing's going to happen to me." Trewer reached for a silver thermal beaker and took a deep swig. "The man fired me six years ago from the engineering department. I worked my ass off for him.

I've gotten my own business going since then, but it's been hard. I can't get a recommendation from him. Nothing! Son of a bitch and his so-called standards. Like no one ever took a nap on the job. I get tired! Other people get tired!"

The accusations must have stung to feel so fresh after such a long time, but Daivid persisted. "Other people will be in danger if the Insurgents come here, not just Mr. Wingle. We need to safeguard them as well. I know you're not really interested in my problems. What will it really take to get your factory line rolling again? What do you need?"

The salt-and-pepper eyebrows went up on the mostly bald, swarthy forehead. "To turn out a thousand units by tomorrow?"

"Tonight," Wolfe said. "Immediately, if possible. There is no time to lose."

Trewer pursed his lips. "Huh. Tomorrow would have been ordinary rush fees. Tonight, double rush. To get me up off this couch, triple rush fees at least. Plus full price for parts plus time. This is my off season. Triple rush."

"Mr. Trewer," Daivid explained patiently, "I represent the Space Service. I work for the *government*. You know I can't get authorization to pay you triple rush fees. Please, be reasonable. Your town could be besieged. Don't you care about your neighbors? The Insurgents are pirates. They'll steal anything of value that they can grab."

"I make small electronic goods," Trewer said languidly. "I have nothing they want." Daivid felt his temper rising. The man was bored and enjoying flaunting his little power, probably the only time in his life he would have a way to screw over Oscar Wingle.

Daivid explained all over again in greater detail how he intended to fight the Insurgents, and what it meant to have the generators in place in his makeshift army. He put every gram of passion and urgency he possessed into his plea. "I cannot stress how important this object is to the success of our mission," he concluded.

"Well, I cannot stress," Trewer said mockingly, "how little I care." He heaved himself up out of his couch and held out his hands to Boland. Boland tossed the power supply to the owner, who put it back in the entertainment center. "There's nothing you can say that will make me gear up again, especially since you can't pay for my time, my materials or my involvement. Now, get out of my house. I'm missing the all-girl porn festival."

Wolfe felt his heart sink. The item would have been absolutely perfect for their purposes. The engineers at Wingle World felt that anything they could jury rig in such a short time would be inferior and might overheat, causing the puppets to malfunction or even catch fire. The greatest benefit of the Trewer unit was that it held perfectly steady temperature. But if the man was obdurate, Daivid couldn't force him to cooperate. They would simply have to think of something else. He signalled Boland to follow him to the door.

"Thank you, Mr. Trewer," Daivid said politely.

"Shove it, Mr. *Wolfe.*"

Wolfe pricked up his ears, his steps arrested. There was something in the scorning, resentful way Trewer snarled out his name that made him hope. He reached inside his tunic and brought out the little database as Boland watched with avid interest. On a hunch, he tapped in the name.

Dad, I never believed I'd say this, Daivid thought, *but thanks.*

He spun back on one heel to face the man in the rocking lounge. The man looked up from changing channels as Daivid cleared his throat.

"Lachlan Trewer," he said, "you owe my father a Class 3 favor."

"You know, sir," Boland said as they guided a hoverloader piled with boxes through the corridors to the engineering department, "you've got to learn to check that thing *before* you go into a situation."

"I don't intend to make constant use of it, chief," Daivid said firmly. As they rolled into the department he put the loader's controller box into Meyers's surprised hands. "There are two hundred fifty generators in this batch. The rest of them will be here by tomorrow afternoon. Careful, they're wrapped in individual padding."

"How—?" she began, astonished.

"Don't ask!" Wolfe shouted, as he stalked away.

"I can help install 'em," Boland offered as the engineers and puppets present descended on the crates. "You're sure these things won't cause a meltdown in the circuitry?"

"Heck, son," Bigfoot Cowboy drawled, picking up one of the small boxes in his padded hands, "we done been through worse weather than that. Our summers get to 43°, 44° sometimes. We're all good for at least 300°. Got to be fire retardant. That's what the marshals tell us, and you always obey the marshal."

"Of course, sir," Boland said, grinning.

"Could be ma'am," Meyers pointed out playfully. "The voice synthesizers disguise the actual speaker pretty well. Why, he could be any gender, any age."

Boland handed off crates from the loader's bed to eager hands. "As long as the enemy thinks they're someone, honey, then I don't care if they're a four-eyed goblin with the croup."

"Got one of those," an engineer said, after a moment's thought.

The next morning, Wolfe and Borden went on a review of the updated puppets, with Sparky and several of the more advanced marionettes tagging along behind. D-45's troop, the 'welcoming committee' who would be stationed closest to the entrance of Wingle World, stood for inspection in the middle of Main Street. A crowd of huge furry cats, dogs, snakes, fish, goats and a few select 'humans' held their weapons at parade rest.

"Watch it with that sword," Wolfe instructed one frog who had his saber slung haphazardly on his humped back. "You can slice your own leg off with the foil edge. Here, let me show you a better way to wear it." He reached over the warty head, and the bulging eyes followed him as he turned the curved edge upward. "Grab for the hilt, and it'll come out business end downward."

"Aye, aye, sir!" the giant amphibian croaked. A few of the others rearranged their gear to match.

Wolfe stood back to have a good look. Like him, many of the Park Irregulars wore the dark blue lightweight 'armor' with protective bubble helmets. Unlike his, few of theirs were real. Only Boland's, Ewanowski's, Okumede's and Ambering's suits had been large enough to lend to the more colorful characters. The rest had been loaned to human or itterim puppets who would draw the most fire in the early stages of the battle Daivid had planned out. When he examined them through his infrared scopes, the heat sensors picked up what it recognized as the red signature of a living being. While the creatures didn't have heartbeats or respiration, the sound of their operator's breath or heartbeat was frequently audible from the sensitive and sophisticated voice system.

"The enemy will assume any strange signal artifacts are just military gadgets that they don't have," Borden reassured him.

"I hope this works," Wolfe said, dismissing the squads with a sharp salute of approval. "This is about all we can do. We're as ready as we can be. We can't put off the bad guys forever."

"I concur, sir. The irregulars will start to lose their edge. I believe the psychological moment will come within thirty-six hours if nothing happens before that time."

"I know *I'm* on edge," Wolfe agreed, twining his fingers together and cracking them impatiently. "I've got to dump this tension, or I'm going to make too many mistakes."

"You know," Sparky piped up from behind them, "Cockroaches is an awful name for a combat unit. It's ugly. Everyone says so."

"I don't care what everyone says," Wolfe said impatiently, trying to think. What was he missing? He'd been over the checklists again and again. Heating elements had been placed in the Palace and other locations where the Cockroaches would be concealed to mask their infrared outlines. He ought to get an hour's sleep, but he didn't think he could close his eyes—or if he did, he wouldn't open them again for sixteen hours. "That's the unit's name."

The blond puppet nudged them both. "You ought to call yourself something like the Wolfe Pack. Get it?"

"Yeah, I get it," Wolfe snarled. "Go jump in a vat of acid, will you?"

"All right," Sparky said in a thick accent, "but I'll be back. Get it? I'll be back?"

"I've seen the vid. Now, will you shut up?" Daivid said peevishly, then paused. *Wolfe Pack.* He did like the idea, but it would be the utter end of hubris to name the group after himself until and unless he earned it. He glanced at Borden, who cocked an eyebrow at him.

"I like it, sir," she said. "Anything's better than Cockroach."

"I haven't earned that kind of right yet, lieutenant," Daivid said sharply.

"You're working on it, sir," Borden said. "You've come a long way from making beds in the barracks."

"Thanks, I think."

Sparky looked Borden up and down, and grinned at her. "Lizzie Borden took an axe, and gave her mother forty whacks. When the job was nicely done, she gave her father forty-one!"

Borden raised her rifle and sighted down it at the puppet.

"Don't do it, gorgeous!" Sparky warned her. "You don't want another one on your conscience!"

"Another what?" Wolfe asked, automatically.

"Sir, I haven't got anything on my conscience," Borden protested, then looked discomfitted. That wasn't true, and all of them knew it. Every living being had done things that s/he regretted. Wolfe doubted that like the subject of the five-thousand year old Terran rhyme that D.E. Borden, Lieutenant (jg), was guilty of the brutal and gruesome murder of her parents. Just being transferred to the Cockroaches meant Borden had some skeleton in her personal closet that she didn't like revealed, but Daivid knew Sparky was fishing for trouble. He mustered an exasperated look and gave it to his junior officer. He aimed a thumb at Sparky.

"Borden, haven't you figured out by now that this pain in the butt just likes to say things to annoy people? I don't know how he located your psychological buttons, but don't let him push them."

Sparky stuck out his tongue at Wolfe. "Spoilsport."

CHAPTER 19

A CHEERING CROWD greeted Oscar Wingle VII as he stepped out of his "personal shuttle" at the gates of Wingle World. A brass band played loud oom-pah-pah music on the side of the dais. Between the twin images of Bunny Hug, the great man hailed his audience. He held out his hands for silence.

"Ladies and gentlemen, I'm glad to have gone away from you…"

"Awwww!"

Wingle/Dudley gave them a playful, warm smile "…so I can fully enjoy the pleasure of coming back again. I am so happy to see all of you here! I've had a wonderful tour of our beautiful planet, and I feel refreshed once again. I'm going back to my secret laboratory in the Carrot Palace in the center of our beloved Wingle World to continue with my latest invention. I'm on the verge of a special breakthrough!"

A young male reporter in a red coat stepped forward. "Can you tell us about it, Mr. Wingle?"

"No, no," he said, draping an avuncular arm over the youth's shoulders. "Let's just keep it a secret for now." He tapped his temple with a forefinger. "I wouldn't want any rival inventors stealing my idea. Thank you all! See you in ten days for the grand opening of Wingle World! Thank you all!"

"Good," Daivid said, in his makeshift bunker among the concrete monoliths in the Carrot Palace, as the interviewer finished up with a little more gushing for the camera. He dusted his gloved hands together. Borden and the rest of the Cockroaches were wearing their ghost armor, most of them underneath costume shells, but he was in his blues so the Insurgents could mark and identify him. "That ought to bring them running. Where are they?"

Beside him, Borden checked her infopad, reading the planetary telemetry grid. "Halfway around the world. They've been flying in a zig-zag for hours since Dudley's last broadcast."

Wolfe activated his communications link. "Everyone on station?"

"Aye, sir," Lin replied.

"Aye, aye," said Boland.

"Triple aye," added D-45.

"*Noms de guerre* only from this point on. The sum is thirteen, and the color is brown."

"Aye," came from the three squad chiefs.

Daivid changed frequencies. "Puppeteers on standby. You probably have an hour. Use it to rest, relieve yourselves or get something to eat."

"We're fine," Connie's voice said in his ear. "You be careful. You're the ones who can bleed."

"Launch the special hoverbus," Daivid said.

"Aye, sir," Streb's voice replied. "They're ready. And—It's off!"

"Turn everything else on!"

"Got it," Glaijet responded from the central command center three stories below the ticket booths. "Rides, ambient music, the works, on—Now!"

All around Daivid the silence was shattered by ten thousand speakers all coming to life at the same time. The most shrill was the calliope music coming from the gigantic carousel only ten meters away that began to revolve, its horses and other colorful painted animals rising and falling as if at the urging of invisible riders. Rainbows of light flashed, creating laser pictures and three-dimensional cartoons on the walls and pavements around the huge building.

"Hi, children!" the voice of Bunny Hug boomed out from overhead. "Welcome to my Carrot Palace! There's room here for everyone! Come and share a happy day with me! Welcome to Wingle World!" A short passage of cheerful music followed, then the message began to repeat.

"Ok, folks," Daivid said, pacing up and back, feeling the excitement dancing in his bones. "All we can do now is wait."

"You there, sonny?" a familiar cranky voice inquired.

Daivid's hand flew to his communication link. He exchanged glances with Borden. "I'm here, Mr. Wingle."

"Good news, boy! I'm finished! This chip is possibly one of the finest inventions I have ever created. Under other circumstances I might have put it up for open auction, but since you're going to so much trouble to safeguard my people, it's yours. I give you my word."

"Thank you, sir," Wolfe said, gratified.

"I'm putting it in a safe place. A very safe place. Now I can keep my mind on my characters. Everything else ready?"

Wolfe smiled. "We're good to go, sir. Keep your head down."

For a moment, the old man sounded just as warmly avuncular as Dudley. "Same to you, sonny. Good luck."

"All right, everyone, they're landing! Anyone who is not a designated observer, into the tunnels."

The four shuttles circled low over the park. Many structures reached up to the skies from the vast complex, but none so high or so majestic as the Carrot Palace. The carrot-shaped flags fluttering from flagpoles mounted upon its four identical tapered orange turrets were over one hundred fifty meters in the air. The building itself was a curious structure. Based upon its eponymous vegetable, the walls of the tall square structure were ribbed and slightly bulgy. In the round spots where rootlets might form on a real carrot were tiny windows rimmed with what appeared to be twinkling jewels, but were most likely only light-emitting diodes in bright colors. Colonel Ayala could not guess from energy emissions which one of those, if any, concealed the workshop of Oscar Wingle. With the din rising from the rides and attractions, sensors couldn't pick up a low-level vibration like a heartbeat.

"Set down," he ordered the four pilots.

"Where, sir?"

Ayala scanned the map on the navigator's screen. "There isn't room near the tower. There." He pointed. "That's plenty of space for us. Easy in, and easy out."

"That gives us six routes toward the Carrot Palace," Oostern said. "We should split up."

"Good advice, Oostern," Ayala said, nodding. "Thirty-five each way under a captain," he said, fanning his hand out over the first five paths, to the southeast, east, northeast, southwest and west. "The remaining forty-five with me to the northwest, the most direct route. The attractions that way are the most all-enveloping, and will give the greatest cover. The rest of you, watch out that you do not attract attention. Report when you're within range of the target. We want to surprise him, and not give him time to destroy the chip before we can get our hands on it."

"Who's got the extremes on the pool?" Boland asked from his point of concealment in the freshly planted bushes around the entrance to Jungle Adventure Land.

"Streb says he'll land right underneath the Carrot Palace," Mose said. "Okumede says they'll land in the parking lot. Everyone else took something in between."

"Here he comes," Wolfe barked, hunkered down uncomfortably with his squad just inside the Carrot Palace walls. "Stifle it."

"Aye, sir," the two men chorused.

"First blood," Jones's voice came.

"No!" Okumede protested. "I was going to say—"

Lin interrupted. "He called it. Let's hear it, Songbird."

"*Ahem.* We Cockroaches find it is urgent/To face filthy rebels Insurgent/ With puppets galore/ We'll even the score/ And act as a Dudley detergent!"

"Fantastic! You get the points, Songbird."

"X-ray, shut up!" Wolfe growled.

"Aye, sir," they all replied.

The four shuttles whisked overhead, sputtering explosively.

"Those engines are missing pretty fiercely," Thielind commented.

"Quiet, Tinker," Wolfe said. "Just because it's loud doesn't mean they can't pick up a stray transmission."

"Sorry, Big Bad."

Though intellectually he knew they couldn't see him, Wolfe ducked automatically as the shuttles screamed in another wide turn, descending rapidly in an obvious landing trajectory. When they dropped out of sight behind the buildings, he followed their progress on a GPS map of the park in his helmet display.

"Any Street," D-45 reported, confirming Wolfe's telemetry. "They're up near the band shelter right in the middle of Anyville, all four in a line. We're on our way."

"That was my guess!" Ambering cheered.

"Pay up," Thielind said to Okumede through an open helmet channel. They lay in wait thirty meters down Any Street in clumps of shrubbery on opposite sides. "You owe Spooky on your side bet. You said they'd split up, and he said they'd stay together."

"I'll owe him the ten credits," the big man replied over the link.

"No chatter," Wolfe warned them. "They might be scanning the frequencies. Necessary info only! I don't want to have to tell you again. This isn't the day room."

"Sorry, sir," they said in unison.

"Park Irregulars, get those parking droids out there. I want those shuttles immobilized as soon as they're empty," Wolfe ordered, changing channels to the one the employees were listening to. "I don't want anyone able to lift off again."

"Right on, Lieutenant!" Engineer Glaijet said eagerly.

"They're down," Thielind announced. "Unloading. Two hundred ten. Two twenty, sir. There are some more bodies on the first ship, but they're too close together to count. Only thirty of them have camo armor. The rest have ablative armor or just uniforms. Grenade launchers, five pieces of artillery. Everyone's got rifles or machine guns. Swords. About six can openers. That's all."

"Noted, Tinker," Wolfe said, keeping his voice calm. "Ready—steady—go!"

The sharpshooter squad led by D-45 had been swelled by a host of puppets from its customary seven to over a hundred. A few of them looked like the real thing—better turned out, in some cases—but most of them, in keeping with Lieutenant Wolfe's plan, were licensed characters to disguise the real Cockroaches among them. Over his ghost armor D-45 was dressed as Waru the Snow Monkey, a wise old wrinkle-faced simian with a white ruff around his face. His second-in-command, Meyers, had a custom-made bear outfit, complete with star-shaped glasses frames and diamond-glitter bracelets. With weapons and ammunition cases, they more than filled the front seat of a personnel transport that ran through the metal-lined tunnels, its wide soft tires rolling in eerie silence.

"You look like a bordello lampshade," he told her over the mastoid implants.

"I do not!" she retorted, bridling. "This is the real me. Cuddly, fun—"

"And garish."

"That's very judgmental of you, Doug. I'm surprised," Meyers replied archly.

"Sorry, Allie," D-45 said contritely as the cart swung wide around a corner. His CBS,P web constricted around him to protect his internal organs, squeezing off his apology. The vehicle came to a halt so suddenly that everyone lurched forward. Above them, a hatch started to slide open, and a ramp dropped down almost to their feet.

"All right, sharpshooters, it's business time," the Egalitarian instructed his squad, living and non. "Everyone stay with your shooting buddy. No one gets left behind. If one of you goes down, your partner drags you back down here. Doc is in the middle of the park near the Inventor's Workshoppe. Don't be a hero.

"Now, remember," D-45 added, unlimbering his machine gun from the strap over his shoulder and snapping off the safety with a crack, "shoot to annoy! Go, go, go!"

Crack!

A single slug winged past Ayala's ear, slamming into the side of an Any Street shop. The brown-and-gray-clad Insurgents dropped to the cobbled streets, taking their weapons off safety.

"Where did that come from?" Ayala demanded. One of the itterim sergeants in camouflage armor pointed over to the right.

"About a dozen bodies in that direction, sir. And another twenty or more off that way." He gestured across the street toward a row of potted plants.

Ayala frowned. "Human? Itterim?"

The noncom checked his scopes. "I can't tell, sir. The readings are all over the place."

"Never mind! Make for the Carrot Palace. You have your orders!"

"Yes, Colonel!" the captains replied. They signalled to their platoons who began to belly-crawl toward their designated paths. More explosions sounded overhead. The soldiers dropped and began to shoot back.

From behind the shrubbery, a yellow fin rose up. A loose-lipped mouth opened and a muzzle emerged, spraying bullets toward the Insurgents. One of the cloth-clad rebels howled.

"I'm hit! It shot me!"

Ayala blinked. He knew he was suffering from lack of sleep, but he did not think that he had reached the stage of hallucination. "Is that—*a fish?*" he demanded.

"It looks like one," Oostern agreed. "And an octopus. And—I don't know what that is, that purple beast. Those cannot be real! Fish cannot swim in air!"

"They're *characters*," Ayala snapped. "Robots, or people dressed up. Return fire!" he shouted at his soldiers. "So Wingle prepared for our arrival in more than one way. He brought in defenders. No more than I expected of such an intelligent man. He would have found out that we were seeking him. These are not important." He looked back at the human who had been shot. "Bandage that and come on. You can't be badly hurt. It was just a fish, after all. Make for the band shell! Go!"

Their rifle squad laid down covering fire. Ayala drew his side-arm and sent blasts of plasma fire at the exaggerated faces that rose up on both sides of the wide avenue as he ran. They were trying to throw him off by making the troops disgusting or bizarre. A clever stratagem, but one that was going to fail, he thought. A blaze of hot fire took an animated bird-of-paradise flower straight in the pistil. It shrieked, beating at its burning petals with its leaves. The lobster behind it saw his arm rise and ducked. The white flame seared above its quivering eye stalks.

The defenders returned fire. A slow-moving charge came whistling directly at Ayala's face. He dove, and it exploded against the wall over his head. He looked up. Nothing remained of the charge but ash and bits of colored paper. Hundreds of cylinders followed. They detonated in a shower of white-hot sparks and screaming worms of light. Confetti rained down on the Insurgents.

"What kind of weaponry are they using? Are they toying with us?" Oostern demanded, crushing the paper in his pincer. Some of the soldiers who wore ordinary uniforms batted at sparks burning holes in their tunics, but no one was killed. "Do they consider this a game?"

"It doesn't matter," Ayala said. "Kill them, and get it over with. We need to get to the Carrot Palace."

From their concealed position they opened heavy direct fire with machine guns and explosive shells. One after another the planters concealing the defenders leaped into the air in pieces. The furbearing forces revealed fumbled with their guns as if surprised to be so suddenly exposed. They appeared to regain their wits, and carried on firing at the Insurgents.

At Ayala's signal, two itterim crawled forward, four limbs on the ground and two each hauling grenade launchers. Charges arched over the heads of the fish and octopi on the front lines, into the heaving sea of pink, blue and red fur he could see behind them.

One of the grenadiers counted. "One, two, three!" And ducked. The explosion shook the very air. Ayala watched, disdaining even to turn down the volume on his audio.

A tornado of multicolored fluff rose on high, accompanied by shrieks and yells of pain. To judge by the drop in the rate of fire coming from the shrubbery, the explosives had hit their mark, taking out a core group of snipers.

"Colonel," Signal-itter Riis said, "our other companies report that they are under attack from costumed troops."

"Go!" Ayala shouted at his soldiers. "Wingle is the target! We will kill all the others later if we must."

Daivid strained his eyes to follow the opening conflict on his scope. The Insurgents had made it away from the band shell, as he had hoped. Security eyes all over the park were picking up different views of the action. He'd never had multi-camera coverage of a battle before. The War College ought to be notified how useful that was for picking out superior vantage points to place heavy weapons.

"Big Bad," D-45's voice said in his ear.

"Go ahead, Numbers."

"They're on their way to the next point."

"Any losses?"

"Three puppets blown up. We made it sound a lot worse than it was."

"Get ahead of them. I want all the companies arriving at the Carrot Palace about the same time."

"Aye, sir. On our way."

Under the gaze of the security eye, the white-ruffed monkey, the aqua bear and their motley crew hustled down a chute, which sealed tightly behind them, leaving no trace of their passage.

You Are Now Entering Fairy Hollow! said the rustic wooden sign on the upright of the ornately twisted arch. *Prepare For Magic!* Beyond the fanciful swirls of giant flowers and jeweled butterflies was a dense artificial forest. Insurgent Company D could see only a few meters of crushed gemstone pathway underneath the thick growth.

Captain Erez Chen snorted as he knocked trailing vines aside with his machine gun muzzle. "Magic. What a load of crap."

His second lieutenant, Naal, a female itterim in her second decade, clicked her mandibles. "When I was small, we came here and believed. All was so real."

"I suppose you believe in dragons, too."

Naal swiveled her long face towards him with an expression of scorn. "Dragons are real. You never been to the frontier? You call them lizzzards."

"Yeah, but Terran legend says they breathe fire. That doesn't happen."

Metallic banging interrupted the conversation. The Insurgents dropped into a crouch. Chen signalled the scout patrol to go on ahead of the rest of the company. The six soldiers, humans and itterim, covered one another into the underbrush. Chen heard the rustle of their passage growing more faint as they advanced, then silence.

He spoke into his radio. "Scout party, respond."

Nothing. He exchanged a frown with Naal.

"Send others," she said.

"Until there's no one left?" he asked. "Hell with that."

"Those were not inexperienced soldiers!" the itterim argued. "If they were taken in silence, then there is something very fierce in there."

"Our orders are to take this route to the Carrot Palace," Chen said, irritated.

"We can take another route, Captain."

Chen merely lifted a hand and gestured forward. The second scout team took point. In silence they passed from Fairy Hollow into Jungle Adventure Land.

"Are they coming?" Boland asked, at ease in his royal leonine disguise on a gigantic gunnera plant made of an indestructible plastic set in a low, dimly lit clearing.

"Aye, chief," said Mose, an occasionally visible flickering outline. Streb, dressed as a spotted orange hyena named Giggles, directed his puppet force to withdraw into the thick trees.

"Why didn't you want to wear a puppet suit, Poet?" Boland asked, admiring his fistful of custom-made claws. They fit very neatly into the trigger of his machine gun, currently concealed in the folds of the cushiony leaf, and he could pick up a hair as if he was using calipers. They fit even more neatly on the controls of his special weapon the park engineers had made for him and the others for this occasion. Thanks to the CBS,P he didn't feel overheated by the addition of a thick fake-fur costume over his already bulky armor.

"I prefer to be an 'éminence grise,'" Mose replied, with a chuckle. "The power suit behind the throne. A successful one is never seen, only hinted at. You're living out your fantasy; I'm living mine."

Boland settled the crown in between his 'ears,' and waited for the Insurgents to arrive. Software, dressed in a coral flamingo costume, stood over him waving a fan that looked like it had been fashioned from her tail feathers. "It's good to be the king."

The scouts emerged into the clearing, their guns at the ready. A huge yellow beast saluted them from a thronelike plant.

"What the hell is this?" one of them asked.

"What is it?" Captain Chen demanded.

The lead scout hesitated. "Well, it looks like a theater setting, sir."

"A what?" Chen asked, pushing forward into the clearing with Naal on his heels. A tall pink bird met them at the edge of the clearing. She gestured toward the throne, where the lion sat beckoning with his long claws.

"Forward!" she said. "Come forward and pay homage to King Tullamore!"

"Bow to the king!" added an ominous voice.

"Bow, or else!" other voices chorused.

"Or else what?" Chen demanded, lowering the muzzle of his gun at the flamingo.

"Or this!" The lion reached around with one paw and came up with a strange-looking weapon. Chen sprang to one side. The stream of bright blue liquid that shot out of the muzzle caught soldiers in the next three rows. They brought up their own weapons—or tried to. Their arms were caught in place. More blue streams squirted out from between tree boles, covering the troops in glue. It hardened quickly, changing from blue to clear as it solidified.

"Break away! Break away!" Chen ordered. The twelve soldiers wearing armor or microplate suits were able to shrug off their chemical bonds and stumble forward. They opened fire on the lion, who dropped his paste-launcher and ducked behind the big leaf with another gun. Rapid-fire bursts of real bullets caused Chen and the others to back hastily into the trees. The flamingo bounded after them and was joined by another flock of birds, all firing guns they must have been concealing under their wings.

"What about the others?" Naal asked, as they ran.

"Leave them!" Chen shouted.

"But they are still alive!" the itterim argued, shocked.

"Our objective is more important," the captain said sternly. "Ayala would say the same. Now, come on! Find another way forward!" One of his bursts of fire took the head off a flamingo. It wavered and fell, but there was no blood. He spun on his heel and shot another one, full in the chest. Its head bobbed at the shock of the bullets passing through it, but it neither bled nor died.

"They are not real!" he shouted. "Colonel, can you hear me?"

"Sir, you'd better hear this," Borden said over the mastoid channel. "Turn to frequency 268.07."

Wolfe looked toward Borden even though she was concealed behind a pile of rubble. "Is that the one they're using?"

"Aye, sir. Listen, quickly."

Wolfe knew better than to question Borden's assessment of an emergency.

"…Machine parts! Wires and gears, components like that. No people in them. They're not a threat. Ignore them. They're playing soldier…."

Wolfe took a deep breath, down to his belly. The secret was out. Ayala and his officers had discovered that they were facing automata, not living soldiers.

"What should we do, sir?" Borden asked.

He growled in frustration. "How can they disbelieve the puppets as fighters? A lot of them are shooting real bullets!" He pounded a hand on the nearest concrete chunk, reducing it to powder. "This *can't* fail now. If the Insurgents think they can ignore our forces, our squads won't be able to chase them here. We need *all* of them here! Squad— I mean, company leaders, listen up! It's time to show them the 'normals.' We're going to have to give ourselves away. Do you read?"

"Aye, sir!" the chiefs responded.

"Your real troopers are pretty badly outnumbered," Wingle's voice said in Daivid's ear. "If you need the park security forces, just say so. The station's over in this part of the park, near my cottage."

"I shouldn't, sir," Wolfe said. "We don't want to draw attention to that area."

"Got it, sonny. Shouldn't interfere. I like a man who knows his own business."

Daivid scanned the park overview, hoping he did know what he was doing.

CHAPTER 20

"PUPPETS?" CAPTAIN MARSEA Gundsdottir laughed, marching through The Doll Kingdom at the head of Company A. The
section of the park, designed to delight young females of all
species, had been decorated almost entirely in shades of pink,
ranging from palest shell to hard-hitting intergalactic distress hot
pink. Every building was a castle, with battlements adorned with
pearls and precious gems. Friendly little faces peered up at them
from wall panels, refreshment stands, and the entrances to rides.
At Gundsdottir's stage of life, the color and the décor made her
feel homicidal instead of social, but the concept amused her.
"That's funny. Heavily armed puppets! I knew the guy was crazy!
Look, there's some of them now! Company, fire at will!"

A dozen or so animal characters dashed out of a doorway,
guns leveled. Gundsdottir's soldiers blithely potted away at them,
making them duck back and forth like targets in a midway booth.
The captain cut the head off a slithering snake, laughing out loud
as it continued to undulate around, unaware that it was 'dead.'

"Wait a minute, ma'am!" Lieutenant Polin cried. "Look!
TWC troops!"

Behind the frolicking animals, a dozen humans in familiar blue
armor and clear helmets fanned out, firing. The Insurgents dove
behind the nearest doll store. Sharpshooters leaned around the corner
to return fire.

"Frax them into a black hole!" Gundsdottir shouted. "Colonel! TWC!"

"What?" Ayala's voice came through full of outrage. "Impossible!"

"I've got a dozen troopers pinning us down here, Colonel! How
could Wingle have gotten CenCom to send a ship here so fast? We
only arrived four days ago!"

There was a long pause. The blue-clad troopers laid down
heavy fire as two of them lugged a black pipe out of a pink play-
house, aimed it, and dropped a heavy gray cylinder down it.
Gundsdottir hastily signalled her troops to split up and move.
"Colonel! How—? Incoming!"

The unmistakeable screech of a mortar shell drowned out Ayala's reply. "Repeat, sir!"

"It's got to be a trick," Ayala shouted. "It must be more robots."

"Well, if it's a trick, it's a good one! They've got artillery!"

"Blast them with plasma! They're only frameworks! If you burn them, they can't shell you any longer. Do it!"

"Yes, sir!" Gundsdottir shouted at her officers. "You heard the man! Blast them all!"

"Oh, slag," Somulska said, finishing a final pirouette in her cat costume. "Mustache, they're ordering the plasma gunners forward!"

Vacarole, dressed as a Florentine Merchant, part of the Walk Through History section of the park, groaned. "They'll incinerate the whole company. Everyone's going to die!"

"Everybody! Retreat! Duck into any building. Move it! Numbers, we've got problems," Somulska radioed her squad leader. "Our cover's about to be blown, and not in a nice way."

"Get out of there," D-45 instructed them. "We'll be there in a sec to give you cover."

"Whoa! Get them!" Vacarole shouted, brandishing his machine gun in one hand and his sword in the other. "Armor-piercing rounds! Attack!"

If the Insurgents were surprised to have come upon a party of TWC troopers, they were even more stunned when a velvet-clad giant in tights and ribbon garters came barreling down upon them. They froze long enough for him to let off several bursts, killing the plasma cannon crew and some of the soldiers around it. Somulska followed as soon as she regained her wits, peppering the enemy. At that range, the 6mm caseless rounds couldn't fail to shred the thin microplate suits. Two armored itterim came after her, visible only as six-armed blurs of pink-in-blue. Some of her shells bounced off their nearly invisible suits, but the armor was old and in poor repair. Black flecks seemed to appear out of nowhere as she picked away at the flexible armor. Eventually she bored holes in them. One fell right away, his machine gun spraying its entire magazine into the tree full of dolls above him. The other managed to hit her repeatedly in the chest then knee then foot. Somulska staggered backward, pain radiating through her body. Her CBS,P squeezed hard against the concussion. She fired back, searching around for her shooting buddy.

"Mustache!" The Florentine Merchant was on his back. The color of his armor was fading from blue to green, and his red silhouette was turning pink. "Numbers, he's down! Send cover!"

"On our way!"

The enemy had been beaten back ten meters by the force of the big humanoid's attack. Suddenly, it realized it was facing one solitary trooper in a torn-up cat suit. In spite of the burning pain in her leg, Somulska went rolling, stopping occasionally to fire off short bursts that kept the enemy off balance until the trigger went limp. She switched her frequency to the puppeteers who ran her squad as she slammed another magazine into her gun. "The rest of you! Keep shooting at the enemy! Keep them busy! I have to get to him. Oh, God, sir. There's blood all over his costume. I think he's dead!"

Daivid almost felt his own heart stop. He switched from park telemetry to the vital signs of his platoon. Nearly everyone had elevated pulse and respiration—all but one. The indicators, except that of brain activity, had gone down to zero. As he watched, the last one descended gently. Daivid felt as though he was watching the man die in front of him.

By that time, D-45 and half of his company had burst out of a tunnel in The Doll Kingdom. They started to drive back the Insurgents and envelop Somulska.

"What's happening?" Wolfe demanded. "How's Talon?" His audio pickup rattled with the sound of metal on metal, and metal on plastic.

The squad leader contacted Wolfe a few moments later. "She's okay, sir. Just a couple of small laser wounds and a few dents she's going to have to beat out later. A couple of the puppets are taking her to Doc. We're going for Mustache."

"No!" Wolfe exclaimed.

"No?" D-45 asked, clearly astonished.

"*No?*" Borden demanded. "Sir, we have to extract his body. It's our code, sir. No one is ever left behind, alive or dead."

"No," Wolfe said firmly. "And he won't be left—later. For now, you have to leave his body there. He's beyond help, Numbers, but he can still serve. Let him lie there."

"But, sir—!"

"Leave him! Get out of there now! Number, taunt them! Get them to follow you. Everyone head toward the Carrot Palace." Wolfe cut the connection, hating himself. He clenched his fists tight.

"*Why*, sir?" Borden asked through the bone implant. She sounded betrayed.

"Because," Wolfe's voice shook with anger, "because we made a mistake, Axe. We gave the puppets body temperature, but we didn't give them bodies. The Insurgents think they're *all* puppets. They didn't believe in the TWC troopers. They will have to, now."

But the incident was not without repercussions. Word spread through the platoon that the CO had failed to honor the remains of one of their dead. He overheard—deliberately, he was sure—Streb giving a very detailed, heartfelt description of a painful and thoroughly obscene punishment the afterlife held for soldiers who failed their comrades in arms. It sounded as though it was aimed at the Insurgents he was chasing toward the Carrot Palace, but Wolfe wasn't fooled.

The Insurgents seemed to be, though. Word had clearly gotten around *their* command that some of the troopers they were facing *were* real. Ayala was bewildered as to where they had come from, and who had summoned them. A chittering, panic-stricken voice Wolfe supposed belonged to an itterim officer gave a warm-body count of the defending force and come up with between two and three thousand, some in uniform and some dressed as characters.

Wolfe, waiting impatiently under cover, grinned mirthlessly to himself. Those tunnels were proving to be a terrific tool. If the enemy only knew the real troopers only numbered twenty-three—twenty-two now—they'd wet themselves laughing. He wished he could laugh. He wished the whole thing was over, one way or another.

A hand tapped him on the back, and he nearly jumped out of his skin. He sprang up, sidearm trained on his assailant. His reactions saved him from firing. It was Sparky.

"You know, everyone is saying what you're doing is wonderful," the puppet said, seating himself on a plascrete block with ease.

Wolfe felt a ray of hope that not everyone hated him just then. His heart slowed to a normal pace. "Thank you," he said sincerely. "We're glad you appreciate our efforts."

The puppet cocked his head. "Oh, not me! I think you're just trying to get attention."

Wolfe groaned. "Why in hell do I listen to you?"

Borden's voice broke in. "Sir! Telemetry!"

Wolfe was relieved to be able to ignore his animated gadfly, even if it was for bad news. Part of the group that Boland's company had been chasing around Fairy Hollow had gotten away from them. According to his tag, Boland was closing in on them through the tunnels, but the Insurgents were going to reach the Carrot Palace ahead of them.

"Into position, everyone!" Wolfe announced to his own company of puppets. "We've got a dress rehearsal!"

Captain Chen raced through Gamehaven with the remains of his company around him. Every time the gaudy arcade attractions rang or flashed, he thought it was more of the weirdly costumed beings coming at them. Only twelve of his thirty-five people left! The others, suspended in glue, had continued to shout at him through their helmet audio until abruptly, they were cut off. He supposed the TWC, or Oscar Wingle's costumed freaks—were they androids or robots, or what?—had killed them all. He would almost certainly have done the same. He knew the Insurgency's policy: if a captive wasn't worth trading and refused to sign on, he or she died on the spot. They didn't have the budget for prisoners.

"Are they puppets, or aren't they?" he shouted at the other captains.

"Dammit, I can't tell," Captain Gundsdottir growled back. Her company was under fire from a fresh wave of fur-bearing combatants. "We killed someone. We've got the body."

"Some of these *can't* be real," Captain Zebediah of Company E insisted. "I've seen crocodiles crawling on their bellies. No TWC personnel do that. They have to work for the park!"

"What about the mortar?" Gundsdottir demanded. "Do amusement venues usually have artillery?"

"Don't try to sort them out," Ayala ordered them. "Destroy anything that moves. Get to the Carrot Palace!"

"Almost there, sir," Chen assured him, his breathing sounding loud in his own ears. He checked the magazine on his machine gun. Still about half full. He had another ammunition box strapped to his back. Every shot had better count.

Naal dropped back to his side, the camouflage of her power suit giving her a bizarrely-colored leopard-spot appearance in the midway lights. "Life signs ahead in the Carrot Palace, sir," she said. "Not many, about twenty. There might be a few other emissions, but there are heat sources blocking my scan. Some have powered armor. I have the traces."

"Good," Chen replied. "Twenty or even thirty is easy. We'll clean them out for Colonel Ayala." Maybe that would make up for losing two thirds of his company to something as low-tech as glue!

The Meadow Pavilion was ahead, a wide-open expanse of rides and attractions. Above it all, soaring to orange heights, was the Carrot Palace. Chen gestured over his head. "Come on!" he signed. Three fingers sent the advance gunners, what was left of them, forward in a crouch around the edge of the Bounding Main, a pirate ship tableau made entirely of inflated cushions to jump on.

"Sailing, sailing!" the speakers sang deafeningly as the Insurgents crept forward across the speaker grates in the teal-blue pavement. "Over the bounding main! Yo ho ho and a bottle of rum!"

Chen growled. "Don't these things impair children's hearing?"

The scouts gestured them forward. Chen's readings were that the life signs were deep inside the Palace. He could take them by surprise. He ordered his small force to creep forward.

The most enormous carousel he had ever seen stood between Company D and their target. Every kind of creature that had ever been discovered was represented as riding steeds on the multi-tiered creation.

"Sir!" Naal hissed. "Dragons!"

"Yes, yes, I can see them," Chen said, flicking a hand at the ride. "Dragons."

"No, sir!" the itterim chittered, pointing upwards. "Dragons!"

"Dragons, just chase them around for a while," Wolfe ordered, watching the whole scene on his scopes. "Pay no attention to the following announcement."

"Aye, aye, sir!" Lin acknowledged with pleasure. She kicked the control that sent the dragon rocketing to the east.

It felt good not to be earthbound for a while. The one- or two-rider scout tanks slightly resembled their namesakes in that they were flown upright, with the pilot standing on two long footrests in between the twin missile launchers, which would be where the dragon had wings. It breathed fire, too, from a plasma gun set in the frame high over her head, above a protective duroplas shield that extended like a mummy case all the way around the front and much of the rear of the pilot's perch. She looked out through what would be its neck, with heads-up display on all four sides of the scope, and the controls were finger studs in the hand rail. Lin played the buttons like a virtuoso as she and Adri'Leta swooped down on the dozen wavering shapes. The Insurgents instantly broke ranks and ran off in all directions. Lin picked out the one with the most intact camo—best gear usually meant it was an officer. She rattled off a few rounds of ammunition, not bothering with a missile or a plasma blast. That would come later. Adri'Leta decided to pursue the forward patrol trying to lose themselves under the Bounding Main attraction.

Daivid turned to frequency 268.07.

"Dragon squadron A, prepare to follow the scouts. Dragon squadron B, await my orders. That is all." He scrolled back to the channels his people were following. "Bluff has been offered. Let's see if it makes them nervous."

Judging from the chatter that Borden was monitoring, the Insurgents reacted with shock to the news that there were armed scout vehicles in the air. D-45 and Boland reported that their prey started watching the skies within moments of the announcement. It made the Insurgents so careless that the Cockroaches had to start missing to keep them on the move.

In a few moments Boland, in his persona as King Tullamore, emerged from a tunnel and attracted the Insurgents' attention by peppering the Bounding Main with bullets. As the inflatable ships sank in the inflatable sea, it was every human or bug for itself, trying to escape from beneath before they suffocated. Boland's team waited patiently until they emerged, sprayed them with fireworks, and got them running again in the direction of their eventual target.

"Dragons!" Ayala snarled as they pressed forward through Pioneer Town to aid Company D. This was no 'amusement' to Ayala. The rides and shops were designed to resemble early generation ships and modular domes, made of reclaimed plastic and fuel tanks from the earliest colonization efforts. He knew dispossessed spacers who were still living in those pathetic conditions. He had lived in one for a short time himself. His next domicile, he vowed, would be a beautiful country estate built by hand by Confederation Senators who would never again impose illicit laws upon innocent people. "Grena-diers and shoulder-mounted missiles to the fore! It is the TWC! Were they waiting for us? Was this an elaborate set-up to catch us? No, it couldn't be. The intelligence on Wingle's invention goes back more than eight months! I've been hearing *rumors* for two years!"

"Don't forget," Oostern put in, "the trap our ships fell into trying to secure the Tachytalk units. That had to have been carefully laid out for our spy."

"So there is no chip?" Ayala shook his head. "There has to be a chip. We *need* that chip, or those TWC bastards will keep us down forever!"

"There must be a chip," Oostern agreed, "or why would they have led us on such a chase?"

"They want it for themselves," Ayala reasoned.

A kick-line of tigers interrupted his musing. The striped beasts, in a multiplicity of colors nature never foresaw, began to dance through the prefab shacks. The gunners opened fire on them. A blue one and a green one were cut in half by the barrage of bullets, and numbers of red, orange, silver and purple tigers fled from the range of fire. Two, white and red, seemed to be resistant to the attack. As Ayala's people concentrated on them, they sprang over the domes and disappeared, bullets nipping their tails. A mix of Space Service troopers and more animals poured out of the buildings around them, shooting sprays of glittering light into their midst.

"More fireworks?" Ayala asked, until an itterim two meters away fell, ichor pumping from his thorax. The soldier twitched feebly, but Ayala knew it was done for. He gave the order to draw and evade. "Those are real troopers!" he shouted, as he elbow-crawled under the swinging doors of the 'Saloon.' "Frag them!"

The WHUMPH! of exploding grenades sent troopers flying into the air in pieces—but none of them bled.

"More robots!" he screamed. "They are killing us with robots!"

He ordered full fire, until nothing remained but a few twitching wires. He stood panting in the ruins of the building. Chairs lay splin-tered on their backs. The metal mirror over the bar was dented and holed. The old-time music maker on the wall had stopped playing its honky-tonk piano tunes. All was silent except for moaning and cursing. A quarter of his company was wounded, some dead.

"I am still reading live bodies underground," Oostern hissed. He stepped forward cautiously, reading his scopes, and scrabbled among the wreckage. He came up with a small black box. "It's hot." He dropped it on the ground and crushed it with his boot.

"So that's how they are doing it," Ayala admired a worthy foe. "So we cannot tell the real ones from the sham troopers. It doesn't matter. We will destroy them all, and kill Oscar Wingle—as soon as the chip is in my hands."

Humming rose over the noise from distant attractions. Ayala went on guard, checking his scope. "Scout! I only read one."

"It's a dragon," Oostern confirmed. "That'll be one of the pair that Chen saw."

Ayala's eyes narrowed. "That won't be a puppet flying it," he said greedily. "Bring it down!"

"Missiles lock on!" Oostern ordered. "On my command—Fire!"

"Ammo!" Adri'Leta squawked, seeing columns of white smoke rising at a sharp angle from the ground. "Missile launchers! Two coming my way!"

"Evade, Mimeo!" Lin commanded. "Can you distract them into another target?"

The clone rode her tank like a windsurfer, leaning and angling sharply, in hopes of dislodging the projectiles from her tail. She did some fancy flying, looping through the angles of roller coasters and parachute drops until the G-force made her cheeks flatten inside her armor, even flying down in between a pair of burning-hot spotlights over a concert arena, but the missiles matched her moves, twin blips on her nav screen.

"No way! They must have brain chips!" Once they'd acquired her, nothing but destroying the missiles themselves would keep them from chasing her to the Crab Nebula and back. Desperately, she set the plasma cannon to follow the first missile. If she blew that one, it might take its partner with it. She rode out over the nearest mountain range, the noonday sun beaming brightly off the snow-covered ridge. No one would get hurt out there.

The missiles, having less bulk to move and depleting propellant with every kilometer, were gaining on her. She fired once, but the target dodged to the side. The streak of white-hot energy carved a trench in the snowpack. Smart brain chips! Where had the Insurgency picked up those? She fired again, framing the missile with shots to top and bottom, not giving the projectile room to escape.

As she had planned, her third shot seared the point-nosed cylinder. She was three kilometers ahead of it when it burst in a blaze of blinding blue light. To her dismay, the other missile streaked forward out of the holocaust. One to go.

By now Lin had freed herself and was coming to the rescue of her shooting buddy. The other dragon spiraled up from the shadow of the Carrot Palace. Adri'Leta traced her streams of fire, angled upward so Lin wouldn't hit her by accident. Sweat rolled down her back. Her body suit changed temperature to cool her, but it couldn't do anything to slow her pounding heart. She didn't want to die!

"Here it comes again," Ayala crowed as the dragon dove down toward them with death in its wake. "Only one missile left! A very skilled pilot. It should be rewarded with a swift death. Fire when it comes in range. Armor piercing. Aim for where the cockpit is open. That will be its back."

"Yes, sir. On my mark," Oostern readied the gunners. "Fire!"

Lin had the measure of the missile now. If she hit it just right, it would tumble out of control and detonate over Wingle Lake, about a kilometer north of the Carrot Palace. She leaned into her scopes, accelerating after Adri'Leta, who was going into a dive preparatory to zooming high over the park and out again. Her hands closed on the controls and gently squeezed.

Telescoped grenade charges shot out of all four barrels, over and under her launchers. They lanced out, struck the missile broadside. Just as it passed over the lake, Lin sent the command and the cylinder blew, loudly and more colorfully than any of the fireworks the puppets had been using for ammo. She enjoyed the spectacle for a second, then swooped around in a circle.

"Mimeo?" she asked.

The other dragon was flying at an angle. The shape at the controls was black, indicating that the suit's power was off line. As Lin watched in horror, the scout vehicle turned upside down in mid-air. The body fell bonelessly, and the dragon sped off alone. Lin swooped down, seeking the dark shape among the innumerable buildings. The lights blinded her.

"Mimeo just got dropped," Lin reported. "I'm going down."

"We've lost one pilot," Wolfe replied. "We can't lose both. Retreat."

"But I'm not leaving her the way you let them leave Mustache," she said fiercely. "No way."

"Yes, you are," the voice said sharply. "That is an order. Retreat. Get whoever shot her to follow you."

"She trusted you. You're letting her down."

"She knew and understood what we are doing here. The mission is bigger than a single individual. It's for an entire population, a whole world! Remember the Space Service motto? There's no 'I' in 'corps'."

"And there's no 'u' in 'asshole', but you're acting as if there is!"

"Chief! Return to base—Now!"

Lin felt tears starting down her face and cursed that she couldn't wipe them off. Was this the wet-eared kid they'd been trying to bring along for a month? He was acting like an *officer*. And was she the same multiply-decorated and much-demoted lifelong trooper who'd been so *amused* by him before? She was trying to do too much, to the detriment of their mission, and he had caught her at it. Their roles were reversed, and she didn't like the feeling. But how could she leave the body of her friend and sister in arms? "I hate you."

The voice was sorrowful but resolute. "I can live with that. Take it out on Ayala later. Get back here. Cuddles will retrieve the other dragon. Poet, how close are you and your company to Pioneer Village?"

"A hop, skip and jump," Mose's voice said.

"Good. Get whoever's there and bring them. I want their asses here when the boom falls. Tullamore, I need your help."

"Aye, sir," Boland's voice said.

"I'm opening all the communication links. Repeat after me..."

Lin bit her lip and kicked the scout vehicle into high.

"Retreating!" Ayala crowed, watching the second dragon fly away in the direction of the Carrot Palace. "I suspect that the air cover we all heard about is just a bluff! Otherwise, would you not expect a full retaliatory strike? We killed one of their tanks, and that leaves only one!"

A party of itterim had rushed out on his command, and came back with the black hulk. Up close it was smaller than it had seemed. Ayala ignored the huge hole the explosive armor-piercing projectile had carved out of the back, and flicked off the helmet. "A human woman," he confirmed, "a real one." Blood poured out from between the paling lips, and the eyes stared half-lidded at nothing. He noted the rank markings on the breast of the suit, visible now that it was powered down to black ceramic. "There are troopers here, but how many?"

"...Fall back!" a tiny voice erupted from the body. The itterim nearest it jumped back, startled. The woman was dead! But the voice was male. She was not speaking. It was coming from inside the helmet. He held it up to listen. "The lieutenant has the chip, repeat, he's got the chip. Everybody fall back to the Carrot Palace on the double. We've got to cover him for our extraction."

Another voice, also male, screamed, "Tullamore, cut circuits at once! The enemy has Mimeo's body—this channel is no longer secure! Everyone cut links."

"Sorry, sir," the first voice said contritely.

The communication link shut down, but too late for the TWC. Ayala smirked. He dropped the helmet beside the limp corpse.

"Prepare to move out," he commanded. "Wingle has turned over the device to a Space Service officer."

"Ooga booga!" screeched a big cream-colored ape, leaping down from a building top. "Ooga booga!" He beat his chest with both fists and capered around the Insurgents.

"Coconut Gorilla!" Oostern exclaimed. The simian knuckled his way up to the itterim and began to pluck at his armor with flexible forefinger and thumb. Oostern was delighted. Coconut Gorilla was a friendly character in the children's threedeeo programs who liked to groom his new friends.

"Don't waste time with those," Ayala snarled. "We must get to the Carrot Palace." He whipped out his plasma gun and opened fire on the anthropoid. But Coconut Gorilla was faster than he was. The bolt lashed out, setting fire to a kiosk covered with crash-couch upholstery, but not the puppet. Ayala found the furry ape beside him. Coconut Gorilla grinned, showing rows of pointed white teeth, and backhanded him in the face with one huge arm.

The blow sent the colonel flying.

"Kill him!" Ayala shouted. He wasn't hurt. The blow had taken him in the helmet. Only the shock of the attack made him angry. Coconut Gorilla shrieked with glee, clambered four-handed up the walls, and ran along the tops of the buildings. Either the bullets missed him, or they had no effect. Three soldiers ran after him, still shooting.

"Ooga booga!" voices chanted from behind the quonset huts. "Ooga booga!"

"That must be a trooper," a lieutenant commented. "How could a puppet be so strong?"

"How could a trooper climb a wall like that?" Oostern retorted. "Beware of the characters. They are more dangerous than we know. I never dreamed they were so strong!"

"Ignore them!" Ayala ordered. "We know where our objective is now."

"Who cares if you're afraid of spiders!" Captain Zebediah of company E shouted at her command. "You're *supposed* to kill them!"

In answer, a huge barrage of shots rang out from behind her, blasting away at the dancing blue arachnids that seemed to taunt them, hanging from trees and buildings, rolling their multiple black eyes. "Control your fire, you six-legged nincompoops! We don't have an infinity of ammunition!"

From the very first moment they had entered Futureland, the itterim soldiers had started getting nervous. Zebediah herself had glimpsed shadows skittering by in the distance. She assumed that the defense forces were stalking them. Who knew that it was psychological warfare? Somewhere in the primitive hindbrain of the itterim lay a morbid fear of spiders, deeper and more paralyzing than even humans' wariness of the hairy, eight-legged abominations.

Snipers had targeted the rear ranks, silently picking off soldiers until one of them died with his pincer wrapped around the trigger of his machine gun, spraying gunfire forward into his own colleagues' unarmored backs. The company spun around, guns ready, to face the clicking, slavering mandibles of three blue spiders the size of tanks. The itterim soldiers had filled the air with bullets, but the spiders lifted upwards on invisible threads and dashed up and over the framework of the gigantic roller coaster next door. After that, only by using the threat of shooting them herself had Zebediah kept the entire company from deserting. A gleaming eye or a jointed, hairy leg appearing around the corner of a building was enough to cause the group to fire off an ammunition-wasting fusilade.

"Squad A, advance!" Aaooorru ordered in his high, clear voice. "Squad B, flank attack!"

Half the character army assigned to him marched in perfect ranks around to the side of the Inventor's Workshoppe, and the other half sneaked off into the bushes. Now that the spiders had the Insurgents surrounded, it should have been no trouble to keep them busy until Lieutenant Wolfe wanted them at the Carrot Palace. Instead, he was finding himself fighting a pitched battle around the Inventor's Workshoppe.

"Do you need some help, shrimpy?" Oscar Wingle's voice asked over his implanted receiver.

"No, sir," Aaooorru replied.

"I can activate the security force. It'd be no trouble. Those idiots are making so much noise, it's going to start coming out of my characters' mouths."

"I—I'll try to get them to be quiet, sir," the corlist replied. "All we want to do is get them moving, but I'm afraid we freaked them out with the spiders, sir."

"Hah! Should have asked your buggy friend. Itterim have this race memory of being eaten by spiders. Deep-seated, really. Humans are afraid of them, too."

The corlist was mortified. "But they call me Spidey! Is it an insult to name me for something that repulses them?"

"No. They like you. It's a *nom de guerre*, isn't it? Supposed to sound fearsome? That's why I keep the arachnids in the Chamber of Horrors. A real pants-wetting experience. You should try it."

"Maybe later, sir," the corlist replied, left with a cultural conundrum to mull over. "Out."

"Colonel Ayala gave his orders," Zebediah shouted, trying to get through to the stupid mantises panting in fear, tongues darting between mandibles. "We have to get to the Carrot Palace!"

"They have us surrounded," chittered her lieutenant. "We must blow through their lines."

"Fine," Zebediah said, her patience exhausted. It was the only thing she missed about belonging to an organized militia: giving an order and having it obeyed without question. She could shoot them herself, or wait for them to settle their problem. "Bring up the shoulder-mounted cannon. We'll knock through that refreshment stand and have a clear run to the major avenue. Fire one!"

CHAPTER 21

WOLFE STOOD INSIDE the arch with his arms crossed as his troops began to pour into the Meadow Pavilion from a dozen different pathways. Bullets zinged over their heads or slapped into the back or limbs of the fleeing figures. He winced when a barrage took out all the lights on the top of the Undersea Adventure ride as the Insurgents tearing along behind Boland the Lion King tried to kill the animals that stuck out their tongues and rolled their eyes at their pursuers.

He knew they wouldn't see him at first. Most of the soldiers racing toward him were in motley collections of uniform pieces eked out with sections of armor. Not all of them had helmets with infrared scopes. They were lucky if the plastic compound was laser-resistant. Most of them weren't expected to live to see the Great Society. Sitting ducks, but that was the Insurgency way.

With sitting ducks in mind, he glanced back at his ersatz army. The characters nudged each other and chuckled, as though they were getting ready for a really special party.

"Is everyone on the way?" he asked Borden.

"Spidey and Scratch are keeping station," the junior lieutenant replied tersely. "They're busy, but all is well so far. The rest are on the way. Thielind reports at least 80% of the Insurgents are in pursuit of our auxiliaries or coming here on their commander's orders."

"Good," Daivid said. "That'll do for now."

Borden was hardly speaking to him. She had broken concealment and climbed out of the rubble to confront him in person—or, more accurately, to confront his moving outline—about the abandonment of the two dead troopers. He'd explained his reasoning again and again, but it sounded worse every time he rehashed it. He had finally ordered her back to her place, refusing to say another word about it. He would probably pay for both the refusal and the dishonorment later, but that was later. They had to live through this battle first. Nothing was certain. They had no extraction, as Boland had broadcast on the helmet channel for the benefit of the enemy he knew would be listening. He had prepared as best he could. Lin, Jones and Ambering were hidden around the perimeter of the square: Ambering on her belly on the roof of the carousel with their big gun, and the other two standing by aboard the dragons.

His belly gnawed at him. He had been too excited to eat more than a few bites of a MERD for breakfast. He could see the rest of the meal in his mind as though it was there before him: hot flapjacks, grilled protein strips, reconstituted fruit compote that wasn't half bad, but all kilometers away out of reach. Even the last of the coffee had gone hours ago. He had water and soft nutrient paste to suck in an emergency, but he'd already discovered it still tasted of Boland's moonshine. Next time, he would see personally to steaming out his suit's tanks.

As the enemy began to fill the winding garden paths leading toward the Carrot Palace, the characters took over the job of leading them on. The remaining Cockroaches and uniformed puppets peeled off and vanished unobtrusively into kiosks and doorways. Wolfe could see it in his mind as if he was watching it on a scope as they dropped into the hidden maze of tunnels and made their way into the building behind him. The Cockroaches were stripping off their costumes—Boland and Meyers probably protesting—and emerging in gleaming invisibility up among the plascrete boulders. Very soon the Carrot Palace would be surrounded.

He thought he spotted Ayala's code tag on a pink shadow now entering the pavilion from the southeast. Closer, Daivid urged him silently. Closer...

"Where did the troopers go?" the Insurgent colonel demanded, racing out with his plasma pistol in hand. Suddenly there was no one in the plaza except the soldiers and hundreds of costumed mountebanks. The Carrot Palace towered above them only a few hundred meters ahead. He saw red traces of body heat, and some mixed signals that might have been chameleonic armor. The lieutenant with the chip was somewhere in that foolish-looking building with the object of his desire.

His company pressed forward into the crowd of performers that swelled as he got closer to the building. Ayala began to lose sight of his men. He ordered them closer together, ignoring the furred, beaked, muzzled and bewhiskered faces that pressed curiously around them.

"Are any of these real?" he demanded. "Are there any living creatures inside any of them?"

"I'll find out, sir," Oostern replied. He signalled to all of the captains, who barked out an order.

Machine gun fire rang out, riddling the shouting, laughing, dancing figures with holes. None of them bled or screamed or fell down.

"No, sir," the itterim acknowledged calmly.

Ayala hollered out orders to his captains. "Surround the Carrot Palace. No one is to get out alive. Advance! Kill the lieutenant and bring me the chip!"

Wolfe waited until all the Insurgents he could see on his scopes were out in the open.

"All right, let them have it! Puppeteers, abandon escort duty!"

In the four quarters of the pavilion, the puppets suddenly sprinted away from the tightly huddled groups of Insurgents. Even from a distance, Wolfe could see the astonished looks on the soldiers faces. He grinned.

"Turn the music up loud!"

"Hi, children!" Bunny Hug's prerecorded voice echoed deafeningly over the pavilion. "Welcome to my Carrot Palace! There's room here for everyone! Come and share a happy day with me! Welcome to Wingle World!"

Wolfe found himself having to shout to hear his own voice. "Heavy duty firepower, now!"

"With pleasure," Lin said over her channel. She and Jones flew out from among the turrets of the Carrot Palace and made a strafing run over the soldiers to north and south of the building. Ambering blasted off shells to the west, landing in the rear ranks of Insurgents. The alloy pavement erupted, sending gouts of molten green plastic in every direction. Soldiers caught in the blast howled in pain. Some fell, beating at the adhesive hot globs with their hands. The rest broke and ran.

"Advance!" Wolfe ordered, springing up. He shouldered his own machine gun. His muscles tensed. He was ready for action. He'd been ready for hours! "Let's give them all a nice, warm Space Service reception! Fire at will! Try not to destroy more of the park than you have to! I've got to answer to Mr. Wingle when all this is over!"

From the north of the building marched Borden with Okumede, Parviz and Injaru fanned out behind her. From the west, Thielind led D-45, Meyers and Somulska. From the east, Boland marched in step with Itterim Haalten, his shooting buddy, and his second in command, Mose, with Streb bringing up the rear. And from the south, Wolfe set forth, leading Nuu Myi, Software and Sparky, who refused to stay in the Palace.

The enemy had to look around to see where the bursts of fire were coming from. To the troops in nonpowered armor, the barrage erupted out of nowhere.

"Hey, stupids!" Naughty Emma shrieked, waving madly from the steps of the Carrot Palace, "they're over here!"

Within a moment or two, the Insurgents realized there were faint outlines dashing back and forth across the archways. The officers, who had superior telemetry, reacted with alarm. Anyone and anything could be dressed up in blue suits and bubble helmets, but up-to-date full camouflage armored suits were not available from any mail-order catalog. To a force already disoriented by having gorillas groom them and flamingoes coat them with glue, the appearance of genuine Space Service troopers was demoralizing. They hesitated.

Ayala shrieked with frustration.

"There are only *four* of them!" he shouted. "Four! Count them! Four! Disarm and capture them!"

The truth dawned on them in a sudden rush, and they were angry for having been frightened by such a ridiculously small contingent. The Insurgents pressed forward, shooting and yelling.

Wolfe pushed Emma into the building, out of the way of the gunfire. He kept an eye on his suit integrity meter as he ran up and back, attracting the Insurgents' attention. Each ricocheting hit chipped away a little at the suit's efficacy. He needed to keep out in the open long enough to establish his psychological advantage, but he knew he was taking a risk. With his chin and his weapon up, most of his chest and neck were protected, but his legs were vulnerable. The experienced Insurgents were aiming at his knees. The plating over his left knee was beginning to give way. It already hurt from the vigorous squeezes it was getting from the CBS,P. A direct hit with an armor-piercing round would cripple him. He couldn't be taken prisoner. There were too few of the living soldiers to protect Wingle World. It was time to call in his special forces.

"Special auxiliaries!" Wolfe shouted. "Advance!"

Out of the building poured waves of blue-clad troopers, but these were not like any the Insurgents had seen before. They were not human or itterim, but raccoons, rams, bears both cuddly and non, unicorns, otters, ducks, ostriches and penguins. They brandished weapons, which they handled with varying degrees of skill in their flippers, wings, claws and hooves. Bullets and skyrockets pinged off in every direction.

"There's Bunny Hug!" Oostern shouted as a tall pink figure in blue microplate and a huge bubble helmet came dashing out of the Carrot Palace with a full-sized machine gun clutched in his huge paws. "They drafted Bunny Hug!"

"I see Nanny Goat," another soldier exclaimed. "And Norgy Porgy," he added, pointing at a rose-colored pig hauling a mortar in his stubby arms.

"Oops!" exclaimed the Bizarro Twins in unison as they accidentally shot a couple of their own fellows. The purple foxes switched guns and went on firing, this time at the Insurgents.

"They're *shooting* at us!" cried a female soldier in a voice full of hurt betrayal.

"They are puppets!" Ayala yelled. "The only real troopers are the ones in the middle! Get them! Get them!"

But the troopers in their camouflage armor with the blue glow disappeared into the midst of the scrimmage.

Daivid and the others took advantage of the confusion to drop into tunnels and come up behind clusters of Insurgents fighting against characters whose memories they had treasured since childhood.

"Bunny Hug, don't you remember me?" a burly, dark-skinned soldier asked, backing away from the giant pink rabbit with his hands in the air.

Bunny Hug's usually benevolent face was creased with a deep frown. "You shot at my friends, Alfano! That's not nice at all!"

The big man was nearly in tears. "I'll never do it again, I swear, Bunny Hug!" He threw down his gun and ran away, disappearing between the carousel and the Noise Factory.

"Get one of the parking droids to pick him up," Wolfe ordered as he engaged a group of Insurgents running away from Nanny Goat and her sharpened knitting needles. Once again he marveled at Bunny Hug's incredible memory for faces and names. A fighter jumped at him waving a molecular-foil-edged knife. Daivid jumped back, but the itterim had the advantage of reach. It gouged into the forearm of his power suit. Daivid shot it three times in the upper thorax, finally knocking its helmeted head off its skinny neck. Suddenly a very tall woman in microplate armor shoved her rifle butt in his face and swept Daivid's legs out from under him with one kick. When he hit the ground, she tried to use her weapon to knock his out of his arms, but he shot her under the chin. The body fell heavily onto his. A moment later, it lifted off him and was flung away. Sparky reached down a hand and yanked him effortlessly to his feet, suit and all. He was stunned by the puppet's strength.

"How did you get along without me?" Sparky asked, grinning.

"Pretty well," Wolfe said. He dropped to his hands and knees, and scuttled towards the nearest tunnel entrance under cover of a squabble between two tigers over who was going to get to eat a very frightened and very young Insurgent corporal. Sparky followed in a series of somersaults.

"You know," the puppet confided as the two of them slid down into the cool darkness of the metal-lined tunnel and double-timed toward the Carrot Palace, "I'd take a bullet for you, Daive."

"I wish you would, you old fart," Wolfe snarled. "You're not taking this seriously."

"You're taking this too seriously," Sparky retorted. "It's just life."

Puzzled, but not willing to take the time to think about it, he activated the mastoid channel. "How many, Borden?"

The junior lieutenant's voice came back after a moment's hesitation. "I estimate that our kills number thirty to thirty-five. Minor to incapacitating wounds, about double that."

"That's enough to demoralize them," Wolfe said. "Time to let Ayala think he's got the upper hand. Meet me on the steps in two minutes!"

One moment Ewanowski was creeping up on the Insurgent position. The next, he found himself flying through the air, landing in a car of the Cyberdrive Roller Coaster, billed as The Fastest Ride

Without Drive Engines in the Galaxy. His neck snapped backwards, only saved from being broken by his web suit, which froze in place around his spine. Half a dozen puppets landed heavily on him and all over the moving train, mostly in pieces.

"Goddammit!" he snarled, brushing them away. He pulled a few of the still-functional ones upright. He hung on as the car swerved wildly and began to climb toward the heavens on a track that looked like a hairpin with rungs. "What just happened? My head's ringing."

"Shell," his shooting buddy's voice came over the implant. "It took out a kiosk and a chunk of pavement. Two of the spiders got blown up. The Insurgents are panicking. They are shooting at anything in sight."

The semicat looked down. "You're surrounded," he said. "We ought to call for backup."

"No need. Squad Two, move in!"

"Spidey, the Surgies are going to—" Ewanowski ducked down inside the car. It swooped down just as the second shell rocketed directly into the midst of the marching marionettes.

BOOM! More chunks of puppet shell, fluff and glitter rained down. Ewanowski waited until the car rocketed out of the center of the carnage, then swung himself out of the car and over the side of the tracks. All of Squad Two had been blown to bits. He let off five short bursts, persuading the Insurgents to give him room to land, then dropped in their midst and rolled, shooting every time he came up, until he was under cover of the sweet-drinks stand in the shadow of the coaster. His camouflage suit meant that most of the Surgies lost track of him, but it was a small mercy. They were heavily outnumbered now. The enemy was throwing everything it had at what remained of the defenders.

"Drop the spiders on 'em again, and scare them away," Ewanowski shouted into his mike. "The lieutenant'll be ready for them at the Carrot Palace!"

"No spiders left," Aaooorru choked. He leaped up on the building. "Mr. Wingle, prepare to evacuate! Go to deeper ground!"

"Can't! I'm busy. I'm sending Security!"

"No, don't—!"

But it was done. Just behind the Inventor's Workshoppe the big double doors of a blue-painted building popped open. From it sped an old-fashioned black van with a red light on top filled with police waving billy clubs. All of them had mustaches, tall rounded hats, and brass buttons down their long blue coats. The vehicle zoomed around the cottage and came to a screeching halt. The police jumped out and began to belabor the Insurgents with their clubs.

The shock was too much for the itterim. Disregarding their screaming captain, they began to fire bazookas and grenades at the cottage, the roller coaster, the puppets, and anything else more than two millimeters high. Ewanowski rolled as far away as he could, shooting at Insurgents, trying to spot Aaooorru. They put anything they had into the big weapon barrels. Fragmentation grenades flew overhead and burst. Explosives landed on every surface and detonated. Gas cylinders burst against walls.

"Dammit," Oscar Wingle said over the helmet channel. "They never had that kind of effect before."

Zebediah was beside herself with fury. The morons under her command were wasting every charge in their arsenal. One missile went rocketing over the head of a multilegged trooper in camo armor, into the foolishly named "Inventor's Workshoppe," and detonated against a wall, exposing a shiny metal conduit, missing the trooper completely. The hole seemed to act as a target for all the bullets, gas grenades and mortar shells that followed. When she got the itterim under control again, she was going to kill them all personally.

Ayala shoved his way through the ridiculous battle going on around him. Something was happening at the Carrot Palace. He counted ten, twelve, fifteen red-in-blue shadows converging on the west steps and heading inside. The lieutenant must still be inside with the rest of the force.

"Oostern, heavy weapons to the Carrot Palace! Companies A, B and C, with me now!" he ordered over his helmet audio.

From all over the pavilion, Insurgents wrenched themselves away from bear hugs, kangaroo kickings and goat gorings, straggling to obey their colonel's command.

Daivid opened his link to the Insurgents' main channel. "Attention, Insurgent forces. I am Lieutenant Daivid Wolfe of the TWC Space Service. I've been sent by my commanding officer to negotiate a surrender."

"Go ahead then!" Ayala howled in his ear. "Save me the trouble of killing you all. Surrender!"

"Not *us*," Daivid said, in exasperation, sticking his muzzle around the edge of the arch and firing off a blast. "You! Try to handle this like mature beings. You're outnumbered a hundred to one."

"Only a hundred to one? Hah! Then here is my answer!"

The BOOM! of a heavy gun firing made Wolfe and all of his squad flatten themselves to the ground. The embossed image of Bunny Hug above Daivid fractured into pieces no larger than his hand and rained down on them.

"That looks funny," Norgy Porgy said. Daivid glanced up at the giant pig. A section of rebar from the pavement had penetrated through the big rose-colored body from end to end. Daivid leaped up and dashed forward in a hail of armor-piercing rounds to leap up to save Norgy, then realized he wasn't really injured. The puppeteer controlling him was safe in a titanium-lined bunker. No one was hurt, but he had nearly gotten himself killed rescuing a doll. He dragged his attention back to what he was doing.

"Back at you," he yelled at his opponent and signalled to Ambering to fire the twinkie-gun.

A huge shell rocketed out of the barrel in a haze of brass. In Daivid's scopes the streak that represented the white-hot core of depleted uranium arrowed through lighter obstructions, such as the Policeman's Booth at the corner of Law Street and Order Boulevard, and into the midst of Ayala's forces. The pavement exploded, sending soldiers and pieces of soldiers flying in all directions. But their guns were not silenced. More shells blasted into the walls of the Carrot Palace. Wolfe dove for cover.

"Give me Wingle's controller chip," Ayala ordered him as the two groups exchanged fire. "I do not want it damaged, and neither do you. Give it up, or we will destroy you and the controller."

"No way," Wolfe said. "If you attack this site, I will destroy the chip. I have it right here." He waved a citrine-encrusted silver box out the door at the Insurgent force. It was actually the soap dish from his hotel room. "That's what you came for, isn't it? You're not going to make it, so you might as well go away!"

"You will give it up to me, at once," Ayala shouted. "Or else!"

"Or else what?" Wolfe shouted back.

"Bring our leverage," Ayala announced grandly.

No one moved. Wolfe took a surreptitious look at his scopes to make certain no one else was sneaking up on them.

"Sir," Thielind whispered urgently into his link, "I'm monitoring Any Street. A clear pod just left shuttle two, lifted straight up. It's full of people. They've got hostages!"

Wolfe felt his heart pounding. "Can you see who they are?"

"No, sir. The infrared's inconclusive, of course. They've all got bags over their heads. I think they wanted to fly that shuttle to the Carrot Palace, but it's surrounded by parking droids. They've pulled off part of the drive housing. We didn't know about the pod."

"No one could have guessed, ensign," Wolfe said. His nerves returned in full force. He stood on the edge of a moral precipice now. Anything he did from this point on would be successful, or a terrifying, criminal failure. The roiling in his gut reached nuclear reactor proportions.

"There's nothing you can say that will make me give up this chip!" he announced, over Ayala's frequency.

"We will see about that," the colonel said. The fighting died around them as the pod set down in the pavilion. Two of the best armed Insurgents pushed open the escape panel and yanked one man at random from the huddle. They pushed the man, blindfolded and with bound wrists, toward Ayala, who took him by the collar of his shirt. He held up a small black control.

"Let them go, Ayala!" Wolfe shouted.

"I'm so glad you know who I am," the scruffy-bearded man said, gazing coolly at the wavering shape that was his opponent, as if he could see right through the ghost effect. "So you know I mean business. All of these charming people," he gestured at the hostages, "were trying to leave this town. I cannot imagine why they wouldn't want to stay in this fine place, with such a fantastic attraction as Wingle World to amuse them! But they will die if you do not give me the chip. I have a box, you have a box. Mine detonates the escape pod. I will exchange it for yours. What is your answer?"

"My answer?" Wolfe echoed, hand plunging to his side and coming up with his pistol. "Here it is!"

"You're going to shoot me?" Ayala scoffed, reading a weapon in the infrared scopes of his helmet.

"Not exactly!"

The PHUT of the Dockery 5002 machine pistol firing was barely audible, but the SMACK! as the round struck the hostage full in the chest might as well have been a nuclear explosion. Ayala stared in disbelief at the gaping black hole that went straight through the body. The man staggered backwards, arms flailing, but he didn't cry out. He didn't fall. And he didn't bleed.

Ayala swept off the hood. The man stared at him.

"You're too ugly to look at," the puppet said derisively, making a face. "Put the hood back on."

Ayala's face turned red with rage. "Kill them!" he shouted, pointing at Wolfe. "Kill them all!"

Wolfe's next shot took the controller out of Ayala's hands. Jones zoomed down out of the sky on his dragon and caught it in mid-air. The sides of the rescue pod peeled down like the skin of a sectioned orange, and the puppets inside ran for cover. Wolfe shot again at Ayala, but the Insurgent chief had hit the dirt and was rolling out of the way.

"Defensive tactics!" Wolfe shouted.

The Cockroaches opened fire. The Insurgents pressed forward from every direction. The Cockroaches fled up the stairs, providing covering fire for one another. As they had planned, the uniformed 'normals' began to pop up a few at a time from behind the plascrete monoliths, shooting out of all four entrances. The Insurgents charged up the stairs, some falling as a lucky shot from one of the puppets hit them. Rebels clambered over the bodies of their fellows, trying to follow the ghostly outlines of the troopers. Most of them shot at the blue-uniformed troopers they could see. Every bullet fired at a puppet, Wolfe reasoned, was another bullet wasted.

"Keep it up," he urged his 'troops.' "Lin, are you ready?"

"Standing by," the senior chief said. She and Jones rode the dragons over the courtyard, drawing fire but steadily urging the Insurgent forces upward and into the Carrot Palace. Hundreds of them crowded the archways. Silhouetted against the sun, they were easy targets. The Cockroaches blazed away at them. The survivors hunkered down behind concrete slabs, returning fire.

"Ambering, prepare to abandon ship!" Wolfe commanded.

"Aye, aye, sir," the gunner shouted as an explosion echoed through the communication link. "Whew! That one took out part of the ceiling, sir. I've only got about two meters of solid roof to lie on."

"All right, everyone!" Wolfe said, "Down the rabbit hole!"

Steadily, the defenders began to withdraw towards the center of the Carrot Palace. He deliberately allowed them to lose ground, encouraging more and more of the Insurgents to crowd inside. He wanted more. He wanted them all!

"I'm over the hole, sir," Borden said over the mastoid link.

"Go, go, go!" Wolfe shouted. "They're coming!"

"What is all this?" Ayala asked, scanning the interior of the Carrot Palace as they swarmed inward, firing at the bobbing heads. "What is all this garbage doing here?"

"Perhaps an art display," Oostern suggested. "Or some kind of sacred site?"

"An art display for children, with broken glass?" Ayala asked, picking up some of the debris and letting it sift from his glove to clink on the heap from which it had come.

Zing! Ayala dove for the floor even before his brain registered that he had been shot at. He picked out the heat images in his display, and aimed over the piles of rubble at the nearest source. It seemed to be vaguely humanoid in shape, but after the force he had faced so far, he was making no assumptions. Where were the blue images?

Signalling to his soldiers to spread out among the monoliths and boulders of plascrete, he kept up a steady return fire, pinpointing his targets. A large group was situated close to the northern door. With a quick hand signal he called for gas grenades.

"Knock them out!" he ordered. "I want that chip. That fool just might destroy it if we corner him."

The grenadiers scurried to obey, launching the green cylinders in an arc that landed them squarely on top of the defenders.

"Cough," Wolfe shouted to the defending puppets then crawled away behind the concrete chunks, trying to stay out of sight of the invading force. The 'troopers' broke into dramatic hacking and wheezing. He grinned. He would have believed in their discomfort if he hadn't known for certain none of them had lungs.

"A-heck-heck-heck," choked Sparky, clutching his throat with pathos.

"You win the acting award," Wolfe informed him sourly. "Now, come on. We have to leave."

"Do my best," Sparky said. "Always—love my work."

"What?"

The puppet posed suddenly, with a raised forefinger as if he was about to speak again, and froze in place. It dawned suddenly on Wolfe that Sparky was not playing around for dramatic effect. Had something gone wrong in the old man's laboratory?

"Spidey, respond!" he shouted.

"Aye, sir!" the high-pitched voice squeaked.

"What just happened? Wingle's puppet just stopped talking. He *never* stops talking." A screaming noise on the channel interrupted the corlist's transmission. "Repeat? What did you say?"

The corlist fired round after round at the party of Insurgents flattened underneath the ruined carousel. His bulbous eyes kept swiveling back to the smoke coming out of the ruined conduit leading down into the tunnel. He activated his link again.

"I am sorry, Big Bad. I have failed. The Inventor's Workshoppe was hit. I am sending a team below to see what has happened."

"I'll go," Ewanowski said, and signed for two of his puppet aides to give him covering fire as he headed for the hidden ramp. "You don't need me up here."

A few moments later, the semicat signalled through from the laboratory. "He's gone. Gas. At least it was quick."

Aaooorru's stalk eyes drooped inside his helmet. He reported back to Wolfe.

"Let them through, Spidey," Wolfe's voice said sadly but resolutely "Follow on. I don't need you there any longer."

Full of anger, Wolfe looked around him for targets. He popped up to shoot, now with his machine gun, now with the Dockery pistol. The screaming of dying Insurgents only made him hungry for more. How could he have been so careless? He couldn't blame Aaooorru. Everything that happened here today was his responsibility, and his alone. The pain in his head as an armor-piercing round creased his helmet brought him back to his senses. He suddenly realized he couldn't see any more trooper ID tags over the red-in-blue shapes in his heads-up-display. He was the last Cockroach in the Carrot Palace.

"Is everybody down?" he asked.

"Aye, sir," Borden said. "We're all retreating from the zone. Quickly, sir!"

"How many have we got in here?"

"At least eighty on my scopes, sir."

"Puppets, retreat! Lin!" Wolfe shouted, diving for the hole. "Blow the place. Now!"

"You're too close," the chief's voice replied. "The concussion will kill you!"

"Just blow it!" Wolfe said, swinging into the tunnel, not waiting for the ramp to lower under him. He dropped to the floor and began to run. It was dark in the passageway except for the tiny red eyes of the emergency lights, so he used his helmet map to navigate. The nearest corner was over ninety meters away. Even with the assist of his power suit he couldn't get there before the blast came. Thirty meters. Forty.

Suddenly, with a roar like a volcano erupting, the floor lifted up and flung him forward. His back pressed into his chest, and the world went black.

"Find them!" Ayala shouted. The troopers had escaped again. No one was left inside the Carrot Palace except blue-suited automata. He strode out into the courtyard, flanked by his officers. "Where could they have gone?"

"This park covers hectares," Oostern said. "There's no way to know wh—"

A noise louder than a starship engine burst behind them. Ayala was only aware of the thunder in his ears as he was thrown out over the Meadow Pavilion and into the empty escape pod. Gravel and debris shot outward, peppering the safety pod. Ayala ducked automatically against the deafening rumble, but he was safe. Outside his shelter, Armageddon was descending.

Individual blasts of white fire erupted all the way around the base of the Carrot Palace. Huge chunks of orange plascrete shot outward, scoring the green cobbled pavement as they tumbled. The sides splintered into long shards and fell. All four of the carrot-shaped turrets tilted in toward the center of the building and almost seemed to turn inside out, then disappeared into the deafening clouds of dust. Ayala was unable to move, but the plastic shell protected him while he watched with utter disbelief as the walls of the Carrot Palace collapsed under their own weight.

When the dust cleared, shards of the orange façade lay in a rough circle on the raised pavement. Cries for help and screams of pain arose out of the ruin. Bodies sprawled, covered with dust on the torn green cobbles. Ayala rose gingerly, his limbs shaking with unaccustomed weakness, to try and help his soldiers. Oostern crawled to assist. One of his upper forelimbs had been torn off, and his head was gashed.

"It was a trap," Ayala whispered, staggering forward. "They brought us here to destroy us! They must all die!"

Daivid felt hands pounding on his chest, and heard an urgent voice calling his name. "Lieutenant Wolfe! Lieutenant Wolfe, answer me!"

Daivid batted feebly at the hands. He pried his eyes open, even though it hurt to do so. "Stop hitting me," he murmured.

"I'm not hitting you," D-45 said.

"What? I can't hear you!"

"I say, I'm not hitting you!" the squad leader shouted. "You got caught in the blast!" The trooper leaned over him as Gire helped him to sit up. Together they helped him take off his helmet. "Your web suit's been giving you CPR. Doc said your heart stopped for a while. Borden's been frantic wondering if you bought it. You okay?"

"I—Yes." Daivid licked his lips, and Gire snapped his fingers. "Nurse!"

A three-eyed green bug-eyed monster sidled up and handed the doctor a water bottle with a straw. He put it to Daivid's lips.

The lieutenant drank greedily. The CBS,P observed his tight shoulders and began running its backrub program. Daivid sighed with relief. He nodded toward the BEM. "I thought you were afraid of them."

Gire beamed. "These are good aliens," he said, enunciating carefully so Daivid could read his lips. "They told me I can dream about them. I think I will. They'll help keep away the bad ones. Your vitals are returning to normal. I would like to tell you to rest for a while, but you won't."

"No, I won't." Daivid put a hand on the floor to push himself up. He turned to face D-45. "Wingle's dead, isn't he?"

"Yes, sir. Gas. Painless. Aaooorru's kicking himself with all his feet, but I keep telling him he is not to blame."

Wolfe bowed his head for a moment. "Any other casualties?"

"None of ours."

"How about Ayala?"

"Still out there," D-45 said. "But we killed about eighty of his people."

"I want him," Daivid said resolutely, taking the helmet back. "Wingle would have wanted me to take him out. Ayala still owes blood for murdering his staff. Let's go get him."

"Welcome back, sir," Lin's voice said in his ear as he strode out into the daylight from the shelter of the carousel. He had to turn the volume up to maximum. The explosion had deafened him so badly that the calliope music from the carousel was a faint whistle in the background.

"Thank you," Wolfe said, admiring the ruins of the Carrot Palace. The entire structure had collapsed in a gigantic ring of orange debris topped by the four giant carrots that had been the turrets. Two of them still had flags to wave. A few pieces had fallen on the pavilion, where they were being used as cover by the remaining Insurgent soldiers. "Nice work! Have you ever thought of a sideline in demolitions?"

"How do you think I make pin money?"

"I was thinking sheep herding?" Wolfe suggested. "How about rounding up the rest of these bastards?"

"I'd love to," the chief replied. Whatever was wrong between them had been put to the side for now.

"Good. All right, all of you slackers!" he shouted. "Lock and load! Special Auxiliaries, ground troops and shock troops, into the Meadow Pavilion right now! Dragons, front and center."

"Aye, aye, sir!" Lin and Jones replied.

"Aye, aye, sir," added a new, raspy voice.

"Let's see how they like these apples," Wolfe said. He threw a new magazine into his machine gun and hefted it, marching into the fray. Behind him came the costumed characters, more and more seeming to arise out of the ground as he closed in on the Carrot Palace.

The two scout vehicles zoomed out of the air, hammering the Insurgents on the ground with tracer bullets. Where troops tried to break and run, they let loose with a burst of plasma fire that scorched the pavement. The Insurgents ran back and forth, peppering the pilots with gunfire that pinged off the protective shields like rain, but they were being herded steadily into the center of the pavilion.

"Stand your ground!" Ayala shouted. "They are only puppets! We still outnumber the real troopers! There are only fifteen!"

"He's good," Borden commented in Daivid's other ear.

"Hope he can use that numerical skill in hell," Wolfe retorted.

From hidden trap doors all over the pavilion, the rest of the Wingle characters arose. Nanny Goat marched proudly at their head, waving the Cockroach banner and her knitting needles. Dimmius Grebs stumped heavily up a ramp as panicked Insurgents shot grenades and bullets at him. With a puzzled, patient look on his face, he picked them up one at a time and flung them at the ruin of the Carrot Palace. The mad unicorn ran around goring soldiers, impervious to bullets that sang his way. Ginophant stomped on anyone that got in his way. He lifted one oversized foot to apologize to one of the Bizarro Twins, who lay flattened on the pavement.

"Ooh, sorry," he said in his deep slow voice, and backed very deliberately onto a mortar team who were trying to load their weapon. "Sorry again."

But far more terrifying was the undulating presence of the huge red dragon. Twice as long as a shuttle, its purple eyes rolling and golden tongue flicking, it snaked in and out of the attractions on low, taloned feet. It could move with the speed of a tank, preventing any of the Insurgents from leaving the pavilion. Every time a group of soldiers attempted to flee, it chased them down, herding them back into the park center.

"Get into the ruins," Ayala instructed them. "We can defend ourselves there! Move!"

Wolfe directed the operation from a distance, monitoring the Insurgents as they made their way to what was left of a magnificent structure, the signature building of Wingle World, and the symbol of a gallant and wise man. He hoped Wingle would have approved of what he had done, and what he was about to do. He watched the Insurgent colonel clamber over pieces of orange masonry. Wolfe tracked him by his red-in-blue signature as he dashed through the building, trying to find a way out. Wolfe bounded after him, ignoring the pain in his knee. He got to the west stairs as Ayala attempted to escape down them, and blasted at him with the machine pistol. He was not going to get away. Firing back over his shoulder, Ayala retreated into the ruins.

The Cockroaches and their allies followed as the Insurgents fell back, covering one another with increasingly wild gunfire. Once behind the crumbled walls, they were able to hammer the Cockroaches with little chance of being hit themselves. Somewhere in there Ayala was undoubtedly trying to plan an escape, maybe already searching for the trap doors that had allowed the Cockroaches to slip out without being noticed, but the tunnels had already been moved. Frantically, the Insurgents fired at the shadows dancing around them. Wolfe tracked the red-in-blue image of Ayala. He was almost in the center of the ruin.

"Dragons, keep everyone in there," Wolfe instructed. Lin and Jones zoomed overhead, peppering the ruins. Heads bobbed up, fired, and ducked down again.

"Ow! Frax a dax," Boland yelled. "One of those crazy bastards just holed me in the side."

"Go below and see Doc," Wolfe ordered.

"In a while, sir. I want to see the fireworks."

"Why not? I want an end to this," Wolfe said, keeping an eye on Ayala's shadow as it bobbed up and down, shooting hopelessly at the troopers and puppets who were just too far out of reach. He wouldn't be able to get out. Wingle's vengeful spirit would be appeased. "Lin, the word is given."

"Aye, aye, sir!"

This time he had the sense to mute the audio in his suit, but the force of the second explosion still knocked him backwards off his feet. The blast was a thing of beauty, catapulting the carefully-collapsed ruins of the Carrot Palace high into the air. Lin must have used every spare kilo of explosive, propellant and flammable substance in the entire city of Welcome, because the shards and chunks of masonry leaped higher than the Carrot Palace had been tall before ending their upward arc. They descended in a hellish rain of destruction. Wolfe and the others ducked underneath any roof they could find to protect themselves from stone and plascrete boulders from landing on them. No one in there could have survived. Wolfe saw no indicators from intact armor. Ayala was dead.

While orange and green gravel and less identifiable pieces were still falling from the skies, Wolfe and his force turned their attention towards the remaining Insurgents, who had been making their way toward the rubble when it blew. He was surrounded by hundreds and hundreds of costumed characters, some badly damaged by gunfire and explosives. Nearly all of these were armed with a projectile weapon of some kind. Their faces inside the bubble helmets were set in stern expressions, the kind of faces that took no quarter and expected none. The Insurgents backed up a pace or two, realizing that they were outnumbered and outgunned.

Very slowly and very carefully, every one of the survivors put their guns on the ground and raised their arms in the air.

CHAPTER 22

THE FIRST THING Lin and Jones had done after the prisoners were rounded up was to go in search of the remains of Adri'Leta and Vacarole. Wolfe was determined that the former would be buried there on Dudley. Her wishes, expressed to him in front of witnesses, would be honored. No more Adri'Letas, and to hell with the faceless foundation that kept bringing them to life.

Sparky was gone forever. Wolfe felt as though he had lost a comrade-in-arms. Not really a friend, since all the puppet had ever done was annoy him, but he wished he could find the 'body' and lay it to rest with honor. He spent some time kicking through the shards of the Carrot Palace in hopes of finding any trace of the puppet.

He turned away to survey what was left of the Meadow Pavilion. The park was a mess. Gunfire and explosive charges had knocked down or blown up numerous attractions and damaged countless others. Hundreds of puppets had been destroyed. He'd ruined Wingle World.

Once the all clear had been given, thousands of people began to pour into the park from all over the region. They gathered up the damaged puppets, and began to survey the ruined pavement, rides and gardens. Wolfe wandered among them like a ghost, unable to surrender his hard-won territory to the people who actually belonged there. Borden found him limping aimlessly around Wingle Lake, and tried to steer him toward the exit.

"Go back to the hotel for a while, sir," she said loudly. "You're still a little hazy from the blast."

"No, I'm not," Wolfe said. "I screwed up. I just tried to tell Aaooorru that it wasn't his fault that Mr. Wingle got killed on his watch. Fortunes of war. He and I both knew that's a heap of slag. I wouldn't be satisfied with it, either, if my CO handed me a line like that."

"It's true, though," Borden insisted.

"It's not. The only thing that would have saved this whole situation from being a complete and utter clusterfrax is if we could have found the chip. Mr. Wingle told me just before the fighting started that he was finished with it. He put it in a safe place. Well, Ewanowski says his lab is a mess. The grenades that hit after Wingle was killed shredded most of what was in there. If the chip is still intact, we will never find it."

"You need a drink."

"I don't deserve one." Though Wolfe had to admit that lying down for a while sounded like a good idea. Once he was rested, he would pitch in and help restore what he'd destroyed.

"Look," Borden said. They spotted a pair of huge pink feet toes up in the midst of a crowd of park engineers. Daivid opened his stride to hurry over.

Glaijet looked up at him. "Sorry you have to see this, lieutenant."

"Bunny Hug is dead?" Wolfe asked forlornly.

Bunny Hug lay on the ground, motionless, his big face frozen in a smile. Daivid felt a wrenching sense of loss, remembering the pat on the head, the hug that was such an important part of Bunny Hug's welcoming and loving personality. He shook the great paw, but it didn't move.

"Well, Mr. Wingle is," Glaijet corrected him. "Of course, it was his character. Bunny Hug is always performed by a Wingle. It's their heritage. It's special to them."

Daivid nodded. Bunny Hug showed a part of Oscar Wingle that he never demonstrated in person—a loving, open, sympathetic side—but he could let it all out in the form of a ridiculous nine-foot-tall pink rabbit. Or a smart-talking freckled youth who always interrupted one's darkest thoughts with a non-sequitur. Daivid felt sad, thinking he never really got to know the man behind one of his childhood heroes.

Daivid finally realized Glaijet was still talking. "…We have to contact his son."

"His son?" he gawked.

"Oscar VIII," the engineer replied. "He's visiting some of our souvenir manufacturers. It's the off-season, you know. Eight does a *wonderful* Bunny Hug. He'll be ready to perform by the time the park opens—if we can get the mess cleaned up in time. Your ensign said he'd help, and we could use it. Oscar IX is still in school. He's learning acting and marketing, though he's got a natural talent for both already. Pretty precocious for a ten-year-old."

Daivid felt his heart lift just a little bit. "So the dynasty goes on." The man gave him a poignant but sincere smile. "The dynasty goes on."

"It's an omen," Daivid told Borden with more energy than he had felt for an hour. "Maybe all is *not* lost."

"I don't believe in omens," the junior lieutenant replied severely.

"It's a mess," Wolfe said, surveying the laboratory.

"I told you so," Borden replied.

The room had looked like a crowded moving van when they had first seen it. In the aftermath of the battle, it resembled landfill. The furniture nearest the burst ventilation duct had been blown to splinters. The communications console, the Waldo device with the enormous magnifier, and every other piece of sensitive equipment had blown and burned. Wolfe scanned the big room to see if anything at all was intact, and nearly jumped out of his skin to see Oscar Wingle VII looking at him.

"Oh, slag!" he panted.

"It's just Dudley," Borden said coolly.

It was. The gray-haired puppet stood in his box with a little smile lifting his mouth under the heavy moustache. Wolfe almost smiled back. He started picking through the ruined cabinets and drawers in hopes of coming across a package with his name on it, or any other kind of identifying mark.

"He was a genius," Wolfe said, after he and Borden had spent a frustrating hour turning over broken boxes and shaking out books. "He would not have put that chip where it couldn't be found. He said he was putting it in 'a safe place. A very safe place.' I wish he'd been more specific."

Grinding and crunching noises made them both reach for their sidearms. Wolfe ducked down behind an overturned desk. A figure emerged from a sliding panel, a silver figure of a woman. She undulated towards them, her hips swaying like those of a real human female. Daivid was transfixed.

"Maria," he breathed.

"Mr. Wingle *was* very specific," she said.

"You speak!"

"Of course," the android said. "I am a prototype. I also think and act. Here. He wanted you to have it, but you had to ask for it correctly. You did." She held out her hand and opened it. On her smooth palm was a small silver cube. Wolfe took it, with admiration for the genius who had invented it, and her. No one could have broken through that ball of steel without destroying the contents.

Wolfe never felt the ground under his boots nor the cold of the snow falling on his head as he danced through the park in jubilation. They had fulfilled their mission! Borden followed him, disapproval writ large on her face. She had taken charge of the chip, not trusting him in his current giddy state. She was such a spoilsport, Wolfe thought. He had to share his joy with *someone*.

"Daivid!" Connie waved to him. She was wearing a blue uniform and carrying a cutout gun under her arm. He waved back. He ran to her and swept her up in his arms.

"I am so glad to see you're all right!" he exclaimed, relieved down to his bones.

"There's something I have to tell you," she protested, as he brought his lips toward hers. "I'm a—"

"A puppet," Daivid finished her sentence for her. He kissed her deeply anyway, and the warm, red lips yielded to him. "I know. I've known all the time, since I went into Tennie's. I was wearing my helmet. It shows the pink heat signature of everyone in the room. You didn't have one."

Connie drew her head back, the eyes wide in surprise. "You knew?"

Daivid smiled. "Yes. I think that's why I let myself fall in love with you. You were—safe. That's why I could let go of the emotional mess I didn't even realize I've been carrying around with me for three years. But the point is, I did. I love you. I love the person behind you. I would like to get to know the real you."

"But this *isn't* really me," Connie protested. "It could never work out." She pushed gently at his chest and he set her free. "I have to go. But I am so glad you feel I helped you break through a barrier." Her dimple showed. "You're all heroes. Congratulations."

"Do you see?" asked the woman sitting beside the bay window in the little house on a corner near the park. Daivid had gotten a good night's sleep, showered and shaved to make himself presentable. The dark blue eyes twinkled, seeming to like what they saw, and the deep dimple by the side of the mouth deepened just for him. "What you think you love is just an illusion. I'm happily married. I have three grown children. I operate twelve other characters in Wingle World. Connie is just a part of me, though she is a favorite. My grandchildren like her to take them through the park. She's got more pep than I have, and she's a lot prettier. I'm getting old."

Daivid came to kneel beside the woman and took her hand. Her hair was almost entirely white, and wrinkles crosshatched the corners of her eyes and mouth and netted her plump cheeks. "Most of love is illusion, as I found out the hard way a long time ago. You're just as beautiful as Connie. Thank you." He kissed her on the cheek then stood up, her hand still in his. "I'll always remember you as the girl I fell in love with."

She smiled. "That is the nicest thing anyone has ever told me. Goodbye, Daivid."

"She okay, looey?" Thielind asked, looking up from the robot controller he was repairing on a worktable.

"Um-hm," Daivid said thoughtfully, scanning the multitude of repairbots all repairing each other and the cleanerbots that clustered around them waving their brush and scrubber arms, all waiting their turn. "Her lawn's a little crunchy from the fallout of the Carrot Palace, but there was no damage to the house. No one was hurt."

"What's she like?"

"Beautiful," Daivid said with a sigh. "But she's married. You knew Connie was a puppet."

Thielind tilted his head. "Aye, sir. Installed her heat generator myself. No one wanted to say. We wanted you to be a little happy. We could tell you weren't. She was really nice, wasn't she?"

Daivid nodded. He noticed that most of the Cockroaches, who were helping out with the cleanup, were very carefully not listening to their conversation. "She was. How's it going?"

It was strange being in the secret depths of Wingle World, in the real inventor's lab, knowing that the man himself, the legend, was never coming back again. The puppets being repaired or created anew under their hands would never know the master's touch. But they'd know the next generation. It didn't make it all right in his heart, but it made things better.

"There you are, Lieutenant Wolfe!"

The three town councillors bustled up to him. The man with arched black eyebrows took his hand.

"We are very grateful to you and your—Cockroaches for saving us all," the puppet said, shaking energetically. "Your leadership saved the townsfolk from a threat we could never have withstood alone. In spite of the ill way we treated you in the beginning, you did us an enormous favor. We owe you a debt of gratitude."

"Oh, no," Wolfe cautioned them, his hands held out in protest. "Not a favor. You don't mean that."

"We do mean it," the plump woman said. "And we know what it means, too. We know who you are. We looked you up. You visited us when you were small. Do you remember?"

"I'll never forget it," Daivid said fervently. "That visit or this one." Very reluctantly, he took the small database chip out from under his uniform tunic and entered the favor as a Class 5 favor.

"Your dad will be pleased," Thielind said absently. The ensign lifted the repairbot down and raised the next one to the worktop. He stroked his fingers gently over the manipulative arms, looking for broken components. One of the tanklike tracks that ran around two of its wheels was missing. It obediently rolled over and opened its access hatch for him.

"What do you do, baby?" he asked it.

"That's a monotrack repairbot," the redfaced councillor said. "Vital to the maintenance of about half the rides. It lays the filaments and repairs them."

"Oh, I see," Thielind said, reaching for a cable cutter. A repairbot on the floor found one and slapped it into his palm like a surgical nurse.

The councillors froze for a moment. Wolfe guessed they were conferring.

"You have an amazing affinity for our machines, Mr.—"

"Thielind," the ensign replied, not looking up.

"Would you possibly be interested in staying on? We could use your help in getting the park in shape. The first day of the season is only ten days away."

"Oh, I'll help until our transport comes," Thielind said. "I'm having a good time."

"But what about after that?" the woman asked. "I speak with the full authority of Oscar Wingle VIII. We're willing to offer you 150,000 credits a year."

The monotrack robot rolled onto one side so Thielind could attach its new tractor guide. "Oh, no, thanks. I'll stay in the Space Service."

"Oh, come on," the redfaced man said. "You can't be pulling down more than twenty thousand a year."

"Eighteen five, actually," Thielind said.

"That's nothing!" the redfaced man exploded.

"Please reconsider," the man with black eyebrows urged him. "What can the Space Service give you we can't?"

"My friends, and my CO," the ensign said simply.

The councillor looked up at Wolfe. "Him? Why? What's special about him?"

Thielind smiled brilliantly. "He calls me ensign."

That last statement didn't hold any special meaning for the townsfolk, but Wolfe was touched by it. The councillors, seeing where the leverage lay, turned to him.

"Would you like a job here?" asked the man with black eyebrows. "That way you can bring your genius here with you. And anyone else you wish." He looked around at all of the troopers, whose eyes were suddenly on Daivid.

"Do you know," Daivid replied with deep satisfaction, "that is the second job offer I've gotten here on Dudley. No, I'm too busy saving the galaxy. But thank you for asking."

"Oh, well," the woman sighed. "It was worth a try. We—We do have one more favor we would like to ask of you. As a tribute, of course."

Daivid nodded. "You want us to help out with a tribute to Mr. Wingle? We'd be glad to. An honor guard at the funeral?" He gathered looks of approval from his troopers.

"Nothing like that," the woman said then paused. "Well, perhaps it is something like that. That would be nice, too. What we would really like to do is to create an adventure ride featuring all of you. It won't open this season, but it could be ready for next year. Visitors would go into an arena and become part of the action, with all of you saving their lives. It would all be perfectly safe, of course."

"You mean make puppets out of us?" Wolfe asked, shuddering.

"Oh, yes. Come back when it's open. You'll love it."

"I don't think so."

"Why not, lieutenant?" Boland asked, a big grin on his face, no longer able to keep up the pretense that he wasn't listening. "I mean, what could possibly go wrong, go wrong, go wrong?"

"No, thanks," Wolfe said. "We don't need to relive the last few days."

"Please consider it seriously," the town councillors urged them. "We really want to create this attraction. We think it will be very exciting, and have broad appeal for all ages. You will escort visitors through a danger scene, and save the world at the end." The woman fixed them all with a hopeful look. "We'll put anyone you like in it."

Thielind grinned. "You could put Lieutenant Bruno in it, as a robot who says, 'You can't have that, you can't have that,' and maybe he gets chop suey poured on his lap. All day, every day."

"I like it, ensign," Wolfe laughed. "I can't wait to tell him he's been immortalized at Wingle World. You have a deal, councillors."

"Er, there's just one thing," the man with the black eyebrows began trepidatiously. "We hate to call your unit the *Cockroaches*, though. It's bad marketing. Our visitors might find the name *objectionable*."

"But that's our na—" Daivid began.

"We're the Wolfe Pack," Boland interrupted, with a look around at all of his buddies. "Whaddaya think of that?" X-ray Platoon in its entirety nodded and grinned at their astonished commander. Wolfe was gratified but speechless. There was no better compliment they could have paid him. He'd been accepted by them, and he was almost too happy to speak.

"We like that much better," the councillors said approvingly.

"So do I," Wolfe said.

The newly named platoon spent the following eight days dining and sleeping in sybaritic bliss in their suites at the Wingle Deluxe. The Welcome town council and the management of Wingle World insisted on splitting the tab of keeping them at the hotel. With the promise of payment, Mr. Codwall turned all of the luxury features on a week early. The Wolfe Pack spent its days at the park, helping to bring it back to its former glory. Another Carrot Palace was erected in under a week, fresher and more beautiful than the one that had been destroyed. Under the care of experienced engineers and willing volunteers, the damage was wiped out so fast that Wolfe had to recount the casualties among his own company to realize that it had all really happened.

The fallen were not forgotten. Vacarole's wife had sent word she was happy to have her husband laid to rest in the Wingle family cemetery. Adri'Leta was buried with full respect and honor, and no grave marker. Wolfe was pleased that he could keep his promise to her.

The rest of the platoon spent its evenings at Tennie's, enjoying coverage of the non-war.

"Another big boondoggle that cost the taxpayers money," one of the regular curmudgeons opined. Wolfe could hardly disagree with him. The news commentators were not complimentary. The Space Service had sent two thousand ships, from fighter up to dreadnought, to face two hundred ships and a disorganized rabble.

"Some Insurgency," Boland had said with a snort.

The *Orion* arrived on the eighth day, after having cleaned up the remaining Insurgency ships, and brought the platoon back to rendezvous with the *Eastwood* a week later.

"Commander Iry wants a debriefing as soon as you have your gear stowed," Ensign Coffey told him with a smile. X-ray Platoon's exploits had gotten more and better press than the action on Benarli, *and* they had brought home Oscar Wingle's last invention, so they were in good odor as far as the brass was concerned. Wolfe hoped it would mitigate Captain Harawe's reaction about the borrowed flitter. It was back in the hold in good condition.

"I'll be there soon," Wolfe promised. He also had a big bag of souvenirs he couldn't wait to distribute to all his friends in the officers' mess.

But first he had a more important duty. He joined his troopers in Gehenna day room. The troopers had made themselves comfortable, unashamedly turning away other units who wanted to use the mess.

"We're heroes, haven't you heard?" Jones asked them cheerfully, slamming the door in their faces.

"They left our drinks alone," Boland said, indicating the shot glasses all of them had set down half full the day they had left. They all took one, and waited while Lin spoke.

"We are here to pay tribute to our honored dead," she said as the others stood with their heads bowed. "Our friends are no longer with us, but their names will be preserved forever." The white lightning burned on the way down, and Wolfe remembered why he didn't chug the home brew.

Okumede cleared his throat. "Here's to Vacarole and Adri'Leta, On Dudley their fates they did meet-a. To our heroes and friends! Our respect never ends, And we hope their repose will be sweet-a."

"Nice," Lin said. "You get the points, Oku."

"To our friends," Wolfe saluted.

Parviz and Streb brought the sheet of salmon-colored hull plating forward. D-45 drew his laser pistol and turned to Wolfe. "Sir, I know they would have wanted it that way. Will you cut the first letter?"

With the greatest of care, Wolfe drilled holes in the shape of a capital "a." He handed the pistol to the next person in line and took a more cautious sip of his drink.

"What's the rest of the traditional custom?" he asked. "Borden wouldn't tell me before we departed."

"We have a drink and a pow or two, and tell stories," Boland said easily, settling back in his chair. "Then we bilk our CO out of his last dime playing cards."

"You're welcome to try," Daivid said with a grin. He watched the memorial taking shape, proud of his unit, proud to be accepted, and overwhelmed by the faith they had shown in him. They were a little unorthodox, but what did that matter? They got the job done and saved a lot of lives. That's what they were there for. That's what they were *all* there for.

"Sir, I've got a surprise for you," Thielind said, taking a box out of his duffel. "This is from the guys at Wingle World. They whipped it up while I was fixing the repairbots. I've been saving it until we got back." He handed it to Wolfe.

"They don't need to give us anything else," Wolfe said, very touched. "We've already got lifetime passes to the park. We never opened our wallets again the entire time we were there. We got to spend *days* whooping it up before the ship came back for us."

"They wanted to. This is special."

Wolfe opened the lid with trepidation. But nothing jumped out at him. Instead, he found a folded square of brilliant golden silk. He shook it out. On it was embroidered the silhouette of a black wolf. Daivid stroked it, admiring the beautiful handwork.

"It's a new banner," Thielind explained. "To go with our new name. To the Wolfe Pack." He raised his glass.

"To the Wolfe Pack!" The entire platoon drank deeply.

"Wait a minute," Wolfe said, holding up the banner and examining it more closely. "This wolf has six legs!"

"'Course it does," Thielind said, his smile brilliant. "It evolved from a Cockroach."

Jody Lynn Nye

Jody Lynn Nye lists her main career activity as "spoiling cats." She has published 25 books, such as *Advanced Mythology*, fourth and most recent in her *Mythology* fantasy series (no relation), three SF novels, four novels in collaboration with Anne McCaffrey, including *The Ship Who Won*; edited a humorous anthology about mothers, *Don't Forget Your Spacesuit, Dear!*, and written over eighty short stories. Her latest books are *The Lady and The Tiger*, third in her Taylor's Ark series, and *Strong Arm Tactic"* first in the Wolfe Pack series. She lives northwest of Chicago with two cats and her husband, author and packager, Bill Fawcett.

Don Maitz

Don Maitz has produced outstanding work in exploring paths of fantastic realism. For twenty five years, he has produced narrative paintings containing fantasy, science fiction, and historical images. His career began with New York City book publishing. Don's artwork evolved within this market and has expanded into many other areas. He has received considerable exposure as the original and continuing artist of the Captain Morgan Spiced Rum pirate character.

His works are internationally recognized and acclaimed. He has twice won science fiction's accolade for best artist, the Hugo award. He has received a Howard award from the World Fantasy Convention, a Silver Medal and Certificates of Merit from New York's Society of Illustrators, and ten Chesley awards from his peers in the Association of Science Fiction and Fantasy Artists. His paintings were included at NASA's 25th Anniversary presentation. He lives in Florida with his wife, Janny Wurts, the noted fantasy novelist and artist. They share a home studio with four cats and three horses.

WOLFE PACK II:
UNCONVENTIONAL WARFARE
By Jody Lynn Nye
coming September 2006!

It sounded like a straightforward assignment. Armed riots had broken out between rival gangs on Perski Station, and the manager had requested military assistance to come and put them down. But why, Lt. Daivid Wolfe asked himself in rueful retrospective, had the brass sent X-ray Platoon, when there were a dozen other units far closer to the station?

The answer came only after Daivid and his troops were on their way: the gangs were in fact 'organized units of established businesses' who were, in the words of their representatives, 'just protecting their interests.' Daivid groaned at the careful phrasing, which he had heard all too often during his childhood, as the eldest child and heir of another 'established business,' or, as it was more normally termed, a Family. Unfortunately, neither of the Families involved were his, but that didn't matter to the brass. They thought with his background he would have more of an insight into making the parties stop fighting. They were so wrong. Daivid protested that adding a member of a third family, even in the guise of a disinterested third party, might be like pouring liquid oxygen into a high static environment. But if he failed, they had a ready made reason for him to take the blame.

He had so far found no satisfaction in the fact that he was right. It was turning into urban combat at its worst as they faced entrenched opponents, on familiar ground, pursuing a non-military agenda. Despite doing everything in the book from interdiction to conciliation, the Dotcoms and the Lins continued to shoot at one another and at his men with equal enthusiasm. Still, the job had to be done. He could only hope that the Wolfe Pack, as X-ray Platoon had renamed itself, would pull off another tactical miracle and calm the tension between the rival organizations.

Daivid had been sent in with the explicit order that he make sure that no more innocent bystanders got hurt. Unfortunately, on Perski Station the civilians are used to doing business with no regard for niceties like government oversight and restrictions, so there are very few *innocent* bystanders. The platoon quickly found out that the local merchants were no happier to see the Wolfe Pack than the Families were, and they were all armed, too.

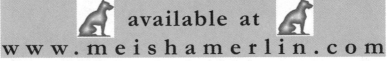